Readers love RUSSELL J. SANDERS

You Can't Tell by Looking

"*You Can't Tell by Looking* is an extremely thought-provoking and timely romance by Russell J. Sanders."

—Kimmers' Erotic Book Banter

Titanic Summer

"Readers craving a coming-of-age novel will find *Titanic Summer* to be a boatload of goodness."

—South Florida Gay News

All You Need Is Love

"*All You Need Is Love* is a beautifully written deeply touching story about coming of age in a very difficult time, and I highly recommend it!"

—Gay Book Reviews

Colors

"Amazing story. Beautifully written. Simply incredible."

—Prism Book Alliance

By RUSSELL J. SANDERS

All You Need Is Love
The Book of Ethan
Colors
Heartthrob
Special Effect
Titanic Summer
You Can't Tell by Looking

Published by HARMONY INK PRESS
www.harmonyinkpress.com

HEARTTHROB
RUSSELL J. SANDERS

Harmony Ink

Published by
HARMONY INK PRESS

5032 Capital Circle SW, Suite 2, PMB# 279, Tallahassee, FL 32305-7886 USA
publisher@harmonyinkpress.com • harmonyinkpress.com

Heartthrob
© 2021 Russell J. Sanders

Cover Art
© 2021 Kris Norris
https://krisnorris.com
coverrequest@krisnorris.com
Cover content is for illustrative purposes only and any person depicted on the cover is a model.

Trade Paperback ISBN: 978-1-64405-918-0
Digital ISBN: 978-1-64405-917-3
Trade Paperback published September 2021
v. 1.0

Printed in the United States of America
∞
This paper meets the requirements of
ANSI/NISO Z39.48-1992 (Permanence of Paper).

For my friends Mamie and Karin, who love, support, and give me strength continuously.

1998

"HEY, YOU'RE on the helpline. What's happening?"

"You are? Where are you? Are you alone in the house? What do you plan to use?"

"Okay, just sit right there. How 'bout you hold the gun at your side while we talk? Will you do that?"

"Yeah, it looks bad right now, but you called, didn't you? I know you want my help—so put the gun down. Okay?"

"You know, calling the helpline is the first step. You're really brave. How old are you, man?"

"Rough age... my friend was your age too. He had everything going for him, man. Sure, there were some things he wanted to change, but he couldn't do that dead.... What's that? I heard a clicking sound. What are you doing?"

"Come on, man. Take your finger off the trigger. Please! Don't you want to hear what I have to say? Death is final, you know. Have you thought about that? Come on. Back off this a minute. Finger off the trigger, guy—finger... off... the... trigger...."

"Good. Trigger released? If you shoot yourself, you can't take it back. Can't you think of one thing that you want to do that you haven't done yet? You off yourself and that's it. No more chance...."

"I hear you, man. My friend thought no one cared about him, either. But there are people who love you, man. Put the gun...."

"But you can't listen with a gun to your head, man! You gotta relax a little. Please just hear me. You are loved, man—I just know it. Huh! I have to laugh at that. One of our friends used to say that all the time... 'I just know it.' But it's true. Somebody loves you. Somebody...."

"Like... like me. I love you."

"What? That sounds strange to you? We just don't hear that enough in this world."

"If I'd said 'I love you' more to my friend, maybe he wouldn't.... I did love him, and I'd bet there is someone out there who loves you too. You have a girlfriend, a boyfriend? What about your mom? Your dad?"

"Well, then, a teacher? A boss, a coworker? We just don't stop to think about all the people in the world who care for us. My friend and me, we knew this girl... man, what a trip. Called us both 'heartthrob.' I don't think I'd ever seen her cry until she heard what happened. She was a wreck, man, of all of it. And this other friend, the lady who said 'I just know it' all the time? We worked with her. She was the nicest person. My friend and I both got fired on the same day. This lady almost quit after what happened. So doesn't that prove that even coworkers can love you?"

"Look, I'm not going to lie to you. It's hard. Life is hard. You can get through this. But if you do this, there is someone—probably lots of someones—who will never get over it. Every day, they'll think of you, remember some tiny thing you did for them, some gesture, and their souls will die just a little bit. Don't do that to someone, man. You can't know how bad it feels."

"But you know, guy, things change. Maybe it will hurt a little less tomorrow, then the next day even less. We don't know the future, man."

"Great. We'll take it one day at a time, okay? I'm glad you called. We can get through this together. You're not alone, man. Believe me… you're not alone."

"You're damn right I'm making sense. Come on. Humor me. Stop this now. Give it some time. Call me again tomorrow and the next day and the next. Eventually, you'll see just how much sense I'm making. Will you do that? Will you let it ride for a while? Just until you can think it all out. I'm here for you. I'll be here for you. And if I'm not here, I've got some good buddies who will want to talk to you. Why? Because they care too. I'll tell them all about you. What's your name, guy? Just your first name—that's a start."

"Great to meet you, Sean. Now, what say you lock that gun away? Just for now. And keep my number right by the phone if you have the urge to get it out again. We'll be waiting to hear from you."

"Awesome! Feeling a little better is better than not feeling at all. Can you do something for me? I want you to empty the bullets out of the gun. Put the phone down and let me hear the bullets fall from the chamber. Then pick the phone back up. I'll be right here. I'll wait… I'll listen."

"Good! That's a great step! Now, put those bullets in a safe place and lock that gun away. And if you feel like getting them out again, you'll call me first? We can get through this together. I'm telling you, you're not alone, man."

"I know, I know… my friend used to say that his life was like a bad TV movie. That's how bad he thought he had it. I wish I'd listened better back then, when he said that. I wanted that movie to have a happy ending. Maybe, just maybe…."

Heartthrob
The Story of a Teenage Actor

Summer, 1963

Scene 1

Fade in: Interior—office of *Kerry!* producer Stan Waldman
Morning

NATE LAUGHED. A tiny little chuckle. He hoped Paul didn't notice. There they sat, he and his manager/dad, in the waiting room outside the office of producer Stan Waldman, a man who would soon decide his fate. Would Waldman hire him, or would he send him away?

Mr. Waldman and superstar comic Kerry Flanagan were casting a new sitcom. And Nate was here, at an honest-to-God contract negotiation. Nate was sick to death of cattle calls, those herds of faces that somehow looked far too much like his, sitting eagerly with headshots in hand, hoping to read the scenes that would bring instant stardom. That's what Paul had gotten for him so far—enormous, get-your-hopes-up-but-not-too-far cattle calls. One had even led to a role on a soap, not quite a featured role, but Nate had made the best of it.

But he sat here now, not because of Paul, who thought he was the best manager in the world—he wasn't—but because Nate took this into his own hands. He knew his imitation of his arrogant father would someday come in handy. As soon as Nate had seen the notice in *Variety* about this new Kerry Flanagan show and seen that Flanagan's character had sons, Nate had brazenly called Stan Waldman's office. Using his best Paul Berrigan, he pitched the idea of Mr. Waldman giving his "son" an audition. Nate was flabbergasted it worked, but Mr. Waldman told "Paul" to send in his son's résumé, and then he put his secretary on the line to set up a sit-down.

That led to a round of auditions. How Paul and his mother, Monica, didn't get suspicious when he left the apartment for these appointments, he didn't know. Probably because they didn't care if he came or went. After all, his life was like a bad movie anyway. That first trip, his mother did ask. He told her he'd gone to see *Dr. No*, the movie featuring Sean Connery as secret agent James Bond, which had just opened and was so popular that Monica was bound to know about it. That excuse worked, so after that, he figured she and Paul decided he'd become a big movie fan.

He took the city bus to the studios, and first came the cold read. He liked the character, so he felt like he did a great job. He managed to convince them that his manager was out of town for a few weeks and that he would call them back. That violated every industry rule. The callback was sacred, and it was always done by the show's reps. But somehow, they believed Nate.

So he called them back with his Paul Berrigan voice, and he was invited back to do chemistry readings. They liked him and wanted to see how he worked with others reading for the roles of the brothers his character had. Those readings must have gone well, because when "Paul" called back in two days, Nate was asked to read for Mr. Waldman and the star, Kerry Flanagan.

That reading went extremely well, despite the fact that Mr. Flanagan didn't seem to be interested in what they were doing at all. Mr. Waldman, however, was quite complimentary. When Nate and his potential costars were finished, Mr. Waldman said, "Give us a minute, Nate. My secretary will be happy to get you a soft drink if you like." Then he looked at the other boys. "Thanks for coming in, guys. We're finished with you today. Stay safe."

Nate retreated to the outer office with the two guys he'd just read scenes with. One of them, the older one, said, "Wow. Sounds like you're about to get hired. They sent me on my merry way and didn't call back to give me the news until three days later."

"A week for me," the younger boy said.

The older one added, "Well, Nate"—he extended his hand for Nate to shake—"see you on set."

"I haven't gotten the part yet," Nate answered.

"You will."

The boys had barely left the office when Mr. Waldman's voice came over the speaker on the secretary's desk: "Send Nathaniel Berrigan back in, please." She opened the door and ushered Nate back into the office.

"So, is your manager back in town? We want to speak to him, and we need him here tomorrow, if possible. Can I call him?"

"Sure thing, Mr. Waldman. He should be back this morning sometime," Nate lied.

"So I can make the call this afternoon?"

"Definitely."

"Pleasure to meet you, Nathaniel."

"Call me Nate. And thank you."

Kerry Flanagan made no move as Mr. Waldman ushered Nate out.

When that call came, Paul blew up like a puffer fish. He was convinced his influence among industry bigwigs had, out of the blue, gotten Nate the audition. What a fool. Nate wasn't very old and hadn't been in the business very long, but he was well aware of the way those bigwigs looked at Paul. They were more than happy to get rid of him as quickly as they could.

But when Paul asked what he was laughing about, Nate just said, "Nothing." And wished they'd get shown in before Paul asked too many questions, got too many ideas.

Paul Berrigan was a total loser. As a manager. As a father. Nate had come to that realization long ago. At first, it wasn't like he was old enough to do much about it. And so he had to pretend Paul knew what he was doing. But Nate was old enough now to take care of himself. He sat in awe of how he'd managed to get this audition. And he intended to get that contract sewn up. If Paul didn't screw it up for him. Paul was good at that.

So they sat. And funny thing—well, it wouldn't be so funny for the secretary who had stepped out of the office ten minutes ago and wasn't back yet—the intercom was open. Paul and Nate could hear everything that was being said in Stan Waldman's inner sanctum.

"Hold up, will ya?" Waldman seemed to be on the telephone. "Ken MacDonald's agent's on the line. He wants us to consider Mac for the role of the publisher."

"That old fag?" Nate recognized that voice. Who wouldn't? It was Kerry Flanagan, star of stars. "No way. Not in my show."

Hearing that, Nate could imagine how quickly the producer must have covered the receiver. America's favorite comic should not be overheard spouting that kind of stuff. Nate knew what the word meant, and he certainly knew most people didn't say that word. They might think it, but they didn't say *fag* out loud. If Paul was a real father, he would have covered Nate's ears—or at least reacted in *some* way, for he surely heard it the same as Nate. *But Paul Berrigan is no father, just a drunken, scheming sperm donor.*

"Sorry, Kerry wants to go another way with the role." Via intercom, Nate heard the sound of receiver meeting phone. Waldman had hung up.

"You know, Ker, Mac might have been good in the part."

"I don't work with queers, you hear? Not now, not ever." Flanagan was adamant. "But from the looks of this office, you do. You gotta fire that flaming faggot decorator of yours. Him and his fancy-schmancy desk you're sittin' behind."

Kerry Flanagan, worshipped by millions, is no Mr. Nice Guy. Queers? Flaming faggots? His fans would be in shock. They might say or think those words themselves, but they certainly wouldn't want to hear them from their idol's lips. Nate was sort of in shock himself. But Nate was smart for his age. He knew that tirade jab was just a control tactic. He was sure of it. The producer was supposed to be in charge, but it was clear the man in charge of this show was Kerry Flanagan. And Kerry was not the Mr. Nice Guy his public image made him out to be. Nate was taking mental notes. He'd remember that when he got in there.

"Look, Kerry, I'm not listening to your bullshit. I like my office just the way it is."

"Whatever you say, Stan. Whatever you say."

"Shall we get on with what you came for?"

"Another kid to read for Brian. Damn, Stan. I thought we agreed on that little shit we read yesterday."

"This is the kid we read yesterday. Are you so out of it you don't remember we agreed to offer him the part? His reading today is just a formality. You know how it goes. Huh?" No answer from Mr. Flanagan. Again, Mr. Waldman's voice: "Berrigan? Nathaniel Berrigan? Nate? He was perfect. We both agreed, and afterwards we decided to call him back today. Remember, before we heard Nate read, I called up my friend who produces the soap the boy was on? Ring a bell? M' friend sent me a loop of some of his scenes. I was impressed. I thought you were. Then the reading with the other kids we cast. Perfection. Ker, does any of this register with you?"

"Yeah, yeah," they heard Mr. Flanagan say. "I remember the kid. Just wanted to make sure you did." That statement was, Nate thought, not very genuine. As disinterested as Mr. Flanagan seemed yesterday, he probably didn't remember Nate. *And despite the fact he supposedly conferenced with Mr. Waldman when I was waiting in the outer office, Mr. Flanagan, it seems, doesn't even remember they're calling me back for a contract negotiation. He may be America's favorite comedian, but I predict he will not be easy to work with. But I don't care. I want this job.*

Paul slapped his leg. Nate knew he was eating this up. To get to hear the private conversation of a powerful producer and a superstar was right up Paul's alley. Nate was more cautious. Especially when they heard Mr. Flanagan was not letting it go.

"Soap, huh?"

Nate heard the derision in Flanagan's voice. *I can win him over. I can win him over. I can win him over. Just don't screw this up. Get me that contract, Paul.*

"Yeah." Mr. Waldman said that as if he had no intention of getting into it again with Kerry Flanagan. *So, Mr. Waldman's in my corner.* "Here's his headshot. Nathaniel Berrigan. I know you remember him. Wonderful read. Great chemistry with the other boys. A few commercials, two years, off and on, on the soap. Experienced. The right age. Quit shitting me, Kerry."

There was a long pause. Then Nate heard Flanagan's voice again, this time with a bit more music in it, a bit happier. "He kinda looks like me." *Yes!*

Nate felt a stir in Paul, sitting next to him. *He probably has a hard-on from that last statement coming out of Kerry Flanagan. It's the cherry on the sundae. Nothing will stop those negotiations now.* Nate smiled at his own good fortune and also at Paul's thinking he might have a cash cow sitting next to him. *Sad thing to think about your own father's thought processes, but that's the way Paul thinks. It's all about money.* So much so that Paul had completely, Nate knew, glossed over the fact that he, Nate, had already been here several times for auditions. Paul had only heard the money phrase: He kinda looks like me. Paul had just sat beside him and heard the same vile things Nate heard, but letting his son work with a man like Kerry Flanagan was A-OK if it led to the big bucks. *But I can take care of myself, Paul. No worries. You don't have to protect me from Kerry Flanagan. No. As if you ever would. This is gonna be my show, my job, my ticket. No thanks to you.*

Then the door to Stan Waldman's private office opened. The tall, impeccably dressed, silver-haired man with the bushy mustache peered out, first to the secretary's desk. Nate figured this was the first he knew his secretary was on a break. Then he turned his gaze to Nate and Paul.

Nate and Paul stood. Paul tugged at Nate, pulling Nate just a tiny bit behind him. *So, he's taking charge. The manager. The man.* Nate smiled.

Holding out his hand, Mr. Waldman bypassed Paul and greeted the son, "Nathaniel...."

Nate shook his hand and began to remind him it's "Nate," but his father pushed him aside, cutting him off. Paul held out his hand to Mr. Waldman and started to speak. But the producer turned and ushered them into the room before Paul could get his clutches on him. *Score one for Stan Waldman.*

But the man's tactic hadn't dissuaded Paul Berrigan. He quickly regained what little composure he'd lost—Nate had seen this happen far too many times—and with his uniquely irritating bravado, stepped to Flanagan first, then to Mr. Waldman, who had regained his power spot behind his desk, and shook hands.

"Glad you could see us. I've guided the kid's career every step of the way. Give him the part, and I can assure you that you will love his work," Paul said. "Nice desk."

Nate almost laughed. *Paul has no sense of "reading the room." He just heard what Kerry said about that desk, and yet Paul still thinks Stan Waldman is the man in charge.*

From the corner of his eye, Nate saw Kerry shoot a *look* at his producer.

"Happy to have you, Paul. Good to see you, Nathaniel," Mr. Waldman said.

"Nate," Nate said, quietly. He didn't want to ruin this, couldn't ruin this. He was willing to let Paul take the lead—until his superego kicked in and the deal started turning sour, at least. That happened a lot with Paul. Nate knew he, Nate, could wow this powerful man and even more powerful superstar with his quiet, humble ways. And his talent. He would clinch this. Still, he was underage, so it was up to Paul, his guardian, to seal the deal. *If I could do the paperwork, control my own money and career, I would. But for now, I have to let Paul do all that legal stuff. My day will come soon—come on, eighteen—and then I can only hope Paul and Monica socked away some of the dough I've made because I'll be out of there. They can sink or swim, as far as I care.*

"Nate—I remember," said Waldman, smiling. Nate liked Mr. Waldman. He seemed to see something in Nate that many in the industry didn't see. *Wow. I can do this.*

"But we use *Nathaniel* professionally," Paul interjected, like he couldn't be left out of the conversation, such as it was. *And once again, Paul completely ignores the* I remember. *Paul is predictable, at least. Can't keep his mouth shut.*

It's my career. Nate glanced at his dad. *I'll handle it. You just keep quiet until your signature is needed on the dotted line.* He wished he could say that out loud.

Mr. Waldman looked at Paul, and he looked at Nate, who thought he saw understanding in the producer's eyes. There was a flicker of *I've dealt with his kind before. I feel for you.*

"Sit, sit." Flanagan took charge, as Nate expected, motioning to a conference table. With a tinge of impatience, Flanagan jerked his head toward the table. "The sides are there. One more reading with Mr. Flanagan here. What say?" Nate saw the piece of paper with the typed lines on it. In the business, that's called sides. He glanced at them when he picked them up. This was a different scene from the ones he'd read before. He had not read with Mr. Flanagan before.

Nate settled into a chair at the table, oozing confidence but still showing humility, while Paul hovered over him like one of those gangster's goons, there to make sure *nothin' happens.*

As Mr. Flanagan took a chair opposite Nate, Mr. Waldman pointed at Paul. "Please, have a seat, Mr. Berrigan," he said. His voice was professional and polite, but he stared down Nate's father. Paul slid into the chair next to Nate, and then Mr. Waldman took his own seat. *Do I detect a bit of cowering here on Paul's part? Good for you, Mr. Waldman.*

Just as Nate expected, Kerry took over. "I'm a TV critic in the show. I have three sons—Nate'd be the middle one, fifteen years old." He directed his words to Paul, knowing Nate already knew all this.

Paul piped up. "Like *My Three Sons.*"

Flanagan shot him a withering look and, all business, impatiently continued reciting the particulars of the show. "Brian's a wisecracker, full of spit and vinegar. Ready?" he asked, looking directly at Nate.

"Show 'em your stuff, kid," Paul said. Paul just didn't know when to quit.

Kerry's eyes darted to Paul, and the disgust on Kerry's face would have shredded a more perceptive man. But not Paul. *Can't you see what he thinks of you?* Nate shook his head a bit—not enough to be noticeable—and then buried his head in the script for a moment. Then he looked back up.

Mr. Flanagan pulled his reading glasses down from his forehead and read.

"Brian, come down here!"

Nate set the sides down, having instantly memorized the lines.

"You summoned, oh master?" In that instant, Nate became Brian, a fifteen-year-old bundle of teenage bravado. Nate smiled on the inside. *I've got this.*

Nate liked acting. It gave him a chance to be somebody else. And getting away from his real life for a while each day was a big relief.

"Cram it, kid," Flanagan continued, *"You're in big trouble! Telisa tells me you didn't come home until two last night. That right?"*

"Now, Dad, you know the Samoan Sumo conks out at nine thirty every night. I swear I got in at two past ten." Nate knew an audience would know Brian was lying, but trying to play his dad. Nate fixed a pleading smile on his face. *This is going great.*

"I know I missed curfew by two minutes," he continued, *"but the elevator was jammed. I'm sorry, Daddy."*

Perfect. Brian's a player, and I've got him playing his dad to the max.

"Well, you just start home earlier next time, Buddy Boy. And watch what you say about Telisa. She's our fourth housekeeper. You boys drove away the other three. I want to keep her. She's the best of the lot."

"Got it, Pops! From now on, she's the island queen!"

And, scene. Actors said that at the finish of a scene if there was no curtain or lights going down. Nate didn't say it, but he thought it.

That was fun! This part's mine!

"Great job!" Mr. Waldman applauded. *You can't get much better than to have the producer give you an ovation. Now, if Kerry is just as impressed....* "Very good, Nate."

"Yeah," Flanagan admitted, the first smile he'd flashed since Nate came in the room brightened his hardened demeanor. "You got what it takes, kid. You got chops." *The ultimate compliment, coming from someone who had more chops than anybody on the planet. And who didn't even remember me from the day before.*

Nate smiled, careful not to blow it by being more like his character Brian than like himself. He was not a teenager with bravado. He just hoped he'd be playing one soon.

"Thank—" But Paul cut him off.

"So, what do you think, Kerry? Can we make this deal happen?"

Nate grimaced. *Shut up, Paul! You're only here for the legal stuff. I set this up. I'm the one who sent in the headshot. Unbeknownst to you, I might add. Leave this to me.* If only Nate could say that out loud, he thought. But he could say something else.

"I love Brian, Mr. Flanagan. And Mr. Waldman, you can count on me to do anything you want with this. It would be such an honor to work with Mr. Flanagan." Nate hoped to impress both the producer and the star before Paul could quash the whole deal.

Mr. Waldman smiled at Nate. Again, Nate saw approval, admiration, and appreciation for Nate having to put up with Paul. Then he narrowed his eyes at Paul and pointedly said, "*Mr. Flanagan*"—Nate was ecstatic that Mr. Waldman was giving Paul a lecture on manners after his calling a star by his first name—"and I need to talk." He stood. "Would you two mind waiting in the outer office? We'll just be a few moments."

"Yeah, sure," Paul stammered. "Thanks for letting the kid read, Mr. Waldman…. *Mr. Flanagan*." *No doubt he's doing damage control. But it's also fun to see Paul react to being dressed down like that. He's almost groveling.* He just hoped Paul hadn't screwed this up for him.

It's too late to kiss up now, Daddy. A frown crossed Nate's face as he looked at Paul.

The producer escorted them to the door, opened it, gave Nate a pat on the shoulder, and as he motioned for them to pass through, he said, "Well, Miss Lehmann, we missed you."

As Nate sat, he saw a guilty look on the secretary's face. She started to speak, but her boss cut her off.

"We'll speak later, Miss Lehmann. For right now, maybe our guests would like something to drink."

He shut the door, and the pretty young woman flashed a smile. "Could I get you something? Water, coffee, a soft drink?"

Paul told her he was fine. Nate, dry mouthed a bit, said, "Could I have a Coke?"

"Sure thing," she answered. "Only take a minute." She left the room. And then the talking in the inner office began again. Apparently, Miss Lehmann had only just arrived from her break when Waldman had opened the door to see them out of his office. She had not, as yet, discovered the open intercom.

The producer spoke first. "So, it's a deal, Kerry? He's pretty good, no?"

"He's pretty good, *yes*, Stan." Just listening, Nate could see the smile on his face. "Best we've heard so far. And yes, I remember him from yesterday now."

"I was glad to see that he jumped right into the part, suppressing the sadness I saw at first in him."

Nate had mixed emotions at that. Yes, he was sad. Living with Paul Berrigan controlling your life would make anyone sad. But he wished Mr. Waldman hadn't noticed that part of him.

"Sadness," Flanagan said. "What sadness?" *Well, at least Mr. Flanagan isn't feeling sorry for me. But I doubt he feels sorry for many people.*

Waldman sighed and continued. "And he doesn't *look* bad, either, does he? It never hurts a show to have a potential heartthrob in the cast."

"You're right. And that *ain't* me. No dame's swooned over me in years. I'm told I was a heartbreaker when I was this kid's age, but I musta grown out of it." Flanagan laughed. "But speaking of heartthrobs— and I'm no expert here—that Samoan kid we cast as Telisa's son will probably turn a lot of preteen heads, too, you know."

"Uh-huh. Tai Atua's face will be plastered across a lot of magazine covers, but Nate will appeal to the girls who like the All-American boy look. Atua and Berrigan will be a nice combination for the show. We shoulda had them read together. But with the chemistry Nate showed with the other two boys, you can bet the sparks will fly when he and Atua are on screen."

"Laughs for Mom and Dad, courtesy of yours truly," Kerry said, "and thrills for their daughters, thanks to the two boys. And the kids? They'll love the shit Atua and Berrigan will get into."

"Got it. So, we're agreed. We bring Nate Berrigan on?"

"Absolutely." And then he added, "Let's just hope we can deal with the dad."

"I can handle him, Kerry. I know his type well."

Nate couldn't believe what he was hearing, and he certainly hoped that Paul didn't let that bit of news squelch the deal.

Miss Lehmann came back with Nate's Coke just as Nate felt Paul's body shiver at the news. He leaned over to Nate and whispered, "We did it, kid. I got you the part." *Well, apparently Paul is so lost in the first bit of news, the second statement didn't even register with him.* Before Nate could take even a sip of his Coke, Stan Waldman appeared in his office doorway.

"Come on back, gentlemen," he said, turning for them to follow him. Nate followed Paul, as usual, and Nate noticed a stricken quiver in the secretary's body as she sat at her desk. Looking at her, he realized they both saw the red light on the intercom at the same time. She quickly pushed a button and the light went off.

Nate pushed the door shut behind him, and then he turned around.

"How'd you like to be a sitcom star, kid?" Flanagan asked.

"Great, Mr. Flan—"

"Wow! Flanagan, you've made the right choice," Paul Berrigan said. "He won't let you down."

Don't blow this, Paul. Nate sighed.

But Stan Waldman was unfazed by Paul. He got right down to business. He gestured for them to sit in two chairs in front of his desk to the side of the one in which Kerry Flanagan sat, looking at them like a king surveying his peasants. He spoke fast, not giving Paul a second of response time. "We're offering a standard contract… three years or run of the show—and I'm certain the show is going to run and run." He quickly scribbled a figure on a pad and slid it over to Paul.

"That's per episode," Waldman continued, rapid-fire, "nonexclusive, except for appearances on other sitcoms."

Nate smiled at the knowing smile on the producer's face. He knew Waldman was reacting to the wide-eyed disbelief plastered on Paul's face. He liked this Stan Waldman, titan of producers, controller of arrogant fathers. Nate knew Paul was hooked.

"If Nate wants to do features during downtime, he's free to do so. One stipulation…." Waldman gestured to Flanagan. "Kerry has to approve all projects Nate takes on. Have to protect the image, right, Kerry?"

Mr. Waldman is no fool; he knows he has to stroke his star. It's in his best interest to keep him happy. Nate had been in the business long enough to know that, and his admiration for Mr. Waldman only grew.

Flanagan nodded.

"Where do I sign?" Paul asked, pulling a fountain pen from his jacket pocket with a flourish. "Want to make it official before you guys see the kid's cowlick," he joked.

Nate rolled his eyes. His producer—for now he *was* Nate's producer—gave Nate a look that said, *I feel for you, son, I feel for you.*

Scene 2

Fade in: Interior—the Berrigan apartment
A few hours later

PAUL STORMED into the apartment, Nate trailing him. Nate was bubbling inside, but he knew it was in his best interests to let Paul do the talking. *Keep the peace. Keep the peace.* Nate said that over and over in his mind all the time. It made his life easier—or so he thought. Besides, after the contract was signed, Nate was so lost in the moment, he didn't hear a word anybody said. Any details would be up to Paul to tell his mother.

And there she sprawled, his mother, Monica Berrigan, in all her glory, on the sofa. From the looks of it, she had whiled away her time thumbing through the latest issue of *Glamour*, smoking cigarette after cigarette.

Looking up, she didn't even stand. Paul had carted Nate off to too many failed auditions for his mother to get too excited. Maybe she didn't care enough. Or maybe she was steeling herself for the inevitable news that he hadn't gotten the part. Or maybe she was just spaced out on the pills she took.

"Well?" she asked nonchalantly. Her flowing orange-swirled skirt whistled against the sofa's green silk brocade as she sat up. She took a long drag off her cigarette.

"We're in," Paul said. Nate was surprised at how calmly Paul had spoken those words. He had expected him to proclaim the news like a town crier.

"What do you mean?" Monica suddenly stood, almost losing her balance. "They hired him?"

Nate moved to the living room archway as his parents talked about him like he wasn't there.

"Babe, we're in the money! Three years or run of the show." Paul gestured like he was peeling bills off a huge wad of money. "That's more than a quarter mil a year!"

"Amazing!" she screamed. "We're rich. Rich, rich, rich!" She danced around the room and stopped at Nate. "Baby, give Mama a hug."

Nate stepped toward her as she grabbed and smothered him. He'd soon be making enough money to get his mom out of there and away from Paul. His mother was just as messed up as Paul, but somehow he didn't blame her. He couldn't pinpoint it. Maybe it was because at some point she made a bad, bad decision—marrying Paul—and now she just had to live with it, anyway she could cope.

"You're going to be a mega-star, baby." She grinned and turned to Paul. "The soap was nothing compared to this."

"You bet your ass, Mama," Paul said, sprinting over to the bar. He grabbed a glass and poured himself his usual—Nate knew the order well—*three fingers of Scotch, neat*. Taking the drink, he sprawled in the nearby easy chair.

Nate's mother eased herself back down on the sofa. "Tell me all about it," she commanded.

Nate resumed his place, leaning against the wall in the archway. He wanted to hear what they had to say, but he knew he wouldn't be a part of the conversation. He never was.

"Flanagan and the producer were blown away by the kid." Paul paused to swallow. "'Course I knew they would be. How could they not, after all the coaching I've given him?"

Nate cast his eyes upward. *Coaching? I'm the one who got the first job, and I'm the one who got this one. With my talent. You, Paul, had nothing to do with it. Especially this one. You still think all those afternoons I auditioned were spent at the movies? I had to read up on* Dr. No, Spencer's Mountain, *and* Paranoiac! *just in case you asked about the "movies" I went to. That last one will prove to be a classic, Paul. You shoulda got me a part in that. Sure, I'm too young for any of the roles, but I could have "played old," and Monica would have loved going to England for the shoot.* Nate chuckled inside, just thinking of Monica drooling over a *trip abroad*, as she would call it.

Monica spoke over her shoulder, never turning her head, plunging a knife into his fantasy.

"Get me my nerve pill, will ya, hon?"

Nate sighed and left the room. He was his mother's gofer. He didn't mind it one bit unless it involved her *pills*. He hated those things. Stepping into his parents' bedroom, he could still hear their voices.

"You can't go a day without that shit, can you?" Paul had a sneer in his tone.

"Don't start, Paul," Monica said. "You don't know how nervous I've been, waiting for you two."

Nate returned with a glass of water and a yellow pill.

His mother took the pill, tossed it into her mouth, and chased it with the water. She handed the empty glass to Nate, brushing the hair off his forehead. He liked the warm touch of her fingertips. If only she did that more often. He felt a bit guilty with his snarky idea of a trip abroad. Maybe his mother deserved it. After all, she was married to Paul.

"This is only the beginning, Paul," Monica said. "Our baby's going to be a big, big star. I can feel it in my bones. After all—we deserve it!"

"You should go do your homework, kid," Paul ordered. "You're going to have a lot of extra work to keep up with everything from now on—the show, school, public appearances. No more sneakin' out to the movies." He pointed his finger. "And don't stay up too late. You have publicity shots at the studio tomorrow bright and early. They're doing yours first. Solo. Flanagan won't be there, so the group shots will come later. Get crackin'."

Nate shook his head. He'd been right there in the room when Mr. Waldman had issued those instructions. He'd heard them, loud and clear. *I guess I was listening. Not lost in the news I was going to be starring in a sitcom—well, costarring, anyway.* But Paul just had to make it sound like he was in charge and Nate was nothing.

Nate left the room but held back in the hall, peering around the corner, listening. It was *his* future they were talking about.

Monica lit still another cigarette, holding the smoldering butt of the previous one to light the new one.

"Our baby's a star, Paul," Monica said, exhaling. She leaned over to tamp the spent cigarette in the ashtray. "If only Mama was still alive to see this. That'd show her. I wanted to be a star, but she wouldn't have it. 'No—no, no, no,' she said. 'It's no life for a child.' Well, she'd be singing a different tune if she saw us now."

"Yeah, she'd be real proud of you and your pills," Paul snapped, going to the bar to freshen his drink.

Nate's mother took a deep breath and held it a moment, as if she were trying her best not to lash out at her husband. *Why does she put up with him?*

In the hallway, Nate fumed. *Lay off her. I don't know why she takes that shit off you.*

Taking a calming drag—calming is what she called it all the time—off her cigarette, Monica said, "When will he get his first paycheck, do you think?"

"First show tapes in three months. Show doesn't air till September. Meanwhile they're going to want him to do the talk show circuit and a big publicity tour. I think we can expect the first check in a coupla weeks."

"That means New York City. That's where all the junkets end up. I'll need all new outfits. Bullocks Wilshire, here I come."

"Hey, now," Paul cautioned her. "Go easy on the spending until after the first check. The soap money's just about run out, and the residuals from the commercials don't show up until next quarter."

Monica tapped her ashes into the potted plant next to the sofa. "I'll just need a few things for the trip."

Paul slugged back a swig of his Scotch and shook his head at her in disgust.

"You know, the kid was unbelievable at the audition. Photographic memory. Looked at the sides, then tossed them away and delivered the lines like he'd been working on them for weeks." *Paul sounds almost proud of me.*

"Ah, talent and brains." Monica exhaled slowly, then tapped out her cigarette. "Comes from my side of the family."

"Yeah, sure," Paul said, "but the looks—they're all Berrigan genes. I tell you, Mon, that boy's going to be a heartbreaker. The bobbysoxers will eat him up."

"This is 1963, Paul. I think that term went out with the fifties. But I know what you mean. Those teen girls are gonna be squealing every time our baby is out in public."

"I figure once the show's on the air, the movie guys'll be falling all over each other to sign him. Maybe even a recording deal."

"Nate's not a singer, Paul."

"Fabian? Paul Peterson? Jimmy Darren? None of 'em can sing for shit. They're just pretty boys, and the girls eat 'em up."

"We're on our way to the top!"

"And no more of this crappy moosepiss I been drinking. Only the best from now on." Paul downed his drink with a grimace.

"We did it," he exclaimed.

In his hiding place, Nate's eyes widened.

We?

Close-up: TV Guide Fall Preview Issue

KERRY! (UNPREVIEWED).... America's favorite clown, Kerry Flanagan, is TV critic Kerry Simon in this cookie-cutter sitcom. Single father Simon is raising three sons. (Can anyone say *My Three Sons*?) Taking the "Uncle Charley" role is Obie-winning Samoan actress Pika Togai, playing Flanagan's housekeeper. Rounding out the cast is Broadway veteran Candida Cameron as Flanagan's boss. Cameron, no doubt, will be the voice of sanity in this riot. Early buzz is that standouts in this fun fest will be newcomer Tai Atua (playing Togai's son) and daytime veteran Nathaniel Berrigan as Flanagan's middle son. Our bet is on Berrigan... the kid's a natural and should develop into a fine comic actor. And the preteen girls in the audience will find he tickles their fancy! Will *Kerry!* KO their hefty competitors *Make Room for Daddy* and *The Adventures of Ozzie and Harriet*? Mondays at 8 PM on NBC

Scene 3

Fade in: Interior—NBC Studios, Century City
First table read, *Kerry!*

NATE FELT like he was being swallowed up by the enormous soundstage. Paul walked him past a set: an apartment that looked like someone rich could live there, an office, and the front of a building with a sidewalk. Unlike the soap, *Kerry!* would be shot in front of a live audience. So the three sets sat side by side and actually weren't as large as they would appear on screen. He knew that from the soap. It must be a camera trick, but tiny sets somehow looked enormous when you watched TV.

There was a tangle, at least that's what Nate thought, of electrical cords that threatened to trip him. Several men were scurrying about, hanging lights.

Then they came to a clearing in all this commotion that Nate found both scary and exciting. *I love this! The lights, the cameras, the sets, the makeup, the people. A busy little world I can get lost in for eight or so hours a day. This is my world. And now a new life begins. No more soap. My character is dead. Although if they need him, he could be resurrected. That's the way of soap operas. And if* Kerry! *doesn't work out, they might just very well bring him back to life in my body. But that won't happen. Some other guy will get the role because I plan to make a lifetime of* Kerry! *Or at least the next eight, ten years.*

"There's your script, kid." Paul Berrigan pointed to a script laid on a large beat-up rectangular table. Scarred folding chairs surrounded it. "I'll wait over there during the rehearsal."

He pointed to a group of the same scarred folding chairs that were placed fifteen feet from the table. There was a sign designating this area for parents. With four kids in the show, the producers had thought of everything.

Nate's eyes followed Paul as he sauntered over to the chairs, and then he looked down at his script. *I'm not letting Paul ruin this for me. He can sit on the sidelines and leave me and everyone else alone. He wouldn't even be here if I hadn't gotten the audition. All me. Let him sit and swell up and think he's the reason we're here. I know the truth.*

There was only one other person at the table. The boy was about his own age, and Nate noticed that, with his copper-colored skin, this boy was strikingly good-looking. Nate shuddered, suddenly feeling inadequate as he sat. *Stop it, Nate. You heard what Mr. Waldman said. You've got it. Talent. Looks. Don't let this kid shake you.*

Nate glanced over at the script in front of the boy. In large letters, someone had scrawled PELE. He looked at the boy and thought, *Makes sense. Well, it's now or never. I hate this shyness that comes over me, but I'm an actor, aren't I? Here goes nothing. Or something, I hope.*

With all the false confidence he could muster, Nate looked at the boy, held out his hand, and said, "I'm playing Brian. I guess you're Pele, if I can believe that script in front of you."

"Yep," the boy said. "I'm Pele. Otherwise known as Tai. Good to meet ya, Nate." Tai grasped Nate's hand, shook once, slid his fingers down Nate's palm, hooked fingertips with him, then held his knuckles out for Nate to knock. Nate followed the ritual hesitantly. *Is this some sort of Dick Tracy-ish secret handshake I've never seen before? After all, I suppose you have to have a friend to have a secret handshake, and I have neither.*

"This is gonna be fun, man," Tai said. Tai's smile was as wide as the table in front of them. Nate couldn't help but like him. "I've been looking over the script. You've got some great lines. Brian's a hoot."

"Oh?" Nate looked at his script, embarrassed. For what, he didn't know.

"Lighten up, man," Tai said soothingly. *Soothingly? Why did I think that? Seems crazy for me to think something like that.* But that's what he thought. This boy, Tai, did have a nice voice.

"You're probably going to steal this show from America's favorite comedian. I saw you on that soap. You're good, man. I'm gonna have to up my game to keep up with you. And I might have to bribe the writers to give me some of those lines of yours." Tai's smile penetrated Nate, and he instantly knew he was indeed going to have fun with this show, if only because he was working with this powerhouse icebreaker.

"One thing I do know, our show is gonna be a big relief after all that crap this summer in Alabama—what was their governor's name? Wallace, that's it—that shit with Wallace trying to keep those kids, just 'cause he didn't like their color, from going to the college was too much, man. Who cares what color you are? Everybody needs an education."

Who is this guy? First he's just the boy I'll be acting with, and then he turns into a civil rights marcher. Should I like that about him, or should I be afraid of him?

Nate mumbled, "I don't know much about that." And he was telling the truth. Nate didn't have a TV in his room. Paul, who probably didn't want to spend the money to buy him one, said, "You don't need to be wasting time watching the boob tube, kid. You should be studying scenes, developing your craft." Paul loved to sound like he was a big-shot acting coach.

"Dude! Next you're gonna tell me you didn't hear Kennedy's civil rights speech. That was awesome, man. The Pres promised us a civil rights bill that's gonna take care of haters like Wallace. Tell me you know all about this stuff, Nate, my man."

This kid—what's his name? Tai—is really on fire about all this. Then it dawned on Nate. *Tai may not be officially black, but he's pretty dark. Maybe this stuff he's talking about affects him. And here I am, stuck in my little cocoon, not even listening to what's going on in the world.*

Before Nate could say anything, though, Tai said, "Okay, man. I'll leave you alone so you can get a sense of this brilliant Brian you're plotting."

Nate opened his script, wanting to get a feel for his character but not wanting to quit talking to Tai. He wanted to tell him he was on his side. He wanted to promise him he'd follow the news more. He wanted to make Tai feel like he cared about him and the world. For the first time in his life, he'd made an instant connection with someone—and Tai was certainly someone he wanted to connect with. He hoped some of Tai's bravado would rub off on him. Nate scanned the pages for his lines. A yellow highlighter was at his place, ready for him to mark his speeches. Those pens were neat. No more underlining, like he'd had to do before these things came on the market earlier that year.

Nate sneaked a look at Tai. But Tai was staring at him, so Nate quickly averted his eyes. Tai, though, was having none of it. He gently slapped Nate on the hand. "Don't look away from me. We're in this together, and our characters are best friends. That's what you and I are gonna be." Tai once again flashed that smile that Nate was beginning to get attached to. Tai returned to the task of highlighting his lines, but before Nate did the same, he eyed Paul, making sure he wasn't up to something that Nate would regret.

Paul had sat down next to a woman, her lap filled with yarn and an uncompleted scarf, calmly knitting. She smiled and opened her mouth to speak. Nate strained to hear what was being said.

"I'm Joana Atua," she said. She nodded toward the table. "My son Tai's playing Pele."

"Paul Berrigan," Paul said. "My kid's doing Brian. I'm his manager." He laughed. "Thought I'd stick around to keep an eye on my little investment."

Nate shot a glance at Tai, next to him. *Did he hear Paul's comment?*

Nate turned again so he could make out what Paul was saying to Tai's mom.

Eyes on her knitting, the woman said, "Oh, we have someone who takes care of Tai's business. I'm just here to lend support. Boys his age act like they know it all, but they're really just little boys still, aren't they?"

Paul mumbled a *yeah* and opened the morning newspaper he had carried in. Nate smiled. *Score a point for the Samoan lady.*

It must have been obvious to Tai that Nate's focus was not on his script. Nate heard that voice again.

"Checkin' out my mama, huh?"

Nate was startled by the question. He certainly didn't want Tai to think he was *checking out* his mother. That sounded really dirty or something to him.

Tai laughed. "Gotcha! That your dad over there talking to Mama? I was concentrating on highlighting, but I think I caught them talking about you and me."

Nate just nodded, hoping Tai would take his response at face value and not do any probing. It was clear that Tai's mother and his father had totally different styles of parenting. Or rather, she actually parented; Paul *managed*.

Over the next half hour, more and more people showed up, taking their assigned places at the table. Two more boys arrived, one younger than Nate and Tai, the other older. They took places across the table. Tai,

like he did with Nate, introduced himself, then said, "And this is Nate."
Startled, Nate looked at Tai as the other boys greeted him and Tai.

The older boy added, "We've met. We read together at callbacks.
Remember? I told you you were getting this part." He smiled.

Nate blushed. "I'm glad you were right," he said with no bravado
at all. He wished, once again, he were more like Tai.

"Now I'm pissed," Tai said. "They didn't have *me* read with you
guys. I guess I don't count."

Nate was surprised at this glint of insecurity in his new friend.

Tai quickly recovered as a large woman as dark as he was sat down
next to him.

"Hey, Miss Togai," Tai said, beaming at the woman.

She patted his hand and said, "Well, hello, my little scene partner."

Tai leaned into Nate and the other boys. "I got to read with Miss
Togai. I guess they thought the two of us needed to fit together more than
I needed to fit with you guys."

The woman must have overheard, because she added, "No, dear,
they wanted to make sure you looked like a son of mine. And don't for a
minute think they didn't want to make sure there was chemistry between
you and the other boys. That casting director is good at his job. He knew
you'd have chemistry with anyone you worked with."

Nate saw Tai's face brighten up into the biggest smile he'd ever
seen on any human being. He was going to like working with Tai. This
guy was something else, friendly, confident, nice, and with just a touch
of rebel. Nate liked that. And he liked Miss Togai, whom he assumed
was playing the housekeeper.

A very pretty lady, old enough to be his grandmother, settled in
next to Nate. She had short, curly, almost white hair and the reddest lips
Nate had ever seen. Unwrapping a chain of bright-colored stone beads
from the glasses she'd taken from her purse, she turned. "Candy," she
said, giving Nate her hand. "I followed you in *Days*. You were terrific.
You were the only reason I ever watched it. And now you're a part of our
little family. You're going to be wonderful in this. I just know it."

Nate shrank a bit, overwhelmed by this talkative woman. He
awkwardly shook her hand and smiled at her. She flashed a huge
smile back. *First Tai, now this woman—all smiles and welcoming and
accepting me. I have to get over this reluctance to put myself out there.
This, after all, is my new family.* He took a breath, pasted a smile across

his face, and said, "I'm jazzed about this. And thanks for making me feel so welcome." *Wow! I'm really getting into this talking thing. And I even managed to throw in some hip language. Jazzed? I didn't even know I knew that word.*

"Aren't you a little pistol," Candy exclaimed, and then she turned to the others at the table. "Well, this is going to be delightful! I just know it!" she gushed. "Candida Cameron." She waved. "But you can all call me Candy. We're going to be one big happy family here. I just know it." Nate couldn't help but swell with joy. This woman, his first friend here— no, his second here—was a hoot—using Tai's word.

"I saw your Broadway show last season, Miss Cam—" Miss Togai was interrupted by a scolding look from the Broadway veteran.

"Candy," the woman corrected her. "And forget me. You are fabulous! And here we are. Working together. What a pleasure, dearie. Who could forget your performance in *South Pacific*? I saw Juanita Hall do Bloody Mary in the original, but you had a whole new take on the role. You deserved that Obie you got, love." She turned her attention away from Miss Togai long enough to tell us all, "For those of you who are not schooled in New York theater, the Obie is the highest award you can win for an off-Broadway performance. Pika here"—*I love how Candy just assumes she can use Miss Togai's first name*—"was a standout in a beautiful new production of Rodgers and Hammerstein's classic. Oh, her 'Bali Hai' stole my heart!" Candy clutched her clasped hands to her chest. "It was a symphony, just a symphony! You're going to bring your music to this table, starting today, my dear. I just know it!"

Nate felt a warmth. This woman, this Candy, was a treasure. He didn't know what *South Pacific* was, what "Bali Hai" was, he didn't know who Rodgers and Hammerstein were, but if Candy loved them and loved Miss Togai for her performance in this play, then he knew he would feel the same about her. After all, he was already in love with Candy. And Tai. Could he call that *love*? Two new friends, both equally as easy to talk to, both who reached out to him and penetrated his standoffishness. *Yes*, he decided, *I can love them both.*

A lanky, balding blond man came from the shadows.

"I knew I could count on you to break the ice, Candy." He leaned over and pecked her on the cheek.

Grabbing his arm and holding his cheek to hers, the actress said, "Everyone... have you met our director, Sam Taylor? Don't let his youthful looks fool you. We worked together on a *Hey Jeannie!* episode. What was it, Sammy? Five… no six… years ago? Don't answer. Humor me if it was longer than that. You'll destroy my youthful image here." Then she focused back on the inhabitants of the table. "Sammy is a treasure! You'll all just love him. I just know it."

God, could I have wished for anyone else sitting next to me? Candy is amazing. I love everything about her. Ten minutes, and in his eyes, Candida Cameron could do no wrong. And on the other side of him was his other guardian angel. *I'm the luckiest guy in the world!*

The director laughed at Candy, his champion, having heard her catch phrase a thousand times before, no doubt.

"Candy is too, too kind," he said, breaking away from her and sitting at the end of the table. "But we are going to do some good work here. From what Stan and Kerry have told me, they've assembled a top-notch cast. I know Candy well. Miss Togai, I'm in awe of your work. Nate, I viewed your loop from *Days*, and I'm excited to work with you."

Nate blushed. Tai leaned over and whispered, "Looks like I *am* going to have to demand some of those lines of yours." Then he squeezed Nate's arm to show he was kidding.

The director continued, "And you guys"—he swept his arm around to include the other boys at the table—"are amazing, if I believe our producer. This is going to be the most fun I've ever had as a director. Let's get down to business, shall we?"

Almost in unison, everyone at the table sort of leaned in toward their director to show they were with him.

"I trust the messenger service delivered the character sketches I prepared for you all? Any questions? I like to send character sketches. Gives you an idea of what I'm looking for without revealing the plot of the first episode. That, I like to keep under wraps until the table read." He looked at each of his cast. "No questions, then?" He nodded. "Good. We'll get started for real as soon as Kerry and Stan arrive." He smiled, then thumbed through papers on a clipboard he had brought with him. "Feel free to ask questions if you have any as you study."

Nate and the others buried themselves in their scripts. Another twenty minutes passed before Stan Waldman and Kerry Flanagan burst through the door to the studio.

"I'm telling you, Stan," Flanagan was saying, "that crap in *TV Guide* chaps me. Spread the word, Stan, and make sure the world knows I'm the star here, you hear?"

Nate, startled, looked up. He glanced over at Tai, who slightly nodded toward Mr. Flanagan with a twisted smile, as if to say, "What's up with him?"

"My people will take care of it, Ker," Mr. Waldman told his star. "I guarantee we can quash any negatives in this week's *Variety*. Just give my guys a chance."

The two were now standing at the table, but right before they arrived, Sam stood. And he motioned for his entire cast to stand.

"Welcome, everyone," Stan Waldman said as Mr. Flanagan sat. Mr. Flanagan commanded attention. There was no doubt he was now at the head of the table. With Mr. Flanagan on his throne, Mr. Waldman motioned for them all to sit. "My assistants are preparing your dressing rooms as we speak," Waldman continued. "Assignments will be made after the read. But first, Kerry here wanted to give you time to get acquainted. Sam"—he gestured toward the director—"why don't you take over?"

"Okay, um—" The director was interrupted by his star.

"Where are the writers?" he barked at Mr. Waldman. "I specifically said I wanted them here at the first read. Get 'em up here now—now, now, now!"

Stan Waldman went toward an assistant standing in the dark.

"Well, until they get here, let's—" The director was interrupted once again.

"Just hold your horses," Mr. Flanagan ordered.

Sam Taylor took a breath, then dropped his eyes to his script. Candy looked at him with pity. Miss Togai looked daggers at Kerry Flanagan, but he didn't notice—or didn't care. The youngest of the four boys looked over at his mother for reassurance. Tai huffed a faint "*Jackass*" under his breath, while the oldest boy drummed his fingers silently on the table. After observing all this, Nate concentrated on his script, trying to block out the whole incident. Mr. Flanagan's tirade reminded him too much of home.

Seven long minutes passed… the only sound coming from Kerry Flanagan's impatient breathing… then three men and a woman came into the studio, trailing Mr. Waldman.

Without even looking at the producer, Mr. Flanagan demanded, "Where ya been? I don't pay you to sit on your asses and drink coffee all day, ya know?"

Nate watched the silent writers pull up folding chairs and sit with scripts in laps. Mr. Waldman also took up a folding chair, a bit removed from the action. He looked as if he'd had his fill of Kerry Flanagan.

"Okay, *now*, Sam!" Mr. Flanagan shouted.

"Great." The director put on a brave smile. Nate really felt sorry for him. Sam—for Nate was really thinking of him by his first name now—had been so happy before this… this…. Nate didn't know what to call Kerry Flanagan now. He wasn't sure this loudmouth deserved being called "Mr.," and yet he was his boss, so he was going to have to just keep quiet and let it all wash over him. At least he had practice with this thing. At home. Lots of practice.

Sam finally said, "Let's just read through, shall we? Page one, episode one… 'The Killer Review.'"

The cast read the script as the writers took notes. Nate had some of the funniest lines. He found just the right delivery, keeping the entire table in stitches. *This is the most fun I've had in forever.*

After twenty-two minutes, Candida Cameron delivered the final line.

Flanagan closed his script and turned to the writers. "I want rewrites in one hour. I'll send my notes to you. And I can tell you right now, giving *her*"—he pointed to Candy—"the last say is unacceptable. The name of this show is *Kerry!*" He stood up and left the stage without a word to the director or his cast members.

Nate looked at Candy, who now simply stared at the tabletop. *He had no right to say that. Not in front of her like that.* But he was also glad Mr. Flanagan didn't tell the writers to cut Brian's laugh lines. But that might be in those notes Mr. Flanagan had promised the writers. *Mr. Flanagan? Why am I giving him that kind of respect? From now on, I will call him Kerry or jackass, as long as I'm not facing him. I can kiss butt then. That's all he deserves. And yes, Kerry could tell the writers to cut or rewrite my lines at any time. Especially if I get all the laughs.*

Sam Taylor diplomatically said, "Mr. Flanagan is a busy man, but I'm sure he is as pleased with the reading as I am. You were all wonderful. Now remember, Monday mornings, we'll do the table read at ten. By one, we'll have rewrites and begin blocking. Tuesdays are reserved for anything that comes up. Wednesdays, we rehearse, incorporating additional rewrites. Thursday morning, camera run-through, Thursday afternoon, dress. On Fridays, we tape… two runs with audience. We splice together the best takes. And gentlemen"—he looked at the boys at the table—"you also have to squeeze in lessons with the show's teacher whenever you can. Tall order, but you boys can handle it." Then he turned his attention to everyone. "Now, you've got fittings. See you on set at one. Don't be late."

Nate was the first to arise, eager to see his dressing room.

Before he and the rest departed, Candy Cameron chimed, "That went well. We're going to make a great team. And Kerry is going to be wonderful. I just know it."

Scene 4

Fade in: Interior—Tai's bedroom
That evening

TAI SPRAWLED across his bed, pencil in hand, studying his script. His mind wandered to the events of that first day. He smiled as he thought of Candy, Miss Togai, the other guys, and of Nate. If only Mr. Jackass Flanagan had been as nice as they all had been. But even if Flanagan was a butt, he, Tai Atua, was in a network TV show. Wow!

What a shock. When he found out about that open casting call and decided to go, he never, ever thought he'd get it. He'd never done any acting before. But he decided if they needed a fifteen-year-old Polynesian, then he was their guy. He got his mother to drive him down there, not knowing what to expect. He didn't even have professional headshots, only some Polaroids he'd brought along with him, not even knowing if he'd need them. The whole thing was a trip. There were at least thirty guys there, all Polynesian like him, reading for this one role. He didn't even know there were that many Polynesians his age in LA. Most of them were a lot better-looking than he was. He almost just turned around and walked out. But Tai had one thing, he thought, that most of these guys probably didn't have. Confidence. He had confidence to spare, so, sitting there, he kept telling himself, *You're gonna get this, man.*

And it happened. He read. They loved him. He got it. He almost threw up from the tension of it all, combined with the reaction he'd gotten from his reading. He was going to be in a TV show. He kept saying it over and over in his head, trying to make himself believe it.

Getting to do the show was a needed distraction. His life was pretty good anyway—his mother and his dad treated him like royalty—but the summer had been filled with all that race stuff. That bozo governor in

Alabama and how he treated those two kids—kids who were not much older than he was and not much blacker than he was. Yeah, he knew he wasn't black like they were, but his dark skin certainly stuck him in their category, at least for some people, the haters. President Kennedy made that awesome speech and made promises, but it takes time to get new laws made, and he sure hoped that time was shorter rather than longer. But meanwhile, he got the show, and he got something else to set his mind on.

His mother was in shock at the money they offered in the contract. It probably wasn't as much as Candy or Miss Togai were getting, most likely not even as much as Nate was offered, since he had experience, but it was more money than he'd ever dreamed he could make. Certainly more than the paper route he had once or that job sacking groceries he'd been facing after school this year. Wow. It was so much that his mother hired a business manager. And once *Kerry!* took off—and he knew it would be a hit—he'd be up for other roles, other jobs.

This whole thing was a trip. Having a job that's not really a job. *This acting thing is fun, I'm making a ton of bread, and I met Nate.* His heart leapt when he thought of him. *Don't, Tai. You know it's wrong, even if you've been doing it for a long time now. It's a sin. Just ask Father Tim. And if you want to go to hell, don't drag Nate down with you. No matter how much you might want to.*

The doorbell chimed, and then his mother called out, "Tai, baby, Kyle is here."

"In my room," Tai yelled back. He sat up, tossing the script aside. *Kyle. I've got to break it off with him. Or at least make him see reason. He's the one who got me into all this. If he hadn't pushed, I don't think I ever would have let myself do it.*

A lanky sandy-haired boy with piercing turquoise-colored eyes, Kyle bounded into the room.

"How's it hangin', dude?" He plopped down on the bed, next to Tai.

"Kyle!" Tai cried out as the bed shook. "Mama doesn't like it when you fall on the bed that hard. You know that. I do have a chair in the room, you know." It was true Mama didn't like it, but mostly he said that hoping to put some distance between Kyle and him.

"Tai, you're such a mama's boy. Little Tai, Baby Tai, Mama's baby," he taunted, grabbing the script.

Tai lunged at him, snatching the script from Kyle's hand.

"Secret, huh?" Kyle fought with him, trying to get the script back. "That show you're on a porno? A blue movie? You ashamed of it?"

No, I'm ashamed of you. If only he could bring himself to say that. *But it's not Kyle's fault he's the way he is. That's between him and his God. My shame has nothing to do with Kyle. I just wish Kyle hadn't been so persuasive.*

"No, Kyle," Tai said, clutching the script to his breast. "It's just I don't want to mess up my first script, ya know, man. It's special."

Kyle laughed. "You're such a dork. But I'm cool."

Tai turned red.

"Okay, hippie boy, before you turn so red that that magic paper there catches fire, tell me about the first day. Anybody groovy?" Kyle asked. *The world has barely heard of hippies, and Kyle thinks they're going to take over. He's sure taken to their lingo.*

"Lots of nice people, Kyle, lots of nice people." Hoping his evasion was successful, Tai, with deliberation, pulled open the drawer of his nightstand and carefully placed his script away. He didn't need Kyle defiling it or his new job—or his newfound friend. He would tread lightly if Kyle asked about Nate. But why would he?

"So—" Kyle prodded him. "You gonna tell your best friend about these *nice people*? Or maybe you want to keep them a secret, too, like your precious script?"

Kyle can be such a hardass sometimes. I'm not sure I even like him anymore. Yeah, when we first got together, we were tight. But then we started.... He convinced me I wanted it. I did it just because that's what he wanted. And I liked it. Then I convinced myself it was okay. I was willing. But it hardly seems worth it to risk eternal damnation with such a hot dog. He throws around his hippie stuff like he's a part of it all. Such a showoff. And can I trust him? He does like to be the center of attention. Like when he takes me to the Strip. Here he is, not more than a little bit older than me, but you'd think he's a fully-grown hotshot. He gets us into all the clubs. It was fun at first—and might be fun now if I was with the right person. But even if I didn't feel like Father Tim would cast me into hell for what we do, I'm tired, tired, tired of Kyle and his steamrolling ways.

Tai turned toward Kyle slowly. "Okay, okay, okay…." Tai took a breath. Then he spilled it all in rapid succession. "The show is great. The director seems like a really nice guy. The producer, Mr. Waldman, must be a saint to put up with Mr. Flanagan." *You don't need to know how I really feel about that jackass. You'd blab it all over, if I know you.*

"A real skuzz-bucket, huh?"

"Well, as my grandfather would say, he's probably going to be a 'hard taskmaster.'"

"And the whole world thinks he's boss."

There's that hippie shit again. "Yeah, he is boss, but not like you mean. He's not so fantastic, but he's *my* boss, so I guess I'll just have to kiss up if I want to keep the job."

"As long as you get the bread, who cares? And starring in a TV show brings in a lot of bread, I would think."

Tai had not told Kyle how much money he was getting for *Kerry!* The business manager warned it was best not to spread that news around. *And Kyle can't keep it to himself. Within a half hour, Kyle would blab my salary to everyone we know and probably a ton of people I've never met. Why, oh why, do I put up with him?*

"Let's just say it's more than you get down at Kentucky Fried."

Kyle laughed at that. And it shut him up on the subject, Tai hoped.

"So, anyway," Tai started again, "Mr. Flanagan is a hardnose, but the rest seem really nice. I really like the director, and the two ladies on the show—Pika Togai and Candy Cameron—seem like they are gonna be great to work with."

"Never heard of 'em. Should I have?"

"Those two are real stars. Not like movie stars or anything. You never heard of them, but they're famous in their own ways. Not as big as Kerry Flanagan, but stars just the same. Miss Togai won a big acting award in New York City, and Candy has been in a lot of Broadway plays and TV shows. She even did a movie with Brando. I didn't tell you about them before because I only knew their names, and I guess I didn't think they were important. But today I found out different."

"Well, I'm impressed." The way he said that told Tai Kyle could care less. "What about the other guys? Any of 'em our age?"

"Well, there are three… one older, one younger, and one that is probably right at fifteen, maybe a little younger, just like us. Well, me anyway, since you're already sixteen. Nate. Nate Berrigan. Remember that name. He's going to be a big star." *Shit, why'd I say that? Mention his name? Careful, Tai. You don't want Kyle getting any ideas. That's all you need, Kyle thinking you* like *Nate.*

But Tai must have smiled when he said the name because Kyle squinched his eyes at him.

"Nate, huh?"

I knew it. Kyle can be so jealous. But he can just can it. I'm not interested in Nate. No way.

Kyle quickly covered, chuckling kinda naughty-sounding. *He's hoping I didn't hear that jealousy.* "Think he'll be any fun?"

"We'll see." Tai pretended he had no idea what was in Kyle's mind at that moment. "Right now, we're all a little lost. Nate, though—that guy has talent with a capital *T*. He looks a little sad, though. Maybe it was just the first-day thing." *Why am I spilling my guts to Kyle about Nate?*

"Probably nothing, man." Kyle blew out a heavy breath. "Just don't get too friendly with him, Tai. You're *my* best friend, ya know," Kyle cautioned.

Tai heard a bit of menace in that *my*. But he told himself he needed to slough it off. He and Kyle *were* best friends. And if he wanted to quit that other stuff with Kyle, he should just tell him. Kyle would understand. *Wouldn't he?*

Tai smiled at his friend. "Yeah, I know. Sandbox to sepulcher. You see, I learned something that day we met in vacation Bible school. Friends forever, right?"

"Twitchin'," Kyle proclaimed.

Tai laughed. "I'm tellin' ya, man, this hippie thing is not gonna last. We're not them. We're just two little boys from the San Fernando Valley. Dig?"

Both boys laughed. "Now I got you rappin' like a true believer."

It felt good to be back in the friend zone with Kyle. *Now I have to forget how good all that other stuff feels.*

"You boys want fresh-baked cookies?"

They looked to the door where Tai's mother stood.

"You bet, Mama," Tai said.

"Then come on in the kitchen. I've got some just out of the oven."

"Burn rubber, TV star. Can't let those cookies cool down!"

Kyle ran from the room, with Tai following.

Back to normal. Just two kids raiding the kitchen. The other stuff will sort itself out.

Dissolve to: Interior—Tai's bedroom

Later that night

TAI LAY in bed, eyes closed, mumbling his lines. The script lay open next to him. After saying a line, he picked up the script, checked his memory, and then he repeated the process.

After fifteen or so minutes, he decided he knew his scenes for the next day. He closed the script and put it on the nightstand.

Checking the alarm, he pushed the button that set it. Then he switched off the lamp next to his bed.

He settled into the covers, closed his eyes, and vowed to sleep, anxious for the next day to begin.

But thoughts played a wicked, Wimbledon-worthy tennis game in his head:

Will I remember my lines tomorrow?

What if I'm not as good as the others?

What if Mr. Flanagan yells at me?

Will the rewrites screw me up?

Will Nate be happier tomorrow?

That last thought stopped him.

Why do I care? I need to worry about myself. Nate can take care of himself.

But sleep still eluded him.

Kyle is a hoot. Where does he come up with all this hippie stuff? He's spent his life in this little LA suburb just like me.

Despite his thoughts keeping him awake, it did feel good to think of Kyle that way. It kind of pushed the guilt away somehow.

He turned over.

I bet Nate doesn't blow any of his lines tomorrow. He's like a natural at acting.

Tai leaned up, hit his pillow a couple of times, then lay back.

Why am I thinking so much about Nate?
He took a deep breath.
Kyle is a good, good friend. What do I need Nate for?
Then it dawned on him.
Nate looks an awful lot like Kyle. Only better-looking. A lot.
He felt a stirring.

Close-up: Television Screen
The *Today Show*
The next month

TWO SHOT: Hugh and Barbara.

Hugh: Well, Barbara, Kerry Flanagan's new show *Kerry!* premieres Monday.

Barbara: Kerry's one of our favorites around here, Hugh. We loved having him on the show yesterday. I can't wait to see his show.

Hugh: As you know, Barbara, we've got two of Kerry's hot new finds right here today… here's Nathaniel Berrigan and Tai Atua.

Wide shot of boys as Barbara hugs both, Hugh shakes hands.

Barbara: What fine young gentlemen you two are.

Tai: (laughing) Thank you, Miss Walters.

Hugh: Did you hear that? *Miss* Walters. They teach some manners over there in Tahiti, huh?

Barbara: (giving Downs a *look*) Of course they do, but it's Samoa, isn't it, Tai?

Tai: Yes, ma'am. But I was born and grew up in Los Angeles, ma'am.

Hugh: And there are those manners again. Good for you.

Barbara: Hugh, that's enough. We're just ignoring Nathaniel here. How are you doing?

Nate: Okay.

Barbara: What's it like working with America's favorite comic, Kerry Flanagan? We all adore him around here.

Nate: He's fun.

Hugh: You don't talk much, do you, Nathaniel?

Barbara: Be nice, Hugh. He's just shy.

Hugh: I'm just trying to lighten things up, Barbara.

Tai: Don't mind Nate. He's quiet, but he'll crack you up in the show.

Hugh: Well, let's see you both in action. We had your boss on the show yesterday and he gave us the basic premise of the show. Here's a clip from *Kerry!* Set this up for us, would you, Tai?

Tai: Let's see…. Pika Togai plays Telisa. She's Mr. Flanagan's housekeeper. I'm her son, Pele, and Nate here is Brian, Kerry's son.

We're all the time playing tricks on people together. In this scene, we have Telisa convinced there is a mouse in the kitchen.

Hugh: All right. Here are Tai and Nathaniel with Obie Award-winning actress Pika Togai in a scene from the new NBC show *Kerry!*

Tape rolls.

Barbara: You guys are simply wonderful. Was that scene hard to do?

Tai: Not at all. Nate's a natural.

Hugh: You're not so bad yourself, Tai. Thanks for being here with us.

Close-up of Downs

Hugh: Remember their names—Tai Atua and Nathaniel Berrigan. Catch *Kerry!* Monday nights at eight right here on NBC.

Scene 5

Fade in: Interior—the Berrigan apartment
The day after the premiere episode of *Kerry!*

NATE SAT in his room, concentrating on the week's script, trying desperately to shut out his very enclosed world. But the walls in the apartment were paper thin. Every word his parents said came through loud and clear. He could almost, since he knew them so well, envision their movements.

"I got all the LA dailies, the *NY Times*, the *Washington Post*, and *Daily Variety*."

That was Paul, who, from the slamming of the door, was his usual hyped-up self.

"Put them all on the coffee table, dear."

Monica, no doubt was lounging on the sofa, cigarette in hand, and didn't want to have to reach too far and exert herself, even if it was for the joy—or sorrow—of reading her son's reviews. And his reviews were the only thing that would send Paul out this early in the morning.

"Let's see. Where's the entertainment section? Ah, here it is. Let's see what the *Times* has to say." He heard a ripping sound, so he supposed his mother had ripped the page out. *Doesn't want to put in too much effort. Holding the whole section up would be too, too much for her.*

"Here it is… '*Kerry!* is everything that we've grown to expect from America's favorite funny man,'" she read, "*… dream cast…. Candida Cameron…. Pika Togai—* Listen to this, Paul. 'However, the real standout here, folks, is Nathaniel Berrigan. Daytimers will remember him from his soap turn. But Berrigan never got to show his comedic genius on that show. Here, young Nathaniel, as Simon's son Brian, is so good that he threatens to upstage his famous costars.'"

"Incredible," Paul shouted.

"I'm so proud of our little baby," he heard his mother say. Nate felt a twinge. *Why have I been so snarky about her as I sit here eavesdropping? She's my mom. She loves me.*

"Listen to this." That was Paul. *No love lost for him. Couldn't even agree with her.* "Berrigan blows us away."

"Who said that?" his mother asked.

"*Daily Variety.* Let's see what they have to say in the *Washington Post.*"

Nate ignored his father's lack of caring about him and listened intently to the reviews. *I'm a hit.*

"The *Tribune* says, 'Finally, viewers have something to rival *The Dick Van Dyke Show*. Van Dyke has a new competitor in the ring. Kerry Flanagan could well become the new king of primetime. And the crown prince is surely Nathaniel Berrigan, a fifteen-year-old wunderkind of comedy.' The *Post* critic loves the show. And our little moneymaker," Paul said.

All he sees are dollar signs. But forget him. I'm loving what these pros have to say about me.

"'All hail Nathaniel Berrigan. We bow to you, oh child of wonder!' Damn. This skirt's in love with the kid. These reviews are screamin' money, money, money. What say? Three fingers to celebrate?" Nate could almost see Paul rush to the Scotch bottle.

"Oh, Paul. Don't you think it's a little early in the day for that? Make mine water." His mother's voice held veiled condescension. She was treading lightly. *Will this set him off? Or will they keep the focus on me and my show?*

Three fingers, neat. That's always Paul's order. Straight up. No ice to melt. Water would dilute the rush. And of course, by the time the day is through, he'll have more "three fingers" than you can count on the hands of Paul, Monica, and me combined.

"Wait—you haven't heard what the *NY Times* has to say: '*Kerry!* is a huge hit, and it's not only thanks to Kerry Flanagan. A lot of credit must be given to the perfect cast that Flanagan has assembled, particularly young Nathaniel Berrigan, who will keep us laughing for years to come!' We've raised a star, Paul." Nate's mother started humming a tune he hadn't heard before. Paul joined in, singing loudly. "We're in the money, we're in the money." Nate sighed.

That's all they think about. Money, money, money. I get incredible reviews, and all they see are dollar signs. I can picture Tai's mother, if she were mine. She'd be hugging me and telling me how proud she is of me and—this is the most important part—telling me not to even think about the money thing because their manager would take care of it all. I wish Tai's mom was my mom, and I don't even know her that well.

I really only know what Tai has said about her. And he thinks she hung the moon. He smiled, thinking of Tai. These past weeks working with him had been the happiest of his life. He wished Tai didn't obsess over the civil rights thing, though.

Just a couple of weeks before the first show ran, Tai came in bubbling over. Dr. King. Tai said his full name, Dr. Martin Luther King, and schooled Nate in what a great man Dr. King was—how he'd given a powerful speech about the rights of black people. It was all about a dream he had for all black people—well, for all Americans, really. Tai's favorite line, which he quoted, was something about Dr. King wishing his little kids would one day be able to say people judged them by their character, not by their skin. *It blew me away that Tai had it memorized, exactly as the man had spoken it. Tai really was impressed.* He wouldn't shut up about it. Not in a bad way, because Tai was so happy over the speech. *I got to thinking and realized maybe I needed to find out more about this civil rights thing. It means so much to Tai, and Tai means so much to me.*

Nate's thoughts were broken by his mother's even louder singing of that song about money. But then Paul cut her off. He must have handed her the water she'd asked for.

"Thank you, dear." A pause. "Now, where did I put my pills?"

It's too early for Paul to drink, but it's not too early for her little yellow pills. Why won't she stop? How can she be "nervous" now? My show's a hit. That has to make her happy. And she's certainly happy about the money. They'll have plenty now. How could she want for anything? She doesn't need those pills.

"You're killing yourself with that crap, Monica." *Like the booze isn't pickling* his *liver.*

"Paul," Monica pleaded, "all this excitement has my nerves in an uproar. I need this right now. Let's just be happy, please. How about that toast?"

"Bad luck to toast with water, Mon, but here goes: To *Kerry!*"

A clink.

To Kerry? That says it all. A toast to the man who will keep Paul in twenty-year-old Scotch. Typical.

Dissolve to: The studio commissary
Lunchtime

TAI WAS almost hidden, sitting just behind the table where Mr. Waldman and Mr. Flanagan sat. The two giants. Not in size, but in stature. With the kind of reviews they'd just gotten, anyone who came in would have their eyes glued to the two whose show would be making big, big money for the studio. And they were so engrossed in their conversation, the two men were totally oblivious to Tai. He was glad he could eavesdrop to his heart's content, get the scoop on what Mr. Waldman and the jackass really were thinking. For once, he was glad that Nate turned down his invitation to get lunch together. They usually left the lot, but today, with Nate declining, Tai decided to go to the commissary. And to his surprise, his two bosses came in just after him, engrossed in conversation, not noticing Tai at that table behind. Didn't they have some sort of executive dining room? But he was glad they were there because it gave him a chance to surveil them. To do some spying. You never knew what you might hear. He just had to stay quiet and not draw attention to himself.

"Could we have *paid* for better reviews?" Mr. Waldman was ecstatic. "It's almost as if we have the critics in our pockets. Kerry, they adore you."

Mr. Flanagan sat to Mr. Waldman's side. From what Tai heard next, Kerry Flanagan was not in a good mood.

"Come on, Kerry," Mr. Waldman pleaded. "Get happy. Listen to this, '… the new king of primetime… Flanagan proves why we're in love with him… the show is destined to be a Monday-night treasure like *I Love Lucy* and *Make Room for Daddy*.' The show is a monster hit. We were number one last night. You sure proved *TV Guide* wrong."

"That we did, my man," Flanagan said, "but what are we going to do about the Berrigan kid?" Tai thought he heard menace in Jackass's voice.

His ears perked up.

"What do you mean? He's great."

"I know—maybe a little too great, if you believe those hack critics. I don't like what I'm reading, Stan." Tai was glad he was listening in on this. He might have to warn Nate.

"Now, Kerry, we agreed that the only way the show would work is if every character was strong. Why else would we hire Cameron and Togai? They got good reviews, too, and you're not worried about *them*, are you?"

Just then, a man in a suit came to their table. "Waldman," he said. "Can't beat those reviews. Know you're proud."

"Couldn't be happier," Mr. Waldman said to the man. "All due to our star here. You've met Kerry, haven't you?"

Mr. Waldman introduced the two, nevertheless. Tai didn't recognize the man's name, but he must have been somebody important. Jackass Flanagan shook the man's hand, but he didn't seem too amped about meeting him.

"Good to meet you, Kerry. Would love to talk to you about a guest spot on my show sometime," the man said.

"Whatever," Jackass said, his demeanor blowing off this man, who must be another producer. "Too busy to think about that."

"W-w-well," the man stammered, "m-maybe when your schedule eases up. I'll leave you two to your lunch." And he walked away.

"Clown," Kerry said as the man left them. "Now, where were we? Yeah. Cameron and Togai. I can handle those two dames. But taking on a kid is different. Those little fuckers can eat you alive."

"Look, Ker." Mr. Waldman's tone was definitely trying to calm his star down. "Thomas has that little girl—what's her name—the one that plays his daughter? Linda, is it? Yeah, Linda. But that's her character. Who's the actress?"

"Who cares?" Flanagan said.

"My point exactly," Mr. Waldman said, pointing. "She steals almost every scene she's in, and we don't even know her name. But Danny Thomas? He's an icon. A strong cast can only be an asset, Ker."

"Well, I'm reserving judgment here." Flanagan huffed. "But if things get out of hand, Kerry Simon is sending his middle son to his room, and the kid's never coming back downstairs. I'm just saying."

"It'll be your call," Mr. Waldman said. "But for now, let's just be glad we're a hit. What say, Ker?"

"Okay, okay. Let's get outta here."

"But we haven't even ordered yet."

"I ain't hungry," Flanagan said.

Mr. Waldman stood, sighing.

Tai thankfully watched them leave without turning around and discovering him.

Now what do I do? Do I tell Nate what I heard? Or is it better to let it ride?

Dissolve to: Interior—Nate's dressing room
A little later

NATE SAT in his dressing room, script in hand. He was feeling a little restless, like the weight of the world was on his shoulders—or the weight of the show, at least—after those reviews. He knew the show was Jackass—to use Tai's description from the first table read—Flanagan's, but he had to live up to the hype the critics had just piled on him. That's why he'd skipped lunch with Tai. His insecurity made him hole up in his dressing room to study, not wanting to miss anything hidden in this week's script. But he guessed he was like his mother. His nerves got the best of him today.

With three episodes already in the can, Paul had stopped coming to the studio with him. It was the same thing with *Days*. As soon as Paul realized that no one was going to hurt his little moneymaker, he backed off and gave Nate some breathing room. *Just bring in the dough and stay out of the way. The story of my short life.* But still, he was glad he didn't have Paul hovering over him. It wasn't like he was some little kid. Even with the soap, he was fourteen. Other kids in the shows had their mothers around all the time, but he didn't need that. And certainly not his *father*—his mind spat the word—hanging around. It was a glimpse of what his life could be like in just a few short years, when he was free of Paul. Taking a cab to the studio was a pain, but he'd soon have his driver's license, with his sixteenth birthday around the corner.

"Hey, man," a voice called from the doorway. *That voice. Tai.*

Nate looked up at Tai and smiled.

"Can I come in?" Tai didn't wait for Nate's answer; he just barged in. Nate couldn't figure why Tai wanted to visit with him. It wasn't like Nate talked to him much. He didn't know what to say to him. Despite all those lunch dates—well, not *date* dates; that would be weird—Nate still wasn't comfortable making small talk. As special as those lunches were, Nate couldn't seem to open up and just talk, something Tai seemed really good at. Except at their lunches, Tai seemed to sit mostly and smile at him. *What's up with that?*

"Did you see the reviews? Mama picked up all the morning papers for me."

Nate mumbled, "Really?"

Tai seemed friendlier somehow. *Like he really wanted to make a— what?—a friendship? Why would he want that? There's nothing special about me.*

But Nate had to admit to himself that a friendship would be nice. After all, he'd never had a friend.

"You didn't see what they wrote?" Tai sounded and looked incredulous. "How could you not see even *one* of them? Don't they get even one newspaper at your house?"

"I guess," Nate said. "I don't really know. Paul probably reads it."

Why was he lying to Tai? No, he hadn't seen the reviews. But he'd *heard* the reviews. *Why am I not just falling all over myself to make friends with Tai? He's nice enough, full of everything I'm not— easygoing, good-looking. But if Tai and I were friends, what would that mean? Would I have to tell him about Paul and Monica? After all, that's what friends do, isn't it? Tell each other things?*

"Paul?"

"My *father*."

Nate saw the questioning look on Tai's face, and he flashed him a "don't ask" stare. There was no way he wanted to go into why he called his father by his first name. Tai grinned. "You, my man, are a big, big star. Everybody loves you. I saw what they wrote. And I also just overheard Mr. Waldman in the commissary. He's head-over-heels over what they're saying about you. Oh, and my best friend Kyle called before I left for the studio this morning. He wanted to congratulate me. Said he'd call the studio to tell me what the kids at his school have to say. I just got paged. It was Kyle. He said everyone is talking about last night's premiere, and most of the girls are raving about you. Kyle said they're all gushing over you, dude."

"Kyle?" The words *best friend* hit Nate. *Best friend? So does that not leave any room for me? Do I want Tai to be my best friend? Or any kind of friend, for that matter?* He stared at Tai. *I think I do.*

"Yeah," Tai said. "Kyle and I have been tight since we met in VBS a million years ago."

"VBS?" Nate questioned. This was the longest conversation they'd ever had except the ones about rights—and those were just Tai talking. In all the virtually silent lunches, he could have talked to Tai but didn't.

"Vacation Bible School… it's a thing that Baptists do. We're not Baptists, Kyle and me, but our moms thought we could have some fun one summer. I think we were about six or seven—yeah, we were seven, because it was the summer after first grade. Anyway, even at seven years old, Kyle and I weren't too tuned in to the other little goody-two-shoes Baptists, but we found some common ground with each other, and we've been friends ever since."

"That's nice," Nate said. *Can you and I find common ground? Isn't this show* our *common ground?*

"Yeah, it is nice." Tai smiled, but then Nate saw something in his eyes. Was it regret? Was it confusion? Was it guilt? *I wonder what that's about.* Gotta be connected to his skin color, something I don't even notice unless he rants about Wallace, praises the president, or quotes Dr. King.

"But enough about me. Let's get back to those awesome reviews," Tai continued. "Some of the critics even liked me, but man oh man, they raved about you."

"I heard." Nate almost hated himself. Here was Tai, gushing about him, and he could only muster two words in response.

"Wait. You said you didn't see any of the reviews."

Now he had to confess. He took a breath and launched into his reply. "I didn't. But the walls are thin at our place. I heard Paul and Monica—maybe I'll explain sometime about why I don't think of them much as Mommy and Daddy—" Tai just nodded at that, and Nate loved him for not asking questions. *Loved? Did I just think that?* "Anyway, they were reading from a whole bunch of papers Paul brought in. They were only reading the parts about me out loud, though." Those were the most unscripted words Nate had every said to Tai. And Tai didn't seem to notice Nate had opened up. He just kept talking about the reviews. *Is this what friends do? Focus on the good and ignore the elephant in the room?*

"Well, dude, you need to see 'em to believe 'em." Tai pulled a sheaf of newspaper clippings from the script he was carrying.

"Listen to this… crown prince… wunderkind of comedy— whatever that is… keep us laughing for years to come… those are scrapbook quotes, man." Tai's smile filled his face and lit the room.

"I don't keep a scrapbook," Nate said.

"Huh?" Tai's eyes grew big, and his jaw dropped. "My mom has two books filled up already, and those came before I even started acting. She's kept clippings and pics of everything I've ever done. I made the local rag because I sold the most candy in Cub Scouts. Mama put it in a book. I got a perfect attendance award for first grade. In the book. I got my first haircut. Lock of hair in the book. I won a middle school debate. Made the newspaper. Clipped and pasted. I can't breathe that she doesn't snap a pic for her precious scrapbooks. 'You'll thank me someday, baby,' she says. My mama's crazy that way."

Nate shuddered as he thought of his mother and her pills, and then he said, "My mom is not much of a *keeper*."

"It takes all kinds, I guess," Tai said. "But you definitely need a scrapbook, man. I'm going to tell Mama to get you one. Here." He handed him the clippings. "These can be your first entries."

"But those are yours, Tai," Nate said, pushing them back toward the other boy.

"Keep 'em," Tai said, thrusting them at him again. "I assure you, Mama has thirty others clipped, which she will send to all the relatives."

"Knock, knock."

The boys looked toward the door. Candy Cameron was there, holding two champagne glasses and a bottle.

"Oh my," she said. "I didn't realize you were here too, Tai. I only brought two glasses." She giggled a tiny embarrassed laugh as she held up the bottle. "I brought some sparkling cider."

Tai grabbed a glass sitting by the dressing room sink and tossed a toothbrush from it.

"To toast our new star here?" He pointed his glass at Nate. "I'll drink to that," he said, holding up the glass.

Nate blushed. He was uneasy with all this, but he kinda liked the newfound attention. Candy popped the cork on the bottle and poured cider into the three glasses.

"To Nate, the newest star of primetime TV," Candy said. "You will shine for years and years to come. I just know it!"

They raised their glasses, clinked them together, and drank.

"But Nate, my love, be careful," Candy cautioned. "Stay on our boss's good side. Kerry Flanagan is not used to competition."

Fade in: The hallway outside Nate's dressing room.
Immediately after

CANDY'S CAUTION rumbled through Tai's head. Was he wrong in not telling Nate what he'd overheard? He'd thought he might tell him, but then he got so caught up in the clippings, Nate's parent comments, and then Candy's unexpected arrival.

Poor Nate. Sounds like his parents will never make the all-time-best list. Not like my mama. And Nate. I'm glad I'm good at reading people. He went from sad to happy to disappointment in only a matter of minutes. The sadness I get—his parents would make anyone sad. The happiness? No doubt that was from the reviews. But the disappointment? When did I see that? Kyle. It was when I was talking about Kyle. Why was I making Kyle seem like such a great guy when I don't feel that way anymore? Maybe Nate didn't like hearing that. But why? Why would Nate be disappointed about my mentioning anything about Kyle? I'll have to think on that.

But Kyle is a problem. He won't be a bit happy when I tell him. But I can't keep stringing him along. We started out as friends, and then the other happened. And oh, how good it was—for a while. But I'm realizing Kyle is not for me. I remember the good times, when we were little kids.

But now? I want to be rid of him. I just don't think of him the same way he thinks of me. Not in that way. And if I'm that way and facing condemnation for it, then it better be for the right person.

Could Nate be the one? He's not giving off any vibes he is that way. But we are still just getting to know each other.

Scene 6

Fade in: Interior—makeup room for *Kerry!*
Friday, November 22, 1963

WOW! THIS never gets old. Nate loved performance day. Nothing beat an audience reaction. When they laughed at him, when they applauded him—he felt like he could rule the world. His world. His life. Away from Paul. Away from Monica.

Like every week, Nate was the first to arrive for makeup. This room, with its makeup tables and the makeup artists scurrying about, was where the magic started happening. Makeup and costumes made it all so real. He was featured on an honest-to-God TV show, and no one could take that away from him. This was what he lived for. So here he was, early. Truth: he was early for everything, whether it was work or anything else. The less time he spent at home, the happier he was. Friday mornings were misery. On Fridays, because it was taping day, they had a late call. That meant he had to hole up in his room and pretend he wasn't hearing what was coming from the living room.

Nate felt almost high from the excitement building in the room. Yeah, no one else probably saw the hustle and bustle of the makeup artists busily setting up their stations, pulling the colors that best suited the characters they were in charge of, and thought there was anything exciting about it at all. Certainly the old hands like Candy and Miss Togai just took it in stride, another day of work beginning. But Nate was different. This was his life's blood. He stood, waiting for his girl to be ready for him. It was time to forget the morning, get into character, and lose himself, forget Nate and be Brian. Being Brian was an easy task; forgetting the morning? Not so easy.

This morning, Paul was ranting, as usual, about Monica's pills, while she was countering with equal volume about his drinking. Nate longed for the Friday mornings when Paul went to the track or headed off to Vegas for the weekend because peace and quiet reigned in the apartment. His mother was hopped up on her pills—which he didn't like, but at least it was peaceful.

Some Fridays, he just came in early to the studio and enjoyed the sanctuary of his dressing room. But doing that was risky, because Paul would question him about leaving so early. Paul was always afraid there was some business thing he'd miss out on, and Nate heading out early could translate to a business meeting Paul was excluded from. Nate didn't know why that was, but there was a lot about his father he didn't understand. Or like.

"Hey, Nate," Tina greeted. Tina was his personal makeup girl. She had long, flowing hair, always tied back with a colorful scarf, and her sparkle showed in her ocean-blue eyes and her electric smile. When Paul first saw Tina, he later told Nate he should make a play for her. Yeah, right. Tina was three years older than Nate. She'd told him she'd gotten a studio job right out of high school, no easy feat because most makeup people were guys. That's the way the industry had always been, and *Kerry!* was at least breaking the mold a little bit, hiring Tina. When Nate protested to Paul she was too old for him, Paul just scoffed. And truth be told, Nate was not worried about the age difference as much as he was confused as to why he wasn't all that attracted to Tina. She would be a catch for any guy.

"Hey, Tina." That was their usual. She said hey, he said hey. Then they got down to business. *Why don't I want to get to know her? She's really a fun person. At least I think she would be. I could ask her out. Not on a date, really, but just to get to know her better. Well, I guess that's what a date is. I've never had one. What would a date be like? It would be fun to go out with someone I know and like already, not some studio-arranged thing, which happens a lot with guys my age. Hollywood is nothing without its publicity. Who am I kidding? Tina wouldn't go out with me. Not only is she three years older than me, but a single "hey" doesn't really lead to the beginnings of a passionate relationship—if I even want one.*

He sat in Tina's chair, facing the mirror. She reached for the astringent and a sponge.

"I know you washed your face this morning, Nate, but I need to cleanse it first to prevent zits."

He'd been through this process with Tina at least ten times, and she always started with her disclaimer. *Maybe if I make more small talk, she won't feel like she has to explain this to me every time. Maybe if I say anything to her, she'll become a friend, at least.* "Sure, Tina, whatever you say." *That was certainly a profound comment, Nate, you doofus.*

She was running the sponge across his nose when Tai came through the door and plopped into the chair at the station next to Nate.

Nate didn't turn because Tina had started to apply his base. He did stare into Tai's mirror, next to him. *He's looking fine as wine today. And happy.* Tai always seemed happy. And that made Nate happy.

"Don't smile, Nate," Tina said. "I need you still. I'm working here."

Before Nate could question himself about where the smile and those thoughts came from, Tai said, "Hey, dude, you're all decked out today and lookin' bitchin'."

Nate was in new clothes he'd managed to get his mother to shop for. He had made her feel bad about ignoring his birthday—way back in April, no less. Why he even wanted new clothes, he didn't know. But he was glad someone—*Tai*—noticed. He was glad his mother didn't balk when he demanded she take him shopping. Shopping and pills, Monica's two loves.

"Thanks, Tai. I got tired of wearing the same old, same old." It took everything he had to make small talk, but somehow it was easier with Tai.

"Well, I like your style."

Before long, the other guys in the cast were getting made up. Miss Togai had come in, and her makeup was being done by one of the leads on the team, a man who had worked during the golden years in Hollywood. He had some stories to tell, and he told them. Liberally. But the stars got special treatment. Which they deserved. *That's why this old guy got hired*, Nate thought, *for his experience.* Nate knew his day would come. After all, his reviews made it clear he would have a long and happy career.

Nate thought about that word "star." Miss Togai and Candy got star treatment here, but Kerry Flanagan would be nowhere in sight. He was a Star—with a capital *S*. He had his own private makeup room, his own superstar makeup artist. *He would not be caught dead among us peons.*

The room was abuzz. The artists were doing their thing, all the while keeping up a steady banter. It was a total cacophony of sound. Cacophony. He loved that word on the SAT list. He wasn't going to need college because of his career, but nevertheless, he had to study for the SAT, part of the curriculum sent over for him. Above the chatter, Nate heard bits and pieces. He'd learned long ago that nothing of importance was being said. Talk of Saturday night dates, talk of their children—that always was a topic of choice with Miss Togai—talk of new colors chosen and why. Nothing earth-shattering went down in the *Kerry!* makeup room, except Tai sometimes expounding on the progress of the civil rights law the president was proposing. But small talk was comforting. For him, just watching and hearing people talk about their lives gave him hope that someday maybe he would have that experience too—provided he ever got out from under Paul and Monica.

In his mirror, he saw Tina suddenly jerk around. He didn't see what she was looking at. "Miss Cameron? Are you all right?" When Tina rushed toward Candy, Nate swung around in the makeup chair. Candy looked totally shaken. She started sobbing as Tina led her to a chair.

"It can't be, it can't be. I just know it," Candy muttered, over and over.

Everyone in the room was stunned, seeing Candy in such a state. The sad mantra she kept repeating left Nate shaken, and as he scanned the room, it seemed to have had that effect on the others as well.

At last Tina, who had been hugging Candy, broke away, her arms still on the woman's shoulders. "What can't be, Miss Cameron?" Tina asked gently, like Candy would break if she forced her to answer.

By then Miss Togai was hovering over Candy, who was sounding like a broken Chatty Cathy doll.

"Candy dear, what is it?" A beat. "Candy dear, what is it?" A beat. "Candy dear, what is it?"

Then Candy regained enough composure to talk, slowly, hesitantly, mechanically, like a robot. "He's… he's… he's…." She was having a really hard time getting it out. "He's dead!" And she burst into an enormous sob.

Nate's worry for Candy had been building, and that outburst took him over the top. He didn't care who was dead, although he was curious. Who he cared about was Candy, who obviously knew this dead person very, very well. And she was shattered by this news she'd gotten. When? Right before she came into the room? How could that be?

"Who? Who's dead, dear?" Miss Togai asked. Her voice was calm and measured. Caring. And loving. Miss Togai's earth-mother persona kicked in.

Candy sat, spent. She took a deep breath. Every eye in the room was on her.

"The president." Candy's voice was so quiet Nate could barely hear her.

"What president, dear?" He had to hand it to Miss Togai. She was good in a crisis. Now, at least.

"Of the country. John F. Kennedy is dead." Loud gasps swept the room. Then total, abject silence. From the quiet came "I just heard it on the radio."

"That can't be. You must have heard wrong, dear."

"I didn't hear wrong, Pika. Someone in Dallas shot him in the head while he was riding in a motorcade with Jackie." And then she started crying again.

"Who would do that to such a fine man?" This time Miss Togai wasn't asking Candy a question. It was more an expression of disbelief.

And then the noise in the room started all over again, but this time the talk was on one subject and one subject only. Some were crying, others were sitting in shocked disbelief muttering to themselves, and still others were wanting more details, while some were just talking about how much they loved this now dead man.

Nate saw Tai and strained to hear what Tai was muttering over and over. He was saying, "The law. The law. It's doomed. It's doomed." Nate wanted to rush over and hug Tai, he looked so distraught. Then Nate's eye caught the youngest member of the cast.

He seemed to be totally confused as to what was happening. Nate got up and went to him. He cradled his shoulders, not saying a word but hoping he was helping him somehow. And it helped Nate, too, for he knew he couldn't comfort Tai. This was someone he could help.

One of the other guys in the cast, the one who played Nate's older brother, held up a transistor radio. "It's true," he said. "Listen...."

From the radio's speaker came the tinny voice of a newscaster: "... President of the United States, John Fitzgerald Kennedy, was pronounced dead today at about 1:00 p.m. at Parkland Hospital, Dallas, Texas. He died from a gunshot to the head. Police are searching for the killer. JFK, as we affectionately call him, was….." Nate thought the newscaster, who normally had a voice of steel, sounded like he was fighting back tears.

The boy switched off the machine. The silence held. Everyone was stunned, now hearing the news for real.

Nate saw Miss Togai cross herself. He saw others in the room with heads bowed. A trio of makeup artists and two cast members joined arms in sort of a group hug. Tai was still murmuring continuously, his head bowed in confusion or prayer or both. Everyone in the room seemed lost. Lost in thought. Lost in grief.

"How will we survive? He was the hope of this country," Candy, now better composed, said. "I was at the inauguration. I loved the man so. And Jackie? Poor, poor Jackie. Not only has she lost her husband, but she has two children to raise without a father." And she broke into quiet sobs again.

Then Nate heard someone clearing his throat. A small throat-clearing sound. One you'd use to get someone's attention. All eyes shot toward the doorway. Mr. Waldman stood there, looking like he was as much in grief as they were.

"I can see you've heard the news."

Mumbles of "yeah, uh-huh, oh God, yes" answered him. Nate looked at Tai to see if Mr. Waldman's words had broken his concentration, but Tai was still chanting his sad mantra.

Mr. Waldman shook his head slightly, like he didn't really want to be there, saying these words, but knowing as their leader, he must. "This news is beyond the pale. The entire nation will be in mourning for quite some time. Under the circumstances, I've decided to cancel today's tap—"

"No, you won't." Kerry Flanagan—the jackass himself—cut Mr. Waldman off. Flanagan stood, fully made up and in costume, right behind Mr. Waldman, having arrived just after him. He didn't show any signs that this horrific thing had any effect on him at all.

"Kerry, you can't be serious," Mr. Waldman said. He didn't turn around. He was trying to maintain his composure, it appeared. Finally, he took one step to his left and turned to Flanagan. "No one will even show up. And our people here—*your* people here—are not up to working today, much less trying to make life seem funny when it's just been proven that it's not. At least not at this moment. I refuse to let this happen. Not today."

"Look, Stan, read your contract. What I say goes. I'm the star, and I refuse to get off schedule just because something happened way out in Dallas, Texas. So a president was killed. It's happened before, and the country survived. Ask Mrs. Lincoln." Nate let out a small gasp. The man was so insensitive. "But if we don't go through with this taping, we'll be a show behind, and that will throw off my trip to Bermuda at Christmas. Not gonna happen."

"Kerry, listen." Mr. Waldman's voice was calm, apparently what was needed if he was going to reason with this egomaniac star of his. "We'll be a week behind, anyway. Surely Monday night's show won't air in the face of all this. Give the kids the rest of the day off. I'll take care of any audience that might show up."

"Stan, look at me." Jackass gestured, his palms running from his head to his toes. "I'm all made up and ready. I'm not letting this change a thing. I'm America's favorite comic, and people can't get enough of me. They wanna laugh. I give 'em that. And today of all days, they're gonna want me to make 'em laugh. The audiences will show. They need me. You'll see. Besides, we can always add a laugh track. Now you people get your asses over to the stage for a run-through. Live audience in—" He looked at his watch. "—one hour, thirty."

And America's favorite had spoken. *If only America knew the real Kerry Flanagan.*

Fade in: Backstage at *Kerry!* set
An hour later

"Can you believe that asshole?" Tai was sitting with Nate. Tai was almost back to himself, battered but trying to focus on the show. At least Tai was ranting about Jackass and not repeating "the law" over and over and over.

"Total asswipe," Nate said.

"I don't know about you, but I don't think I'm gonna conjure up any laughs before that audience."

"Me neither." And to his surprise, Nate began to cry.

"What's up, dude?" Tai placed his hand on Nate's arm. "Don't cry. Working for that shitpot is not the end of the world."

Tai's concern really ripped Nate apart. Just a little over an hour ago, Nate had his chance to comfort Tai, and he'd held back. Now Tai had jumped right into it when Nate needed him.

"It's not that. Believe me, Kerry is no worse than my parents. It's that… it's that…."

Tai now leaned over and looked him in the eyes. Tai's eyes, the color of rich, warm, dark earth, were comforting, bolstering.

"It's just that I loved Kennedy. Sounds crazy. I don't know if many kids our age ever gave him a thought. But I really think he would have led this country to awesome greatness. He'd already started to do that." Nate had no sooner said that than he regretted it, for it would surely remind Tai of the impending demise of the civil rights law. And Nate did not want to plunge Tai into despair again. He had enough for them both. But Tai seemed so intent on keeping Nate on an even keel that he ignored the implications in what Nate had said.

"I know. I kinda feel that way too. And everybody in the makeup room? You saw 'em. A lot of people feel the same way. Kennedy was a great man. The news hit me hard, but you know what? He was such an awesome man that folks are going to keep doing his work. I was convinced the law I want so much was dead with him. But it's not gonna be. In Candy's words, I just know it."

"From your lips to God's ears. And now we have to push aside how we feel, and thanks to a self-centered prick, try to *entertain*. I never thought I'd think of *that* word as a curse word." Tai moved his hand up and down on Nate's arm. It was soothing. "Flanagan was wrong *and* right. No one's going to show up, and they will have to use canned laughter with this episode."

Tai continued rubbing Nate's arm. It was almost like a caress, something he hadn't felt since Monica got into the pills and fell out of love with her only son. He found he liked Tai doing that.

"Obviously you haven't peeked out. Audience is already arriving. They'll be here. Nothing will stop people from getting to see America's favorite funny man. Not even the death of their favorite president. Who knows? Maybe they just need some cheering up, and I guess it's up to us to do it."

They heard "Places" called. Nate looked for Tina to repair his makeup from the tears, and then, like the trouper he knew he could be, he took his place, waiting for the announcer to introduce him to the audience. When he went out on stage, he was amazed. The place was packed, as usual.

The crowd roared like usual when Nate was intro'd. That put him on track.

Tai was right. Maybe they were there to see Flanagan, and maybe they were there because they needed cheering up. Either way, it was his job to do the best he could, to get roaring laughs out of each and every audience member. He could do that. What is it they say? Laughter is the best medicine. Well, he was gonna give 'em a giant dose of it. Thanks to Tai.

And that caress.

Scene 7

Fade in: Interior—Nate's dressing room
Early February

"I LOVE, love, love this job!" Nate spouted as he and Tai sat talking on their break.

"Tell me how you really feel about it," Tai quipped.

Tai's happy face made Nate feel glad. He'd thought about Tai's obsession with civil rights. Black people were pushing for it more and more, and Nate had thought Tai was maybe on their side because he was different too. Nate, though, also wondered if there was another reason that Tai was so obsessed with all people being equal. But with Tai as happy as he was today, Nate was just glad they were there, and they were able to sit and talk and make him forget his home life.

"Let's face it. If I weren't here, I'd be in my bedroom alone—or purgatory, as I like to call it. You haven't experienced my so-called parents. So yeah, I guess I get a little too excited about being here sometimes."

"Hey, guy. I love this job too, and I have great parents. There's something about being here every day, joking, carrying on, being with Candy and the cast, being with you. Makes me forget the world. It's a rush."

"I guess we have to thank Mr. Flanagan, but the rush would be better if he weren't here. But again, if he weren't here, we wouldn't be here."

"Ain't that the truth," Tai said with a humph. "Can you believe that photo session we just had?"

Nate let out an unbelieving laugh. "The Kerry family without Kerry. I pity the photographer and the entire publicity department. There we were, posing our hearts out in front of that green screen. And why? Because our star couldn't bother to be there."

"Yeah. Said they could insert him into the pictures later. And even if it looks fake, his fans will never notice. He's their god. He can do no wrong."

"He's a piece of work, isn't he?"

"Worse than that, he's a jackass," Tai said.

Nate laughed at that.

Tai joined in. "You know, I call him that."

"What?" Nate asked.

"Jackass. Not to his face, obviously. But I have been known to almost slip up. Yep. Jackass Flanagan. I've called him that for quite some time now."

Nate laughed. "I call him that too. Ever since that first day when I heard you call him that at the table read."

"You're kidding? You heard that?" Tai asked sheepishly.

"Sure did. And since that moment, he's been Jackass Flanagan to me."

"I'm surprised little Natie can use such a vile word. It's unseemly. I just know it."

"I'm not as innocent as you might think. And quit making fun of Candy, Tai."

"I'm not. I love her. I like to hear that. Just one 'I just know it' and I know all's right with the world."

"Yeah, Candy's awesome." Nate paused, smiling. "Hey, can you believe that episode we taped the night of JFK's death aired last night and got the biggest ratings we've ever gotten?"

"I guess it proves what Jackass said: people were needing to laugh. And maybe we were, too, because that taping was our best performance ever. It was a smaller audience than we're used to, but they laughed harder than twice that many people. Of course, you had the best lines, and that audience ate you up."

"Ah, I'm sure it was only because they wanted to forget that horrible day for a while, Tai."

"Don't kid yourself, Nate. You've got a gift. I try hard, and I hope I succeed, but you? Well, you're just a natural."

"Tell that to Paul and Monica. I'm just their cash cow. That's all they see me as." Nate frowned, thinking of his parents.

"Now, buddy, don't be that way. Your folks are probably doing the best they know how." Tai truly wanted to bring Nate out of his sudden funk. "I'm sure they care about you a lot."

"Okay, let's see. Paul cares about his Scotch, his gambling, and his so-called *connections.* If he doesn't perish from alcoholism, the girls in Vegas may kill him with some disease one of 'em may be carrying. Monica? Pills, shopping, and Pall Malls. I know you heard what the surgeon general just said about smoking. It's a killer. Cancer. So if she doesn't die a gasping death, she may kill *me* with her smoke. No, neither of them puts me high on their lists. I come in a poor fourth. But you know what? When I'm on that stage, I don't think of them. Not one bit. I just think of Brian, and I am Brian. I don't even think of what a butthole Kerry Flanagan is. I think of Brian's dad—who loves him— Kerry Simon."

"Wow, your mind doesn't stray anytime? Not even a little bit?"

Nate shook his head. "Nope. Total focus."

"You blow me away, dude. I wish I could do that. Sometimes I get offstage after a scene and I can't even remember it. That's how distracted I get. From now on, I'm gonna *be like Nate.*"

Nate looked at his watch. "Well, if you're gonna be like me, I say it's time to get on set for the table read."

Tai glanced at his own watch. "Mickey says we still have ten minutes. And Mickey Mouse don't lie."

"Whatever. I'm headed out." Nate stood and started to leave.

"Hey, wait, dude." Tai grabbed Nate's bare arm. Nate liked the way it felt.

"What, *dude*?" Nate punched the hippie word Tai used all the time.

"I was just thinking. Before we take off, could you give me your phone number?"

"My phone number?" Nate chuckled with irony. "You want it?" *Thank God he asked. I would never have offered, but I do like the idea of his having it.* "I don't even know if it works. Nobody's ever called me. You see, Monica got me a separate line. She said a star needed his own phone because his friends would be calling him all the time." He laughed. "That's how good she knows me."

Nate looked around for a piece of paper but found none. There was a ballpoint pen, however, on the dressing table. He picked it up. He grabbed Tai's arm and scribbled a phone number on it.

"There," he said as he wrote the last digit, "if it's busy, you've dialed the wrong number." He looked Tai in the eye and smiled.

"Hey, man. Everybody at the table will see this." He pointed to the numbers.

"So? They'll just think you hooked up with some hot chick," Nate said with a smirk.

Dissolve to: Nate's bedroom
That night

NATE'S PHONE jangled. He almost didn't know what was making that funny sound. Then he realized it was the phone that had sat on his bedtable for at least the last three months with never a ring.

He picked up the receiver. "Hey, Tai."

Tai, on the other end of the line asked, "How'd you know it was me? You have special powers or something?"

"No, I have a friend who's the only one who possesses my phone number. Stood to reason it was you calling."

Tai laughed. "I thought you were joking."

"Sadly, no. But I'm glad you called. I can now report to Monica that my phone is working. And that I apparently have a friend."

"You're a gas, dude. You know I'm your friend. Sandbox to sepulcher."

Nate squinched his face. "Huh? What's that supposed to mean?"

"Just a saying my friend Kyle and I use. If you remember—I think I told you—we met when we were really young—hence *sandbox*—and we vowed we'd be friends till we both croak—hence *sepulcher*, one of those grave things, you know?"

"You're a trip, Tai." *His voice fills me. How strange. I guess that's what friends do for you. Make you* feel. *Real feelings, not the ones I conjure up on stage.*

"Maybe I *am* trippin'. You never know. Maybe I'm over here smokin' weed. High as a kite. What say you to that, m' friend?"

Nate heard the sly humor in Tai's voice, but he couldn't just let this lie. "That stuff can kill you, Tai. Everybody's *getting high* these days. But I'm not seeing how anybody's better for it."

"Well, aren't you Mr. Moral Example?" Tai laughed. "Don't worry, my mama would kill me dead if I ever did that stuff. The only high I get is from her cookies. Best in the world."

Did Monica ever bake him cookies? Nate seemed to remember something, far back in his mind. *If only Monica were like Tai's mom.*

"Okay—let's get down to business. The reason for this call, dude. You heard of the Beatles?"

"Who hasn't? I don't think I've heard one of their songs yet, but they're all over the news. Gonna be on Sullivan this coming Sunday. But I don't have a TV in my room, and I'm certainly not going to watch it with Paul and Monica. I can just hear what they'd have to say. *Look how long their hair is. What is that noise? Don't those boys have parents? They're a disgrace.* Then if I told them how much money those guys are raking in, they'd have me in the recording studio that very night."

"Bummer, dude."

"You're right, Tai. Having my parents is a major bummer."

"Nah, dude. I meant the part about your not having a TV in your room. But I can render a solution to that problem. What say you come over to my house Sunday night for the viewing. I, thanks to a mama who worships me, do have a TV in *my* room. We can watch in total privacy."

Nate winced at Tai's *worship. I wish I had that.*

"So, you game? Mama will make snacks. I can promise some of her famous cookies. Can't turn that down, now can you? Grab a cab and be over here by six. I'll give you the address tomorrow."

"I'll be there," Nate said. He felt his entire body tingle at the thought. *The Beatles. Leaving the apartment. Tai.*

"Far out. It's a date." And Tai hung up.

A date?

Fade in: Tai's bedroom
Sunday night

"YOU WERE right. *Best* cookies on the planet," Nate exclaimed, stuffing another one in his mouth.

"I told you Mama's cookies were a gas." Tai got up to turn on the TV.

"Look, it's starting," Nate said.

"Yeah, but I bet they're not on right at the beginning."

Tai sat back down and grabbed another cookie. But before long, Ed Sullivan was introducing the guys.

"Yesterday and today," he said, "our theater's been jammed with hundreds of photographers from all over the nation, and these veterans agree with me that this city's never witnessed the excitement stirred by these youngsters from Liverpool who call themselves the Beatles. Now, tonight, you're gonna twice be entertained by them, right now and the second half of our show. Ladies and gentlemen, the Beatles!"

And there they were. John, Paul, George, and Ringo—in the flesh on America's favorite TV show. Nate looked at Tai. Tai looked at Nate. There was sheer joy on each face.

Nate certainly hadn't known what to expect, despite Tai's weeklong chatter about this event. And event it was. The audience was packed with young girls. There was a smattering of older people, but mostly there were young girls who started screaming the minute they saw the Beatles for the first time. It was almost hard to hear the beginning of their first number. As Nate listened, he realized this song he'd never heard before must be called "All My Loving." After all, they kept singing those words every few lines.

Before long, though, he and Tai both were making up words for the ones that weren't repeated enough to pick up, singing along at the top of their lungs, bouncing up and down on Tai's bed in time to the music. This was the most fun Nate had ever had.

The long-haired hippie freaks—that's what Nate'd heard a DJ call them—went right into another number when they finished "All My Loving." This one was slower, sweeter. But you couldn't tell from the squeals coming from the audience. Nate knew that song. It was "Till There Was You," a song from a Broadway show. Monica played the album all the time.

Nate watched Paul. He liked him the best. There was something very different about this good-looking guy. What was it? His guitar was backward! *He must be left-handed.*

He punched Tai. "Look at Paul. His guitar."

"Yeah, he's a southpaw. Didn't you know that?"

Nate didn't know that. *I gotta get out of my room, put down the books, quit studying my script until it's tattered. I want to be like Tai. A normal kid.*

The next number had to be called "She Loves You," because they sang that line over and over and over. And after each time, they sang, "Yeah, yeah, yeah." Nate laughed.

After about the second time, he and Tai were turning to each other, singing loudly "Yeah, yeah, yeah" along with these boys on stage who were not a whole lot older than they were. Tai had said they were in their early twenties, and that was only four or five years older than they were. Tai also had filled Nate in on the guys' entire history. John was only sixteen when he started his first band, and Paul was only fifteen when he joined them. And now they were the hottest group on the planet. Nate wanted that kind of fame. *I want girls screaming like that over me.*

The Beatles finished their set, and things calmed down on the TV. While they waited for the return set, Nate and Tai consumed more cookies and talked.

"Far out, man. Those dudes blew me away. Can you believe it? How great are they?" Tai was all worked up, riding the high of what they'd just seen.

And Nate was right behind him. Who needed marijuana when they had the Beatles? Nate had never felt such a rush in his entire life. It was like his world had opened up and he was finally alive. And he loved being this alive. "This is the most fun I've ever had, Tai. You see those girls in the audience? That one that was screaming and chewing gum all at the same time? What a hoot. And that older woman. She was coming unglued as much as all those thirteen-year-old girls. These guys have something. They got more talent than I've ever seen. That audience is worked up, dude!" Nate was shouting, he was so excited.

Tai laughed at Nate.

Nate felt himself deflate. "What? Why are you laughing?"

"You called me dude. The fab four are turning you into a bona fide hippie freak." Tai laughed again.

Nate felt crushed. *Why is Tai making fun of me? He gets me all worked up over these guys, and then when I use one little word of his, he laughs at me. I knew I could never be normal like Tai.*

"Wait, Nate. I see that look on your face. I'm sorry. I'm not making fun of you. I'm happy you're lovin' this. Okay, dude?" He punched *dude* when he said it. And then he punched Nate on the arm.

Nate smiled.

"What a gas—a total gas! Which one's your favorite? Tell me," Tai demanded.

"I like Paul." Nate was surprised at all he was sharing. He'd found words to open up to Tai, thanks to the Beatles. "That smile. And the way his hair bounces around when he sings. And that voice. Smooth as velvet."

Tai smiled at Nate.

"What?" Nate asked.

"I've never seen you this happy, dude. Makes me happy. I love you, man."

Just then, Sullivan was introing the second set. They opened with a song all about wanting to hold hands. As Tai and Nate watched intently, singing along with their made-up words, Tai put his hand in Nate's.

They were having so much fun with this song about holding hands, Nate didn't think a thing about what Tai had done.

That song ended, and the group burst into a raucous number that could only be called "When I Saw Her Standing There." Tai jerked Nate off the bed, and, still holding hands, they danced, mostly just jumping up and down, singing at the top of their lungs. Nate felt warm and happy and safe and full. All feelings he was not used to. These guys made him feel every bit as amazing as they were making that audience of little girls feel.

The Beatles crashed their final chord, and Tai leaned over and kissed Nate. On the lips.

Suddenly, for Nate, there was no air left in the room. He couldn't speak. He didn't know what to say.

Immediately, Tai broke away. He held up his hands in a defensive position, his palms facing Nate. He spurted, "I'm sorry. I'm so, so sorry. I don't know why I did that. It was wrong. I know it was. It'll never happen again. I promise."

Nate still stood like a statue. Mute.

"Say something, Nate. Please. I know what I did was wrong, but you're killing me here."

Bewildered, Nate found his voice. "I think it's time for me to go home." He headed toward the door.

Tai grabbed him, swung him around. "Don't go. Please don't go."

"I have to." Nate was still in shock. He didn't know if he should forgive Tai or not. He didn't know if he liked the kiss. Or not.

"Nate, just tell me we can still be friends. Just tell me that, and then you can go."

The look on Tai's face tore Nate apart.

"We can still be friends, Tai. You're my only friend. I can't lose you." His words were mechanical, but somehow he knew he spoke the truth.

Tai let out a huge sigh. "We can talk about this. But not now. Just know I'm sorry. Know that I know it was wrong. And please, please, know it will not happen again. Okay?"

"Okay." Nate was spent.

"So now, we'll get you home. I'll go call a cab. You can wait outside if you want."

Nate did want to wait outside.

Dissolve to: Interior—cab
Immediately after

NATE FELT blindsided. *What was that all about? Was Tai just caught up in it all? Did I let him kiss me? I could have pulled away at any time, no matter how quick it was.* He hadn't had much religion from Monica and Paul, but he at least knew that sort of thing between two guys was wrong. But it felt good. *Maybe I was just so happy, being with the first friend I've had in my entire life. Maybe that's all it was. Two friends having fun. Yeah, sure. Holding hands? I could forget that easily. But a kiss is pretty personal. Friends don't kiss friends. But I liked it. Could I be—what do they call it?—queer? I don't think so. It's wrong, and I don't like to think of Tai in that way. He's my friend, that's all.*

But I liked it.

Scene 8

Fade in: Interior—Nate's dressing room
The next day

"KNOCK, KNOCK."

That voice couldn't be imitated. Nate turned, knowing it was Candy standing in his doorway.

"Want some company, my little love?" Candy purred, a smile in her voice, pouring sunshine into the room, as usual.

Nate did indeed want company. He'd gotten to the studio even earlier than usual because he had slept very little the night before. He'd been sitting there, his brain about to explode with all the thoughts that wanted out. *What happens when I see Tai today? Am I mad at him? Was he just high on the Beatles? Or was that kiss something that was planned? And what about it? Two guys kissing isn't right. It's a sin, isn't it?* His total absence of religious training didn't allow him to quote the chapter and verse of the Bible that laid it all out, but Nate was reasonably sure something like that could land you in hell. Yep, it was definitely a sin. *And Tai knew that. Surely he knows that. All his talk of vacation Bible school and that mention once of his priest? There is no way he's clueless about what he did.* Nate sighed. *But it did feel good.* It was something he liked. It was something he might want more of. *If it didn't mean eternal hellfire.* Or did he even care about that?

"Come on in, Candy. I need some distraction. And you're some great distraction. Have I told you I love being around you?"

"Not in words, no. But I see it in your eyes. We share a special bond, my little love. I just know it." She came closer to him, stopped, and peered into his eyes. "And I see something I don't like. You're wrestling with something. Tell Candy what's bothering you."

Nate instantly averted his eyes, afraid and embarrassed she had seen something in them. *She can't see what's really bothering me, can she?*

"Don't turn away, love. You're troubled." Her voice was lovingly stern.

Nate had never known anyone quite like Candy. If she said she saw something, then she saw something. He had to cover. And fast.

"I suppose it's nothing. It's just my mother and my father." *What? Why bring them into this mess?* Recklessly, or at least that's what he thought, he was now going to have to spill some serious beans to Candy. *Why can't I keep my mouth shut?*

"What about them, my love? I've not met your mother, but I remember your daddy came around a few times when we first started all this. He was a bit brash, but he seemed harmless to me." Then she got a stricken look on her face. "Oh my God, he's not hitting you or something, is he?"

Nate's first thought was that he could steer this conversation far, far away from the truth if he told her his father was a violent son of a bitch. But luckily, he realized pretty quickly that would not end well. Candy would not let go of that. Not at all.

"No," he said quickly. "Nothing like that. It's just my parents don't take a lot of interest in me—what I have to say, what I do. It's been getting to me a little." He tried desperately to keep his face a mask of indifference, for if he thought more deeply than his words conveyed, he might cry. And Candy could not see that. No way.

Candy grabbed him and hugged him. "Oh, my little love, parents sometimes forget they are raising little human beings. They bring you into this world, and at first, it's like you're their precious little toy. Sometimes, some parents never get past that. They don't realize their children grow up with the feelings and emotions that come automatically with the years piling on. But don't you fret. Eventually they'll look up and see a fine young man standing in front of them, and they'll be pleased as punch they made you. That you're part of them. Your folks love you, Natie. I just know it."

There was so much comfort in her voice and her magical hug, Nate felt guilty he didn't tell her the truth. *But would the truth have gotten that reaction from her? After all, being with Tai in that way is just not right.*

She released her hug. "Now, when I went past the table, Tai and most of the gang were already there, boning up on this week's episode. What say we join them?"

Nate felt better, just basking in Candy's love. When *Tai* came out of her mouth, though, all his dread returned. But he couldn't just crawl into a hole. He had a job to do, and just because he didn't *want* to see Tai didn't mean that he didn't *have* to see Tai. *And maybe I* want *to see Tai.*

Candy and Nate went hand in hand to begin the day's work.

Dissolve to: Table
Immediately afterward

"YOU TWO finally ready to get your asses in gear?" Kerry Flanagan called to them as Nate and Candy came into view.

Nate sighed. The one time he was a tiny bit late was the one time that Jackass Flanagan wasn't a giant bit late. Flanagan liked his grand entrances.

"So very sorry, Kerry dear," Candy said, taking her chair. "I'm afraid I'm the culprit holding everything up. Natie and I were coming from his dressing room in plenty of time to get here when I realized I had to stop at the necessary. My little love was gentleman enough to wait for me while I did my duty. Please forgive us our little transgression." *You have to hand it to Candy. She's quite the actress. And a quick thinker.*

Flanagan huffed. "Yeah, yeah, yeah." Nate's mind wandered back to the previous night and the Beatles's *yeah, yeah, yeah.* Nate squelched a laugh. Laughing right now—at Jackass—would definitely land him in hot water. Then he realized if he could laugh about anything that happened the night before, then maybe he could laugh at—or at least forget about—the kiss. *Please, oh God I don't know, make that the case.*

Sam, the director, said, "Okay. Let's get this party started."

The table read began, and it went without a hitch. Surprisingly, there was little chatter from Jackass Flanagan. *Maybe, just maybe, there won't be a lot of rewrites on this script.*

When the last word was read—always the line came from Kerry Simon, Jackass's character—Sam said, "Well, well, well. I think we have a winner this week. Your take on this, Kerry?"

"Not bad." He paused. "We'll get rewrites to you in time for this afternoon's blocking, but I think there may not be as many as usual. Maybe you guys"—he turned to the writers—"are finally earning the dough I pay you." Then he spoke to the cast. "But don't get complacent, you hear? We'll see if these gags work as we rehearse, but if I think of better ones, there'll be cuts and insertions." He paused. "Plan on it."

Then he stood abruptly and simply walked away.

Nate's first reaction: Kerry has left the building. That was a play on *Elvis has left the building*. Nate had heard that announcers would announce that at the end of Elvis Presley concerts to make people leave, rather than stay, hoping for an encore or, better yet, a chance to meet their idol. But maybe this didn't apply here. Nate knew that each and every one of his fellow cast members would leave Jackass Flanagan standing there if the director told them they could go.

"You guys are great, even if our star doesn't tell you often," Sam said.

Or ever, Nate thought.

Nate's apprehension returned. There was no way he could talk to Tai right now. He hoped to slip out a side door, avoid a confrontation. There would be no lunch date today with Tai. *There was that word again—date.*

Before Nate could even stand and turn, Tai was next to him. "Wanna get lunch? I've got Mama's car. We could go to the Farmer's Market. We've got time. Blocking's not until one thirty."

Nate had forgotten Tai was a licensed driver now. Tai was a few months older than Nate, and getting his license was all he talked about. Nate felt a little guilty that he must have forgotten and, knowing himself, never even asked Tai when his birthday was exactly. He also was surprised Tai hadn't told him, but sometimes they got busy at the studio, and sometimes they didn't talk much when they had lunch together. Before that kiss, Nate had enjoyed just being with Tai. They didn't need to talk. *I just liked the being.*

Nate opened his mouth to spout out some bogus reason why he couldn't go to lunch with Tai. But he made the mistake of looking at him. Tai looked so needy, like he truly wanted Nate to realize the kiss was just an impulsive thing. *But what if it wasn't?*

With what they called "mixed emotions," Nate nodded he'd go to lunch with Tai. He didn't want to have to talk about the kiss, but he didn't want to avoid talking about it. *Why is life so hard?*

Then Nate turned chicken. He called to Candy, who was already walking away. "Hey, Candy!" She turned around. "Want a couple of dates for lunch?"

A huge smile blossomed on her face. "I'd be honored, my little loves. My treat. I'd bet you boys have never been to the Brown Derby, now have you? I know you've seen that Lucy episode where she meets William Holden there. Well, dearies, every star needs to eat at the Brown Derby once in his life, and today's the day for star dates. The tourists will be all atwitter, wondering how an old buzzard like me got two wildly handsome TV stars to escort her to lunch. This will be so much fun. We've got oodles of time. My car and driver await. Come, my loves. You're in for a treat. I just know it."

Nate felt a little ashamed of himself. He knew this was not the lunch Tai had planned, but it bought him some time. Some processing time.

Scene 9

Fade in: Interior—Tai's bedroom
A few days later

TAI BROODED. Nate still was avoiding him over that kiss. It was affecting everything in his life. His dealings with his parents. His sleep. His work on set. If he didn't break through to Nate and get him to talk to him, his life was over. Not suicidal over, but not worth living over. Nothing he did was working. The lunch with Candy was fun, but that was mostly because Candy kept the conversation going, telling tales about the Brown Derby and old Hollywood—not that she had worked there during the thirties and forties when the star system was happening. In those days, the studios kept a close watch on their stars, and if they got into a jam, the studio people were quick to get them out of it and keep everything out of the papers. A star got into a fight? No one ever knew. A star got a little handsy with his costar? Taken care of. A leading man had pool parties with hunky guys? Totally secret.

These days, though, the TV studios weren't as protective. And especially to people with run-of-the-series contracts like him and Nate. So maybe he was wrong to kiss Nate. Nate probably freaked out as much for the career danger that might come of it as for the fact that Nate likely wasn't into guys.

Tai wished he *was*, because he liked Nate. Liked him a lot. But then again, Tai also wished he himself was not into guys. Life would be so much simpler. He wished Kyle had never turned him on to all that stuff. *Maybe I'd have a girlfriend right now instead of mooning over Nate.*

Shit. That's what my life has turned into, a pile of steaming, foul-smelling shit.

And on top of all this, he had to deal with Kyle. *Shit, shit, shit.*

When Kyle called earlier and started with his usual "What's up?" Tai, falling for it every time, made the mistake of telling Kyle exactly what was up: his parents were going out for the evening and Tai would be home alone, studying his script. The minute he said it, he knew he shouldn't have.

Kyle pounced on it. "I'll truck it on over. What time they leaving?"

Oh God. Why can't I be as good as Candy at making up stuff? Her visiting the necessary story for Kerry was awesome. I saw through it when I saw the tiny glance at Nate she gave before she spouted it to Jackass. Whatever the reason she and Nate were late had nothing to do with her bathroom habits. Probably talking about me. And that kiss.

"I really have to study, Kyle. This week's script is heavy on my character, and I need to learn my lines."

"Don't bullshit me, lover boy. You've got a mind like a steel trap. You don't need to study. But I need me some Tai time. So, what time shall I cruise on in?"

Getting him to back off, stay away, will take more energy than I have right now.

I can't imagine it happening, but maybe Kyle will be a distraction.

Reluctantly, Tai said, "They say they'll be leaving at six." Then the guilt. *Why am I letting him come over? I know Kyle. I know what he'll want to do.* Tai formed an instant mental picture. *And I know I will like it. I'm a bastard. I should tell Kyle I need to go see Father Tim, go to confession, and won't be home. Like he'd buy that. No, Kyle will be here, things will lead to things, and I will like it. And the guilt will eat me up. But—if things happening were with Nate instead of Kyle? I'd like it more. Kyle's been the only one all these years. I want to blame him for who I am. But why? Here I am, having fantasies about Nate now. I want him. Yep. I do. Nate. Instead of Kyle. But if Nate... would I feel as guilty?*

"See you at six fifteen, lover."

And that's how, precisely an hour and half later, Kyle was sitting on Tai's bed, mindlessly plucking Tai's guitar. *At least Kyle didn't come in itching to get started with it.*

Still pretending to study his script and desperately trying to make Kyle feel like he wanted him there—he had mixed feelings; after all, Kyle was his longtime best friend, but he also was his partner in sin or crime or whatever you wanted to call it—Tai, from his chair, looked over the top of the script page at Kyle as he picked at the guitar strings. Kyle's hair was falling in his eyes as he concentrated on the melody. *Just like Nate's hair. Whenever Nate bends his neck the least little bit, his hair falls down over his eyes. The writers even incorporated that into his character.* He smiled, thinking about it. *Stop it, Tai. It's not fair to Kyle to think about Nate all the time he's here.*

Kyle looked up and saw Tai staring at him. "What you smilin' at? Do I have cooties or somethin'?"

"You crack me up. Nah, I was just looking and thinking."

"I know. It's because you can't get enough of my beauty because I'm your main squeeze." Kyle grinned. Kyle's turquoise eyes sparkled. *Nate's eyes, only these pools of seawater didn't have the hurt, the sadness in them.*

Tai looked down at his arm, thinking of Nate but also fearing Kyle might read his thoughts if their eyes were still locked together. *The numbers Nate wrote faded long ago, but I copied them into my address book. Not that I needed to. Those numbers are burned into my memory.*

Kyle propped the guitar next to Tai's desk, just across from the bed. Then he stood, walked over, took Tai's script, tossed it onto the desk, and gently pulled Tai toward the bed.

"Now, how 'bout we mellow you out?" Kyle pulled a joint from his shirt pocket.

"No, Kyle. Put that away. I've told you over and over, I don't do drugs."

"It's just pot."

"I don't care. Hippies can smoke weed, eat mushrooms, shoot up for all I care. But nothing like that is happening in my bedroom, you hear?" He wished he'd added sex to that long list, but he was weakening.

"Okay, dude. Don't wig out." Kyle put the joint back in his pocket. "I can mellow you with my magic fingers, huh?" Kyle began to rub Tai's thigh.

Stop. He reached to move Kyle's hand. But it felt so good.

Tai tensed. "No, Kyle. I really do have to study tonight." But he let Kyle keep rubbing him.

"I was just hopin' for some lovin', Tai baby." Kyle continued caressing Tai's thigh as he leaned over and kissed him gently. Tai's brain said, *This is wrong*, but he felt his resistance melting. Kyle knew what he was doing, in more ways than one. He was good at getting Tai to let his defenses down.

If I know this, why can't I stop him? But what Kyle was doing—his hand, his breath, his lips—made Tai feel great. Kyle turned him on. He was very good at making a guy feel great, and Tai was losing all his resistance. *I don't even like Kyle anymore, and yet I can't make myself stop him.*

Maybe I can distract him. It was a futile thought, but maybe, just maybe, it would work. Kyle's folks were in the middle of a divorce, and things were getting ugly. *Get Kyle talking about that and he'll forget about the other. And I can at least not have to confess this night to Father Tim.* In his mind, Tai rolled his eyes. *Like I've ever confessed this stuff to Father.* He thought of earlier, when he'd fleetingly planned to tell Kyle he was going to confession. *No, if I don't burn in hell for doing this, I'll certainly be cast into purgatory by Father Tim for revealing all this—if Father Tim has that power.*

Tai gently pushed Kyle's face away, not wanting to hurt him or make him mad. He just wanted to avoid what they had done so many other times. He was confused. They'd done this a lot of times, and it never made him feel this way. Suddenly he was so against it, and his mind was reeling. He'd thought he was going to hell deeper and deeper each time they'd done it, and yet he still had gone ahead with his sinful ways. Why did this time seem so different? *Do I really feel like it's wrong? Or do I want to save myself for Nate now? Even if it never happens?*

"Let's slow down, Kyle. I know you want it"—he knew he had to add the next part, even if he was able to avoid the deed altogether this evening—"and I do too, but we haven't seen each other in a week or more, so let's do some catching up, huh?" *Well, that sounds stupid.*

But Tai plowed on with his quest to stop Kyle now and maybe forever. He clutched at the one thing he knew would stop Kyle in his tracks. "What's the latest with your parents?"

He was sitting so close to Kyle that he felt a change in Kyle's body. If his onetime friend had been turned on, Tai had managed a shift to neutral.

"The latest?" Kyle frowned. "The latest is that my mother, Dear Sweet Mommy, is bookin' it to Vegas to shack up with her barely twenty-year-old squeeze. And she's drainin' Dad for just about every penny he has. So it looks like Dad and me are movin'."

"Moving?" The news caught Tai off guard. He and Kyle had lived a block apart forever. That was one of the first things they figured out they had in common—they lived on the same street.

So he and Kyle would be apart for the first time in all these years. He'd miss his friend. But then again, if Kyle weren't so available, maybe he could break himself of the *Kyle* habit.

"Yeah," Kyle said, exhaling. "Dad found some flophouse apartment for us in a sleazy high-rise just off Sunset. Not exactly where the stars hang, but it's clean and cheap. But it's just a half hour, maybe less, from here, lover."

Tai's brain stumbled over that word, as it always did. He and Kyle had only been involved for a few months—lots of sex during those few months, but still, it wasn't a lot of time. All those years of friendship, all those years of knowing each other. But they had only hooked up for the first time in the last year. *I'm not your lover, Kyle. And I think I'm glad you're moving, as much as I'll miss the friendship part of it all. If we are still friends, that is. Your moving will give me a chance to regrow my cherry—if that's even something that can happen.*

"I can't believe you're moving, Kyle. Things won't be the same around here." It was the nice thing to say.

"Don't worry 'bout it," Kyle scoffed. "It's no biggy. We've got the phone. You're driving already. We'll see each other a lot. I've even already got plans for my seventeenth birthday, just the two of us. I'm definitely planning ahead, even if I'm moving from this valley abode."

Birthday? Kyle's next birthday is months away. July? August? September? They'd always made a big deal out of Kyle's birthday because he was the older of the two of them. *Shit! Now I feel guilty because my rattled brain can't even remember when my supposed best friend's birthday is.*

Kyle just kept on, though. "And my hunky stud here"—he tapped Tai on the nose—"is a TV star! If he can't get his mama's car, he can spring for cab money anytime we need to see each other."

"Right," Tai said. "Big star, big bucks. At least my folks don't spend all my money, like Nate's do." That came out before he could even think.

"Why'd you have to bring *him* up?" Tai thought he detected a tinge of jealousy in Kyle's voice. He was trying to hide it, but it was obvious to Tai that Kyle thought Nate was a threat. And maybe he was.

"I just feel sorry for him. He and I have become good friends, and I don't like what I've heard about his parents. His mom's a train wreck. His dad's a total loser. Nate needs a friend."

"Dealin' with shitty parents are what agents, lawyers, and *adults* are for. Last time I checked, you are none of the above." He spat that last statement.

Tai didn't want to get into it with Kyle about Nate. After all, his oldest friend had just told him he was moving. That was enough for Kyle to deal with.

He hugged Kyle. A quick, friendly hug. One that Kyle couldn't interpret as anything else but friendship. "Let's not talk about Nate and his problems. It will all work out with your mom. As for you and your dad, your new place will be great. You'll probably even have a hunky neighbor who, the moment you lay eyes on him, will make you forget your old friend Tai."

"I can't ever forget my lover."

There was that word again.

Kyle stood. "Well, if you're really aching to study and you don't want my dope, I guess I'm outta here." He walked to the door, opened it, and left. Tai felt bad at how he'd treated Kyle, but he was glad his method worked. He was happy to be rid of him.

Tai was already getting up to get his script when he heard Kyle's voice again. Kyle was sticking his head back into the room. "You sure you're not burning with desire for me?" This time Kyle had a smirk on his face, and Tai could read that smirk. It said, "I'm okay with not doing it tonight, but just in case...."

"Isn't it Andy Williams night? I know you never miss his show. Now, you just head on back to your house and flip on that TV. About time to hear, 'It's Andy Williams, brought to you in Living Color.' I hear the NBC peacock is beautiful." Tai delivered that speech, tongue in cheek, with great flair—like a TV pitchman selling his wares. And fully knowing Kyle was not anywhere near a Williams fan. Andy's fans were mostly old ladies.

"Your loss, lover." And Kyle exited. Tai waited a few moments, fearing Kyle might magically reappear, but he heard the front door slam, so he knew he was safe.

That word again. Lover. Maybe with us thirty minutes apart, I can break my Kyle addiction. That's all it is. If Kyle really does like men, then that's on him. I feel sorry for him, but there's nothing I can do. Me? I can get over it. Kyle's the only guy I've ever done anything with, so that doesn't make me queer.

I just want to be friends with Nate. That's all. He needs a friend. I'm going to go to rehearsal tomorrow and do whatever I need to do to make it up to him.

Scene 10

Fade in: Interior—the *Kerry!* set
The next day

NATE, EVER his eagerly early self, was sitting in his off-set chair, talking to Candy and waiting for things to rev up. They'd blocked everything the day before, and this was rehearsal day—or as his fellow cast members liked to call it, "hell day." This was the day Jackass raised the biggest stinks. Lines got changed instantaneously—sometimes even back to the originals from the table read—blocking would be redone by Flanagan himself because "the camera needs to be on the star, and I'm the star," and by the end of the day, everyone was exhausted and ready for the next day's tapings. Miracle of miracles, Flanagan was the picture of Mr. Wonderful when audiences were present. Any rants were left for backstage, far away from audience ears. He had to maintain his image.

Actually, Nate had shown up even earlier than usual this morning because, just before he left for home the day before, Mr. Waldman's secretary had come to the set to tell him he was to show up in Mr. Waldman's office the next morning. He barely slept, wondering what that was all about. He didn't dare tell Paul. What Paul didn't know wouldn't hurt him. And Paul was lost in a drunken haze most of the time these days anyway. He almost phoned Tai to tell him about the meeting, but then the memory of the kiss stopped him.

But here he was, sitting with Candy, filling her in on his news.

"Natie, that's wonderful," Candy gushed. "You're going to have so much fun. I just know it."

And just then, Tai sauntered up. "What's so wonderful?" he said to Candy.

"Oh, my love, it's not for me to tell. This is Natie's big news."

Nate began hesitantly, not knowing how Tai would take this news—or even if Tai really cared. Nate, confused and afraid of his feelings, was trying to keep his distance from Tai.

"Well," Nate began hesitantly, wanting to spill his good fortune to this boy who had once been his best—his only—friend, "you know Ford Motor Company is our sponsor. Mr. Waldman called me into a meeting with a Ford guy this morning. The man told me they're bringing out this incredible-sounding new sports car. It's called a Mustang. They want me to do the commercial that introduces it to the entire USA. The guy said he thought my fans would like the car a lot."

"Wow! That *is* news!"

Nate saw Tai start to lunge at him, pull him into a hug, and then back off. But he saw genuine happiness for him in Tai's eyes. He could have been jealous. After all, Tai was just as popular on the show as he was—especially with the young audience. They could have picked Tai to do this. Probably a better choice even. Tai, at least, knew how to drive. But the look in Tai's eyes made Nate feel that old connection, feel like he could share all his news with him. He was glad about that. His first thought when they told him was he couldn't wait to tell Tai. Then the reality of their situation kicked in, and he had a momentary pang of sadness.

But now, he knew he could spill it all.

"Tai, you won't believe it. Not only do they want me to do the commercial, they're giving me one of the cars."

Tai whooped and raised his hand, and Nate gave him a high-five.

Then Nate continued, bubbling over, "The man said the car is supposed to be one middle-class people can afford. A sports car that people like the ones who watch our show can afford to buy. He showed me pictures of it, and it's a gas. I get a convertible—red with white leather seats."

"Wait a minute. I just thought of something," Tai said. "You don't know how to drive. You're not even old enough yet."

"That's another amazing thing. The unveiling is April seventeenth. My birthday is April sixteenth. I got my learner's permit already, and I can enroll in driving school this weekend. I'll be ready when I get the car."

"You're not going to any school," Tai said. Nate was about to say something like "Try and stop me" when Tai added, "I'm going to teach you to drive. I'll tell Mama tonight, and she'll work out a schedule when I can teach you. Mama's all the time saying I'm the best driver she knows, so I know she'll let me do it. Saturday start okay?"

Nate's heart was almost bursting. Their friendship, something he treasured above everything else in his life, was back on. That kiss was history, and Nate knew he could forget it.

"Saturday it is," Nate said. He added, "It's a date," and then, with a flashing pang, he wished he'd left that part off.

Before Tai could add anything, Sam called, "Places, people."

As Tai and Nate sauntered to their places, Tai leaned over and said, quietly, "You've got good news, I've got good news. I heard the House is makin' great progress on the Civil Rights Act. President Johnson is really stepping up to the plate. He's keeping Kennedy alive with this."

Nate still was having a hard time with Tai's wanting this thing so much. He just didn't see Tai suffering a lot of discrimination, but he knew that it was a good thing for black people, and he knew how much Tai wanted it. "Great news, Tai," he said. Tai's smile as they parted to take their marks made him shiver.

The rehearsal began. Nate felt like no amount of shit from Jackass could bring him down from this high he was on today. He had his best friend back, and Jackass could just rant and rave and bellow and scream and parade around and pull his weight all he wanted. Nate was immune.

And shit did rain down on them. If they weren't totally used to this kind of midweek rehearsal, they might have walked out. That was the consensus among all of the cast, even Candy, who never seemed to let anything get her down, and Miss Togai, who was the absolute professional at all times. The younger among them—Nate and Tai included—had threatened such a rebellion, a walkout. But Candy and Miss Togai had talked them down. *Sometimes you need professional adults to quell a riot stirred up by the rabble-rousers. Kids all over the world right now are taking charge, and that's a good thing, but oh, the shit that would have been stirred up if Candy and Miss Togai hadn't made us* Kerry! *young ones see reason.* Walking out was not an option, not with Kerry Flanagan as their boss; they all just tried as hard as they could to endure.

The last line was said, Sam looked for the star's approval to dismiss, got a nod, and then he started to give his regular "Knock 'em dead" speech that he gave every week the day before taping. Kerry cut him off.

"Just in case you guys start wondering why, I turned 'em down flat." Nate scanned the roomful of blank stares. No one, not even Nate, who should have guessed, knew what Jackass was talking about. "I don't do sales. And no amount of bribes from any sponsor will get me to hawk their wares. No, that's for you peons."

So that's it, Nate thought. *Uh-oh, he's about to spill the beans.* Nate's mind roiled. *They're all gonna hate me.*

"So—" Their star-boss took a deep, disgusting-sounding breath. "The good people at Ford"—sarcasm dripped—"are putting out some new cheap-shit sports car that anybody can buy. They needed a pitchman, and after I turned 'em down, I suggested Brian do it." He used Nate's character name.

You don't even know my real name, do you? Or you don't care to use it. That would make me seem important, now wouldn't it?

The youngest cast member, who had not developed any good sense yet apparently, mumbled, "Who's Brian?"

Flanagan scowled at him. Then he pointed to Nate. "The kid here." And then Kerry Flanagan, America's favorite funny man, simply turned and strode away.

Watching that, Nate kind of got the idea that every bit of that speech was completely false and that Jackass was saving face, just in case. The guy from Ford never even mentioned trying to get Kerry Flanagan to do their commercial. He definitely made it sound like Nate was their first and only choice.

Nate figured Ford would have sought Flanagan's approval for their offer to Nate, if only to appease their star. He also figured Flanagan would never have refused their deal with Nate, if only to not upset the sponsors. Business was business. And besides, Jackass could raise a stink, but there was nothing in his contract to prevent Nate from doing commercials.

As soon as Flanagan was out of sight, Miss Togai enveloped Nate in her earth-mother arms and gushed, "I'm so happy for you, dear." The rest of the cast huddled behind her, eager to offer their high-fives, good wishes, and the only thing Nate could call it—love. Nate was relieved. He was afraid they would be upset they weren't chosen. And they might be if they knew what he was getting for his efforts. Candy, with her driver, didn't need a new car. Miss Togai probably didn't need one either, but she might like the exposure the commercial would bring. Tai already knew, but the other guys would kill for a new sports car—even the youngest, who wouldn't be able to drive it for years.

Leave it to Candy to spill the beans. "Tell them the rest, Natie. We all love you. They'll be so happy for you. I just know it."

So now it was up to Nate to tell a guy who was just two years older than he was and probably had been driving for those two years at least, a celebrated Samoan actress who could knock the socks off any commercial, and a kid who couldn't drive but who would scream like one of those girls on the Sullivan show at the Beatles when he saw the new Mustang, that he, Nate, was going to be one of the first people in the entire US to drive this new, fabulous car.

"Don't hate me, but I not only am doing the first commercial ever for the new Ford Mustang, but they're giving me one of the cars for doing it."

At that, five cast members—the people who played his two brothers, Candy, Miss Togai, and Tai—and Sam, their director, plus an assistant director, a prop man, and anyone else within earshot wrapped Nate in a giant hug.

It felt so good. Here, here on this set. Love. He'd go home and tell Monica this news, and she'd probably say, "A Mustang? I heard they were introducing a cheap car. Why couldn't they give you a Lincoln town car for doing this?"

And Paul? "Why in the hell did they talk to you without me being present? How much they paying you for this commercial?" Nate didn't care. He was told there was pay, but just getting to do it and getting the car was payment enough. Screw Monica and screw Paul.

This here, right now, this moment with his only friends, was magical.

The only love he ever got was here on this set.

Scene 11

Fade in: Interior—Tai's home
Saturday morning

TIPPY-TOEING, NATE had snuck out of the apartment. Nothing was going to keep him from his first driving lesson, keep him from Tai. He was alive with excitement.

Not that it was all that hard to sneak out. Paul left for Vegas the night before, and Monica was rarely up before noon, since she spent most of her life these days in a drug-induced stupor. Nate figured the only thing that woke her as *early* as noon was a craving for a Pall Mall.

Now, as the cabbie pulled in front of Tai's house and Nate gave cash to the guy and then stepped onto the sidewalk, a shiver overtook him. *I'm returning to the scene of the crime. This is where it happened. The kiss.*

He stood, at first totally stone-statue-like, and then he felt a tremor. It came from the soles of his feet and rumbled all the way up to the tips of each of his hairs. *Was that an earthquake?*

Nate looked around. There was no sign that God had wreaked havoc on the quiet neighborhood.

Then he realized what his body was trying to tell him: *Shake it off, Nate. We both were having a good time, rocking out to the Beatles, and Tai just got too excited. He made a move that he would never have made if we weren't both feelin' the love, the love those four guys were spreading with their "She Loves You" mantra.*

Nate shrugged, smiled, and made his way up the sidewalk. Tai was his best friend—his only friend, actually. Candy was his friend, but she was not his and Tai's age, and a guy needed a friend his age who would understand what he was going through and not try to fix it because he couldn't. That's what Candy would never understand. She couldn't fix Paul and Monica.

He knocked on the door.

Instantly, the door flew open. "Hey, dude! *Afio mai.* Welcome—in Samoan. Come in, come in." Tai was bubbling over, bursting with energy, a smile as wide as the Grand Canyon.

"Were you waiting at the door?"

"Nah, man." Tai smiled wickedly. "I was spyin' on you from the living room window. I was about to come get you if you hadn't finally started up the walk. What were you doing out there?"

"Nothing, man. Just thinking."

"'Bout what?"

Nate had to come up with something quick. *No way am I telling him what I was really thinking about—I'm through worrying about that kiss, and I don't need to get Tai riled up over it again.*

"By the end of this day, I'm going to be a driver. This is the best day of my life." Nate hoped he'd covered.

Tai narrowed his eyes and laughed. "You don't know. I may not be a good teacher. Maybe I'm just actin' the part." He laughed again. "Let's hope your confidence in me is well-placed. A month ago, I was standing in your shoes, but Mama swears I'm a great driver now. And she should know 'cause she taught me. Now, like I said, come in."

Nate walked past Tai and stood as Tai shut the door.

"You hungry? Mama's got a mean breakfast laid out for us."

"Breakfast? I figured you'd be ready to roll as soon as I got here."

"Hold your horses, Mr. Mustang. Plenty of time, plenty of time. I knew you'd be here early. You always are—early, I mean. What's that you say? If you're on time, you're late."

Nate felt warm all over, hearing Tai quote him. He was not sure where he learned that saying, but he did know where he learned to be early. Monica was never on time for anything in her life. He hated being late when she escorted him to his days on the soap. And back in those days, he was too young to take himself to the studio. He had to have a guardian, and with Paul out, in his own words, "making things happen"—translate, at the track, throwing Nate's money away, or at least what the Coogan law allowed Paul and Monica to keep for Nate's living expenses—Monica was the designated caregiver of their young actor-son. Nate remembered all the times at the end of the shoot each day. She was stoned out of her mind on her little yellow pills. By the end of the day, he was *her* guardian, not the other way around.

With a sweeping gesture, Tai said, "So, follow me to the feast." He followed Tai to the kitchen, where a table was filled with a zillion different dishes. Well, maybe five or six, but there were scrambled eggs, crisp bacon the way Nate liked it, a stack of pancakes, hash browns, and huge sugary cinnamon rolls.

"Nathaniel, it's so good of you to join us." At the sound of Mrs. Atua's voice, he tore his eyes away from the table.

"It is nice of you to have me, Mrs. Atua. And please, call me Nate." Monica had never taught him manners, but he'd played enough kids to know he'd said the right thing.

"My pleasure, Nate." He liked she didn't argue about his name. Nathaniel was a contract name, a name Paul insisted on because he said it was a star's name. *I feel like a Nate.*

"And you can call me Ruthie, Nate."

"Sorry, Mrs. Atua, but I don't think I can do that." *Where did that come from? Monica would jump at the chance to call this woman by her first name, to make her her bosom buddy.*

"All right, Nate. How about Mama Ruthie? That's what Tai's friend Kyle has always called me. You're my son's friend. Seems appropriate to me. It won't offend me, and most importantly, it won't offend you. So—Mama Ruthie?"

Nate smiled, and it felt like a smile that relieved all his anxiety, relaxed his tense muscles, and made him feel good all over. He hadn't realized how much he was walking on eggshells until that smile freed him. "Mama Ruthie"—the name rolled off his tongue, so he knew it was the perfect thing to call this woman he barely knew, this woman who was embracing him with her words, her actions, her heart—"this is the most amazing spread ever been put before me. At home, I'm lucky to get a bowl of cereal. And that's if I get it myself." He wished he hadn't said that, especially when he saw the look on Mama Ruthie's face. It was a mix of a scowl of disapproval and a look of sadness.

"I love cooking, and I love entertaining. Especially my baby's friends. So you just sit down over there—pick a spot—and I'll pour us some OJ."

Nate looked at Tai, who motioned to the chair on the far side of the table. When they both were seated, and with Tai's mom getting the juice from the refrigerator, Nate leaned over conspiratorially. "Where'd she buy all this stuff?"

Tai leaned in closer. "Buy? Who buys breakfast? She made it all. Mama's been slavin' over that stove since the crack of dawn."

Nate wouldn't accept that she had made it all. *Monica can't boil water. Surely Mama Ruthie couldn't do all this, all in one short morning.* "You're shittin' me. She got those cinnamon rolls at some bakery, right?"

"You kiddin'? Her cinnamon rolls have a huge reputation. When I was little, you know how mothers would bring store-bought cookies to school for class parties?" Nate knew that all too well. Monica always brought the ones in bags—cheap bags, at that—not even the ones from a bakery. "Well, my mama showed up with her cinnamon rolls every time. Got so she had to make extras because other teachers were sneaking over to get them for their coffee breaks. No—look around you. Does this kitchen look like all this came from take-out cartons?"

Nate scanned the room. She hadn't left any messes, like Monica would if she ever lifted a finger in the kitchen, but there were skillets in the sink, soaking in soapy water. There were pans gooey with cinnamon sugar glaze on the counter next to the sink. And there, next to a contraption that looked like a squeezer of some sort, was a pile of half oranges, the life smooshed out of them. That impressed Nate most of all. Who squeezes their own orange juice?

After pouring juice, Mama Ruthie called out, "Fetu! Breakfast!"

The door to the backyard swung open. A tall, bronze, muscled man appeared. "Let me just wash up." He headed toward the kitchen sink.

"Uh, uh, uh, love. You know the rules. Seventeen years you've lived with me. What's the first rule in my kitchen?"

Together, they recited, "No filthy hands in the kitchen sink." And then he kissed her.

She shooed him away. "Go. Guest bath. Now!"

The man emitted a laugh that was not ridicule, more like love, and rushed from the room.

Mama Ruthie shook her head back and forth. "My Fetu, my crazy husband. Always testing me. But he knows the rules. You bet he does." She winked at Nate.

She took a place at the table, removed a cloth napkin next to her plate, and spread it in her lap. With that ritual completed, her husband returned, leaned over, and gave her a huge smacking kiss on her cheek, and then he took his place.

Nate was ready to dig into this banquet, but he held back. He needed to get the lay of the land. And he was glad, because next came something he'd never done in his entire life. The family—including Nate—joined hands, and Mr. Atua said grace. He thanked the Lord for the food, and then Mr. Atua added, "And Lord, please change the heart of Mr. Branwell." At the sound of amen, his three friends crossed themselves.

Shoveling in a forkful of scrambled eggs before Nate could even get all the food arranged on his plate, Tai said to his dad, "Mr. Branwell still holding out on the contract?"

"No shop talk at the breakfast table," Mama Ruthie said.

But her husband answered Tai, "Yes, son, Mr. Branwell does not like the men I have on my crew. He's barely happy with me."

Tai turned to Nate. "Mr. Branwell doesn't like the black men Dad uses, and he only hires Dad's company because he knows my dad does a great job. But as soon as President Johnson gets his Civil Rights Act passed, those problems will go away."

"Tai baby, eat your breakfast and leave the worrying to your daddy and me," Mama Ruthie said gently.

Mr. Atua spoke. "Listen to your mother, Tai. Everything will be fine." Then he quickly shifted to Nate. "So, Nate. Glad you're here. We watch the show every week, and you always make me laugh." He looked slightly at Tai. "Too bad my lazy son here doesn't have your talent."

Nate's initial reaction was that there was a crack in this perfect family he'd just met. But he looked at Tai, and Tai was grinning. Then he saw Mr. Atua reach over, grab Tai's chin, and shake it gently back and forth, laughing the entire time. This was clearly a father who loved his son. *So there are such creatures on this planet.*

"I hear my son is teaching you to drive today," Mr. Atua said. "You *do* have plenty of medical insurance?"

"Stop it, Dad. You'll scare Nate. I'm not gonna let him crash or anything."

Mama Ruthie swatted her husband's arm. "Fetu, stop with your teasing. Tai will be a great driving teacher. He could teach you a thing or two, the way you rush around, changing lanes like God wasn't watching."

"I'm a safe driver, Ruthie," Mr. Atua defended himself. "You're the one who could cause a wreck, being so cautious. You drive like an old lady. A beautiful old lady, but an old lady, nonetheless." He leaned over and kissed her nose. She swatted him away, like she was annoyed, but Nate could see she was happy, happy.

"Well, this old lady driver'll be in the back seat today… just in case. I have every confidence in my Tai's driving skills, but he is new to the game, so I'll be a silent partner, just sitting and doing my knitting while Tai turns Nate into a driver worthy of a brand-new car not even on the market yet."

Nate beamed at her mention of the Mustang.

"Can't wait to see this wonder car," Mr. Atua said as he grabbed a second cinnamon roll off the platter.

With breakfast finished, Nate, Tai, and Mama Ruthie headed for her car. Tai got in the driver's seat, Nate rode shotgun, and true to her word, Mama Ruthie took the back seat, her knitting bag in hand. "Don't mind me, boys. I'm not here," she announced with a chuckle.

Tai turned to Nate and whispered, "She thinks I can't handle this. But don't worry."

"I hear you up there, baby. I know you can handle it. I'm just here to make sure, in the event of an unforeseeable occurrence, Nate doesn't have to file that health insurance claim." She laughed. "My Fetu is a card. Yes, he is."

Tai got right down to business. He gave Nate all the basics he needed to know before taking the wheel, showing him where the light switch was, how to operate the windshield wipers, explaining how important the mirrors were, and explaining how to use the *footfeed*, as he called it. Then he laughed. "Modern people call it an accelerator, but my"—his voice got louder as he directed his comment toward the back seat—"my old mama calls it a footfeed." And then he laughed hysterically.

"Laugh all you like, smarty-pants," his mother said. "That's what my grandfather back in Samoa called it when he taught me to drive. I mocked him too. Believe me, that was the last time I ever laughed at my grandfather. He was a stern man, he was. But I loved him. Anyway, he learned to drive when they actually called the accelerator that, and he let me know right quick he was not going to teach me anything if I thought he was a joke. So"—she waved the back of her hand at Tai—"just keep mocking me if you want me to take this venture over from you, little man." Nate heard the smile in her voice and knew Tai was not in any trouble whatsoever.

"Yes, Mommy," Tai said. Then he turned back to Nate and flashed a sly smile.

From the back seat came, "I see that smirk."

No way. Tai was not facing her at all. Must be some sort of Good Mama powers she has.

Tai just shook his head. "Okay, Nate, I'm taking us to a huge parking lot down the road a piece. It's at a corporation that has thousands of workers, and none of them work on Saturdays. So we will have plenty of room for you to practice before we get out on the road with you at the wheel. You can pop some wheelies, burn a little rubber...." He looked over his shoulder, as did Nate. From the rearview mirror, Nate saw Mama Ruthie narrow her eyes, and then she continued her knitting.

Tai just smiled.

As promised, Tai arrived at the parking lot within minutes. He pulled in and stopped the car. He and Nate got out and switched places.

With each of their seatbelts in place and firmly buckled, Tai started his lesson. "Okay, check your mirrors. Look good? Now, here's the keys. Put the key in the ignition, and when you turn the key, give the car a little gas." The engine immediately purred, and the driving lesson was on.

For forty-five minutes, Nate maneuvered the car around that enormous lot. He followed every instruction Tai gave him. Tai must have been doing a good job because Nate felt confident, and Mama Ruthie hadn't uttered a word. And there were no wheelies, no burning rubber.

At last Tai announced, "It's time, honored student, for you to *hit the road.*"

Nate sat there a moment, working up his courage. Suddenly, a police car pulled up.

An officer got out and strode to their car. He motioned for Nate to roll down the window. "What are you two up to?"

Nate answered, "My friend is just teaching me how to drive."

The policeman looked over at Tai, eyeing him with disapproval. Nate was surprised the officer didn't notice Mama Ruthie in the back seat, nor did she say anything.

"You a licensed driver, boy?" The officer's voice had an edge to it, a tone he hadn't used with Nate.

"Yes, sir," Tai said quietly.

"Speak up, boy. I didn't hear you."

Tai answered a little louder, "Yes, sir. Would you like to see my license?" Tai smiled. Nate saw the smile, and it seemed filled with fear.

"Get it out, boy. Pass it over here."

Tai extracted his license from his wallet and handed it over. The policeman examined it, sighed, and handed it back. "Just wanted to make sure you two weren't up to something."

At that, Mama Ruthie finally spoke up. "I'm the boy's mother, Officer, and I can assure you this is just a driving lesson."

The policeman seemed startled, having not noticed she was there until she spoke.

He tipped his hat. "Sorry, ma'am, just doin' my duty." But the look he gave her wasn't all that friendly, Nate noticed.

The policeman went back to his car and drove away.

"Never you mind, Tai. You did everything right. Just always be polite and do what they say."

And for the first time, Nate realized something. *No wonder Tai wants that law passed. That guy was fine until he saw Tai. He didn't even ask to see my license, but he looked at Tai's like he was hoping something was wrong with. It's not just black people who need rights. That policeman just proved that.*

Nate shivered at the thought. But he decided he was ready to drive, and since that was why they were there, for him to learn, he started the engine.

That simple act put things right again. Tai was back in a good mood. "Head on out, dude. We got some serious drivin' to do."

Nate steered the car out into the road they'd come in on. As he drove, he tried to remember everything Tai had told him. He controlled his speed, keeping his foot on the footfeed—he loved that word—firmly, giving the engine gas at a steady rate. He signaled turns, looked both ways, even did a perfect parallel parking at least three times in their journey, just to show he could. His concentration, coupled with Tai's watching his every move, neutralized the encounter with the policeman.

"Ready to take on the 405?" Tai asked.

Nate's heart lurched, his eyes widened, and he felt a bead of sweat trickle down. He was nowhere near ready to tackle freeway driving. He glanced at Mama Ruthie, hoping for a lifeline. "You're sure he's ready for that, baby?" she said. Nate relaxed.

"Why not?" Tai replied. "You took me on my first lesson."

"Whatever you say, baby. You're the teacher."

Nate tensed up again. But if Mama Ruthie thought he was ready, he guessed it was a done deal. He just had to do it. Either that or look like a wimp to Tai.

Tai directed him to the freeway, and on the way, gave him a few tips: "When you enter, enter with purpose or those bozos will mow you down. Check your mirrors. You only have a short distance to merge into traffic. And God help you if you hesitate. When you think it's safe, gun it. You can always adjust your speed when you're in the right-hand lane. Okay?"

Shaking in his boots, Nate answered, "Okay." And there they were, the frontage road. *God, oh God, please have the entrance closed.* But God wasn't listening. There it was, the freeway entrance. Wide open. A giant mouth, ready to swallow its next victim. Nate took a deep, deep breath. It was now or never.

Nate felt Mama Ruthie's breath on his neck. She had evidently leaned forward to monitor this maneuver. She hadn't said a word, but she was doing her duty as official observer and director of damage prevention.

Nate steered. Gunned it. Successfully merged into the right lane, cars whizzing past him. Mama Ruthie actually applauded. Tai laughed. Nate accelerated and was soon matching the speeds of the other cars. Well, at least the ones going the speed limit, and those were few and far between. Tai reminded him the right lane was considered the slow lane, and as long he went the speed limit, he was okay.

Tai let Nate travel the 405 about three miles before he instructed him he needed to get off. He told him to use his mirrors, slow his speed as he exited, and watch for other drivers as he merged onto the frontage road. And with that task successfully completed, Tai directed Nate back to their starting line, via neighborhood roads.

Nate expelled the breath he'd been holding for what seemed like the last fifteen minutes at least. He felt totally competent as a driver and totally spent as a human being. This lesson had drained him. He looked for the police officer, not wanting another nasty encounter, and then he pulled into the lot and stopped the car at the very spot in the giant lot where he had begun his adventure.

"How ya feel?" Tai asked.

"Honestly? Kinda shook up. But I feel like I know how to drive now, thanks to you," Nate said. Tai beamed, and Nate loved making him happy.

"You're a great student," Tai said, pushing him playfully. "Now I'm taking the wheel."

Nate let out a huge rush of air. "Good. I'm wiped."

"I know just how you feel. It's a combination of *Wow, I didn't know I could do that* and *Good, I'm glad it's over*. You'll lose that last feeling as we do more practice. Won't he, Mama?"

"Sure will, Nate. My baby took to driving like a duck to water. I could feel all his apprehension leave after the second practice session."

"So—we'll take Mama home, and then I'll drive you home," Tai said.

"You don't have to do that," Nate protested. "I can take a cab."

"Nonsense." That was Mama Ruthie talking again. "I will not send you home in a cab, not now that you're family. And I bet I can rustle up a bag of cinnamon rolls for you to take with you."

Nate was stricken by her use of the word family. *Am I really that now? A member of Tai's family?*

Tai pulled up to his house, and all three got out of the car. "Need a pit stop?" Tai asked. "I need to drain my wiener, dude."

"Tai baby, I know I taught you better," Mama Ruthie said. "What will Nate think of me, you using such language?"

I'll think my family—he still wouldn't let himself truly believe that word applied to him—*here is a very normal, loving one.* And then he thought of Monica and Paul.

The boys both took advantage of the bathroom break, and then Mama Ruthie showed up with the promised bag of cinnamon rolls. "Here you go, Nate baby." She handed him the bag, and then she engulfed him in a hug. "Uh! You give good hugs, Nate. I'm gonna like having you around here."

Tai, once again in the driver's seat, Nate, once again riding shotgun, headed toward Nate's apartment. Nate felt more loved than he'd ever felt, even the other day when the whole cast gave him that group hug.

"Your mama's the best ever, Tai."

"Not too shabby, is she?"

"And your dad, he's pretty awesome too."

"The old man? He's a gas. Great guy. Doesn't deserve the hassle of working with Branwell. But money is money, as Dad says. And he says for every Branwell, there are a zillion others who don't even see color."

"Yeah, well, I wouldn't say that policeman is one of them."

"Oh, Nate, you wouldn't believe how often we have to watch ourselves. And we're just brown. Think of the black people who have to deal with that shit day in, day out. No, that law's gonna change everything. I just know it."

Nate didn't even laugh at the "I just know it." He was too stricken by Tai's statement. Living in his cocoon, his white cocoon, he had never thought about the discrimination in the world very much. But he felt for Tai and his family, and for every black person he'd ever seen on the street, shopping, walking, driving. But he also thought of how much easier the world must be for Tai, even with the hate some must have for him just because his skin wasn't white, because Tai had Mama Ruthie and Fetu. Funny, he felt like calling Fetu "Papa Fetu," and he didn't even know if that was acceptable.

Nate said, "You're lucky."

"Lucky?" Tai looked at Nate like he was crazy, after the conversation they'd had about civil rights and how people of color were treated. Nate clarified, "You have Mama Ruthie and your dad—two wonderful parents."

Tai's gloom brightened into an enormous smile. "Yeah, I guess I am." Tai's pride seemed to burst from him.

He's right to feel so good, Nate thought. *His parents are the exact opposite of mine.*

Then Tai added, "Mama meant it when she said you were family now. You do know that, don't you?"

Hesitantly, Nate answered, "Yeah." But as much as he wanted to believe, he wasn't ready to accept it. *Mama Ruthie meant what she said, but am I worth it?* He banished the thought.

"If I'm family, what do I call your dad?"

"Pops is fine, dude."

"Pops it is." *Pops and Mama Ruthie.* That had a nice ring to it.

"I'm glad you came over today, dude. Not just because I liked teaching you how to drive, but because this whole day was such a gas.

Well, except for that racist cop. But forget about him. He's a *so'ona fa'alavelave*. That's shithead in Samoan."

They both laughed at that.

"I haven't had this much fun with a friend in a month of Sundays. Thanks," Tai said.

"I'm thinking the same thing, Tai."

Close-up: Tai
Voice-over

NATE, NATE, Nate. I hope you had as much fun as I've had today. I hope you realize we can just be friends. I need you as my friend. Kyle's past that. I don't think things will ever be the same with Kyle again. Once you cross over to the dark side, you never can go back. And what Kyle and I did was pretty dark. At least Father Tim would say so.

Close-up: Nate
Voice-over

OH, TAI. I wish I had a family like yours. I wish we could be friends forever. But something always screws with my life. Usually it's Paul. Or Monica. But I'm too happy right now. And that will lead to my downfall. God or whoever will not allow me to be happy. That's too much to ask for. As Candy would say, I just know it. But Tai, I do hope our friendship doesn't get messed with. Because I like your family. And I like you. I like your jokes, I like the way you throw in all those hippie words, I like the way you never seem to be down, I like your smile, the twinkle in your eyes, and who am I kidding? I liked that kiss.

Scene 12

Fade in: Interior—Nate's bedroom
A couple of months later

SEASON FINALE shoot tomorrow. I really should be looking over my lines. I've never flubbed, but it couldn't hurt to review. Others in the cast have incurred Jackass's wrath when they messed up. He blows up—after the audience leaves—every week over some shit. He's immune to the no-fuckups rule, but no one else is. Jackass breaks character all the time to mug at the audience. Sometimes he even blows a line on purpose just to get a laugh. But God forbid anyone else even flubs a line by accident. So yes, I should be studying my script, if only to make sure I don't land in his line of fire.

I also could be doing my homework. The on-set tutor pulled him away from the set, as she did Tai and the youngest member of the cast, as often as she could. She would quickly explain an assignment, and then they were on their own, pretty much. That's how schooling in the industry worked. He'd do the assignments, and they'd get sent to his official public-school teacher—who he saw only the last few weeks of the school year, after the last show had been taped and he was free to attend school. No wonder he never made any friends. Joining a class the last two weeks or so of a school year, like he'd be doing next week, didn't allow much time to make friends.

Yeah, Nate should be studying or doing homework, but his mind was full of the last few months. When he was on the soap, he thought a lot about how his life was like a bad TV movie. If it weren't *his* life, it might be laughable. His addicted mother, his gambling drunk of a father, his abject lack of friends, his shyness beyond normality—all added up to *After School Special: A Tragic Life, the Sadness of Being a Child*

Actor, or whatever they might want to call that piece of art. He laughed. *Probably be a big ratings-grabber.*

But being on *Kerry!* changed his life. He may have summoned up the courage to land the job for himself, but he was still that shy kid when *Kerry!* began. Candy wouldn't allow it, though. She, in her own special way, was his lifesaver. She and her *I know it*s gave him hope that he could make it big and survive doing it. He used to think that maybe being a star meant you had to be like Kerry Flanagan, in it all for yourself and the fame and fortune it could bring. *But Candy is a star—not as big as Jackass—and she is wonderful, happy herself and intent on making him happy. Thank God for Candida Cameron.*

With Candy in his heart, he thought of Tai. Tai was secure in himself. He didn't let anything bother him. Granted, Mama Ruthie and Pops were the best parents in the world, but Tai, too, had to endure Jackass's demeaning rants, and they just rolled off Tai's back. Nate wanted to be like that, but some days, Jackass got to him, and he just wanted to crawl away to the safety of his dressing room.

Having Tai in his life, having Tai as his friend—still his only friend besides Candy—had made him the happiest guy in the world. Nothing could bring Nate down when he thought of that. Tai was so patient with him when they practiced driving. Despite that first lesson, which went pretty well after the police intrusion, Nate had made some bonehead moves the second time out. Tai never raised his voice, never tried to take over the wheel. With Mama Ruthie his silent partner—yes, she still rode in the back seat every time—Tai continued to help Nate get better until Nate was letter perfect. He passed his driving test with flying colors.

Then Nate filmed the Mustang commercial. Being on a drama-free set was a dream. The director of the commercial was kind, considerate, and patient, like Sam, the show's director. But the show had Kerry Flanagan to stir up shit all the time. The commercial was Flanagan-free. Nate had never filmed a commercial and had no idea how it went, but it wasn't that different from shooting *Kerry!*—only without the egomaniac.

The day after the commercial aired, the rep from Ford showed up after *Kerry!* rehearsal. Mr. Waldman brought him to the set, and together they led Nate to the parking lot. The Ford guy presented Nate with the keys to his very own, brand-new, hot-off-the-assembly-line Mustang convertible, cherry red with snow-white interior, just as promised. A photographer snapped stills of the whole thing, and the next day, Ford took out a full-page ad in the *L.A. Times*, featuring Nate and his new car. Mr. Waldman held up five different newspapers from across the nation for Nate and the whole cast to see. He was beaming when he said, "Cast, these are only five. I'm told Nate's ad has made twenty-five major papers, all across America."

Everybody cheered, and Nate was glad Jackass Flanagan had already left. *No telling what he would have said.*

Nate drove the car home the day he got it. He parked it in the building lot and was on cloud nine when he came into the apartment. Neither Monica nor Paul asked a thing about how his day had gone, and since he didn't want to spoil the high he was on, he didn't even mention the car. In fact, it might be days before they even noticed he was gone a lot, and that would be when they said something. Even then, they wouldn't care enough to go see the car.

He never asked how Monica had missed the *Times* ad. She did like her newspaper, but he figured she just looked at the department store and boutique ads and the gossip columns. At any rate, both his parents would see his car when they needed Nate to drive one or both of them somewhere. Monica would gripe about how it wasn't a town car, and Paul would speculate how much he'd get for it if he sold it. Nate was glad they didn't even know he had it for the time being. Amazing. He could leave for rehearsal without either of them asking how he was getting there. So much for parents of the year.

The next day, rehearsal ended, and Nate took Tai for a spin.

"Dude, this is one hell of a car, not your daddy's car, for sure."

Nate winced. It was, in fact, his daddy's car because he was too young for the title to be in his name. He could only hope Paul never figured that out or it might be bye-bye Mustang. He tried to crack a joke to hide his apprehension. "Tai, my father's car is a four-door sedan. Can't get much different from this."

Tai laughed. "I have no idea what your father drives around, dude. It's a saying—not your daddy's car—means just what you said: this Mustang is not anything like what any daddy would drive. It's for cruising, not for cartin' little Junior and baby Missy to Cub Scouts and ballet lessons. This machine is outta sight."

"You kill me, Tai." *I'm happiest when I'm with you.*

"Rev it up. Hop on the 101. Let's see what this baby can do, dude."

Nate cut his eyes at Tai. "Is this my driving teacher talking? The one who was so cautious and careful?"

Tai flashed a sly smile.

"Well, I do have insurance. I called Paul's guy this morning before we got started. 'Johnson, Paul Berrigan here.'" Nate was doing a perfect imitation of Paul, and Tai was cracking up. "'My kid's a licensed driver now, and he just got a car. Need to put him on the policy.' Then I gave him all the pertinent info, and Pete Johnson, insurance agent of the month at his agency, was none the wiser. He never knew he wasn't talking to Paul Berrigan himself."

Both of them laughed at that. Then Tai asked, "And what happens when Paul gets the bill?"

"Are you kidding me? Paul Berrigan is usually so drunk he doesn't question a thing. Just writes the checks, careful to take out his cut of my money from the bank before he gets any bills."

"He takes your money?"

"That surprises you? As Paul says, 'The Coogan law says guardians get a reasonable amount of a child actor's salary in order to provide a roof over his head, clothes to keep him warm, and food for his belly. So that's my money, and I'm entitled to do with it however I want.' If I know Paul—and I do—he doubles the rent, invents clothing bills, and feeds me royally—in fantasy, that is. The only meals I get at home are the ones I cobble together. I eat a lot of tuna fish and peanut butter and jelly."

"I can't believe it. He's stealin' you blind, dude. My parents don't use a penny of the money I make. They sock it all away into a college fund. They say I might not be so lucky after the show folds, and I'll need to get my degree. I kinda agree with them. And you know my folks, however they explained that to me, it wasn't mean or anything—just practical. That's why I have to bum rides, call cabs, and use Mama's car when I can. No money for a car. All goes to the fund."

"You do know someday soon you'll be able to get the money the Coogan law socks away for you? That's the only thing that keeps me from raisin' a stink about Paul and Monica and my money. Let 'em spend what they bleed from me now. I'll be eighteen soon, and the Coogan money is mine. I can wait."

Tai smiled and said, "I know all about the Coogan law. Down payment on a house. My parents have it all thought out. Besides, dude, I'm not making the star salary you're making. You're rakin' in a lot more, I dare say, right now than I am, and it's only gonna get better. Your career's gonna soar. Me? I might just be a flash in the pan, a falling star, a man on a ride to Skid Row. A used-car salesman waiting to happen. At least for that I'll use my acting skills I'm honing."

Tai sounded so pitiful that Nate knew he was kidding. But he was right about one thing—nothing was going to stop Nate from having a long, brilliant career. And Tai would be right there with him. What had Tai said, "Sandbox to sepulcher"? And *Kerry!* was their sandbox, fun but messy.

With the friendship they had, Nate was sure they'd be together all the way till their final breaths.

With no extra studying, lines, or schoolwork happening, Nate yawned, relaxed by his Tai-thoughts and ready to get a good night's sleep. There'd be no tossing and turning that night. Not with Tai in his thoughts. And his dreams.

Dissolve to: The *Kerry!* Set
The next morning

THEY HAD finally come to the taping of the final show of the season. For Nate, it was bittersweet. He'd met two good friends, Candy and Tai—he sighed—he had brought joy to a lot of audiences, he'd spent countless happy hours away from Monica and Paul, and yet… what was he going to do now? Now that it was ending. No one knew if they'd have another year of this or not.

Sam called them all together right before they were letting the audience in. Some were still in mid-makeup procedure, so this cast meeting must be important.

Nate looked around. Kerry Flanagan was nowhere in sight. He would rush in at the very last minute, just in time to be introduced to the audience.

Their director took a sweep of the gathered group, making sure everyone but his star was there. Then he took a breath. "Okay, guys and gals, big announcement. It's hush-hush, so no blabbing." Sam paused, for dramatic effect, no doubt. "*Kerry!* has been picked up for a second season!"

A loud roar shot up from the cast. The news quickly spread to the crew, and everyone was hooting and hollering and high-fiving and hugging and just general hell-raising.

"Quiet down, quiet down." Sam motioned for the noise to stop. "I don't blame you. I did a happy dance when I heard that too. But remember, it's not for publication. The network gets to make the big announcement. Okay?"

A burst of *okays* pierced the newfound silence.

Nate basked in the news. A second season. A friend like Candy. A brand-new Mustang. Tai.

Life was good.

Tai.

Take that, Paul. Take that, Monica. Take that, *A Tragic Life.*

Scene 13

Fade in: Interior—NBC Studios
Season two—*Kerry!* the first table read

CANDY LEAPT up when Nate arrived. She and Tai were already at the table.

"My little love!" she shouted. "A Maggie nominee! You'll win, I just know it!"

She smothered Nate in a hug.

There was a time when Nate would have struggled to pull himself out of her grasp, not because of Candy herself, but just because he felt stifled by such enthusiasm. Those were the old days, the soap opera days. That time was long gone. He relaxed and enjoyed Candy's mighty hug.

"Yeah," he said, finally pulling away from her, "you're nominated too, Candy, and you're gonna win too. *I just know it!*"

By this time, Tai was standing. He leaned over and put his arm around Nate's neck. "Hearing that announcement last night, I was bustin' with pride. Hearing your name was almost as good as hearing mine would have been."

Tai was playing to the crowd here, making Nate feel good in front of his costars. Tai had phoned him the minute he'd heard the nominees. In fact, Tai was who had told Nate he was nominated for the *Teleplay Magazine* Maggie.

"Well, your time's coming, Tai," Nate said, smiling.

He and Tai had seen a lot of each other over the break. They'd put a lot of miles on the 'Stang, going to the beach and back and toolin' around town. For Nate, it was a chance to stay as far away from Paul and Monica as possible.

He loved being with Tai. He was glad they were friends. Tai had never again mentioned the kiss. There were times when Nate wondered about that. There were also times when Nate wondered if he didn't like that kiss. And then he instantly banished those thoughts. Not because that sort of thing was a sin—and he was sure it was—but because he didn't want thoughts like that to come between him and Tai.

They had also not talked a whole lot about the cop incident. Nate didn't ask about the contract thing Pops—he loved calling Fetu Atua that—battled out with that nasty client. Summer was for having fun, and both Nate and Tai avoided the heavy stuff. Tai didn't ask about Nate's parents, and Nate didn't bring up the civil rights thing.

But Tai was bursting when he phoned Nate on July 2. It was a Thursday, and Tai and Nate had been planning a Friday trip to the beach, so Nate didn't think anything about it when his phone rang. But Tai was shouting, "It's done, it's done," and laughing and crying at the same time.

Nate was alarmed. This was unlike Tai. Tai was the even, always happy one of their duo. At least most of the time. Hearing what sounded like tears mixed with laughter was weird.

"What, Tai, what? Is something wrong? You sound happy, but you sound like you're cryin' too. You're worryin' me, Tai." Nate's words tumbled out so fast Tai could not have responded if he'd tried. But he was still laughing and crying hysterically.

"Tai, you're scarin' me. What gives?"

He heard Tai take a deep, deep breath. "The Civil Rights Act. Johnson just signed it on TV. You gotta get a TV in your room, dude. Johnson used a ton of pens—I think they said seventy-five—so everyone there could have a souvenir of the signing of the most historic act ever. Man, I wish I had me one of those pens. Anyway, Nate baby, no more discrimination!"

Nate not only was happy about Tai's news, but he heard that word he used. Somehow Nate thought discrimination would not end in a flash, but it might help Pops get his contracts, and it might stop that shitty cop from pulling his stunts. So Nate was happy Tai was happy, and oddly, Tai calling him baby, as crazy as it sounded, made him feel warm all over.

The warmth of that moment was a huge wave of emotion he surfed all the way up until this moment when work started again and Nate was released from day-to-day bondage in the prison he called home.

He, Tai, and Candy sat down at the table.

"Have you read this script, dude?" Tai held up his copy. "You've got the best lines of anybody."

"You certainly do, my love," Candy echoed. "And I'm jealous!" She giggled and poked Nate on the arm.

Nate *had* seen the script. And he secretly was glad because Candy and Tai told the truth. It was the best script yet for his character. *That's if our leader lets me keep all those great gags.*

The other cast members slowly gathered, offering congratulations to both Candy and Nate on their nominations.

Nate noticed that the other guys were all tanned from their summer vacations. If it hadn't been for Tai, his summer break would have been like all the others he'd had—holed up in the apartment. Tai changed all that. His skin was as tanned as the others. It felt good to know he was as normal and red-blooded as his brother cast members.

Pika Togai eased her considerable frame into her chair and sighed. "Oh, how I wish I were still on the beach."

"The beach, dear?" Candy gushed. "I thought sure you'd have done a movie during the hiatus. A star of your caliber must have had a lot of offers to choose from."

"Oh, oh, oh," Pika said, "I leave the twenty-four seven work to the young ones here, Candy. I don't have the energy anymore. No, I enjoyed my time just lying around, soaking up the sun."

"I know what you mean, dear." Candy gestured her assent. "My agent wanted me to do a six-week Broadway run, but I said, 'No, no, no—these old bones need respite.'"

Movies? Broadway? I guess stars like Candy and Pika are in demand during the hiatus. I would have liked to keep working, but no one offered. Or maybe Paul didn't try to get me anything. I should have looked for something myself.

Conversations abruptly ceased as Kerry Flanagan came blustering in.

"Season two, huh? Let's get started," he barked, sitting down. "This year we're bringing the focus back to Kerry. The new writers and director will see to that."

So much for welcome back.

Stan Waldman diplomatically spoke up. "Welcome to our new writers...." He pointed to the three at the end of the table. "And welcome, too, to our new director, Marv Freeman. Marv created *Life Unaware* and *Plant Service*, two of TV's longest-running shows. We're looking forward to his input on *Kerry!*" Mr. Waldman led applause for the new director, who had come in behind Mr. Waldman.

Let's hope this Freeman guy is as good as Mr. Waldman says he is. I already miss Sam.

Nate noticed that Kerry Flanagan was looking impatient. *You'd think he'd be happy. He fired Sam, and he fired the writers. That alone should be enough to make Satan himself ecstatic.*

"Pat yourselves on the back, people. A Maggie nomination for Best Comedy. You all made that happen." Mr. Waldman was very happy indeed.

As they whistled, stomped, and applauded, Nate noticed Kerry looking daggers at Mr. Waldman.

"And more applause"—Waldman gestured to Candy and Nate—"for our supporting Maggie nominees." The people at the table erupted with whistles and whoops and beating on the table at this announcement. Flanagan was the lone dissenter, sitting with hands folded. "We are very proud of them."

Candy interrupted, "Nate and I are very proud of our nominations, Stan, but let's not forget that our star is going to win Best Actor in a Comedy. I just know it."

The table once again erupted, but this time the enthusiasm was not quite as loud and raucous. Appeasing their boss was more important to them than lauding him.

"Okay, okay." Kerry held up his hand. Oblivious to his cast's obligatory praise, he silenced them. "Maggies aren't everything. We have a show to do. Page one…."

Scene 14

Fade in: Exterior—the red carpet outside the Roosevelt Hotel
The Maggie Awards

THE LIMO the network sent pulled up in front of the auditorium.

"Oh my," Monica said, repairing her lipstick, "I can't let Sirena see me all messed up."

Nate peered out the window at the crowds. He could see out, but they couldn't see in the tinted windows. *Neat. This is cool—who would have thought I would be here after just one year on the show? The Maggies are almost as important as the Golden Globes or the Emmys.*

His mother primped her hair, checked her makeup, popped a pill, and then said, "Now."

Paul frowned at Monica, then tapped on the window, and the driver opened the door to the limo. Monica, Paul, and Nate stepped from the car.

Girls screamed at the sight of Nate.

"Wave to the fans, Nate baby," Monica said out of the corner of her mouth as she waved and smiled to the people situated in bleachers to their left.

Nate smiled and shyly waved.

Together, the three walked up the red carpet.

Sirena Cartwright, interviewer to the stars, thrust a microphone in Nate's face. Nate knew her report would be on the *Today* show the next morning.

"My, my," Sirena said, "you do look handsome tonight. What a dapper young man." She turned to her camera. "Ladies and gentlemen, Nathaniel Berrigan from *Kerry!*" She turned back to Nate. "How do you feel about your nomination tonight? Are you excited?"

Nate opened his mouth to answer, but Paul interrupted, almost stepping right in front of Nate. "We're very happy, Sirena. This nomination is a great tribute to Kerry Flanagan."

Sirena looked at him a moment, then asked another question of Nate. "How does it feel to have all these girls screaming for you? If I were only ten years younger…."

Nate looked down at the red carpet.

Monica grabbed the mic. "We love all our fans, Sirena."

Sirena quickly recovered the mic and said, "Well, good luck, Nathaniel."

"By the way, I'm wearing Givenchy, Sirena. He's Audrey Hepburn's designer," Monica said, but Cartwright had already turned to greet another nominee.

"Well, that was rude!" Monica wavered a bit as Paul grabbed her arm and steered her toward the hotel doors.

Nate trailed behind his parents, sighing.

Cut to: Interior—Blossom Ballroom, the Hollywood Roosevelt Hotel

AN USHER showed them to the *Kerry!* table. Nate sat, Paul and Monica beside him. Shortly after, Candy Cameron arrived, looking beautiful in some sort of red-and-yellow flowy dress. She sat next to Nate. Trailing her was Tai—who, like Nate, was in his first tuxedo—and Mama Ruthie, looking gorgeous in a simple lavender-colored dress he knew she'd made herself. Other *Kerry!* cast members rounded out their party. Flanagan himself was one of the hosts of the show, so he was backstage.

As Nate scanned the room, Tai reached behind Candy and squeezed his shoulder. It felt good. Support from a friend.

Candy leaned over and hugged Nate from behind. "This is your night, Natie. I just know it." She kissed him on the cheek.

Nate squeezed her arms and said, "Thanks."

"Look!" Monica said to Paul. "There's Marjorie Lord. I just love her on *Make Room for Daddy*. Nobody even remembers Jean Hagen. She played Danny Thomas's wife the first season. But Marjorie's been the wife ever since. She's a doll. We were at that luncheon together last month."

Nate couldn't believe his ears. *Monica thinks she's the queen of Hollywood and knows all the stars.* He watched as his mother gave a friendly wave toward her *friend* Marjorie. Lord looked at her with a "Who are you?" look.

"Looks like you made a big impression on her," Paul wisecracked.

"I heard she's very nearsighted without her glasses. She probably didn't recognize me from so far away," Monica defended herself.

Nate just shook his head.

The lights dimmed. A disembodied voice came from the speakers.

"Welcome to the historic Hollywood Roosevelt Hotel in Hollywood, California. This is the fifth *Teleplay Magazine* Awards, televised for the first time in living color, here on NBC. Your hosts tonight are America's favorite funny man, Kerry Flanagan, and from *The Dick Van Dyke Show*, Mary Tyler Moore. Appearing on tonight's show will be Donna Reed, Carl Betz, Danny Thomas, Andy Williams, Donna Douglas, Max Baer Jr...."

Dissolve to: The stage
About twenty minutes later

"AND NOW, here to present the award for outstanding performance by a supporting actor, comedy, the star of *The Beverly Hillbillies*, Irene Ryan, and Marshal Matt Dillon himself, the star of *Gunsmoke*, Jim Arness."

Arness led Ryan from the backstage. Granny Clampett—as Nate knew her—was all decked out in a flashy wine-colored dress with a long pink flowing thing trailing behind. She looked a lot different from the old woman she played on her show. Arness, though, looked pretty much like the marshal, in a tuxedo but with a black cowboy hat and boots.

As they arrived at the podium, Ryan stumbled and Arness caught her.

"Sorry, Irene," Marshal Dillon said. "I stepped on your train."

"Oh, Jim." Granny blew him a kiss. "You can ride my train anytime."

The auditorium erupted in laughter.

Arness gestured as if he were pulling a train whistle. "Woo! Woo!"

More laughter.

Ryan gazed lovingly into his eyes. He pecked a kiss on her nose and said, "Irene, shouldn't we get on with the award?"

She feigned confusion and then said, "Oh yes, the award!"

She held up the envelope and read the nominees. "Nominated tonight for Outstanding Male Performance in a Supporting Role in a Comedy are Sean Tricker, *Get Molly* on ABC, Albert Russell, *Talk is Cheap* on CBS…"

Nate watched the monitors as the camera zoomed in on each of the nominees as their names were read. He studied each, as he'd done every nominee so far. He'd thought about how to act if his name was called. But he was sure he wouldn't have to worry about that. The other nominees were too good.

"…and Nathaniel Berrigan, *Kerry!* NBC."

The camera panned in on Nate. He cut his eyes around, looking ill at ease with this close-up.

"He's mighty fine," Ryan said. Laughter erupted from the crowd as Ryan acted like that was an accident. "Oops," she said. "Is this thing on?" She pointed at the mic.

"And the winner is…." Arness paused for dramatic effect as he ripped open the envelope. He looked out at the audience and smiled, then announced, "Nathaniel Berrigan."

The camera once again zoomed in on Nate, who had a stricken look on his face. The crowd applauded wildly. Nate stood, in shock. Tai grabbed him and gave him a hug. Candy kissed his cheek. The other cast members whooped, with the boys shouting, "Nate! Nate! Nate!" over and over. The orchestra struck up the *Kerry!* theme.

Monica pushed Nate into the aisle. He walked slowly to the podium onstage, where Irene Ryan gave him a big hug, holding on longer than he expected. When he heard the laughter, he knew she was mugging for the camera. At last she released him. Arness handed him the gold statuette.

"I-I-I…." Nate stood there, unable to speak. He stared at the award.

"Go ahead, dearie, tell us how you feel," Ryan coaxed him.

Finally, Nate found his voice.

"I don't know how I feel right now. I'm in shock. I never thought this would happen. I suppose I should thank Mr. Flanagan and Mr. Waldman for hiring me and my fellow cast members who are so nice, especially Candy Cameron, who is very supportive, and Tai Atua, who has become my best friend." He started to walk off, then turned back to the mic. "Oh yeah! And thanks to *Teleplay Magazine*." Nate held up the trophy as the orchestra played him off the stage.

Cut to: Interior—the limousine

MONICA LIT a cigarette as soon as they settled back into the limo. She kicked off her shoes and stretched.

As Paul poured a Scotch from the bar, he said, "Well, we did it! This win is gonna be big bucks for us."

"You think?" Monica took a drag off her cigarette and exhaled noisily.

Nate, sitting between them, waved the smoke from in front of his face.

"Of course," Paul said, knocking back the Scotch and pouring himself another. "This means endorsements, guest shots, maybe even a movie deal. Why, I wouldn't be surprised if I couldn't coax a raise out of Waldman."

Nate stared out the window. All this talk of raises didn't interest him. After all, Paul spent all the money anyway. No, he just wanted to keep working—anything to keep *Daddy* happy and off his back.

"A raise? You really think so?" Monica asked. "He still has two years to go on his contract."

"Yeah," Paul said. "But who knew he'd cop a Maggie? *Kerry!* can't do without him now. In-dis-pen-si-ble! We got leverage, babe."

"You hear that, sweetie?" Monica gushed to Nate. "We're coming up in the world."

She pulled off her diamond chandelier earrings, then rubbed her earlobes. "Maybe you could buy me these baubles now, instead of renting them."

She waved the earrings in front of Paul.

"You could be dripping in diamonds if you didn't blow so much on pills." Paul spat the words.

"Paul. That's not fair. You *know* how my nerves are."

As Paul turned from her, disgust in his eyes, Scotch spilled from his drink onto Nate's lap.

"Hey," Nate yelped. "Watch it."

"It was an accident, baby," his mother said, trying to smooth things over. She brushed the Scotch from Nate's pants. "Tell Daddy you're sorry for yelling at him."

"You oughta be *thanking* me," Paul said to Nate. "You slobbered over everybody on that goddamn show, but you didn't even mention me. Without me, there'd *be* no *Kerry!*"

Scene 15

Fade in: Interior—men's room, NBC Studios
The day after the Maggies

NATE HAD stopped by the tutor's cubicle to turn in some homework for her to send to his public-school teacher, and then he'd reported to publicity to shoot some stills of him holding his Maggie. He was allowed to take the trophy home and use it for the publicity stills, but then it would get sent back to *Teleplay Magazine*, where they would have it engraved.

Gushing with pride and love for him, Candy posed. One shot had them looking at each other, devotion sparkling in her eyes. He ate it up.

With the shoot finished, he headed back to his dressing room. But first, he realized he needed to—in Tai's words—drain his wiener. He stopped into the men's room. Nate preferred to do his business in a stall. That was left over from his shy stage. *Who am I kidding? I'm still shy. I'm just better, thanks to Tai and Candy.*

He was about to zip up when he heard voices outside the stall.

"That's it, Stan." It was Kerry Flanagan, and from the sound of it, he was livid. And Stan had to be Mr. Waldman. Nate knew he shouldn't be eavesdropping, but he didn't want to show himself, not with Jackass so angry. And, too, he would have to barge right in, breaking up their conversation, which might make Flanagan even madder. So he stood silently in the stall, listening. "*Finis.* Over. He's outta here." *Who?*

"Ker," Mr. Waldman said, "you can't fire the boy. He won a Maggie, for chrissakes! What would people say?"

They're talking about me. He wants to fire *me. Oh my God.* Now Nate was really listening.

"Don't care, Stan," Flanagan barked. "I'm the star of this show, not some snot-nosed kid."

"And you also play the father figure. How would it look if Kerry Simon got rid of his middle child?"

"Send him off to boarding school. Let him get his own apartment. Hell, throw him in front of a bus—I don't care. Just get ridda him."

"Now, Kerry, calm down." Mr. Waldman tried to placate his star. "We can't do any of those things. Simon loves his kids—he wouldn't farm one out. And Brian's too young to get his own place—he's sixteen, for God's sake. And killing him? The fans would crucify us. No, there's no way to get rid of Nate."

You tell him, Mr. Waldman. Oh God, please, convince him.

"I don't want him there, you hear me? I'm the executive producer. I say what happens here!"

"If you get rid of him, you'll have to terminate Cameron too. After all, she won the supporting *actress* category, if you recall."

"Fine, fire her ass too. No more *I just know it*s."

Nate almost jumped out of the stall to yell, "You can't fire Candy. She's the best thing on this shit show." But he caught himself. That would serve no one. And it really wasn't a shit show, so saying that would really get him canned, immediately.

"I'm afraid I'm overruling you, Kerry, for your own good." Nate was impressed at how calm Mr. Waldman could be. And he was glad Mr. Waldman said what he said. *I'm not getting fired. That's a good thing.* "No one's being fired. And I suggest you issue a statement praising the boy and gushing about how proud we are that he picked up a Maggie. It's only good PR."

Nate heard the trailing voice of Kerry Flanagan say, "This isn't ove—" as the two of them must have left. Nate opened the stall door just enough to spy around. They were gone. He left the stall, washed his hands, and went through the door into the hallway. There he almost bumped into Paul.

"Pau—" he stopped himself. "Dad, why are *you* here?"

"Got some business with Waldman and Flanagan," Paul barked, brushing past Nate.

My God. That raise business in the limo. I've got to stop him. "Dad, no." Nate grabbed for Paul's sleeve, but he was too far ahead of him.

"Dad, listen to me," he called as his father reached Mr. Waldman's office door.

Paul stopped at the door and turned to Nate. "Watch and learn, kid, watch and learn." And before Nate could say any more, do any more, his father had pushed through the door. Nate ran and got into the outer office before the door closed.

But Paul had pushed past the secretary and was already standing in the open doorway of Stan Waldman's office.

If I had a gun, I'd shoot him in the back right now. I swear I would. And no one would convict me.

"Hey, Stan." Paul's tone was full of bluebirds and sunshine.

Nate stepped into the office right behind Paul, but there was nothing he could do to stop him. His father was a steamroller, and he was about to roll right over Nate's career.

Paul strode forward, grabbed Mr. Waldman's hand, shook it vigorously. Nate saw through Paul's act, so Mr. Waldman surely did. *But that won't stop Paul from knifing me in the back.*

"Good morning, Paul, Nate." Mr. Waldman was all business charm. "Paul, you, of course, know Kerry Flanagan."

Paul turned to Flanagan. "Glad you're here, Ke...." Then Paul caught himself.

He remembers how he offended Jackass that first meeting. I wish he'd piss Jackass off now so he'd get thrown out of here before he can screw things up.

"*Mr.* Flanagan." Paul held his hand out to Kerry, but the comedian ignored him. After a moment, Paul retracted his hand and held it to his side limply.

I'm no fan of yours, Jackass Flanagan, but I like your style—in this case, anyway.

"Have a seat, Paul. Nate, take the other chair." Mr. Waldman pointed to the chair opposite Kerry Flanagan for Paul. He sat, but Nate stood, waving an *I'm okay* sign to Mr. Waldman. Mr. Waldman nodded, no doubt feeling Nate's pain. Then he said to Paul, "What brings you here?"

"How 'bout that Maggie?" Paul asked. "Some kid, huh?"

Flanagan glared at him. Mr. Waldman smiled at Paul.

"We're all very proud of Nate," Waldman said. "Good job, son," he said to Nate.

"His mom and I are just bustin' with pride, I tell ya." Paul beamed.

What a total butthole. Maybe that will fool these two men, but I know different. They don't give a crap, unless it means more money in their pockets.

"So—are we here just to chew the fat about last night, Berrigan?" Flanagan didn't try to hide his snide demeanor.

Ignoring Jackass Flanagan's tone—or rather not even noticing—*That's Paul for you*—Paul said, "Well, that's why I'm here, actually. Lotta buzz at the parties last night. I've even fielded a few calls from producers this morning." Paul shifted in his chair. "The kid's hot. And Monica and I want to capitalize on that. Nathaniel Berrigan is a big, big asset to *Kerry!* right now."

Why can't I stop this train wreck? Don't do it, Paul. Keep your fucking mouth shut.

Oh, how Nate wished he could say those words aloud, but he was powerless.

Paul cleared his throat. "And, ya see, when we signed that contract last season, none of us—you, Stan, or you, Kerry, or the wife and I—had any idea of how big the kid would become. So...." He paused and swallowed. Nate wished he'd choke to death, right then and there. Then Paul looked at Mr. Waldman and Kerry Flanagan to *just be clear*. Nate knew that look, and it always accompanied Paul's *let's be clear* speech. "I think it only fair that you give the kid a raise. Considering the prestige of the gold statue, I think that double his salary per episode is fair and just."

Flanagan's mouth dropped, but not before Nate caught a glimpse of a smile.

Nate wanted to crawl into a hole, a hole where he was still under contract securely and there was no Paul Berrigan.

"Paul," Mr. Waldman began, "as I said before, we are very proud of Nathaniel." *He's using the official name. That can't be good.* "And we agree he is a big asset to the show. But a contract is a contract."

Paul gave Kerry Flanagan a look. *What? Do you, my incompetent father, think Jackass Flanagan is going to back you up on this? That ain't gonna happen,* Daddy. *Not after what I heard in the toilet.* The bastard looked as if cogs were turning in his brain, but he remained silent, letting Mr. Waldman do his dirty work for him, Nate figured.

"I'm afraid that a raise is out of the question," Mr. Waldman said.

Good. If Paul will back away, my job's still safe.

"Look, Stan, Ke—er, Mr. Flanagan, the kid is gold to you right now." *Quit talking, Paul! Get out while the gettin's good, bozo. But not Paul Berrigan. He doesn't have good sense. No, he has no sense at all.* "The publicity he will generate alone will shoot the show back to number one. We deserve some compensation—"

Mr. Waldman interrupted him. "Maybe if you came up with some reasonable perks, Paul. We might be able to provide some extras for Nate. But a raise? No, I'm sorry—"

Flanagan cut him off. "Step outside, Paul," he said. "Let me talk to Stan a minute."

Paul and Nate left the office.

I don't trust Kerry Flanagan, but maybe Mr. Waldman can talk some sense into him before this train—my train—derails.

The two sat down in the outer office.

"They're gonna make us an offer, kid. Just you wait and see."

Nate was so angry with Paul he kept his mouth shut. He was not going to tell Paul what he'd overheard until he knew the outcome of all this. And if he got fired, Paul would never hear the end of it.

Dissolve to: Interior—Waldman's office
Immediately afterward

"WHAT'S UP?" Waldman demanded. "First you want to fire the boy, now you want to give him a raise? If we double his salary, we'll also have to double Cameron's, and since she signed on for a hell of a lot more, we're talking about a sizable chunk of change, here."

Flanagan smiled a Cheshire cat smile.

"Don't you see, Stan? This is our way out."

"No, Kerry." Waldman shook his head wearily. "I don't see."

"Look—that ass Berrigan just told us he was fielding other offers. Yeah, right. Like that's going to happen overnight. Anyway, we'll tell him we have no intention of standing in his son's way. Release him from his contract. Let him pursue these phantom offers. It's perfect."

"The network will never back this plan, Kerry."

"Don't you worry about the network, Stan. The only person at the network who could be a problem is Holcombe. That queen almost licks my boots every time he sees me. I can handle that old queer anytime. No, Holcombe won't give us any trouble."

"What about the show? How would we handle this? And don't give me any of that 'throw him in front of a bus' bullshit."

"Okay—how 'bout this?" Kerry grinned. "Nate's character Brian's on his school's ball team, right? Suppose he goes to a *special* game. Hawaii, maybe. The plane goes down. Is the kid dead, or does he survive? We could milk it forever. Meanwhile, we get mileage out of the mystery and lose the kid all at the same time."

"Our audience doesn't want to deal with a tragedy like that. We're a sitcom, Kerry, not some nighttime soap."

"Look, Stan. I'm America's funny man, right? We can spin this with laughs. What if, say, the kid is kidnapped? We could play it for laughs, find out he engineered it himself to get attention. We do it all with phone calls, maybe a voice-over or two—we hire somebody to imitate the kid's voice—and when all is said and done, Simon packs him off to boarding school to teach him a lesson. I know we could pull it off."

"Um… it might work." Waldman rubbed his chin. *I don't want to lose Nate, but there is no reasoning with Kerry Flanagan. And his idea might work.*

"Might?" Kerry countered. "It's a ratings bonanza!"

"Are you sure you want to do this?"

"Yeah, I'm sure. We get rid of the kid, and I get to do a *pissed-off/ concerned father* scene that'll snare me an Emmy. And I know just the writer who can write it so it's funny as hell. It will be the best work I've ever done."

Stan Waldman sighed. He picked up his phone, punched in his secretary. "Send Mr. Berrigan and Nate back in, please."

Dissolve to: Outer office
Immediately after

"Mr. Waldman will see you again now," the secretary said.

Nate once again followed Paul into the office, feeling like the guillotine blade could very well be about to fall.

The moment they got through the door, Paul asked, "So, is it a go?"

"I'm afraid," Mr. Waldman began hesitantly, "that we can't—"

Paul interrupted him. *Just accept it, Paul. You fucked me over.*

"Five thou per more, how would that be?"

Flanagan broke in.

"What Stan is trying to say, Paul—" The star turned on every bit of fake charm he could muster; Nate saw it, but Paul was oblivious. "—is that we couldn't live with ourselves if we held Nate back in any way. We want him to be free to take any of those other offers that you have lined up. So we are releasing him from his contract."

"But—but—" Paul sputtered.

This would be funny, seeing Paul like this, if my heart hadn't just been ripped from my body.

"No, no, no," Flanagan said, gripping Paul's shoulder. "No need to thank us. Having Nate with us this long has been a pleasure, but we all knew that a talent like his could not be contained on a simple sitcom. He's destined for the big screen, Paul. Looking forward to seeing his first flick."

"I suppose we could discuss some of those perks you mentioned." Nate saw Flanagan smile as sweat poured from Paul's forehead. *So you got what you wanted, didn't you, Jackass?*

Paul was babbling now. "A personal assistant?"

"Oh, Paul," Flanagan gushed, his concern faker than a TV preacher milking the crowd for money, "your boy is going to be a big, big star. You don't want him shackled to a TV contract, do you? The really big projects don't want to have to shoot around a sitcom schedule."

"Nate's awfully young for a movie career." For a second, Nate had the urge to guffaw. Paul was grasping at straws when the haystack was already on fire.

"Nonsense." Flanagan slapped Paul on the back. "Was Mickey Rooney too young? Judy Garland? Elizabeth Taylor? Who's to say that they would be stars today if they hadn't started in the business as kids? No, you need to grab that gold ring when you can, Paul."

Mr. Waldman took a sheet of paper from his drawer and thrust it in front of Paul.

"Standard contract release, Paul. Sign here." Flanagan grabbed Paul's hand and thrust a pen into it. He guided the hand to the paper. In a daze, Paul signed.

"Now," Mr. Waldman said, after signing the paper himself, "Kerry, your autograph, please."

Kerry Flanagan signed with a flourish as Paul visibly shrank.

I wanted Mr. Waldman to stop this. But no one can stop Kerry Flanagan. What Jackass Flanagan wants, Jackass Flanagan gets. And Nathaniel Berrigan, child actor, is now Nathaniel Berrigan, fired and unemployed child actor. Damn you, Paul!

Scene 16

Fade in: Interior—the Berrigan apartment
The same day

"WHAT'D THEY say?" Monica demanded as Paul plodded into the apartment. Nate had followed him home in the Mustang, and now he was right behind him, standing and waiting to take in what Paul would have to say about all this.

Paul beelined to the bar and poured himself a Scotch. He took the drink, gulped it down, and poured another.

"Why am I thinking this is not good news?" Monica stood. A menacing look on her face, she asked, "What did you do, Paul?"

He fucked up, that's what he did.

But Nate didn't say anything out loud; he only watched.

"They didn't buy it, Mon." Nate had never seen Paul look so defeated. Those few words said so much. Paul had failed, miserably crashed and burned, and despite his usual bravado born out of just being Paul, he knew he'd blown it. And it hurt him to admit it to Monica. That was Nate's assessment, and it was right on the money, he thought.

Paul took a swig of Scotch. *Does he hope to drink himself into oblivion, or is the Scotch just a prop? A reason not to talk.*

Monica's eyes narrowed. She measured her words. "What do you mean... they didn't buy it?" She blew up totally. "They're not giving Natie a raise?" she shouted. She strode to him. She positioned herself so that their noses were almost touching. Amazingly, her next words were quiet, almost menacing. "How did you screw this up? You said it was a sure thing."

Funny how she had to walk right past him to get to Paul, but she didn't even acknowledge Nate's presence.

"It's worse." He pushed his way past her, plopped in his chair, breathed in heavily, exhaled loudly, and then took another drink.

"Paul, you're scaring me." Monica took her Valium bottle from a pocket, popped open the cap. "Is this a two-pill or three-pill confession, Paul?" She barked, "Tell me what happened—now!"

Slip that entire bottleful into his Scotch, Mother dear.

A swig of Scotch. A long, loud, defeatist huff of breath. "They let him go." The voice thin, the delivery weak, bewildered.

Monica threw up her hands, almost an invocation to the God she never worshipped. "Oh my God!," Monica screamed. Then she tore into Paul. "No—that can't be right. They wouldn't fire him. He's a Maggie winner, for God's sake. You misunderstood." She shook out three pills and tossed them back on her tongue. Then she grabbed Paul's Scotch and washed them down. She gave him back the drink, then staggered to the couch and fell back on it.

Reality must be setting in. It takes a while with my mother, but she does get it finally, the message piercing her drug-addled brain.

"I'm telling you, Mon, they canned him. They made me sign a contract release." Paul pressed the cool Scotch glass to his forehead.

"I want to know exactly what happened, Paul Berrigan." She was mustering her attack impulse once again, Nate could tell.

Nate was amazed that neither of them said a word to him. He was just their commodity, a thing to buy and sell. He was the dress that Bullock's wouldn't take back, the Ferrari test-driven overnight that the dealership was demanding payment for. Nate was simply merchandise, an item no longer needed because they'd found a flaw. He was worthless to them unless he was earning their booze and pills for them.

Monica sat, staring Paul down, her gaze demanding he spill. She said not a word for the longest time. But Nate knew Paul knew what she wanted and would get, come hell or high water.

Finally, Paul took a deep breath and began again. He went through the office encounter, step by step, ending with the signing of the release. "I should have suspected something when that bastard Flanagan was so nice. He caught me off guard. Before I knew, I was believing everything he said."

"You're such a fuckup, Paul Berrigan," Monica said, pointing a finger at him. She let that sink in, and then her demeanor brightened. She stood, started pacing. "But maybe we can turn this around. The offers last night? You'll just have to talk to some of those producers. You can get the kid another job."

So now she's calling me kid. I thought that was just a Paul thing. I actually thought there might be a tiny bit of mothering in my mother. But she's no better than her husband.

Paul put his palms over his eyes and said nothing.

When Paul was not forthcoming with anything, she turned toward him. "What is it?" she barked.

"There *were* no offers." Nate had to strain to hear that. He knew what Paul was likely going to say, but he wanted to hear it for himself. And yet Paul said it so quietly, it was as if he was afraid of Monica's reaction.

Now she stood right over her husband. There was utter contempt in her voice. "You told me that producers were coming up to you right and left last night."

"Well, don't believe everything I tell you, okay?" That statement was not as full of force as the words implied. Paul actually seemed afraid of Monica. He took another gulp of amber courage.

"You're a bastard, Paul." She tossed those words like a knife, and when she hit her target, she turned from him, like he was useless. But she wasn't finished berating him. As she strode away, she punctuated her words with each step. "Natie won a Maggie! And what do you do? You get him fired! Fired! Like he's a nobody." Nate watched as his mother exhibited more force than he'd seen in her in years. Paul slumped lower and lower in his chair. "You're no good, Paul Berrigan. A loser. You talk big, but when I need you the most, where are you? Lost in your lies." With her back to Paul, her words seemed to carry even more force. They pounded Paul. If it weren't for the fact she was more interested in the money they were losing than in his welfare, Nate would be happy she was berating his father so. "Our baby could be a star, but you can't make it happen." She stopped.

Paul looked up at her, defeated.

Then she turned and fired her final bullet: "Just like you can't make it happen for me in our bed. You're Mr. Limp Dick all the way, aren't you, Paul?"

Enraged, Paul shouted, "Shut up!"

In one motion, Paul stood, rushed to Monica, and slapped her.

Her defiant steely blue eyes stared a hole through him.

Paul sighed, dropped his eyes to the floor, and slowly made his way from the room.

There was a *click* as the front door shut behind him.

Nate turned. He stared at his mother. Even for her, that limp dick line was a low blow. He didn't know what to say. He watched her calmly walk to her purse and rummage through it. She pulled out a crumpled newspaper clipping. She looked at it, and then she went to the phone and dialed.

Nate had no idea what she was up to, but he was too tired over it all to care. He turned to leave. But he stopped when he heard her say into the phone, "Information?" His curiosity got the best of him. He stopped and listened.

"I need the number for a law firm in Hollywood… Tingle, Handley, and Merriman."

Is she hiring a lawyer to get my job back?

He heard her dial a number.

"Mr. Handley, please," Monica said.

The person on the other end must have asked who was calling because he heard Monica say, "Monica Berrigan, Nathaniel Berrigan's mother."

After a pause, Nate heard, "Mr. Handley, this is Monica Berrigan. My son is Nathaniel Berrigan, star of *Kerry!*"

Another pause.

"Well, Mr. Handley, I saw in the *Times* that you were Leta Holloway's attorney."

A shorter pause.

"Mr. Handley, sir, I would like to hire you."

It was a one-sided conversation Nate was listening to, but he surmised Handley had replied to that bit of news. Then Monica continued.

"Fine, Mr. Handley, I'll be happy to set up an appointment with your secretary, but I can tell you now, I do have a case. Paul Berrigan is a sniveling, bottom-scraping alcoholic, and I want a divorce!"

Nate didn't know whether to cheer or be very afraid. After all, he was out of a job, and his mother was ready to cut ties with his father, who in his inept way, might, magically, be able to get him another job if he weren't distracted by divorce proceedings. His life had just gotten exponentially worse. Nate guessed it was up to him now to find gainful employment for himself.

Kerry! Kid K-O'd

ON THE heels of carting home a golden flame Sunday night, *Kerry!* cast member Nathaniel Berrigan was released from the popular sitcom. The sixteen-year-old heartthrob's contract was torn up yesterday by producer Stan Waldman and star Kerry Flanagan.

Waldman's office released this statement:

> *Nathaniel Berrigan is a huge talent.* Kerry! *has been immensely enriched by his participation. But Nathaniel's father and manager, Paul Berrigan, asked for and received a release from the contract. Apparently his recent Maggie win puts Nathaniel in line for some important projects that would not fit into our shooting schedule. We wish him well.*

The *Kerry!* cast members are evidently reeling from the news delivered to them at rehearsal Monday. Contacted at home, Candida Cameron, herself also a winner Sunday night, said, "We are devastated to lose a member of our little family. But we are confident that Nate's star will not burn out anytime soon. He is going to be a huge success in films. I just know it."

Star Kerry Flanagan's publicist said that the comedian is devastated to lose such an "incredible" talent, but that the *Kerry!* show will continue to be as high quality and as entertaining as ever.

Scene 17

Fade in: Interior—Nate's dressing room
The next afternoon

NATE EMPTIED the closet of his belongings. He really didn't have much to pack. He hadn't brought many things to the studio. He stuffed a few shirts, a change of pants, and a *Kerry!* baseball cap into the cardboard box he had brought with him. Then he paused, got the cap out of the box, and tossed it into the garbage. *Won't need that anymore,* he thought. He was numb. He didn't know if he should cry or be angry. And should he be mad at Paul or Kerry Flanagan? Or both? It just wasn't fair. He was fired because he won an award. An *award,* for God's sakes. Jackass Flanagan should be proud of him being in his show. And Paul? Paul should have kept his mouth shut.

What if I'd caught up to Paul before he went into Mr. Waldman's office? Would it have made a difference? Would Paul have backed off? Kerry would not have had his *out.* If he still wanted to fire Nate, he would have had to come up with a different reason.

Paul hadn't come home last night. Monica, after her epic phone call, sat in the living room, most likely totally drugged out and convinced she was going to take Paul for everything he had. *But does he have anything? Everything he has is mine. Surely that will come out in any divorce.*

Eventually, Monica came into his room.

"Hey, baby," she said. Her words were slurred, and she had an *I got him* look on her face.

"Your fucked-up father got you fired."

She was truly out of it. He was standing right there when all this went down—in Mr. Waldman's office and when Paul told Monica. *Is she so full of her little yellow pills she has no recollection of my presence? Or did she never even notice I was there?*

He pretended the plaintive melodies pouring from his stereo were drowning her out.

She walked over and flicked the Off button on his sound system. "Cease the tuned-out teenager act, will ya? Did you hear me? You're off the show, thanks to your dear old dad."

Her speech became more distinct, no doubt fueled by her hatred of Paul.

"Yeah," Nate said.

"*Yeah*? Is that all you can say?"

Nate just stared at her.

She raised her voice, as if his lack of response had to do with a sudden loss of hearing. "You're canned," she bellowed. "Your daddy tried to get us a raise, and instead he got you eighty-sixed."

"So?" Nate didn't want to talk to her. He wanted her out of his room. He was well aware of Paul's stupidity. He just wanted her to leave and hoped his one-word answers would silence her. But she persisted.

"Don't you understand, baby? No... more... money." She punched each word.

Nate looked at her, then reached over and switched the stereo back on. He couldn't show her his disappointment. That would just add more fuel to her fire, and all he wanted was peace.

Monica shook her head. "You're a strange kid." She turned to leave his room, muttering, "Strange, strange, strange, strange."

Then she swung around and dropped her bomb. A bomb that wasn't nearly as explosive as she must have hoped since Nate had already heard about it in that phone call the night before. She screamed over the music coming from his quadrophonic speakers.

"I'm filing for divorce," she shouted. "I'm tired of your father's screw-ups." There was a self-satisfied smirk on her face.

Nate refused to let her see the panic he was feeling. He no longer had a job, and if Paul moved out, he would be forced to go to public school and then spend the rest of his waking hours nursing a drug addict. He was trapped.

Then he thought of Tai, his best friend. *Will he desert me now I'm off the show?*

But there wasn't a chance in hell he was letting Monica see any of this in his face. He was stone.

With no reaction from Nate, Monica left his room, shaking her head.

And here he was in his dressing room, packing up.

When he pulled the scrapbook Tai had brought him from the closet, he sat. Thumbing through the book, he thought, *I'm gonna miss this show. My friends, the work.*

A tear slid down his cheek. He wiped it on a sweatshirt he had stuffed in the box.

"Hey, dude." He looked and saw Tai backing up in the hallway. "I didn't know you were here."

"Hey, Tai," Nate called halfheartedly. There was no way Tai really cared about a loser like him.

Tai came into the dressing room and slapped Nate on the back.

"Congrats, buddy," Tai said. "Wish I could do a movie."

"Huh?" Nate's face screwed into confusion. What was Tai talking about? He was canned from the show. He wasn't leaping into movie stardom. "A movie?"

Nate stood and stowed the scrapbook in the box.

"Yeah," Tai answered. "That's what they told us. You were leaving to do a movie. Said you got the offer on Maggie night."

Nate breathed in heavily, then let the breath out in a series of sarcastic chuckles. He had to laugh. It was better than the crying he'd been doing. A movie? *So Mr. Waldman had thrown out Paul's lie and the cast had bought it. And why shouldn't they? They had no reason not to. After all, Nathaniel Berrigan was an award winner.*

"Sure, I'm going to do a movie—with Troy Donahue and Sandra Dee," Nate said, packing the empty sparkling cider bottle that Candy Cameron had toasted him with all those months ago.

"Sandra Dee? She's hot. No shit?"

"Yes, shit." Nate paused. Nate couldn't keep this up. Tai didn't deserve to be led on like this. "There *is* no movie. Paul got me fired."

"What?" Tai's eyes widened, and Nate couldn't tell if it was disbelief or concern.

"That's right," Nate said. "Paul got me 'released' as they put it. I am now totally free to take all these *fabulous and glamorous* nonexistent movie offers."

Nate felt a tear form. He sniffled, hoping to stop it before it rolled down his cheek. But Tai must have seen it. He put his arm around Nate's shoulder.

"Something'll turn up, though, dude. You won the Maggie. Producers aren't stupid. They know your value. As for Paul, he's a royal shit."

"Uh-huh." Nate looked around. Making sure he had everything in his single box was a way to distract him from the fact he was leaving for good.

"I'm gonna miss you, dude," Tai said. He had dropped his arm from Nate's shoulder.

"Tai, did I ever tell you that you are my only friend?"

Tai laughed. "Nah, that can't be. Everybody loves you."

"Everybody? That's only if you believe *Tiger Beat*. You're the only person I've ever been able to talk to."

Tai's face lit up.

"Not my mom. Not Paul." Nate paused. "Candy is nice to me, and I think of her as a friend. But I don't talk to her. Not really. Is there anyone else? Let's see." He thought, then answered sarcastically, "You, Mom, Paul are the only people I ever really get a chance to talk to. Mom's too drugged up to listen. She scares me, her and her pills. And Paul? Well sometimes I think Paul doesn't even know my name."

"What do you mean? He's your dad." Tai's voice said he was trying to cheer Nate up.

Nate scoffed. "You know what he calls me, Tai? My *father* calls me *kid*…. That's right. *Kid*. And Mom's not much better. Most of the time she calls me *baby*. Like I'm her little doll. But at least I like that—sometimes. But Paul… no, he doesn't deserve to be called Dad. As much as I used to think I loved Mom and she loved me, these days I think they're just two people, two random people. Two people I happen to live with." *And now even that is changing.*

But he wasn't ready to tell Tai about the divorce thing.

Tai smiled, but it was sort of a helpless smile. Like Tai wanted to say something that would wipe all the sadness away but he didn't have a clue what words could heal Nate.

At last Tai said haltingly, "I feel for you, dude, I really do." He paused, like he was gathering more words. "You're making progress, dude."

Nate wasn't sure what Tai meant by that, but he felt comfort in those words.

Tai took a step toward Nate and gave him a sideways hug.

"Thanks," Nate said. Then he shrugged and picked up the box he'd packed. "Well, I guess I'm outta here."

"Wait a minute! We are gonna see each other, aren't we? Just because you're leaving here doesn't mean we can't hang out together," Tai said.

Nate felt warm all over at the thought. "You've got my phone number. Call me. But—"

In unison they chanted, "If it's busy, you've got the wrong number."

Tai added, "I know, I know. Nobody else has the number."

They laughed. It was the first genuine feeling of joy Nate had experienced since the morning before.

And he'd shared that feeling with Tai.

It felt good.

Scene 18

Fade in: Interior—Nate's bedroom
The next Monday evening

NATE LAY on the bed, the silence stifling. He was bored to tears. Being out of work was driving him crazy. He had gone back to public school, and he felt like a fish out of water. Some of the girls treated him like he was Elvis or one of the Beatles or some other heartthrob celebrity, which was annoying, and some of the guys mocked him because he'd been fired, so they figured he wasn't the hot shit the girls thought he was. But those were only a few of his new classmates. The vast majority of them were so wrapped up in their own lives they didn't pay any attention to Nate whatsoever. So, what he'd hoped would be a chance to get out of the apartment, away from Monica, and make new friends was a total bust. He was even bored with the classwork because he was used to pretty much teaching himself and doing it all without any help.

And Monica was useless. At the moment, she was in her bedroom, ultra-calm from her *nerve pills*—read that *passed out*. She took the pills, she said, to calm her nerves. Well, her pills were making *him* nervous. What if something happened to her? They were all alone in the apartment since Paul left. And alone was the operable word because Paul didn't show his face nor call for several days. Until last night. He actually showed up at the apartment.

And who was he kidding? He hated, hated, hated not seeing his friends in the show. Those hours were like a work program from this prison his life was. He wouldn't even have to speak to any of them. Just to be around Candy, Miss Togai, the guys in the cast gave him a sense he belonged somewhere. And then there was Tai. He missed seeing him every day so much, and his firing was not all that long ago. Give it another month and nobody, but nobody would even remember who he was.

His phone rang, and for a moment, Nate wondered where that sound was coming from. It just didn't ring very often. But he knew who it had to be. He brightened up just a bit, clinging to this tiny bit of hope, a call from Tai.

He rolled over and picked up the receiver.

"Tai?"

"Hey, dude, it sorta creeps me out that you know it's me on the other end of the line."

"Well, it had to be you or somebody selling magazines—although I don't know how they'd get my number," Nate explained.

Tai laughed.

Nate sat up. For the first time in days, he felt alive. His heart burst just hearing someone from his real and only world that mattered to him. It could have been anyone from the show on the other end of the line and Nate would have felt like a life preserver had been tossed out to him, but it wasn't just anyone. It was Tai.

"You really never gave it to anybody else?" Tai queried.

"Don't know anybody else."

"Trippin', dude," Tai said, a disbelieving whistle escaping his lips. "So, how's it hangin'?"

"Okay, I guess," Nate said. Nate was not going to spend this precious call whining about his lack of a life. "What's happening with you? You just calling to cheer up your loser friend?" Despite his resolve, he let self-pity get the best of him.

"Stop it, Nate. You're not a loser. And do I need a reason to call?"

"Well, no," Nate answered. He let himself smile at the thought Tai would call just to shoot the breeze. "But I wasn't expecting you to call." Nate immediately thought that sounded unfriendly, so he quickly added, "But I'm glad you did."

"Look, man, you're my best bud—I called to check on you, that's all."

Nate felt his smile stretch wider. *This is what friendship's like, huh?*

"It's crazy around the set, dude. Everybody—I mean *everybody*—misses you. After they announced you were leaving to make features, Candy said, 'That boy is going to be a big movie star…'"

Nate joined in with him: "I just know it." They giggled together. It felt corny but good. Something they shared. And it was a breath of fresh air in the gloom of Nate's cell.

"I didn't tell any of 'em about Paul's screw-up. I figured if you wanted them to know, you could tell them yourself. Man, I can't believe he got you fired."

"Yeah." Nate thought about that, and there was comfort in what he was thinking. "I bet he's kicking himself over it. If he doesn't get me work soon, he'll have to give up his very expensive bottles of Scotch."

"Is he trying to get you something?"

"Hard to tell. He didn't come home until last night. He left last Monday. Came back all *kissy-wissy*, tail between his legs, *Oh, honey, I'm sorry*. It was disgusting."

"Wow, dude." Tai sighed. "Where'd he go?"

"Where else? His home away from home. Vegas. Would you believe he came home with some ashtray he got from a new casino called the Tally-Ho. Said it was a present for me. He gets me fired, and I get a stolen ashtray. Some trade, huh?

"So what did your mom say to him?"

"She dropped the bomb."

"What bomb?"

"The divorce bomb, Tai."

"How'd your dad take it?"

"Like usual… lots of Scotch. Then she kicked him out for good."

"It'll blow over, Nate. She'll let him come back." Tai's voice said he was trying to be nice, to make Nate feel better. But Nate was convinced this was a permanent move on Monica's part, and he wasn't sure he cared. As long as Paul at least tried to get Nate another job, he was fine with him being an absentee father/manager. Maybe Paul not being around would sober up Monica, and she would get back to the job of mothering him.

"Not this time, Tai. I think she's serious. She's kicked him out before, but she's never filed for divorce. She's already talked to a lawyer… Handleman, Handy, something like that."

"Louis Handley?"

"Yeah, that's him."

"Oh," Tai said, "she *is* serious. That guy's good. He handles all the big divorces in the industry."

That statement took Nate by surprise. "You an expert on movie star divorces?"

Tai chuckled. "I read."

"Well, I hope he knows how to squeeze blood from a turnip, as Monica likes to say, because I'm out of a job, my dear, sweet mother is incapable of holding down a job, and Paul? I'd bet he lost every penny he had at the Tally-Ho, otherwise he wouldn't have come back crawling. I've read everything I can find in the trades, and there are no jobs out there for the taking. Not for me, anyway. I'd be out pounding the pavement, begging for auditions, but there just doesn't seem to be a pressing need for a teenage heartthrob right now."

"Well, hang in there, dude. Just because your mom's pissed at your dad, it doesn't mean he's not workin' for you still. He got you the *Kerry!* gig. He'll get you something else."

"Yeah, sure," Nate said unconvincingly. *Tai places too much faith in Paul Berrigan. He doesn't know I got that gig all by myself.*

"I miss you, dude." There was a pause, and this sank in. Nate's heart swelled. Tai continued, "Look, man, let's meet up sometime. Talk to you soon."

"Yeah—so long."

Nate reluctantly hung up the phone. He missed Tai. And that *meet up* couldn't happen any too soon for him.

Scene 19

Fade in: Interior—Tai's bedroom
Immediately after

TAI CRADLED the receiver, then stretched out on his bed. He sighed, a giant, loud breath of desperation he felt because he was powerless to help Nate.

There was a knock on the door.

"Come in, Mama."

The doorknob clicked, and then his mother backed into his room, carrying a tray. "How'd you know it was me, sweetie?"

"Ma...." Tai rolled his eyes. "It's eight o'clock, isn't it? You never miss my snack." He smiled. "You're such a good little mommy." As she stood beside the bed, he leaned up and pecked her on the cheek.

"Well, you may be a big, whopping, sixteen-year-old man now, but you're still my little sweetie. And I'll never miss your evening snack. Not even when you're forty years old. I'll just balance the tray on my walker." She teetered a little as she placed the tray on his bed.

"You plan to be living with me when I'm old and gray, Mama?"

She laughed. "Well, if I'm going to be bringing you milk and cookies for forty years, you *better* take care of me."

"Yeah, Mama—I'll always take good care of you." He paused. "As long as you keep baking." He broke off a chunk of cookie and gobbled it up.

"And someday, I'll need to make a bigger batch. For my daughter-in-law and my grandchildren."

Tai looked down at the bedspread, hoping his guilt didn't show. He thought he was over that stuff with Kyle. He'd avoided Kyle for a long time now. Kyle had moved on, Tai was convinced. But when he thought of Nate, all those old stirrings welled up, and Tai was beginning to think maybe what he felt with Kyle wasn't something he could just turn off. Turn off, yeah, with Kyle, but with Nate?

"Enjoy, sweetie. Sleep tight." She gently pulled his chin up, kissed his forehead, then left the room.

Mama, Mama, will I have to someday tell you there won't be any grandchildren?

Tai was startled by the phone's jangling. He quickly swallowed milk as he reached for the receiver.

"Tai here."

"Hey, lover boy. I tried earlier, but the line was busy. What's going on?"

"Nothin', Kyle." Tai frowned. He'd just convinced himself he was rid of Kyle, and here he was on the line. "I was just checking in with my boy Nate."

"Nate, huh?" Tai heard the change in Kyle's voice. He'd made a point not to give Kyle any reason to think Nate was the reason he was trying to break it off with him. But Kyle was no dummy. Maybe he could cover—with the truth.

"Yeah, man. Things are rough for him right now."

"How's he doin' since he got his ass canned?" There was too, too much pleasure in that question.

"That's just between you and me, okay? I shouldn't have told you that." *Why did I tell Kyle Nate got fired? It just slipped out, and I knew when I said it, it was a mistake.* "I should've kept my mouth shut."

"Okay, okay." Tai didn't like the tone he heard.

"Officially," Tai continued, "he is *pursuing other interests.*"

"Well, good. That means he's not around *pursuing you.*" He laughed.

"Nate's not like that. He would never have the slightest interest in what you and me do—" he caught himself. He wanted to say "in what you and me *used* to do."

"Yeah, sure, lover. No way he could resist. That Samoan diver's body of yours is total temptation. He'd fall sooner or later."

Tai felt trapped. *Kyle has a mean streak. If I outright break it off with him, there could be hell to pay. Kyle has spent far too long as my "one and only." Kyle has his claws in me, and he is not giving up easily.* So Tai tried to finesse himself out of the mire.

"There you go again," Tai mock-teased. "That jealous streak of yours is gonna get you in trouble, Kyle."

"Okay, okay—what you got goin' for the weekend, lover boy?"

Kyle is on the make, and I've got to think fast. Keep it casual, Tai.

"Nothin'. I could use some R and R." *Kyle was a really good friend until the sex started. Maybe we can get back to those times. I may be playing with fire, but if I just stay cool with Kyle, we can get back to where we were before—a friendship without benefits, as Kyle calls that stuff we do.*

"Me too. My boss's ridin' my ass this week. You'd think stocking soup cans and bagging groceries was some sort of religious calling."

"Yeah, well, working for him couldn't be any worse than working for *America's Favorite Comedian*. What an asshole. Like today, Kerry—"

"Let's change the subject, man. You up for a burger Saturday night?"

That's Kyle. His job's fair game for conversation. Mine? He doesn't want to hear it. But still, going out for a burger sounds good—and harmless. I hope I don't live to regret it.

"Sure, man, I can get Mom's car." *Burger. Cruising. No heavy stuff.* "We can cruise the Strip."

"Sure. Burger it is."

"Pick you up at seven thirty, dude. Be waiting in the lobby. I hate the way your super looks at me. He's always carrying that pipe wrench, and there's something not right about him. I always think he's just a brain-bashing waiting to happen."

"The guy's harmless... just not too bright, but he does keep everything working in tip-top shape." Kyle paused. "And he's kind of sexy in a *don't mess with me* way."

"Yeah, man... well, you can have him." Tai wanted to keep sex out of the conversation. "See you Saturday."

"Seven thirty on the dot. See ya."

Tai hung up his phone, lay back, and closed his eyes.

Oh, Nate, Nate... if only you were interested. Tai felt his body warm. *If you'd just notice how I feel about you, Nate.* Tai immediately felt guilty. He was going to give that stuff up, right? But every time he thought of Nate, he got turned on. Been that way since the first day he'd seen Nate on the set, at the table read. And Tai knew he'd only kept Kyle on the string this long because he was a substitute, a Nate clone. *He does look like you, Nate.* Tai felt the blood rise within him. *Kyle* does *look like you. But there's something missing in Kyle. Your eyes, your hair, your skin. But not your smile.*

No, no one has your smile. You fill my soul with that smile.

Close-up: *Daily Variety*
Three weeks later

Teens Steamroll NBC Execs

EVER SINCE heartthrob Nathaniel Berrigan was released from hit sitcom *Kerry!* NBC exec offices have been flooded with letters. It seems Berrigan's fans were not taking the explanation given for his release. They want their Nate back.

This reporter was told that presidents of Berrigan's fan clubs throughout the US have been rallying their troops. Their goal? To get their number one boy his job back. The prezzes wrote letter after letter to their most loyal members, urging them to write letters to NBC. And demanding that they tell all their friends to write letters. These flowery and sometimes angry missives are arriving daily in the NBC mailroom. Postal workers are delivering bag after bag of them, all demanding that Nate be restored to the show.

Word is that NBC has caved. How in the world his sudden reappearance will be explained is still up in the air. But our soothsayers predict Berrigan will be back as soon as they can do some retooling and get an episode shot featuring him. Does this mean his replacement character will be 86'd?

Scene 20

Fade in: Interior—Nate's bedroom
Monday afternoon, mid-October

NATE'S BEDROOM door *swooshed* open. *Paul. Can't you just knock before busting in for once?*

"Hey, kid," he barked. "Got good news." He swaggered, weaving a bit from the Scotch, across the room. "Your old dad negotiated a new contract for you. You're goin' back to *Kerry!*"

"Okay." Nate's heart leapt, but he refused to let himself believe Paul. Or let Paul see his reaction if this thing was true.

"*Okay?* Is that all ya c'n say?" Paul slammed his hand down on the dresser. "Look, kid, I been bustin' my butt to get you back on that show." *Yeah, sure.* "How 'bout a li'l enthusiasm here? Don't you wanna know what happened?"

Nate breathed out. If it was true, he *did* want to know the details. Paul must have sold his soul to the devil to make this deal. *Or sold my soul.* "Okay, tell me."

"The network was flooded with letters, demandin' that you come back. They had no choice but to re-hire you. And, thanks to me, at a considerable increase in *moolah*."

Oh, goody, more Scotch for you, more pills for Monica. Certainly won't change my life. Not in the money department. Someday—someday I'll have access to the Coogan account, but until then, I have to just sit and watch you steal me blind. But go ahead. Someday will come soon enough. Nate stared at Paul and bit his tongue; then he asked, "When do I go back?"

"It was in this morning's *Daily Variety*. You show up Monday for the table read. You'll be filming an episode for next month, but they want ya to film some promos Friday mornin'. Now, chop, chop. Ya need to get dressed. You and me? We're going out to celebrate."

"What about Mom?" Nate asked. "We can't just leave her here."

"She'll be okay. She's *napping*," Paul said, sarcasm dripping.

"I don't care," Nate said, staring Paul down. "I'm not leaving her here." *I just got my job back. I don't need Monica choking on her own vomit or slipping into the netherworld from her little yellow pills.*

"Suit yourself. I'll celebrate without ya."

Paul left the room. He didn't even seem pissed Nate wouldn't go out with him. He was just looking for a chance to drink fancy Scotch and be seen around town.

That's nothing new, Nate thought as his phone chimed.

"Hey, Tai," Nate answered.

"You slay me, dude."

"I swear to you—you're the only one who ever calls me."

"Like I've said before… weird," Tai said.

"Have you heard the news?"

"What news?" Nate heard a coy tone in Tai's voice. It was obvious he'd heard. But he played along.

"I got my job back."

"You're shittin' me."

"Stop it, Tai. *You're* shittin' me. You knew all along. Admit it."

"Well, I may have read something in *Daily Variety*." He paused. "And there might have been some chatter on set today."

"Then you knew before I did. Paul just told me."

"So, when you coming back?"

"On set next Monday."

"Wow! That's so bitchin'. Now I wonder what they'll do with diva Dana," Tai said.

"Diva Dana?"

"Yeah, I never told ya 'cause I didn't wanna upset ya, but when they wrote you out, they hired a girl, Dana Warrenton. She was introduced to us as a *seasoned* actress. La-di-da. She's only our age, dude. She plays Candy's ward—her housekeeper's daughter she's raising. None of her episodes have aired yet. But she'll stir the pot for sure. She's black. I guess with all the civil rights stuff going on in the world, somebody at NBC rightfully thought they needed to step up to the plate and insert a colored person. I'm glad. Shows the Civil Rights Act is workin'. I'm surprised Kerry Flanagan allowed it—well, legally, he can't stop it, but anything for ratings, huh? That's gotta be what Jackass is thinkin' 'bout this. She'll bring in the white libs and the black audience."

"You already have them covered, Tai. The black girls, white girls, and all the others absolutely adore you. Maybe Mr. Waldman and Jackass just want to cover all their bases, hiring this girl."

"Well, I warn you, the gal's a real pain."

"So that's why you call her Diva?"

"There's not a bigger one around. She's always throwing around things like 'When I was in…' or 'In my last Broadway show, we did….' Funny, though, I've never heard of her, and you'd think if she's such a *seasoned* actress, a black one at that, she'd be famous. I think she's all talk, and probably has a fake résumé. But I'm not in casting, and I'm not Mr. Waldman. Ain't my problem."

"Do you think they'll keep her with me coming back?"

"Prob'ly. They made too big ado out of her to us. They've been keeping her under wraps. I'm surprised word to the public hasn't gotten out about her. I woulda told you before about her, but we were sworn to secrecy. It would have been my ass if word got out. Not that you'd have said anything, but still. I think they're planning a big push right before next Monday's show. That's the first she's in. There'll be a big weekend blitz. I expect they'll blow her up big and then do the same when your first new episode airs. Besides, I'd imagine she's under contract like the rest of us. They can't fire her for no reason. And 'specially just because you're comin' back."

"So—I guess the table will get more crowded now," Nate said. Nate was apprehensive about his return, especially with this fresh news Tai had laid on him. *How will I shape up next to this bigger-than-life star they've hired? Especially since we're about the same age, and she sounds a lot more experienced than I am. That's no fake résumé—not if they're bankin' on her boosting the ratings.*

But Tai knew how to change his mood quick.

"Man, Candy is going to be so happy. That woman loves you, dude," Tai said. Any mention of Candy could put a smile on Nate's face. "I told her what happened. But I swore her to secrecy."

"What did she say?"

"I hate to talk about your old man, but she said, 'So that joker got him fired. He's not good for Nate…'"

They joined together, laughing, "I just know it."

"She cracks me up!" Nate said. "But she's been a good friend."

"Yeah," Tai agreed, "I like her a lot." Nate wished he'd shared his phone number with Candy. Surely she would have called to check on him. Tai continued, "Now, to change the subject, how are they bringin' ya back? They shipped you off to boarding school after that stunt you pulled, dude. Well, Brian, not you. But you know what I mean."

"Wait a minute—I watched that episode where Jackass banished me. It was painful as hell to hear him talking to me—on the phone, no less—reading me the riot act, while I was supposedly already in a school in Scotland, of all places. You were great in that episode, by the way." Nate didn't mention he watched the episode just to see Tai in it. "I suppose he can bring me back just as easily as he shipped me off." Nate laughed. "Three weeks on an isolated island off the coast of Scotland. Not a bad vacation for Brian, really. If I know the writers, Brian will *not* have learned his lesson."

"And now Brian will not only have me as his partner in crime but the new girl too. Maybe they planned this all along, dude."

"We both know they didn't, Tai. But I wouldn't put it past Jackass to milk it for all it's worth."

"True, true. Well, I, for one, am glad you didn't fall off a Scottish cliff into a watery death. I've missed you on the show."

The warm feeling from when Tai hugged him returned, and Nate said impulsively, "And I've missed you." Flustered, he paused, then said, "Well, I'll be back bright and early Monday, so get ready for me."

"See ya."

"Oh, wait!" Nate shouted, hoping to keep Tai on the line. "I forgot—I'm doing some promos Friday morning. Maybe they'll schedule you for those too."

"Hope so. I'd definitely show up early on a taping day to see my bestest friend. If not, I'll look for ya Monday. So long, my friend."

"Yeah—so long." Nate hung up the phone, smiling.

"Friend," he said, again and again.

Close-up: *The Hollywood Reporter*
October 23

Sitcom Maggie Winner Returns

CENTURY CITY: At a substantial salary increase, *Kerry!* Maggie winner Nathaniel Berrigan will be back at work. Insiders tell us that Berrigan's per-episode take has been doubled.

Young Berrigan, who took away the Maggie award for best supporting actor in a comedy just a few short weeks ago, was reportedly released from his contract to pursue other projects, but after an alleged almost half million letters flooded NBC offices demanding his reinstatement, the powers that be took notice. Negotiations began almost immediately, and Berrigan's manager, his father Paul, with producer Stan Waldman and star Kerry Flanagan by his side, reached the new salary agreement. "We had to ensure that my son would be compensated in line with his new star status, since we will be turning down some lucrative offers in order to continue with the show," said the elder Berrigan.

How will *Kerry!* writers orchestrate this sudden return? Last we heard of Berrigan's character, Brian, his on-screen dad, Kerry Simon, was angry enough at him to put him on a slow boat to Scotland. But Simon's emotions, no doubt, will come into play, and we will be treated to a heartfelt reunion. Kerry Flanagan is a master at comedy. Will he orchestrate a sudden burst of sentiment? Who knows? Good luck pulling that one off, guys.

Berrigan is scheduled to return in time for November, that time when Madison Avenue admen are gearing up for the Christmas rush and viewers seeing those ads is crucial. Could this all have been just a ratings booster? We have to wonder.

Scene 21

Fade in: Interior—NBC Studios
The following Friday

IT WAS like a maze in a carnival. If Nate hadn't been there before, when he shot stills for the seasons and when he won the Maggie, he'd swear he was navigating a labyrinth. The photography studio was stuck far away, down endless corridors of the huge NBC complex.

At the door marked PHOTOGRAPHY, he stopped and took a deep breath. He had no idea who would be there, so he was a little nervous. *Who am I kidding? I am a lot nervous.*

How would he explain to his friends why he had been gone? Did they just blindly buy the crap they were told? According to publicity, he was supposed to be on the string for some lavish movie contracts. How would he explain dropping all that? They'd think he was a fool, coming back to *Kerry!*

He stepped into the room, bracing himself for a zillion questions. But besides the photo assistants, there was only one person in the studio—a girl about his age. A black girl. She was tall, maybe a couple of inches taller than him. She had curly black hair and was wearing enormous hoop earrings, a T-shirt that stopped inches above her navel, the shortest skirt Nate had ever seen, fishnet hose with rips and tears in them, and platform heels that reached to the sky.

That would explain her height.

The girl looked straight at him, giving him a once-over from neck to toes, and then she spoke, a touch of contempt in her voice.

"Well, look who's here... the celebrated Maggie winner, come crawling back."

Nate stopped in his tracks, took another breath. He smiled. He was not going to let her get to him. *Who is this person, and why is she being so shitty?* Then it dawned on him who she was—the one Tai called the diva. *Appropriate, Tai.*

"Don't tell me—you're Dana Warrenton," he said, his precarious mood crumbling a bit but his determination intact. He put indifference in his voice. "I've heard a lot about you."

"So you've seen my work?" She primped her hair and posed. "Caught a preview of this week's show, oh prodigal star-returned?"

What a piece of work.

"Actually, no," Nate said. "Tai told me all about you." He put as much meaning into that *all* as he could.

She dropped her smile. "Well, don't believe everything you hear. And don't get any ideas, Heartthrob. You quit. They hired me." She paused, apparently to let that sink in, like she was the savior of the show. "My agent worked an ironclad contract for me. I'm not going anywhere. Looks like you weren't the hot property you thought you were. But I'd bet that was just a ploy. Didn't work out. Came crawling back." She paused. "Don't think you can drive me away, even if you have the powers-that-be around here fooled."

Nate wanted to lash out, but he thought better of it. She seemed like a royal bitch, but he was going to have to work with her, so he said, "Whatever you say."

Just then, Tai came through the door. He stopped. It was clear Tai was assessing the situation. After looking Nate in the eyes, he spoke.

"I see you two have met," Tai said. He looked again at Nate. "Was I wrong?"

Nate didn't say anything.

Dana did, however. "So, you warned him about the strong black woman come to take over, huh?"

Before Tai could respond, an assistant spoke. She apparently had not heard anything that had come before her interruption because she gave orders like she'd just stepped into a friendly gathering. And she was *no-nonsense.* "Okay, you three. Tight schedule here. We've only a short window of opportunity. First, we shoot you three. Then Kerry—er, Mr. *Flanagan*—will be here at nine to join you. He'll only sit for a short half hour, so keep the ball rolling. Finally, you report to the set to shoot promos. The whole cast will be there waiting. They had to show up early. That means overtime for everyone. So don't drag your asses. You're very well aware you'll be taping right after lunch. Now—" She pointed. "—

wardrobe back there. Chop-chop." She clapped as she said those last words. "Your clothes are waiting for you. Get crackin'"

As Tai and Nate changed, Tai said, "The diva's a total trip, idn't she?"

"Trip? I'd use a stronger word. Begins with a *b*. Totally full of herself," Nate said. "I don't think I'd wanna cross her."

"The walls in here are thin, Heartthrobs." They heard Dana's voice coming from the other dressing cubicle. "I can hear you," she sang out. The melody was sweet, but Nate pictured her as she delivered it. Pure ice.

Tai scrunched up his mouth and silently mocked her *I can hear you*. Nate laughed.

After a makeup person gave them cursory paint jobs, they did a variety of shots. Like the assistant, the studio photographer was all business, so the three teens posed in silence, like trained circus dogs, on command.

Then Kerry Flanagan swept in.

Without a word, he stepped into their shots, and the photog kept shooting.

When they were finished, Kerry left abruptly, never saying a word.

"Okay," the assistant said, "*fini*. Here, that is. You're due on set right now." She barked those last two words and clapped again. "Stop at the assistant director's desk to get your sides for the promos. Then learn your lines while makeup freshens you up."

Dana headed for the set. Nate and Tai walked together, trailing behind Dana, whose stride was bigger and quicker than theirs. *And*, Nate thought, *I want to stay as far away from her as I can—for the time being*.

Dissolve to: Interior—the makeup room

CANDY LEAPT up and embraced Nate the moment he walked into the makeup room. It was the first time he'd seen her in three weeks.

"You're back, my love," she chimed. She kissed him on the cheek. "I've missed you so very much, dearie. And the show has too. The ratings will soar with you back. I just know it."

Nate gasped for air under her effusive squeeze. But this greeting was worth a little smothering. He had missed not just Candy but the show itself. He was so glad he was back.

Caught in Candy's grasp, Nate spied Dana's reaction to Candy's statement.

"Oh yeah, teenage girls across America are planning Welcome Back viewing parties even as we speak," Dana snarled. *Boy, that girl has a chip on her shoulder—a giant one. I'm going to have to steer clear of her or make friends, whichever becomes the easiest.*

"Dana dear," Candy said as she released Nate, oblivious to Dana's dose of sarcasm, "you are absolutely right. I just know it."

Tai rolled his eyes at Nate.

"Life, as we know it, has not changed," he said with a grin.

Dana had rolled her eyes at Candy too. Nate had a hard time reading her. Did she agree with him and Tai that Candy was a hoot, or did she find their *I know it* friend to be a drag?

Dissolve to: Interior—the *Kerry!* set

KERRY FLANAGAN was on set looking impatient when Nate and Tai arrived, having finished their makeup.

"Welcome back, my love," Candy, with her giant smile, gushed at Nate—Nate could tell it was a calculated effort to one-up Jackass, who had not said a word to him. "We all missed you so much." She punched every word. Candy was Nate's champion. She was not about to let Jackass Flanagan bring them all down.

The rest of the cast echoed Candy's sentiments. Nate's heart leapt, knowing he was missed. And secretly, he was glad his friends were, in their own way, standing up to the tyrant known as America's Favorite Comedian.

The youngest, who frequently spouted without thinking, said, "Did you really get a bunch of movie offers?"

Think fast, Nate. "Yeah, but I was missing my little brother here, so I turned them all down," Nate said, touching the boy on the nose.

The boy blushed while everyone laughed. Everyone except their boss.

"Can we get on with this?" Flanagan yelped.

Just like old times. But at least Jackass's not giving anyone else a chance to make inquiries as to my movie star status. Thank God for that.

They shot three promos, touting Nate's return to the show. Nate marveled at Flanagan's instant transformation in the promos. With a smile wide enough to fit an entire freight train in it, Jackass looked straight into the camera and told the world how happy he was Nate had returned to the cast.

If promos could win Emmys, Kerry Flanagan would have one in the bag for that bit of acting prowess.

When they finished, the director said, "Okay, gang. We're shooting, as usual, this afternoon. You've got an hour forty-five for lunch and prep. It's been a long day, for some of you, longer than usual." He shot a look at Tai, Dana, and Nate. "See you back at two, sharp."

The cast members scurried off, leaving Nate standing on the set with Tai.

"Hey, man, commissary okay with you?" Tai asked.

"Okay?" Nate said, lost in thought.

"For lunch. We only got an hour or so before we have to get ready to shoot, and time is ticking away."

"No, Tai, you only have an hour. Today? I have forever. I'm not in this episode, remember?"

Nate's heart broke, just thinking about how his friends would soon be in front of the cameras, in front of that life-affirming audience. And he would be left out in the cold.

"Oh yeah, man, I forgot," Tai said apologetically. Then he smiled. "Well, let's go celebrate your return, then, dude."

"You go ahead, Tai."

Nate saw a look of disappointment on Tai's face.

"Expected home, huh?" Tai asked.

Nate expelled an ironic chuckle. "Not likely. No, Tai, I think I just want to stick around here and soak up the atmosphere. I've been away far too long."

Tai put his hand on Nate's arm. "I can imagine how you feel, dude." He squeezed Nate's arm, and Nate felt something.

Why do I feel like this when Tai is near me? When he touches me?

"Okay, if that's what you want. See you later." Tai gave him one of his signature sideways hugs and left.

Nate sat in the canvas chair marked DIRECTOR. He closed his eyes and breathed in heavily. *This is where I belong. I can't let Paul screw this up for me ever again.* He looked up at the lights hung in the fly space. *Home? I'm home here. Sure, Kerry didn't welcome me back, but*—he shrugged—*who expected that? Everyone else was glad to see me. Here—this is where I belong. With my family.*

With Tai.

His eyes focused on the stairway to nowhere on the set. *Those stairs lead to my room. So it's just a platform behind a door—it's more home to me than the place I share with Paul and my druggie mother.* He winced. He hated thinking of his mother that way. But that's what she'd become. *Why do you let him do it, Mom? You've let him ruin both our lives.* He let a tear slide down his cheek. *I used to think that you could help me, but now you're just hopelessly lost, Mom.*

Nate wiped the tear.

No, I'm on my own. No help from Paul, no help from Monica.

It's just me.

Scene 22

As Nate settled into his seat at the table, he inhaled deeply. *Smells like work—and that's a whole lot better than the smell of Monica's Pall Malls and Paul's Glenlivet breath. Thank you, thank you, thank you, God. While I was gone, Dr. King won the Nobel Prize, but that achievement wasn't mentioned in the Berrigan household, and the* My Fair Lady *movie opened and was a smash hit, but Monica was too strung out to drag me out to see it. So the world went on without me, but this, this, is all that matters to me. I'm back where I belong.*

"Like old times, eh, dude?" Tai hovered above him.

"Yeah," Nate said. "It's good to be back." A tear escaped and rolled down his cheek. He quickly swiped it away. Tai touched Nate's shoulder as if he were acknowledging Nate's reaction in all its tenderness. *I'm back, I'm happy, Tai's with me—what more could I ask for?*

Tai sat and opened his script. As the two silently read, other cast members showed up, spoke greetings, then settled down to peruse scripts. Last to arrive was Dana Warrenton, strutting in, her body crying out *diva* with each step.

"Ah—the prodigal son," she intoned, snide and nasty, as she sat. Everyone else ignored her, but Nate had his eyes on her soon after he sensed she was making her entrance. Their eyes locked, and Nate detected something in her that he hadn't seen at the photo shoot. He didn't yet know what it was, but something was hidden deep inside the diva. He smiled at her. She narrowed her eyes as if to say, "What are you smiling at?"

Is she pissed no one noticed her grand entrance? Or is it she definitely doesn't like me? Or maybe it's that she sees I'm onto her. Am I onto her?

Kerry and Marv, the director, showed up almost simultaneously and the read began.

Candy had the first line....

Harriet: Telisa, is it true? Brian's coming home?

Telisa: Yes, Miss Bowerman. Mr. Kerry is on his way to pick him up.

Harriet: What happened?

Dana's character, Harriet Bowerman's ward, Lena, had the next line.

Lena: He was really in Scotland?

Telisa: Mr. Simon was so angry, he found a school to send him to far, far away from here.

As usual, the director read the stage directions: *Kerry Simon comes through the door, Brian trailing behind.* Then he paused, waiting. Nothing.

Marv said, "Okay, Kerry—it's your turn."

The bastard had been sitting, face buried in a newspaper, ignoring the rehearsal thus far.

Kerry: Here he is. And he's promised to be on his best behavior. Or else it's back to Scotland.

Dana: Did you have to wear a kilt? I heard they don't wear anything under those things. Wasn't it awful breezy in Scotland? I've heard the winds blow anybody.

Everyone laughed. Nate looked at the diva. It was hard to tell, but he thought she might be blushing. At any rate, she was rattled at her mistake. She was definitely embarrassed.

"Look at that line again, Dana," Marv said. I believe it says *I've heard the winds blow anything."*

"Yeah, Warrenton," Tai asked. "What's on *your* mind?"

"Now, Tai," Candy said. "Be nice. She just saw the line wrong."

Nate noticed a tiny tear escape Dana's eyelid. Pretending to scratch under her eye, she erased it.

What's up with the diva? Bothered by a little mistake? Her? Hard to believe. I think my earlier assessment of her may be right.

"Okay, okay," Dana said, with what Nate read as false bravado, "I guess I just wasn't paying close enough attention. Sorry."

So the diva was back. But Nate felt just for a second, he'd seen inside her soul.

Dissolve to: Interior—a table at the commissary

TAI WAS chowing down on a burger, while Nate was devouring a fish sandwich.

"How 'bout the diva?" Tai chomped on a french fry. "Do you think that was an accident? Fifty bucks says she read the line wrong on purpose."

"Maybe," Nate said, setting down his drink. "But I don't think so. She looked sorta embarrassed."

"Embarrassed? No way. Not the diva." Tai wiped his mouth.

"Did you ever think that you may have her pegged wrong? That maybe she's not the diva you think she is?"

"No way, dude," Tai said. He gulped the rest of his Coke, then stood. "I gotta run. Have to drain the wiener." He turned to leave, then swung back. "By the way, did I tell you how glad I am you're back?"

Tai smiled and left; Nate continued eating. Finished, he was about to get up when Dana walked past him.

"Hey!" Nate said, her back to him. "Don't worry about what happened this morning. We all screw up sometimes."

She swung around and threw a penetrating, withering look. "You think I give a shit? I've got more important things to wig out over than something little like that."

"Okay, okay," Nate said, throwing up his hands. "I get you. No problem."

She narrowed her eyes. "You get me? What's that supposed to mean?"

"Nothing," Nate said quickly. His attempt at being nice backfired on him. He wouldn't make that mistake again.

"Look, Heartthrob." Dana leaned over and poked him in the chest. "Don't think you've got me all figured out after one morning's rehearsal, you hear?"

"I don't think that," Nate said. He took a deep breath. Despite his resolve not to cross her again, he couldn't help himself. "But I saw that tear," he said quietly.

Dana's eyes widened just a bit; then quickly she brushed him off.

"I had something in my eye," she blurted out.

"Uh-huh." Nate nodded. He deliberately wiped any expression from his face, letting her read into what he would say next. "If that's the story you want to go with… but remember, it's okay to make a mistake sometimes."

"Thanks for the permission," Dana said. Then she turned away and headed straight for the door. But before she turned away, Nate once again saw that vulnerability in her eyes.

What's up with her? She wants us to think she's hard as nails, but that's not what I see. No, the diva's not as tough as she wants us to believe.

There's something about her I like.

Close-up: magazine page
Fave! Magazine

You Demanded, They Listened

AN ALMOST *half million of you wrote letters, demanding that Nate Berrigan be brought back to* Kerry! *That's a lot of letter writing!! And why did you do it? Because Nate is hot, hot, hot! Says costar Dana Warrenton: "Nate heats up the room just by being there."*

Just who is Nate Berrigan? Fave! *shadowed Nate for a day on the set of* Kerry! *just to get the lowdown on who this enormously talented guy is.*

A Teen Phenom

First of all, sixteen-year-old Nate is every bit as delicious in person as he is on screen. From his curly blond locks to his turquoise eyes, Nate makes you want to just reach out and hug him. He is Lovable, with a capital L. But Nate also has Talent with a capital T. As we watched him rehearse, we were blown away by his photographic memory and his quick wit. Nate Berrigan is the perfect package!

Public Outcry

After winning his Maggie, Nate left Kerry! *to do other projects, but public demand brought him back. "It's funny," said Nate, "you don't really know how much people like you until something like this happens."*

A Typical Day

We were curious how a heartthrob like Nate spends his days when he is not on set. "Well," Nate told us, "I really don't do anything much. I listen to music—I love the Beatles, Bob Dylan—and I read. I've been catching up on Heinlein, and I read To Kill a Mockingbird. *And I study. It's hard keeping up with schoolwork when you are working on set most of the day. But my dad says school's important, so I work hard at it."*

School

Nate is finishing up his sophomore year, but don't look for him at your local public school. He and his school-age costars attend classes right at the studio. Whenever they are not needed on set, they are whisked away to their teacher, who, the kids say, is tougher than any public-school teacher.

What's Next?

So, what's next for Nate? "Right now," he says, "I'm just focused on Kerry!" And his love life? Well, girls, you may have a chance. Nate is not dating anyone in particular, and in fact, he says, "I'm still searching for the right person." So, you all have a chance!! Who will win his heart?

Scene 23

Fade in: Interior—Nate's bedroom
A few weeks later

SATURDAY. NOTHING to do. Nate hated the weekends. Two days of endless nothing. Except, of course, for monitoring Monica to make sure she didn't OD. The good thing was oftentimes, Paul was nowhere to be seen on weekends.

During the week, at least, he had work. He had the show. If he steered clear of Jackass Flanagan, he had everybody else, especially Candy, the diva, and Tai, all of whom kept his spirits up.

But weekends were the worst. He'd thought he might call Tai, but something stopped him. Tai had his own friends, and he didn't need Nate hanging around. He was trapped in the apartment with a mother who could barely function, so drugged-up that most of the time, she slept. And as long she woke up from time to time, her sleeping was actually a good thing. But it didn't relieve his boredom.

The most horrible part was that Nate felt like if he left his mother, went for a spin in the 'Stang for a precious hour, or walked, even for a few minutes, to get a Coke at the 7-Eleven just at the corner, he might come back to find her in trouble, passed out with a broken leg or worse, even dead.

I'm just a kid. I want to feel grown-up, and I have a responsibility at the show to hold up my end of the bargain, but here? I'm just a kid who's saddled with a drugged-out mother and an absent father.

During the week, there was the housekeeper. Poor Mrs. Duggan... she had to mop up after his mom and babysit her too. He didn't know how she managed. Or why. Surely there were other jobs out there that didn't require puke pickup in their descriptions. Mrs. Duggan was a saint. A saint who likely would be gone in a blink of the eye. The Berrigan household didn't keep many housekeepers for very long. Mrs. Duggan was the best of the lot, so maybe she would stay around a while. The worst was when one quit and it took a while for picky Monica to get another one. Or even pickier housekeeper candidates to agree to be hired.

He picked up the remote, punched Power, and within a few seconds the new, big TV—another of Paul's *keep-the-kid-happy* toys—filled with picture and sound. He flipped through the channels... cartoon, cartoon, prayer, *Lone Ranger* rerun... ten channels of crap, nothing that he wanted to watch. Nothing, on this Saturday morning, that provided even a tiny bit of distraction from this bad movie he called his life. Of course, there was rarely anything he wanted to watch, even on a supposedly good TV day. Here he was, a genuine TV star in his own right—those girls getting his job back for him proved that— and basically, he hated TV. How could television's drama compare to his own real-life drama?

Since his mother filed for divorce, Paul didn't come around much. Particularly on weekends, when he was most likely in Vegas. But when he did, his visits always ended in yelling and name-calling. Nate's head throbbed, listening. "You never loved me, you slut" from Paul. "All you ever wanted from me was to get the kid a high-paying gig to keep you in designer dresses and your beloved pills."

Monica would counter with "Yeah? And all you do is waste that money on casinos and Scotch. And probably whores, for all I know. What is it you really do in Vegas, Paul?" The words changed somewhat during their bouts, but the gist was the same.

That's the way it goes at Berrigan manor these days. He'd heard the NBC chairman, in an interview, say, "Our drama is top-notch. We know what we're doing." *Well, they don't know drama at all until they've camped out here a few days. And, God forbid, winter break from the show is just two weeks away. What fun. I used to like Christmas, back before the Scotch, the Valium, the drunk daddy, the passed-out mommy.*

"Natie?" he heard his mom call from her bedroom.

He sighed as he switched off the TV.

Nursing time.

Dissolve to: Interior—Monica's bedroom

Immediately following

"WHAT YOU need?" Nate called as he entered the room. He tried to wash all the disgust from his voice, but as good an actor as he was, he still heard traces. He was tired of being a nursemaid when he should have been a son.

Oh God. She's done it again. The strong stench of urine assaulted him.

"What is that smell?" he said, wondering why he even needed to ask, holding the palm of his hand over his nose, for he knew the odor well. It had happened before.

"Natie baby, I think I had an accident in the bed. I was asleep, and then I woke up."

I'm the son; you're the mother. This is supposed to be the other way around. You take care of me. Nate sighed heavily. He pulled back the satin comforter covering his mother. He tugged at her arm.

"Come on. To the tub." He hated the disgust he felt right now. A strange mixture of distaste for his mother and a desire to help her overwhelmed him. As he pulled her from the bed, he thought of the intense hatred he had for Paul. *Paul should be here doing this. It's his job. She's his wife. This is not something a son should have to deal with. But she does need me.*

He inched his mother to the bathroom. He gently lowered her to the edge of the bathtub. He told himself he wasn't being gentle because he had any love left for her, but rather because he just didn't want to get accused of abusing her if she broke a hip or something.

"Get undressed." He absolutely, totally despised this part. Even if she peeled the clothes off herself, he still had to stand, watch, and supervise. *To have to watch my own mother like this. Disgusting.*

Monica looked into her son's eyes; then she hung her head. Nate felt something wet drop onto his foot.

Nate almost melted. He felt a mixture of anger *at* her and sorrow *for* her. "Are you crying, Mom?" Nate felt so helpless. "There's nothing to cry about. We just need to get you cleaned up." He surprised himself with the gentleness in his voice. He thought he was well past caring about her.

He wanted so badly to want to help her. She was his mother, for God's sake. Why couldn't he feel an ounce of love or compassion or caring?

"Oh, baby, I'm so sorry you have to do this. I don't know what happened. I'm so ashamed. This has never, never happened to me before. Maybe I'm sick."

Never happened before? Have you blocked out the last time? And the time before that? And God knows how many times poor Mrs. Duggan has had to deal with it that I don't know of.

The tinge of tenderness he had felt faded. "Yeah, okay. Now, just get undressed. I won't look." He averted his eyes as much as possible so she would see he wasn't looking. But he had to look. He had to make sure she didn't hurt herself. *The last thing I need are cops, ambulances, hospitals.*

He knelt to switch the faucet on. Then he remembered those last three words she'd spoken. *Sick? Yeah, you're sick all right. After all, you take enough* medicine, *don't you? I wish I could flush every pill in this apartment down the toilet. But you'd just find a way to get more.* He surprised himself, for his internal dialogue had turned from anger to concern.

He glanced around at his mom, who was holding her arms crossed over her exposed breasts and keeping her legs tightly closed. He quickly looked away, fidgeting with the faucet handles.

"Can you get into the tub yourself?"

"Yes, Natie," she said, sobbing.

The tears. Why, oh why, oh why?

"Don't cry, Mom, it's okay." *It's not okay. It's not right. It's not what I should be doing on a Saturday morning. But if I don't help her, who will?* He stood, his back to her. "I'll take care of you. Now, you slip into the tub and get nice and clean, okay? I'll be just outside the door if you need me."

Briefly, trying not to look at her, he offered his hand to steady her as she got into the tub.

He left the bathroom, then, as promised, stationed himself outside the door. He heard his mother's crying, which, he realized, oddly comforted him because it told him she wasn't slipping under the water, passed out and drowning.

After a few minutes, there was a splash, which sounded to him like his mother was standing up. But just to make sure, he called out, "You okay in there?"

From behind the door, "I'm fine, Nate. I'm just drying off. I'm feeling much better now."

She sounds better. The bath must have sobered her up, enough, at least, to function somewhat.

She stuck her head around the crack in the doorway. "Could you hand me a robe, baby?"

Nate looked around and found a silk robe slung across the foot of the bed. He plucked it up and took it to her.

A moment passed, and then Monica emerged from the bathroom, tying the sash on the robe. "I need my nerve pills, baby. Could you get them for me?"

And the tiny bit of concern for her he had vanished. *Do you never learn? Those things are killing you! You wouldn't have pissed the bed if you weren't hopped up on those pills. You wouldn't have been so humiliated by it all. You wouldn't have had to force your* teenage son *into helping you, a grown woman, take a bath.*

He wanted to lash out, to shout those very words, his face an inch from hers, trying desperately to break through to her.

But he was helpless, unable to pierce her stupor, unable to make himself feel better about the whole situation. Nate felt there was nothing he could do but kiss her on the cheek, something he rarely did these days. It was an impulsive gesture. He wanted to make himself feel better by being nice to her. She was his mother, after all. Maybe she would take it as a grand gesture, one that would motivate her to quit this shit. But the instant he delivered the kiss, he knew it was a stupid, fruitless thing to do. She was too far gone. She was not going to change.

He grabbed her sleeve and said, "You can have my bed." It hurt to say the next words. "I'll get your medicine, and you can rest in there."

He led her to his bedroom, flung the covers back on his bed, and tucked his mother in. "I'll be right back."

He went to retrieve her pill bottle and a glass of water. He stared at the bottle. A little brown bottle filled with little yellow bullets, all set to kill his mother as if they'd been fired from a gun. *I could just empty these into the toilet. But what would she be like if she* didn't *have her* medicine?

The thought was too scary.

He continued into his own room and gave his mother two of her coveted Valium. Then he tucked the covers securely around her. He wanted to make a prison for her, a prison of covers that would, for a few brief hours, keep her locked away from him. "I'll just be in the other room, if you need me."

He went to the home phone. He didn't know where to start. He dialed *0*. "Operator, can I get the desk at the Tally-Ho casino in Las Vegas?"

As the operator placed the long-distance call, thoughts raced through Nate's mind.

You better be there, Paul Berrigan. I'm sick of this mess, and you're going to start cleaning it up.

"I have your party on the line, sir." The phone switched to another voice. "Tally-Ho, how may I direct your call?"

"Can you page Paul Berrigan? He is probably on the casino floor."

"One moment, sir."

Nate waited. After a few minutes, the woman came back on the line. "Sorry, sir, but no one answered the page. Perhaps Mr. Berrigan is gaming somewhere else today."

"Have you seen him today?" Nate was desperate. He didn't know how that question was going to help him find Paul.

"Mr. Berrigan is one of our regulars, sir, but no, I haven't seen him since I was on duty yesterday. Perhaps you could try the Desert Inn."

After five more phone calls to five different casinos, Nate was defeated. One clerk actually said Paul was staying at their hotel, and she asked if Nate wanted to leave a message. But what would he say? "Get home. Your wife wet the bed." Somehow Nate knew that would only fuel Paul's fire. It wouldn't tear him away from his Scotch, his blackjack, his whores.

"No—no message."

Nate exhaled, a deep, long wind. Disgusted with his life, with Paul, with Monica, he began to strip Monica's bed of its wet sheets.

Scene 24

Fade in: Interior—the *Kerry!* set
The season wrap party

"So, DUDE, did Paul ever get you anything for the break?"

Tai was scarfing down a piece of cake.

"Yeah, sure." Nate laughed ironically. "He got me a subscription to *Tiger Beat*, a copy of the new Heinlein novel, and a box of chocolates. Oh, and a new stolen ashtray."

Tai looked at Nate like he was crazy. "A new stolen ashtray? You don't smoke."

"Oh, this one is from the Tropicana. Paul says the casino's a classic, so the ashtray will be worth something someday. Fun, huh?"

"That sucks, man." Tai wiped his mouth with a paper napkin printed with the *Kerry!* logo. "My agent lined up a movie for me. It's just a little part, but they're shooting in Samoa, so I'll get to finally see my homeland—the last week in June, the first in July. Mama and I are staying to visit with relatives another week after the movie wraps. I'll be back right before the show starts up again for next season."

"Sounds like fun." Nate set a champagne glass on a nearby table. They'd provided sparkling cider for the under-agers to toast with. "I'll be catching up on my Heinlein. I might even read *Mockingbird* again." It was impossible not to hear the sarcasm in Nate's voice.

They both laughed, remembering the quote from the *Fave!* story.

"Where'd they get that, man? I know you've never even picked up *To Kill a Mockingbird*. You bought the CliffsNotes when it was assigned to us. And I'd bet good money you've never read a Heinlein book, either."

"I had to tell them something," Nate said, a chuckle in his voice. "I'm surprised I even knew who Heinlein is. But I couldn't very well tell them I hole up in my room while my mom is strung out on downers and my dad is swilling Scotch." Nate was no longer smiling.

Tai put his hand on his shoulder. Nate shuddered a tiny bit. Every time Tai did that, Nate wanted him to never move his hand again. "Come to Samoa with me. You could hang out on the set."

"Hey, yeah, and I could probably get Paul some whiskey. Do they make a special Samoan Scotch? Any distilleries in Samoa?"

Tai laughed. "It's not like it's a deserted island, dude. They may very well make Scotch there, but I doubt it. But if they did, I somehow think you wouldn't be able to buy any. Unless you've got a fake ID I don't know about. So what say, truck it to Samoa with me?"

Nate sighed, thinking of the last incident with Monica. It hadn't repeated itself for months—at least not on a weekend when Nate was in charge of her. But still, he didn't feel like he could leave her. To die. Or stir up scandal. "It sounds like fun, Tai, but I'd better stick around here. Maybe I can scare up some work on my own. But even if I don't, believe me, staying here is easier than asking Monica and Paul for traveling money. Want to come and watch me pack?"

"Sure," Tai said. But as soon as they were inside Nate's dressing room, Tai grabbed him and enveloped him in a hug.

What brought that on?

"I'll miss you, man," Tai said. Instinctively, Nate laid his chin on Tai's shoulder. He knew Tai was only showing friendship, but... *Tai's arms feel so warm and safe.*

Tai was not pushing him away. Nate refused to wonder about that. He just enjoyed the feelings.

"Fond farewells?"

The boys quickly broke apart at the sound of Dana's voice.

"You two look like two friends going off to separate battle fronts," she quipped.

"A summer with Monica and Paul *is* pretty much a battle," Nate said.

"What?" Dana plopped down in front of Nate's mirror. She primped her hair.

Nate had never told Dana about his parents, and he wasn't about to do it now. "Nothing."

"I've got to go, man," Tai said. "Sure you won't reconsider?"

"No," Nate answered, "but thanks anyway."

Tai smiled wistfully at Nate; then he left.

Dana stared at her image in the mirror. "Whaddaya think? Should I go natural with my hair?"

Nate didn't answer.

"I'm thinking I might join Dr. King's movement during this break. Maybe I need a new, more natural look. As Dylan says, 'The times they are a-changin'.'"

Nate didn't even want her in his dressing room, much less to shoot the breeze about civil rights. She'd never mentioned them before. Not two months before when those people in Montgomery, Alabama, marched. Not even when Dr. King marched in Selma later in the month. No—Dana was likely just talking off the top of her head here. She had something else she wanted to ask.

And then she dropped her bomb.

"So, Heartthrob, what is it you're not reconsidering?" She kept her face fixed in the mirror, nonchalantly picking at her hair.

"Nothing, Dana," Nate said, "just nothing."

"It didn't look like nothing, the way you two were holding on to each other for dear life."

Is that a loaded statement? What's she fishing for?

"We were just saying goodbye." Nate took his backpack from the closet. "It's the end of the season, you know."

"Don't I know it! I'm looking forward to some R and R." *So the civil rights talk* was *just a ruse.* "It's exhausting being a… diva." She smirked at his reflection in the mirror.

Nate blushed.

"What? You don't think I know you and Tai call me Diva? I'm not stupid, ya know. You're well aware I heard you in the dressing room the very first time we met. And I know you've never stopped."

"Okay, you caught us. But let me just say, we don't mean anything by it. At first you were pretty hard to take, but you've grown on us."

"Like a fungus, huh?" Pulling a clip from her head, she gathered all the loose strands of hair. She pulled them into a sleek, sophisticated updo, proving the *natural* hair was just talk. "So, when are you two going to get it on?"

"Huh?" Nate choked.

"You know—do the nasty, bang your baskets, pump the pole?"

Nate's eyes widened, and he started to sweat. "Tai and I are just friends, Dana," he managed to spit out.

"Sure you are," she said. "You can't fool the black girl. No how, no way. This girl's seen life, believe you me. I know what I see, and I saw the way you looked when he hugged you. You've got it bad, Heartthrob."

"That's enough, Dana," Nate said. He had to stop this talk.

"No, apparently it's not enough. You look pretty unfulfilled to me, Heartthrob."

"Tai is not like that."

"Who are you kidding?" Dana asked. "Just give him a little encouragement. He'll jump at the chance. A woman knows these things."

"Change the subject, please." He wanted that to come out as firm command, but it came out more like he was pleading with her.

She smiled.

"Okay, but listen up, Heartthrob. You two will be an item someday. The times they are a-changin', remember? Won't be long before, just like us black folks gettin' our rights, you gay folks will get yours. And you don't want to wait, just because some laws say it's wrong, just because some do-gooders *think* it's wrong. If Dr. King had waited, our folks wouldn't have come as far along as we have. And God bless Rosa Parks. Someday there'll be a gay Rosa Parks, and you guys won't be stopped." She finished her lecture and paused. Then she smiled again. "But don't worry, your secret's safe with me."

"Tai and I don't have any secrets, but you go on thinking that if it makes you happy," Nate said sarcastically.

"So," Dana said, "my dad has this cool beach shack in Malibu. How about coming out sometime this summer? I'll be staying with my mom the first month, but maybe we could meet end of July?" As quickly as her storm had come, it had abated. She was back to being just normal, sometimes irritating, sometimes ingratiating Diva.

She looked at Nate, who was standing there, silent.

"Please say yes," she said quietly. The quiet was the key. It said to Nate she didn't have as many friends as he'd pictured her having. He knew her dad was rich, but maybe a black rich man was as much a fish out of water as a teen sitcom star with impossible parents. Maybe Dana didn't have any friends, and that's why she was asking Nate to visit.

Nate paused before answering. He was thinking about Monica and what might happen if he left her alone.

"I just don't know, Dana," Nate said. "I might be needed at home."

"Give me a break, Heartthrob. By July, your mom will be begging for a reason to get rid of you for a weekend. Trust me."

"You don't know my mom," Nate said quietly.

"All moms are alike, Heartthrob."

Nate took a deep breath.

"What? Your mom beat you or something?"

Nate didn't say anything.

Dana's eyes got really big. "She does beat you? Geez! I was just kidding."

"She doesn't beat me, Dana," Nate said. Then he looked her in the eyes. "I'm going to tell you something. You've gotta promise you won't tell anybody, hear? Not even Tai—especially not Tai."

Dana held up her hand and swore.

Nate just stood there. Finally, he spoke.

"My mother does not beat me. She is usually not alive enough to do anything like that."

He saw the diva screw up her face, wondering where he was heading.

"My mother, Diva, is a pill freak. Tai knows that, but there's more. She is usually totally out of it. It scares me sometimes."

Dana put her hands on his shoulders. "Oh, Nate," she said, "I would never have guessed that. That's tough."

"She is so out of it sometimes. She staggers around. She passes out. She can be so sound asleep—translate that to mean a drug-induced coma—that she pisses herself. That always wakes her up, and she yells for me to clean up the mess. It's awful." Nate paused, fighting back tears. Tears for his mother, tears for himself. "So you see, I don't know if I should leave for a weekend or not. Weekends are the worst usually, for some reason. And our housekeeper has weekends off. It's just me and Mom."

"Look, Nate, my dad *knows* people. You say the word and he can get you some help, get her into rehab. He'll do that. Let me help." Her voice was full of concern and determination.

"No—no, no, no—my mom would never go into rehab. Believe me!"

"I'm just saying, Heartthrob… you give me the word, and I can get my dad to put things in motion."

"Okay," Nate said, wanting to bury this topic fast.

"Now, Heartthrob, we'll put everything on hold. Who knows what can happen by July. Just say that you'll *try* to come to the beach house."

Finally, Nate spoke. "Okay, but cool it with that other talk, too, you hear?"

"What other talk?"

"About Tai and me, remember?"

"My lips are sealed, about both things," she said. She ripped half the back page off a script that lay on the dressing table, tore it in two, scribbled a number on it, and handed it and the other piece to Nate. "Write down your phone number, and I'll call you."

She folded the scrap of paper and tucked it in her bra. "Toodle-oo, dear!" She did her best Candy imitation as she left the dressing room.

That's number two—my phone's going to be ringing off the wall.

Nate smiled. Getting that off his chest felt right. A giant burden had somehow lifted, and he felt good.

Then he thought of what she had said.

He and Tai? No way. We're just friends. Tai isn't like that. *And neither am I.* Am I?

The diva made it sound like it was okay. Not a sin. Not something unnatural. Like lots of people loved someone of their own sex. Like it might even become all right someday. Like they wouldn't get arrested for it. *But even if I'm that way, Tai's not. So Diva's blowin' in the wind with that. She quoted Dylan, I can too. She definitely doesn't know what she's talking about.*

But Tai's hug did make him feel safe.

Close-up: newspaper page
The *Los Angeles Times*
May 15

Around Town

GET READY for this town to heat up this summer. One of TV's hottest stars will be in the middle of a major smackdown.

Nathaniel Berrigan, teen star of NBC sitcom *Kerry!* will be heading to divorce court.

No, the teen phenom hasn't married on the sly. His parents, Monica and Paul Berrigan, are splitsville.

Word has it that Mama Berrigan has engaged the talents of divorce lawyer extraordinaire Louis Handley to handle the battle. Handley is no stranger to high-profile Hollywood disentanglements. His biggest hit was Leta Holloway's court date last fall.

Papa Berrigan needs to watch out. Handley's hammer will fall and crush anything in his path.

Look for the fireworks in early June. We'll keep you posted.

Scene 25

Split screen: Tai and Kyle, each on phones
July, after Tai's return home from Samoa

"Yeah, it was pretty intense," Tai said. "The character was a lot different from Pele."

"Glad to hear you had a good time in Samoa, lover boy. I got pretty horny, waiting for you to get back."

"C'mon, man." Tai laughed, but inside, he didn't like hearing this. A month without Kyle had given him lots of time to think. And he knew they would never get back the friendship they once had. No, he had to break it off entirely. "We talked about that before I left. No exclusive rights. Remember? You should have found you someone." They *had* talked about it, but Tai left LA thinking that Kyle was probably not listening.

"I didn't want anybody else, lover. All I wanted to do was to fly to Samoa and keep an eye on your cute little butt. But I know you stayed true to me." A pause. "You did, didn't you?" Tai heard a snicker, a lecherous tiny laugh. Tai had not found anyone else. But that was because the only one he wanted was back right here in LA.

"Nothing to worry about, man. I didn't even look at another guy the whole time I was gone." *When am I going to tell him?*

"You're not playin' me? Saved yourself for me, huh, lover?"

No, not for you. Tai's courage was waning. He had to break the news, no matter the consequences. But he failed in his resolve.

"Yeah, man." *I'm a royal shit for lying to you, man, but am I lying? I didn't do anything because all I could think of was Nate, Nate, Nate. And that will never happen.*

"So—when can we hook up? Like I said, I'm cravin' you. Ready to put in some work here? Know what I mean? Tomorrow night?"

The thought panicked Tai. *I'm not craving you. That's the problem, here. You were fun to be around when we were just friends, but I should never have hooked up with you, Kyle. I don't want to be with you anymore. Why can't I just tell you that?*

"You still there, Tai? You're not saying anything. How 'bout it? Tomorrow?"

If I'm chickenshit and not going to tell him, I've got to think fast! "Nah, man, I have to spend the weekend with family. My dad hasn't seen me in a month, remember? It's family night. You know—Bob's. That was the first place Dad ate when he came to LA, and he trots us out there every chance he gets. He swears by their food. So tomorrow night I'll have my butt in a booth at Bob's Big Boy, chowing down on burgers, fries, and milkshakes. Probably a hot fudge sundae, too, just for good measure." *Good save!*

"I've had better. Ditch the family, and we'll get a great burger at *our* place. I'm missin' you something fierce, Tai."

I have to tell him. Why can't I do it? Kyle's a good guy. He'll be disappointed, but he'll get over it. "No can do. I told you it's family weekend. That means aunts, uncles, and cousins on Saturday afternoon, Saturday night, and Sunday. Samoans are very family oriented, dude. You know that."

"Sneak away Saturday afternoon. Dad'll be out of town with his new squeeze. We'll have the place all to ourselves. We can make beautiful love all afternoon. C'mon, lover boy."

I hear the smile in your voice, Kyle, but I know you are dead serious. That scares me. And it ain't gonna happen. It's now or never. I've got to tell him.

"That's just not the way it works in my family. They expect me to be there." Tai paused. Took a breath.

Before Tai could say anything, Kyle spoke. "So when *can* we see each other?" There was both desperation and a bit of anger in his voice. "I'm begging, lover boy. I need me some Tai."

"Kyle? Truth? I can't do that stuff anymore." *There. It's out.* Tai breathed a sigh of relief.

"Cut the crap, Tai! I'm serious. I want to see you. I missed you. Didn't you miss me, even a little?"

"Kyle, you're my oldest and dearest friend." He stopped to let that sink in, hoping it would ease the next idea into Kyle's brain. He took a breath to give him enough air to spit out what he needed to say—a steady stream of words he couldn't break for fear of never finishing. "We can't do this anymore it's not right it's ruined what we had before all this we can't see each other again not as lovers not as friends." He gulped air. *Lord! If he doesn't accept this, I don't know how I can make it any plainer.*

"Then meet me tonight, just for a little while. No strings, okay?" Tai felt his heart fall. *He is not letting go.*

Tai measured his words, hoping they would sink in. "No, Kyle. I meant what I said. It's over." Tai hung up before Kyle could say anything else.

Close-up: Tai
Voice-over

I'VE JUST destroyed my first and best friend. What's wrong with me? I know that everything we did together was wrong, so Kyle and I are not good for each other. And I know Kyle has grown into someone I don't much even recognize anymore. Both are good reasons to get rid of him. But the biggest reason—the sin? All I can think of is Nate. And if I plunge further into hell and act on what I'm feeling, I'll take Nate with me. And that's even worse than keeping on doing it with Kyle. I hate myself.

Tai lay on his bed, staring at the ceiling.

I've got to get rid of these feelings. I can't keep on like this. The new season will be starting soon, and I can't be around Nate until I can at least control how I'm feeling.

But how can I just throw these feelings away? God, I need help. I need help, I need help, I need help.

Fade in: Tai, at rectory door
Soon afterward

TAI KNOCKED. *Please be here, Father Tim. I need help.*

The door opened. In front of Tai stood Paulie. Paulie was the youth minister at the church. His given name was Paul, but when he worked with the kids, he insisted they call him Paulie. Tai had gone to Paulie's catechism classes when he was confirmed two years before. He hadn't seen much of him since, except from a distance, at mass. With the show, Tai didn't have much time for youth activities at the church.

"Tai, good to see ya, dude." Paulie held out his hand for Tai to shake. "What brings you here this cool, moonlit night?" Paulie always had a way with words.

"Is Father Tim here? I need to speak with him." He hoped his face showed none of the anguish he was feeling, but it must have, for Paulie pulled him into the foyer.

"Sorry, Tai. The Father is at the hospital. One of our oldest parishioners is getting last rites. But *I'm* here to help, if I can."

Tai had always liked Paulie. He was a good guy, and he thought he could trust him. There would be no seal of the confessional, like there could be with Father Tim, but then again, he hadn't come here to make a formal confession.

"Come on," Paulie said as he motioned toward an office near the door. "I can see something is troubling you. Let's talk. Maybe I can help."

He led Tai into the office. Two chairs sat in front of a desk. Paulie turned them so they faced each other and then told Tai to sit.

Tai sat. He felt a huge weight on his shoulders. It was like Atlas trying to carry the world. He had to tell someone about all this. But he couldn't make himself tell the absolute truth. Since he was going to hell anyway, lying was the least of his worries. He put his best acting face on.

"I have this friend…." Tai looked at Paulie's eyes to see if he believed him. After all, in the movies, situations like this always started with those four words. Paulie's face was totally neutral. That gave Tai a bit of courage.

"I have this friend who—" Tai stopped. He couldn't do it. He didn't know what to say, but as he sat there in anguish, Paulie spoke quietly.

"Tai, I see hurt in you. Nothing's so bad that it can't be vanquished by telling someone. I'm here for you. And I promise there is no chance I will betray your confidence. I may not operate under the seal of confessional as conferred by the Church, but in my heart, I truly feel my position here, my calling here has that seal, just as if I were a priest. I'm not a priest. We're not in the confessional. But Tai, you can tell me anything."

Tai took several deep breaths. He felt like he was dying, that his trip to hell was just beginning, right there, right then. But Paulie let him have his moment. He didn't try to soothe him and comfort him or tell him that everything would be okay. He just let Tai process his panic. And in that moment, he was enveloped in Paulie's acceptance.

"I'm a terrible person, Paulie. I've sinned. Gravely sinned." *Those words don't even sound like me. But they are how I feel.* "Paulie, I've done things. Bad, bad things." And then he paused before he could make himself *say the words.*

"Nothing," Paulie said, his voice barely audible, "is so bad that it can't be righted. You can have absolution from any sin, Tai."

There was something so positive, so consoling in Paulie's voice that Tai found the words.

"I've done things with my best friend. A guy. Sexual things." *Now Paulie would rain down the hellfire. In Candy's words, I just know it.* But Paulie said nothing.

After a few moments, Paulie said, "Go on."

I've come this far, I might as well take it all the way. "And even after I just told the guy we were through, and I didn't want to do those things with him anymore, I still want to be that way with another guy, someone I work with."

"Tai, were you in love with your friend you did these things with?"

"No. He was my best friend, but I wasn't in love with him. That's one of the reasons—obviously not the biggest reason, the *sin* reason—that I broke it off with him. I didn't want to hurt him any more than I already have." Oddly, Paulie smiled at that revelation.

"Tai, that's love you showed to him. It's not the love that is tied to a sexual relationship, but it's love nevertheless. You care about your friend. Jesus Christ said we must love one another. Every act of kindness is spreading the Christ's word in this world."

So, there it is. I suppose I would have gotten something like this from Father Tim, who always preaches about Christ and his almighty love. But Father Tim is never talking about sex, and Paulie, in his own way, just condemned me. Those words—sexual relationship? No doubt he will go on to make me see that that can only happen between a man and a woman. That's the truth, isn't it? And I can't live with my feelings I have for Nate unless I confess them to someone and get them erased from my brain.

Tai shook his head. "You're not understanding all this, Paulie. There's something else I haven't told you. I broke that thing off because, if you remember what I said, I have feelings that won't go away for another guy."

"And do you love him?"

Tai thought a moment. In all his fantasies about Nate, sexual and otherwise, he'd never attached the word love. But as he thought about it, he knew that's what it was.

Tai burst into a smile. It was liberating. No matter what Paulie said now, it wouldn't erase that smile. If Christ said love one another and love was the most important thing we could do in life, then he knew whatever he might do with Nate—if Nate were willing—would be right.

"So, Tai, in my opinion—"

Tai cut him off. He didn't need to know his opinion. "Thanks, Paulie." Tai stood. "I know now what I have to do, what I'm meant to do."

Scene 26

Fade in: Exterior—Dana's father's Malibu beach house
Late July

THE MUSTANG rolled up before a massive gate. The divorce didn't stick, he guessed. Monica would probably call it off because Paul came crawling back; Monica let him slither back in. But at least Nate was free to spend a weekend away from that sordidness called home. He looked at the gate and what lay beyond. *Lord. Dana never said her dad was* this *rich. Who would have thought a black man could have this much money? When Dana said rich, I thought he was just richer than a lot of other black folks. I guess I should have heard Malibu and figured a beach shack, as she called it,* would *be a mansion.* He rolled down the window as a guard stepped from a small gatehouse and came over.

"Mr. Berrigan?" the guard asked, all business but with a smile.

"Yes," Nate answered.

"Dana's waiting for you." The guard went to a latch on the side of the gate, pulled on it, and opened the gate.

Nate whistled under his breath. *Leave it to the diva. Secrets, secrets, and more secrets.* He pulled the car through the gate.

"Wow," Nate said. But, dumbstruck by the enormity of it all, he fell silent after that single-word reaction.

He wound his way through about a mile of driveway shaded by a true rainforest, filled with palm trees, huge-leafed plants, and delicate flowers. The forest opened onto a circular drive in front of a glass-and-steel structure, bigger than any house Nate had ever been to.

The diva, wearing a pink-and-green bikini which made quite a statement on her glistening black-diamond skin, came running from the house screaming, "Heartthrob!" and pulled him from the car. She reached into the back seat and grabbed Nate's knapsack. Then she encircled Nate with a huge hug. Her sun-exposed skin was warm against Nate.

"I'm so glad you're here!" Dana pulled Nate up the steps and into the house. "Did your parents give you any flack about staying the weekend?"

Nate ignored her question as they entered the house. *Monica was in her usual coma when I left, and Paul was consuming Scotch and blubbering apologies to a wife who was too out of it to listen. So, no, they gave me no flack.*

Nate gawked at the entry hall. The ceiling must have been twenty feet tall, and the house itself was very open. There was a steel-and-glass staircase that led upstairs, and across from the front door, sunken down two steps, was a living room furnished with leather couches and chrome tables. Everything was lush. He wasn't used to this kind of wealth.

"Well, did they?" Dana poked Nate's shoulder.

Nate refocused. "Did who? Did what?"

"Monica and Paul. You cleared staying the weekend with them, didn't you?"

"Oh!" Nate said, nodding. "Paul's with his friend from Scotland, and Monica? Well, let's just say she won't miss me this weekend. She's curled up with her friend Val."

The diva flashed him a look of wonder.

"Val as in Valium."

"Poor Heartthrob," she said, rubbing his shoulders. "Forget about them. They don't deserve you." She waved her arm like one of those girls on *The Price Is Right.* "Welcome to our little beach shack."

"Are you kidding? This ain't no shack. Who's your dad, the Crown Prince of Abu Dhabi?"

"My *old man*," she said, her voice filled with contempt, "is Byron Stone, CEO of Stone Enterprises, Ltd. He's richer than most crown princes. And this"—she gestured again—"is only *one* of his many homes. If you think this is fancy, you should visit the one in Gstaad."

"Wow." Nate whistled. "But your name is Warrenton, not Stone. What gives?"

"Mom is Samantha Warrenton, caterer to the stars. Some *almost* eighteen years ago, she catered a Stone Enterprises *soiree*"—the sarcasm dripped from her mouth—"and I came after the dessert, if you get my drift."

"You're kidding me."

"No, my love, I'm not," Dana said. "Mom never married dear old dad, and in fact, he's listed as *unknown* on my birth certificate because she didn't want him to know about the fruits of their little fling. You can just imagine the flack that would have caused. White industry giant gets black gal caterer knocked up. Mom made the quick and ironclad decision that she could take care of herself and her baby girl without any help from anyone. But *Daddy* found out eight years ago, and he declared he would not have cared at all that his little girl was a much darker shade of skin than he. Very pre-civil-rights-movement attitude. Very progressive, Byron Stone. Father of the Year material. Mom still refused his money, but he threatened to sue for custody if she didn't let him into my life. So here we are. He's never around, but he showers me with largess. So, quite often I get to reap the benefits of his riches, if not his love. And believe me, he is generous. He's been trying to make up for those lost eight years ever since he found out. I can't figure out if he loves me in his own way, or if just can't stand the fact that his blood courses through my veins and he has very little control of it. But enough. This weekend is for fun, fun, fun."

She pulled Nate's wrist, and together they started up the stairs.

"I'm going to show you your room so you can get changed. We're out at the pool."

"We?" Nate panicked a moment. "You mean your dad's here too?"

Dana tossed off a wicked laugh. "Oh no—no, no, no, Heartthrob. Dear old Dad's in Tokyo... won't be back until next Wednesday. No—for this little episode of your life, I have brought in a special guest star."

"Who?"

"Never mind who," she said, pushing him through an open door. "See you downstairs in five. Just go through the kitchen and out the sliding doors."

Dana jumped back and ran down the stairs. He heard her footsteps as she made her retreat.

Nate was in a huge bedroom with a balcony that overlooked the rain forest. Attached to the bedroom was a bathroom with a giant tub and a shower stall that must have had twenty shower heads. He opened the closet. It was half the size of the enormous bedroom and was stuffed with men's clothes.

Damn, she put me in her dad's room. I sure hope he doesn't show up early from Japan.

Nate pulled his swim trunks from his knapsack. He shucked his street clothes and slid into the trunks. He looked around for a towel. There was a giant beach towel slung across the lavatory with a crudely lettered sign that said, "Take me, Heartthrob."

He grabbed the towel and headed downstairs.

At the bottom of the staircase, he turned left and wound his way to a wall of glass that looked out on a sapphire sky and the equally blue Pacific Ocean. Seagulls swooped over the waves.

He saw a terrace down a short flight of stairs. There was a swimming pool surrounded by beach loungers and tables with umbrellas. Dana lay sunning herself in one of the lounge chairs.

He found a door and slid it open. The diva turned and waved.

Nate took the short flight two steps at a time.

Dissolve to: Exterior—the pool

"So," HE asked, "where's this special guest star?"

In the pool, a lithe body swooped from underneath the water.

"Surprise!"

Tai was a topaz jewel, shining in the sparkling water.

Scene 27

Fade in: Interior—the Malibu beach house
A few hours later

TAI WRAPPED the stringy pizza cheese around his tongue, then gobbled half a slice.

"I love anchovies, man," he sputtered, cheese hanging from his lip.

"You're the only person I've ever met who does, Samoan." Dana reached over and dabbed Tai's chin with a napkin. "You're overflowing here."

Nate rolled his eyes and sighed. "Thank God you made a pizza just for us, Diva."

"Right on, Heartthrob."

The three laughed.

"How in holy hell did you learn to make pizza this good, Dana?"

"I didn't grow up with Hollywood's premier caterer without learning a few tricks, Samoan boy."

"You could open a restaurant with this stuff. It's fit for the gods, Diva."

"It helps that this place has the best equipped kitchen in Malibu—maybe even LA itself. My daddy, who can't boil water, believes in the best of everything.

"I think we need us some music," Dana said as she leapt up and vanished. Within seconds, a stereo system blasted out the Rolling Stones. "It's their new album," she shouted as she came back into the room. The turntable might be in a far-off location, but the entire house was wired for sound.

They sprawled across the sofas, devouring pizzas and grooving to the music after a day in the sun.

As Tai reached for another piece of pizza, he said, "So, dude, were you really surprised to see me?"

"Huh?" Nate shouted.

Tai tried to shout over the music. "Glad to see me?"

Dana jumped up once again and left the room. She came back almost immediately. She'd obviously run to turn down the sound system. "That's better, huh?" she said. "We can talk now. You were saying, Tai my little love?"

As much as they all three adored Candy, the boys never failed to crack up when the diva imitated her.

"I was asking Nate if he was glad to see me," Tai said.

"You bet." Nate wiped a smear of tomato sauce off his cheek with the back of his hand. "When you didn't call me after you got back from Samoa, I thought you were mad or something."

"Nah, man." Tai swigged root beer. "The surprise was the diva's idea."

Dana jumped up, saying, "Thank you, thank you," as she curtsied to each of the boys.

Both boys, at the same time, said, "Sit down, Diva." Nate added, "We've already praised your cooking skills. Any more applause and you'll begin to think we like you."

They all laughed at Nate's joke. Then Tai's eyes met Nate's, and he held his gaze for just a moment. *What am I seeing here?*

Dana leapt up once again when the last song on the record ended. "Let's dance. Huh? You two ready to get happy?" She ran from the room.

Nate worried she had seen his moment of wonder. Or was it discomfort? He quickly let his eyes stray from Tai to his pizza, and he gobbled up the piece as Dana came back.

The Beatles were now shouting, "I Wanna Hold Your Hand," and Dana pulled Tai and Nate up from their respective seated positions. "Dance, boys, dance," she ordered. And she started jumping, gyrating, laughing. The two boys stood there. She took both their hands and jerked them into dancing with her. When the song ended, "I Saw Her Standing There" started, and their dancing became even more joyous. Nate was happier than he'd been in weeks.

The album segued into "That Boy," and Dana pulled Tai and Nate together, joined their four hands, and retreated. The song was a slow one, a song about how one boy loved, lost, and wanted to love the same person again. Nate felt a bit awkward with the song, the idea that the diva expected him and Tai to dance together. But Tai pulled him close, and all his inhibitions melted, at least until the song ended. As Tai held him, a bit too close, Nate thought, he felt something wrong was happening.

Unsettled, Nate pulled away. But he hoped Tai didn't take offense. He never wanted to forget that dance. He pretended exhaustion as he sank back onto the couch.

Tai looked at him. Nate saw confusion in Tai's face. Nate was so puzzled by that look, that dance, that feeling that had come over him, he reached for another slice of pizza and stuffed most of it into his mouth, fearing what words might escape. Meanwhile, both Tai and the diva took their former places.

"That was fun, wasn't it, Heartthrobs?" Her tone seemed to be covering something. Was it triumph? Was it wonder? Was it fear she had ignited something she hadn't intended to? All those thoughts ran through Nate's brain as he chewed and chewed and chewed, hoping this bite of pizza would never be ready to swallow. But eventually he could chew no more. He had to swallow and break the silence in the room.

"Is your dad going to mind my borrowing his bed?" Nate said. *That's a good question. Totally unrelated to anything that just happened. It's a safe topic.*

"If he does, it's his own fault," Dana said. "This whole house only has two bedrooms, his and mine. Daddy *discourages* overnight visitors."

Nate eyes widened, panic seeping in. "Then where is Tai sleeping?"

"With you, Heartthrob," Dana said. "Unless you want him bunking with me." She adopted an ultra-proper British accent. "No, my dear, that would nevah do. Much too impropah. A young lady must guard herself against the advahnces of young gentlemen." She dropped the accent. "You're stuck with the Samoan, Heartthrob."

Tai looked at Nate and smiled. Nate gulped.

Dissolve to: Interior—the bedroom

TAI STRIPPED down to his underwear. Nate's eyes lingered. Then he caught himself and looked away.

"Right side of the bed okay for you, dude?"

Nate hesitated. No side of the bed was good, not with Tai in it with him. Feelings were stirring, rising. Feelings that had started with "That

Boy." He was going to have to fight to keep from revealing whatever it was he was thinking about Tai. *What am I thinking? What is this? It's wrong, isn't it?* "Sure." *I could have grabbed a pillow and said, "I'll just sleep out there on the balcony." Like that would happen.*

Tai slid under the covers and yawned.

"Fun day, huh?" Tai rubbed his eyes. *He's so nonchalant. Like nothing happened between us. I thought I saw he was uncomfortable for a moment down there in the living room, but he certainly doesn't seem to be now.*

"Yeah." Nate folded back the covers on his side and got into bed, trying to stay well away from Tai's sleek, muscled body.

"I'm beat." Tai switched off the bed lamp. "Night, dude."

Please, oh please, just let us drift off into cleansing sleep. I don't know if I like what I'm feeling or if I think it's filthy. Just let me sleep.

The room was thrown into darkness. There was very little outside lighting, and none of it seemed to be spilling into this room. Nate tensed, eyes wide. Feeling totally knotted up, he turned his body to relieve the pressure. But turning on his right side, like he usually slept, brought him to a position where he could see only Tai. A sliver of moonlight filtered through the open windows. It seemed to land right on Tai, a spotlight focused on this perfect body lying beside him. A gentle breeze wafted in. The intoxicating scent of flowers from the rain forest jungle outside the balcony set Nate's nerves on edge.

Tai was out immediately, it seemed to Nate, but he himself barely slept. After turning again onto his back, Nate was as tense as ever. He tried desperately to induce sleep, but it was coming only in fits. As soon as he'd doze off, Tai would move or turn over or snort, and Nate's stirred senses would remind him that he was sharing the bed with Tai.

At first, Nate slept without cover, the folded-back top sheet acting as a barrier. He was afraid to join Tai under the sheet. But as the night wore on, the breeze intensified. Nate felt a chill, so he reluctantly pulled the sheet up over him.

He turned over on his left side and commanded himself to sleep, praying the feelings stirring in him would go away.

Tai slung his left arm and leg over Nate's body. Nate's eyes popped open. Tai's skin was touching his, and he was getting aroused. Not a gradual thing. He felt himself grow hard and ready. He couldn't let that happen. He tried to will his erection to go away. *Tai doesn't know what he's doing with that arm, that leg. And I can't let myself think he does know.* The sleeping body inched closer to Nate. Tai's nose was nestled up against Nate's neck. In his sleep, he lightly cooed.

Nate trembled. *Oh my God. This can't be happening. I've never even been on a date with a girl. How can I be turned on by Tai? But I am. And I like it.*

Slowly, Tai's droopy eyes opened. He smiled. "Nice, huh?" he mumbled. Nate hoped to see Tai fast asleep, talking in his slumber, dreaming perhaps. But Tai was wide-awake. Then his eyes closed. Tai was asleep once again.

The stirrings in Nate grew stronger. He was about to explode with Tai so close.

Do I push Tai away? Then how would I explain myself? No, it's not nice. You were too close to me. I freaked out. I don't want you touching me.

Nate's thoughts paused. A revelation.

But I do want you touching me. I want you touching me and kissing me and holding me. I don't care if people say it's wrong.

It's nice. I like it.

And I like that I like you touching me.

It feels good.

It feels right.

Scene 28

Fade in: Interior—the Berrigan apartment
Sunday evening

WHAT A weekend! Malibu, the diva, the water, and… Tai. Nate whistled as he opened the door to the apartment, still riding the high. *Yeah, it was a great weekend. And with the show starting again next week, every day will be great… with Tai.*

"Where have *you* been?" he heard.

Nate's good humor vanished. *You had to spoil it, didn't you, Paul?*

He looked around the corner into the living room. Paul sprawled in his chair, Scotch in hand. *I'm so sick of this. Can't I have a life?*

"What do *you* care?" Nate spit. "Been off stealing more ashtrays, I see." Nate pointed at two ashtrays with different logos on the coffee table.

"Watch your tone, kid," Paul slurred. "I got those last week. Your mother has been frantic, hysterical. You just left. Didn't tell us where or when you'd be back." Paul could spout that shit all he wanted, but Nate had told him. He just was too drunk to remember. Nate just wanted to go to his room and distance himself from this man who was trying to be a father, much too late in his life. *Why do you care?* Nate rolled his eyes. *As if I believe you. Oh yeah, of course Monica was frantic. Sure. She's probably still passed out from before I left. Or did she rouse herself enough to yell at you? I suppose the divorce is cancelled now, isn't it?* Paul scowled. "I asked you a question, kid."

"I was with friends. I told you that before I left." Nate stared at Paul, daring his challenge.

"Yeah, righ'," Paul barked. "Like you *ha'* any friends." Paul's speech was slurred. *What a great role model you make, Daddy.*

"That's how much you know." Nate turned to leave.

"Don' turn your back on me. 'Splain yourself, kid." Nate almost laughed at Paul's drunken, unintentional Ricky Ricardo explanation demand. But luckily, he thought better of it.

Nate sighed, a from-the-depths, exasperated huff of air. "I spent the weekend with Tai and Dana, from the show, okay? Dana's dad has a beach house at Malibu."

Paul sat up, suddenly sober. Or as sober as a jolt of rich-scent could make him. "Malibu, huh? What is he, rich?" He swigged his Scotch. "That black gal has a rich daddy? How rich can he be? Who is he?"

"You"—Nate shook his head—"haven't heard of him."

"Try me," Paul said.

"He's just a businessman. His name's By—" Nate was interrupted by Monica, who floated in, swathed in a brightly flowered caftan, holding her head with one hand and her constant cigarette in the other. If she hadn't looked so haggard, she might have looked beautiful, like the old days.

"There you are, my sweet," she cooed at Nate. "I told you, Paul, he'd be back soon. Did I leave my nerve pills in here?" She sidled to the bar, hands extended to break a fall, if needed.

You've already had your quota for the day, I see.

Monica found her pill bottle, popped the cap, took two of the little yellow pills, and tossed them into her mouth. She turned, carefully maneuvered herself in Paul's direction, grabbed his glass, and chased the pills with Scotch.

"Hey!" Paul yelled, reaching for the glass.

"Don't be selfish, Paul. I'll pour you another." She stumbled the few steps to the bar, poured more Scotch, and returned the glass to Paul. Then, brushing Nate's cheek as she passed him, she fell onto the sofa.

Another typical day with the Berrigans. They avoid each other, then they fight, then they avoid each other, then they fight. And meanwhile, Monica supposedly is divorcing Paul. Or isn't. It's hard to keep score. My guess is that's never gonna happen. She'd never survive without him. And he likes having a wife to use as an excuse if any of his floozies try to get serious. She'll drop the case, and another chunk of my money will be wasted, paying off that high-powered lawyer. Nate turned toward his room.

"Wait a minute, kid, I haven' finished wi' you. You been gone since Friday e'ning. Your mother and I had no idea where you were." *I could have been in my room and neither of you would have had a clue as to where I was.* "Now, I wan' some answers." *And just why do you deserve any answers?*

"I said I told you both I was going, okay?" Nate huffed. He gestured toward his now prostrate mother. "Would she have remembered anyway?" He pointed at Paul. "Would you remember anything in your Scotch-induced fog?"

Paul ignored Nate's remark. *Score one for me.*

"So—like I asked before—who's this colored millionaire?"

"Byron Stone." Nate shifted his weight. "And they prefer *black* these days. Besides, Dana's dad is not black, he's white."

"Byron Stone." Paul said the name like he was thinking it over. With a sudden burst of sobriety, he bellowed, "*Byron Stone*? He's one of the richest guys in the world. How in the hell is he the dad of that little pickaninny?" Paul was salivating.

You're such an asshole, Paul. You think Dana is less than you, far less than you, but if she has a filthy rich white daddy, then you're all ears, just listening to figure out how you can cash in on this new development.

"That's for them to tell you, not me," Nate said. *There wasn't chance in hell he was revealing any Stone family secrets to Paul.*

Then instantly Paul's tone and demeanor changed. "That Dana's an okay-looking girl, kid. You could do worse. Good for you!"

Not ten seconds ago, she was a plantation field worker in your eyes, but now that she's the daughter of a billionaire, she's an okay-looking girl? You are such a putz, Paul. A racist putz, at that.

Nate closed his eyes and shook his head. "I'm not interested in Dana, Paul. We're just friends."

"Since when d' ya call me Paul? S'Dad, to you, kid. Won' stan' f' none of this Paul crap coming out of your mouth. And wha's wrong with the girl? The times are changin'. You could be with a Negro. Especially a rich Negro."

"So, I rush out and marry Dana just so you can get your hands on her alleged fortune? Ain't gonna happen." Nate paused, then added for good measure, "Paul."

"What are ya—queer?" Paul spat, like that was the ultimate insult. "You'd *have* to be to not like the daughter of a man who has that much money."

For an instant, Nate was struck by Paul's word *queer*. Then, as hateful as the word sounded—and he knew Paul meant it that way—he knew that's what he was. He *was* queer.

Nate quickly turned away. "I'm going to my room," he mumbled. He had to get out of this man's, his father's, presence before he said or did something he would live to regret.

"Think 'bout it, kid. Money like that can buy a lot of happiness, if ya get m' drift!" Paul shouted as Nate went down the hall to his bedroom. "And can the Paul shit. Show some respect. After all, if it weren't for me...."

Here's your respect, Nate thought, slamming the door.

Scene 29

Fade in: Interior—Nate's dressing room
Season Three *Kerry!* The first day back

"MY, MY, my, Heartthrob… you've just been glowing all morning."

"Cut it out, Diva," Nate said. The all-knowing Diva. Capable of discerning the least little thing, especially if it involved him and Tai, it seemed. He had to be careful to keep his feelings for Tai from showing. That would be hard because he was so happy they were back at work. He could spend every day with Tai and avoid the chaos his parents called *home*. "I'm glad we're back is all." Nate tossed the script he was studying onto the counter. "You don't know how much *fun* it is—*life with Monica and Paul.*"

"I can imagine," she said. She sat on the sofa across from his chair and unscrewed the top from the nail polish she'd been shaking.

"Oh—and just so you know, Paul will be publishing our engagement notice any day now."

Dana looked up from her nails, a trace of a smile kissing her lips.

She is the all-powerful Diva. She knows exactly what I'm talking about.

"The perfect merger—the handsome son of Paul Berrigan and the lovely daughter of zillionaire Byron Stone." Nate scrunched his face into a twisted smile.

"So your da-da doesn't care if his very white son is saddled with a—unbelievably gorgeous, I might add—*Negro* girl?"

"He's more interested in the half of her whose father is one of the richest men on the planet. Money trumps race every time with Paul."

The diva tossed off a snicker. "Yeah, tell him not to get his hopes up. Mr. Stone's lovely daughter might be willing"—Dana thrust an exaggeratedly loving look at Nate and gestured toward him—"but the handsome Berrigan scion only has eyes for someone else." She clasped her hands to her heart—careful not to smear the fresh coat of polish she'd been applying—and pasted a faux abject look of dejection on her face.

"Cut it out!" Nate blurted just as Tai appeared in the doorway.

"Cut what out?" Tai asked as he dropped next to Dana.

Nate turned beet red.

"Paul Berrigan has instructed his only son that he is to marry the millionaire maiden, *moi*!"

Tai burst into uncontrollable laughter with Dana acting suitably indignant.

"Pity the poor guy who has to take on the diva," Tai said, in between spasms.

"Enough, enough," Dana demanded. "I have young escorts pounding down my door, I'll have you know."

"Escorts?" Tai asked. "You mean like the ones on the back pages of the tabloids?"

Dana whacked him on the head with her hand while Nate sat, smiling. *Who'd have thought friends could be so much fun?*

Dana stood. "I'm headed to the *classroom*." She said that with contempt because both boys knew their classroom was a tiny little used-to-be storeroom, set up just to satisfy the State of California Board of Education. "You guys ready?"

"Give us a minute, will ya?" Tai said, and Dana smiled at him, nodding.

"Sure," she said. "I'll just finish my nails in my dressing room where there are no rude interruptions, and then I'll meet you in the hall of matriculation." And she left.

Tai and Nate sat quietly, looking at each other.

After a moment, Tai said, "About last weekend, dude—"

"Fun, huh?" Nate interrupted him. *I don't know where he's headed, but I do know I don't want to talk about it. I liked his being close to me, and I can't stand him telling me it shouldn't have happened, or he was thinking of some girl in his dreams, or he goes crazy when he's asleep.*

"Fun? More than fun—that's what I wanted to talk about—"

"The diva's a riot, isn't she?" Nate stalled Tai.

"Yeah, she is, but I wanted to talk about us—"

"I caught hell when I got home," Nate said. "Paul was pissed. He didn't know where I was, even though I told him I was going away for the weekend, like he was sober enough to listen. Monica supposedly was distressed over my leaving, like she was even awake enough to be that, and Paul lit into me the minute I got back. I can't figure out why he came home, but I guess the divorce is going away after last week's negotiating meeting. Monica probably thought she could get more money out of him, but the only money Paul has is mine, and most of that he has lost at the blackjack table—"

"You told him where you were, right? That you were with me?"

Nate's stream of consciousness didn't stop Tai as he hoped it would. But oddly, after Tai spoke, he paused. *Is he waiting for an answer, or is he letting that* with me *sink in?* He looked at Tai, hoping to read something in his eyes. And the look must have shifted gears in Tai's brain, if any gears needed shifting.

Tai added, "And the diva?"

Suddenly Nate felt safe. The conversation had been changed. He no longer had to worry about his feelings for Tai being revealed.

"Yeah… that's when he started in about Dana being such a good catch and all."

"What *did* you say about that?" Tai probed.

"I didn't say anything." He thought he saw Tai's face drop a little.

"Look—last weekend with you—"

"Ah, my little love—" Candy barged into the dressing room, cutting off Tai.

"Oh! You have company, my other favorite person." She kissed Tai on the cheek, then turned to give a peck to Nate. "I can come back later."

Thank you, thank you, thank you, Candy, for breaking up this little truth fest. I have no idea what Tai was about to say, but it couldn't have been good.

"We were just heading out to class, weren't we, Tai? Why don't you come with us later to lunch, Candy? Dana's coming too."

"Oh, it would be such fun. I just know it," Candy said. "But I'm meeting my agent. Before you run off, though, I have a proposition, dear. I have tickets to a gala premiere of the new Elvis film tomorrow night. My niece Karin—such a radiant child—is just dying to go. Well, I thought to myself, why would she want to attend with her old auntie when I could arrange a date with a darling young man, one she is head over heels in love with, if I can gauge by all the *Tiger Beat* clippings she has on her wall." She looked at Tai. "Sorry, love, but I'm afraid little Karin only has eyes for Nate, here." Then she looked at Nate again. "Would you be a dear, sweet, and go with her? It would mean so much to me."

Nate swallowed. *A date?* He wanted to say no, but Candy was so nice. She was more like a mother to him than Monica. From the moment he'd met Candy, she'd loved and protected him.

"I-I-I guess so…," he sputtered.

"Oh, the two of you will have a lovely time. I'll call Karin this evening and make all the arrangements. She'll be ecstatic—I just know it! I may have to shout on the phone over her squeals." She hugged Nate, who looked helplessly at Tai, who was staring at the floor.

"Now, dearie," Candy said, thrusting a pen and paper at Nate, "give me your phone number so I can call you with details." Nate wrote down his number. *That's three.*

"I'll arrange for a car and driver. And don't worry about what you wear. These things are never formal anymore, alas. Wait for my call, now." Like a whirlwind winding down, she swept from the room.

Tai stared at Nate, a look of disappointment darkening his face. *What's up with that?*

Scene 30

Fade in: Interior—motel room
The night of the gala premiere

TAI YANKED the covers up over his naked body. Nate out on that date with Candy's niece. It tore him apart. He was steeled, no, joyous, to tell Nate how he felt, and then this…. He sighed. *Well, Nate's better off with Candy's niece. There's no way he would want to get into a sordid relationship with me. I was sure I knew it was okay, after talking to Paulie. Jesus* understood. *Even* approved. *Yeah, sure. You fell for that one, Tai. I open my mouth to tell Nate, and Candy comes in with her plan—God's plan. He stopped me. God, why? It felt so right, and now look at me. I'm a total wreck. God, you gave Nate to me and then took him back. I felt so good about it all, and where am I now? A sleazy motel. A lumpy bed with stained sheets. Kyle. He only had to phone, pretending I'd never broke it off with him, and I run to him.* Tai yanked the sheet again, trying to control it somehow. But he knew it wasn't the sheet he was mad at.

"What you thinking 'bout, lover? You're awful restless."

Tai looked at Kyle next to him. *Nate could be kissing* her *right now, instead of me. How can I tell you that's what I'm thinking about?* "Nothing." And he grabbed at the sheet again.

"Whoa, lover! Careful. We don't want to have the sheet police come after us for destruction of property." He chuckled. Then Kyle grabbed Tai's cheeks and planted a kiss on him. "Let's start thinking about us, okay?"

Tai smiled, summoning his best acting skills. *What am I doing here? I don't want this. I should just leave. I could leave. Nothing's keeping me here. I could just up and bolt from this bed. From Kyle. Why am I punishing Kyle for something he doesn't even know about? Why am I punishing me?*

Tai lay there, uncomfortable and thinking, as Kyle covered him in kisses, down his right side and up the left. Grabbing the jar of Vaseline, the boy spoke. "Turn over, lover boy, this is what I've been craving."

As Kyle tried to tug Tai over onto his stomach, Tai suddenly realized what he was hearing. It smacked him straight between the eyes. He stared at Kyle. He wanted to shout, but he was afraid. Afraid of riling Kyle up. So, calmly, he said, "I've told you before, that's off-limits."

And that did it. "You think I'm *unclean* or something?" Kyle spat the words, obviously pissed off Tai was rejecting him.

Yeah, I do. The acting skills kicked in again. He couldn't afford to bring out Kyle's wrath. *I've seen that before, and that time, it wasn't about me or anything I'd done.* Again, he replied calmly and coolly. "It's just that I'm not sure what can happen. It's not like there is a training manual out there. There may be a sexual revolution going on, but what you want to do is not covered in the Kama Sutra. At least I'm pretty sure it's not. It just seems risky to me."

"I'm clean, lover. No diseases."

Tai could hear a measure of anger in Kyle. He didn't want that to grow.

"So, how do you know *I* don't have a disease?" Tai asked.

Kyle smiled, seemingly amused at the thought. "I trust you, lover."

"It's not a matter of trust, man. It's a matter of safety." Tai kept his voice even, putting every bit of *reasonable* he could muster into it.

"So—I'm pretty sure you haven't caught the clap from a street whore because not only would you not indulge like that, but you are totally not interested in girls. So if you have caught something, it has to be from another guy." Tai heard the tension building with every word Kyle delivered. "And it seems the only guy you're interested in these days is your beloved Nate." The vitriol Kyle put into *beloved Nate* was like acid pouring from a vial. "Am I right? Is he the one you're worried about? Have you two indulged during our short breakup you orchestrated? Is that it?" Kyle's overthought words masked seething anger, but Tai saw it in Kyle's eyes. "Did you fuck him? Did he fuck you?"

With sudden horror, Tai focused on Kyle's earlier words and completely ignored the two stabbing questions. *There's no way Nate could have the clap.* Then Kyle's rage registered. *Kyle is getting much too close to the truth. He's right. I am holding out. For Nate.* He started to speak—what, he didn't know—but Kyle cut him off.

"I'm horny as hell, lover boy! And you haven't answered my questions."

Ignoring that, Tai said, "I'm just not ready for that yet. Give me some time, dude," Tai pleaded, hoping to placate an already too-worked-up Kyle.

"Are you stalling?" Kyle's tone told Tai this could turn uglier fast. Too fast.

He had to do something. And it better be now. Before Kyle exploded. Maybe he could blow him. But even that thought repulsed Tai. He wanted nothing to do with Kyle. Not anymore. He only wished he'd decided that before coming here. But Kyle was escalating, and he not only turned Tai off, he scared him. With revulsion, he ran his fingers across Kyle's cheek, hoping that might calm him down. "No, no—nothing like that."

But Kyle was not buying it. He jerked Tai's hand away. "Look, Tai. You brought me to this sleazotel. Yeah, I'm the one who called you, but you jumped at the chance to get back together. Quit stalling and get it on." He stuck his fingers in the Vaseline jar. "Turn over. Now."

"That's the way to a guy's heart—sweet talk." *Oh my God. That just came out. I'm a shit. Just tell him, Tai. Tell him it's over and whatever happens happens. Damn. I should not have said that. But it's there, hovering over us, like a bomb about to drop.*

"Not my style, *lover.*" Menace. It filled his voice. Overflowed. "You know me. I. Want. It. When. I. Want. It."

Thoughts raced through Tai. Later, he would look back on this and wonder why those thoughts weren't about flight, about survival, about getting the hell out of there. *Unfortunately, I do know your style. I knew it when I set this up. But maybe I wanted this. Maybe I wanted you to beat me up, pummel me, knock some sense in me—or knock me senseless, but that would be hard to do because my being here proves how senseless I am.*

"Come on." He poked Tai on the butt. "Turn over. Now!"

Maybe I deserve this. Maybe I knew this would happen all along. Defeated, Tai slipped over onto his stomach. He waited for the inevitable. Dreaded the penetration, welcomed the punishment. Then his left brain must have kicked in. He'd learned, in one of those science school packets, that the left side of the brain was for logic and reasoning. But instead of jumping out of the bed, he just lay there, thinking. Maybe it was a coping mechanism—he'd learned that from one of those packets too. Maybe it was his way to disengage from what was about to happen to him. *Why am I letting Kyle do this? What am I even doing here? Is this going to make anything right?* He steeled himself for Kyle's power trip. The act that would prove Kyle had total control over him.

No. I've got *to tell him, once and for all, this* thing, *this* whatever *we're playing at, isn't working. That I do not want to and I won't let him do this. Not ever. I'm not giving myself to Kyle, ever again. And certainly not this way. And not now.* As Tai's mind raced, he felt panic build inside him. *What will he do if I tell him? And why am I so chickenshit? I can fight or I can let him—*

A fingerful of frigid Vaseline jerked Tai to reality. He turned over and sat up, facing away from Kyle, hanging his head. *Now!*

Fury. Rage. Blind anger. Kyle could hurt him now far worse than if he'd just let him have his way with him. "What's the matter, you shit? I'm all ready for you. You think I'm planning to end this night with a case of blue balls?" His words were darts.

What will he do? What will he do? What will he do? It doesn't matter. Whether Nate wants me or not, I don't want what Kyle dishes out. He can beat me. I don't care. But I won't let him have his way. I may deserve anything he does, but this will end. Right now.

Kyle grabbed Tai's arms, jerked him. "Lay back down. I want you!"

Pulling away and standing but still hoping to avoid the brunt of Kyle's wrath, Tai took a deep breath, and then: "I can't do this, man."

"What do you mean you can't do this?" Kyle was frantic. Shouting. Not caring about the thin walls of this cheapjack crap of a place. Each word was like a hammer. "I need you. Just relax and let it happen." Then he seemed to ease off a bit. He became a little softer, a little kinder, a little the old Kyle. "I can wait a few more minutes if you're not ready yet."

What? Wait a few more minutes? Is he backing down? This was his chance. He might not get another one before Kyle's rage revved up again.

"I don't need more time, Kyle." Tai carefully measured each word, hoping to get through to him and truly not wanting to hurt this boy who had been his best friend for eons. "It's just...." He paused. "It's just...." The words came rushing out. "I don't want to do this, none of this, anymore, you hear?"

He expected Kyle to be enraged. But what he saw on Kyle's face was disbelief. Wonder. And hurt? Did he see hurt?

"I don't understand, Tai. What is it? You got somebody else? It *is* Nate, isn't it?" Kyle's voice trembled.

I wasn't expecting that. Kyle—the Kyle who once was my best friend—is still in there.

"No." Tai thought of Nate, closed his eyes, and let out a little puff of air. "No," he said dejectedly, "there is no one else."

"So you expect me to believe that there's no one else and that it's not me." A simple question that went from hurt to howl in ten seconds. "What? Did you suddenly just turn into a frigid jerk?"

Now Tai knew he had to get away. Kyle would never understand. But they had been so much to each other. He had to try. *Why am I risking my life for this?* he asked himself. Then he knew his answer. *I know Kyle, and Kyle would never hurt me.*

"Look, dude." Tai bent over and retrieved his briefs from the pile on the floor. Standing on one leg and then the other, he pulled them on. He needed the mechanics of the simple act to get him through this. "I don't know what it is. I just know that I have to be alone right now." During all this, he had not looked at Kyle. He continued averting his eyes. "I'm leaving. You need cab money?" Tai reached for his wallet, pulled out a twenty, and thrust it at Kyle, still not looking him the eye.

He swatted Tai's hand away. "Keep your dough, you prick!" He threw the Vaseline jar across the room. It hit the wall. The top came off. A glob of goo slid down the faded wallpaper. "So that's it for us? You walk out and it's all over?"

During Kyle's Vaseline tantrum, Tai had slipped on his shirt and jeans, picked up his shoes. He had walked toward the door. He stopped, reaching for the chain on the door. "Yeah, man." Tai sighed. He'd finally done it. For good. "I'm sorry."

"Oh, you're *sorry* all right." And then something almost unexpected. Tai had resigned himself to the fact that his best friend no longer could feel. But Kyle started sobbing.

Tai's resolve faltered. "Come on. Let's just admit it was fun while it lasted. Huh?" *What a lame thing to say. If Kyle hadn't hit him by now, the punch was bound to come after that.*

But Kyle was still on the bed, not moving from it. "Oh yeah, lover—it was fun, fun, fun." Sarcasm. Deep, dark, lead-like sarcasm.

Tai felt like all had been said. It was over between him and Kyle. "I said I'm sorry. What else can I say? See you around." *You are a shit,*

Tai. How could you add that last? Kyle will either kill you right here and right now, or he will kill himself when you're gone. But Tai was not thinking straight, and at that moment, lost in his own misery, he didn't care what happened.

He turned, stepped toward the bed, silently dropped the twenty on the bedspread, turned back, lifted the chain on the door, opened it, and walked through.

The broken automatic door closer left the door wide open.

Scene 31

Fade in: Interior—Nate's dressing room
The day after the gala premiere

"So, like, what's up, Pele?"

"Nothin', Zits. Just hangin' out. How was yesterday, Playboy?"

Nate sat next to Tai on the sofa, his script in his lap, eyes closed, as Tai fed him his cues.

"It was a gas. Took the chick up to Central Park with a basket of food your mama packed for us. Found a spot where they wasn't too much action, and we made our own action so much we forgot to eat. Not enough time."

"Did you kiss her?"

Nate looked at his script.

"That's not the line, Tai," Nate said, reading the script. "Says here, *'She worth seeing again?'*"

"Forget the script," Tai said, grabbing the pages from Nate. "Answer my question."

"What question? We were running lines, remember?" *What's up with Tai? He's bothered as hell today. What did I do? He's trying to cover, but I knew something was up the minute he came in.*

"I asked, did you kiss her?"

"Kiss *who*?" Nate stared at Tai.

"You know who—that skirt clinging to you at that premiere."

"Oh man." Nate laughed. "You read the rags too, too much."

But Tai wasn't ready to let go, Nate decided, because he popped off: "Well, did you?"

What's bringing this on?

"No! Of course not. We just met, there were thousands of people around, and I've…." He stopped.

"What?" Tai probed. "Huh?"

"It's...." Nate blushed. He was embarrassed, and Tai must have seen it. He had a sudden attitude change, as if he'd been baiting Nate and now was different somehow because he hadn't gotten the answer he'd been fishing for.

"What's embarrassing?" Tai leaned over and tickled Nate. "Tell me."
That's better. Back to old times.

"No, man." Nate giggled, pushing Tai away.

"Tell me," Tai said, grabbing Nate and tickling him harder. "Tell me, tell me, tell me."

"I've never kissed anyone," Nate blurted out, gasping for breath after laughing so hard. "No one, not a soul, never, never, never," Nate rattled off, laughing. *Was that a lie? He didn't kiss Tai, Tai kissed him that night with the Beatles.*

Tai looked into Nate's eyes, holding his arms down at his sides. "Are you telling the truth, dude?"

"Yeah," Nate said, suddenly not laughing. *Why did I reveal that? It's personal.*

Tai continued staring into Nate's eyes. Nate felt uncomfortable. Tai was boring into his soul, and he didn't know what to think about it.

Then slowly Tai's lips met his in a gentle kiss.

Nate took a deep breath as their eyes remained glued to each other.

An eternity passed.

Silence. The world had slipped away. Nate kissed him back. Oh, did he kiss him back. Now, now—he had kissed someone. No mistaking it.

"I wanted to do this last weekend at the beach house, but I was afraid," Tai whispered.

"Don't," Nate murmured.

Tai dropped Nate's arms and edged away.

Nate felt a tear slide down his cheek. He'd finally been kissed, really kissed, and Tai was retreating. *Did I do it wrong?*

"I'm sorry," Tai said. "I shouldn't have done that. It's just—" He stopped, then started again. "Kyle and I broke up this weekend, and I hoped...."

Broke up? Does that mean...? "No." Nate reached for Tai. Nate looked at Tai and wondered, *Why do I keep saying no?*

Then he found more words. "I meant to say, 'No, don't be afraid.' I have enough fear for both of us."

Tai grinned and took Nate's hand.

"I don't know what's happening here," Nate said. "I suppose it's wrong." He wiped another tear from his cheek. "But—" His words stumbled. "But—" He paused. Then it tumbled out of him. "I wanted this to happen. I've wanted this for a long, long time. Way back. Back before that kiss that night after the Beatles, I think. I never, ever thought it was wrong. God—if Monica and Paul knew, they'd probably kill me. And Kerry—he hates fags. We'd both be toast. But whatever—I just don't care."

"Don't even think about them," Tai said, placing a finger on Nate's lips.

More silence.

Finally Tai said, "I tried to tell you earlier this week. It was all I could do to keep my hands off you last weekend."

Shyly, Nate said. "I felt the same way, but I didn't know if you were *that way* or not."

"Oh yeah…." Tai sighed and nodded. "I've been *that way* for as long as I can remember. And it's *gay*, by the way, not *fag, faggy, fags*. I hate any version of that word."

Nate gazed into Tai's eyes. He saw love. He saw more devotion than he'd ever felt from anyone else. He felt like the world had opened and Tai was his guide.

"So, when did you first know?" Nate asked.

"It just happened. Between me and Kyle. We were first best friends, and before we knew it, we were *doing stuff*. A lot of guys start out that way. Some are curious, and it doesn't last. For me, it lasted. Oh, did it last.*"*

"And are you still *doing stuff*? You said you broke up this weekend. What's that mean?"

"It means I told him it was over—the friendship and all. I knew what I was feeling for you—what I *am* feeling for you—is the only thing I want in my life. I didn't know if you were willing, but if you weren't, then I would just go without. Not having you was better than having anything with Kyle."

"And how did he take all this?"

"Wudn't happy. Pretty pissed, actually. And hurt. But he'll get over it. I've known Kyle for a long, long time. He doesn't hold on to anything. Believe me."

"I hope you're right."

"I am. Trust me."

Trust. I would trust you forever, Tai.

They kissed again. This time Nate took the lead. They held each other after that long, beautiful kiss.

Then Nate stood and went to the door.

"Dude," Tai protested. "Where ya going?"

"I wanna be sure the door's locked," Nate said. He stepped over to the door and pushed the lock button on the knob; then he turned to Tai and smiled.

"Now—teach me."

Fade to Black

A Knock... later

STARTLED BY the sound, Nate jerked. Tai jumped up, smoothing his clothes.

"You guys in there?" It was Dana. "Lunchtime, boys. Our beloved tutor was hell-bent on fetching you two for class, but I covered for you. What ya doin' in there?"

"Just a minute, Diva," Tai shouted. They got up, and Nate looked in the mirror, parting his hair with his hands.

With his hand on the doorknob, Tai turned. "Well, now you can't say you've never been kissed." He grinned, then opened the door.

Dana looked from Tai to Nate to Tai and back again to Nate.

She smiled.

Scene 32

Fade in: Interior—lobby of Nate's apartment building
A few days later, night

NATE CHEWED his fingernails and paced the lobby of his building. It had hit him in the middle of his shower: *This is a date. This is not just "hanging with Tai." This is a real, live, two guys who like each other, spend the evening together date....* He had stepped from the shower and dried off, but his pits were still wet. He swiped them with deodorant twice, just in case. Now here he was, waiting for Tai's arrival.

Never, ever in a trillion years did I imagine this. I guess I hoped. I wished. But damn, I never thought past all that to an honest-to-God date. And feeling this nervous. Or this happy.

A cab pulled up in front of the building. Tai stepped to the curb.

Nate pushed his way through the door of the building and met Tai on the sidewalk.

"Dude," Tai called. "Ya ready?" He turned and motioned toward the open door of the cab.

Nate walked up to Tai. "I didn't think about it earlier, but while I was waiting, I realized we could take the Mustang."

"Nah, dude. I asked you out. I provide transport. Now hop in. I got this all planned."

Nate climbed in, with Tai piling in after him. The driver turned from the front seat, watching them. Nate felt an uncomfortable shudder overtake him as the guy stared.

"Nate," Tai said, motioning toward the driver, "Joe, my chauffeur."

Nate's mouth dropped as the cab driver extended his hand. "How's it hangin', Nate?" Joe chuckled.

How's it hanging? Is he just being friendly, or does he see something in this?

Nate shook Joe's hand. Then he looked at Tai, puzzled and embarrassed at the greeting.

"Joe, cut it out. I told you Nate was special," Tai said. Then he turned to Nate. "My friend Kyle intro'd me to Joe. I call Joe whenever I need a cab. Easier that way. Joe knows me. I know Joe. We go way back, don't we, Joe?"

The driver smiled and said, "Yeah, Tai, m' man, we sure do. You and Kyle been callin' me forever."

Nate nodded as Joe pulled away.

"Where we going, Tai?" Nate asked as Joe maneuvered to the inside lane.

"Sit back and enjoy the ride, babe." Tai leaned into Nate, his topaz eyes filling with tears.

Alarmed, Nate blurted, "What's wrong, Tai?"

"Nothin', dude. I'm happy. Crazy happy. You don't know happy when you see it?"

As Tai leaned in and pecked Nate on the cheek, Nate squirmed. "Tai…," he said, "Joe!"

"What about Joe?" Tai mumbled, staring into Nate's eyes. "Like I said, man, Joe *knows* me. Took me a long time to come out of the closet. Truth be told, I've only really been out a short time, but all those months when Kyle and I were messing around, Joe was there for us."

Panic darkened Nate's face. "Then he knows about me too?"

"Well, we didn't discuss *this* specifically, but yeah, I think Joe has surmised that Kyle and I are dead, and we, you and me, are on a date."

Sweat broke out on Nate's brow. Tai brushed it away with his thumb.

"Don't *worry*," he reassured Nate. "We can trust Joe. He's one of us. And he's my friend." And once again, Tai closed in on Nate.

And once again, Nate squirmed.

Tai held up the palms of his hands in surrender. "Okay, dude, I know this is all new to you. I'll back off… for now." He gently took Nate's hand and kissed it. Then he sat back on the seat. Nate sat silently, processing everything.

Finally, Nate said, "You never did tell me where we're going."

Tai expelled a tiny laugh. "We're gonna have fun tonight. I'm taking you to paradise."

"And where would that be?" Nate asked.

"A little place just off the Strip."

"The Sunset Strip? Never been there. Taking care of Monica keeps me sequestered like a jury member on a capital murder trial."

"The Strip's a gas, dude. And lots of gay guys roam the Strip," Tai exclaimed. "Sit back. Enjoy the ride."

Joe pulled onto Sunset Boulevard, and Nate marveled at the sights.

"We have here the Boulevard, home to LA's covert homosexual scene," Tai intoned, playing tour guide, complete with imaginary megaphone. "LA's hunkiest hunks parade, cruising for love, carnal or otherwise. And along the way, they play, they eat, they shop."

Excited, Nate pointed out the window. "What's that?"

"That, my friend, is a bar. You know, one of those places where homo sapiens drink, dance, and carouse. Cast your eyes up the street. There's another. And once we get on the Strip proper, your vision will feast on tons of 'em. And in those palaces of hedonistic revelry, you'll find all sorts of people… tourists, stars, hippies, rock musicians, and yes—" He dropped the tour guide act. "—some gorgeous guys who are like us—those who practice 'the love that dare not speak its name.'"

Tai, Tai, Tai. First the tour guide, now an English accent. What a clown. His *clown.*

"What?" Nate giggled.

"It's Oscar Wilde, British, one of your more famous queens in history."

"Queens?"

"Yeah. Men who are larger than life, who don't care if the world thinks they are just a bit different. Wilde was put on trial and went to prison for being gay."

"When? Is he still there?"

Tai laughed. "No, dude. That was way, way back. In England. It can still happen in the US, but times are changing. Keep a low profile and most people leave us alone. Someday—maybe soon—we'll have the right to be ourselves. The Civil Rights Act will eventually take care of that. All people, all equal. Right? But at the moment, we have to pick and choose where and when we're open about it all."

"And we can do that in the places you're talking about on the Strip? Is that where we're going?"

"Yes and no. We're not going there tonight. Why? We're both underage, and no bouncer for any of those clubs would let us in. Used to let me in when I was with Kyle. He looks older. I doubt you and I could get past the goons. But some gay guys get in. And in those clubs, they dance their pants off. With some very high-profile celebs, I might add. Some of whom are deep in the closet but have female arm candy in tow just in case they need to act like they're sweet on a gal. But they cruise the ordinary guys, might pick them up, take them away in their limos, ditch the doll before getting the guy back to their pads, and then... well, you know. But even if a gay doesn't hook up with a movie star, a rock star, a high-powered something-something, two ordinary guys can still meet up and go for a little alone time. And that applies to hetero hookups too. The places are pickup heavens, for straights and gays alike. Guys meet, greet, and leave together."

"Where do they go?"

"Depends. If they can, they go back to their apartments and houses. If that's not possible—maybe they still live with parents, have a straight roommate, or are married—then there are motels where they can get cheap rooms for the night and the clerks ask no questions."

"Sounds kinda sordid."

"Can be. But it's the price we pay if we want to be ourselves. But don't you worry. All we're doing tonight is going for some chow."

"How do you know about all this?"

"Kyle. How he found it all, I have no idea. I just know he is, as they say, much more worldly than I am."

"You guys have been friends for a long time, you said. When did you know? When did you two start—you know."

Nate saw a *look* cross Tai's face.

"My friend, it's a long story, probably something we should save. Let's just say that I loved every minute of my friendship with Kyle, but after we started *this* up—" He waved a finger in the air. "—not so much. He's not the guy I always thought he was. You can know someone for years and years, then you find you don't really know 'em at all."

"Did he turn you gay? That's the word, right?" *It feels weird saying it.*

Tai didn't answer immediately. Nate could tell he was thinking, carefully forming his words, like he had come to some sort of life-shattering idea.

Finally, Tai spoke—measured. "Nate, m' friend, no one can *turn you* gay. You either are or you aren't." He paused again. "Before Kyle and I ever started messing around, before I even knew he was gay, I… knew… I… was."

He said that like it was the first time he's ever admitted it to himself.

Tai continued, with more confidence. "I felt it." Another pause. A deep breath. "Just like you probably have felt it. Before you ever know the word, before you ever know guys can like other guys—and girls like other girls, I might add—you find yourself getting a little stirred up when you see a guy who you like to look at or like the sound of his voice or get a feeling that you've never had before. Am I right?"

Nate thought a moment. Tai was right. If he'd been able to admit it to himself, he knew he was attracted to Tai long before that weekend.

"It's a lot to take in, Nate. Stick with me. I'll be your guide. Right now, just sit back and enjoy."

Weird. I really should be uptight right now with all the new stuff swirling around me. But I will sit back and enjoy. *Tai makes me feel it's all right. It's like I have permission, given to me by the one person who has that power over me.*

The cab made a right turn onto a side street.

"Where we headed, Tai?"

Tai laughed. "'Where we headed? Where we headed? Where we headed?' Is that the only question you can come up with tonight? Didn't I tell you to sit back and enjoy?" He brushed his hand across Nate's cheek. "Relax, babe."

That was the second time Tai called me "babe" tonight. I like it. "Stop mocking me, Tai. I really want to know where we're going." *But I really don't care. As long as it's with Tai.*

"To one of my favorite spots. You hungry?"

"Sure," Nate said. "I'm always hungry."

"Good, because you are about to have one of the best burgers on this planet."

"But we just passed Hamburger Hamlet. Now, *that* I've heard of."

"Oh, dude, have you got a lot to learn. Yes, most along the Boulevard would swear by the Hamlet, but I say there's a place much, much better."

They pulled up to a small storefront. Across the window, in colorful lettering, it said *Big Dick's*.

Tai tossed some bills to Joe and leapt from the car. He held out his hand to Nate, who followed him. Then Tai stuck his head back into the cab.

"Back in about an hour? 'Kay, Joe?"

"Anytime, guy," Joe said.

Then Tai motioned toward the building.

"Welcome to the finest hunks of meat in Hollywood." He led Nate to the entrance of the hamburger joint. As he pushed open the door, he cracked, "And the burgers are pretty hunky too."

Dissolve to: Interior—Big Dick's Hamburger Joint

TAI AND Nate had no sooner passed through the door than a gorgeous man behind the counter called out, "Hey, hey, hey! If it isn't the Samoan TV star. How's it hangin', Tai?"

"Long and hard, just for you, Bart."

"Where's your friend? Thought you guys were Siamese twins. Never seen one of you without the other."

"Kyle's toast, Bart." He pointed to Nate. "This is Nate. I promised him something hot and heavy." Tai chuckled.

"Well, you've come to the right place, Nate. And no introductions are needed. I've seen your show." He pointed to a TV on a shelf above the counter. "M' boy Tai here and you are my favorite TV stars. I've seen you hundreds of times. You are *fan-fuckin-tastic*, my friend."

"Thanks," Nate mumbled.

"Now, what can I get for you two?"

Tai turned to Nate. "Bacon cheeseburger?"

"I guess," Nate said, barely recovering from his embarrassment.

"You can't go wrong. It's *my* favorite, anyway," Tai told him. He turned to Bart. "Two bacon cheeseburgers, medium, double bacon, extra crisp. And the giant basket of fries."

He turned back to Nate. "They're hand cut, not those frozen things some places try to pass off."

Turning back to the counter, he finished the order with "And two of your giganto-enormous chocolate malts."

"You got it, m' man." Bart finished the order on his pad with a flourish, ripped it off, and clipped it to a pulley system to send it back to the kitchen.

Tai and Nate settled into a secluded corner booth, Tai practically sitting on top of Nate.

"You a regular here?" Nate asked. *Stating the obvious! What a dork I am!*

"Couldn't you tell?"

"Yeah, looks like you *are* known." Nate smiled. "How'd ya find this place?"

"You heard what Bart said. Kyle."

Nate paused, pulling some napkins from the napkin holder. *Is this thing between Tai and Kyle really finished? And what does Kyle think about that?* He looked around. *What if Kyle shows up?* He decided not to think about that. "Who's Dick?"

"Where? I don't see any dick," Tai deadpanned.

"Tai!" Nate squealed. He'd led a sheltered life, but he did know that *dick* had another meaning other than a man's name. "Cut it out." He pushed at Tai playfully. "*Big Dick*. Who's he?"

"The late Big Dick started his place back in the thirties, long before any guys like us started coming out of the woodwork. Back then, gay guys kept to themselves mostly." Tai was back in his tour guide mode. "Little did the very large man, Dick, know that the name of the place would eventually take on a whole different meaning. Dick ran the place until the fifties. Then his son took it over. Bart bought the son out a couple of years ago. Now—" Tai paused, no doubt for emphasis. "—Big Dick's is the premier eatery for *those in the know*."

As they waited for Bart to bring their burgers, Nate flooded Tai with questions.

"Okay, truth time—how long have you known you're gay? Why didn't you ever tell me? How come you don't mind coming into a place like this?"

"Whoa, dude. One question at a time." Tai stopped him. "How long? Prob'bly as long as I can remember. I think it's something that's in you from the time you're a toddler, being gay or straight, that is."

"Really?" Nate couldn't believe what he was hearing. Feelings he had long held were coming into focus, making sense.

"Yep, really," Tai answered. "And I never told you because everyone's funny about this. Some people can handle it, some can't. I didn't want to ruin our friendship. I had my suspicions about you—some of us have something like a radar sense—especially after the Malibu weekend, but I decided to take it slow and see what happened. I'm glad I did." He smiled at Nate and caressed his cheek.

Nate shuddered. *That feels so good. But what if someone sees us?*

Tai must have sensed Nate's apprehension.

"Don't worry, Nate. We're safe here. Almost everybody who comes here is like us. And those that aren't? Well, that's why I chose this booth. No one can see us from the main area."

Nate wanted to feel safe, but it was hard.

"So you weren't asleep that night?" Nate asked.

"Asleep? How could I sleep with your hot body curled in mine? It was all I could do to keep my cool, dude."

Nate let out a deep breath. "So it wasn't just me. I was so afraid that I would screw up after that. I had these feelings, but I wasn't exactly sure what they were. I didn't know what to do with them. And if I believe Paul and Monica, I'm bound for H-E-L-L if I let the feelings out. They've never given me *the talk*—about girls *or* guys. But believe me, they wouldn't want me to be this way, if only for the fact that it might screw up my career and *their* paycheck."

"Forget Paul and Monica." Tai turned Nate's face toward his and kissed him. "This is all that matters."

Nate pulled away. "Which brings us to my third question. Aren't you afraid coming into a place like this?"

Tai tried to lighten Nate's mood. "What? Bart only serves certified USDA-inspected meat. Don't think there's anything to worry about."

"You know what I mean."

"Look, Nate, this is a gay place. Bart's gay. His customers are gay. They're not gonna rat on one of their own—or two of their own as the case may be. And the *paparazzi*? Those vipers? They're too busy staking out the places on the Boulevard and the Strip. The big bucks are not made snapping pictures at Dick's. Believe me, a picture of some Hollywood giant is far more lucrative than a picture of two teenage sitcom actors." His eyes twinkled as he touched the tip of Nate's nose. "We've got nothing to worry about. Believe me, dude."

Nate frowned.

"Okay, what's swimming in that beautiful little head of yours?"

Nate slowly formed his words, not wanting to ruin this magical night but needing to know. "So—" He paused. "—this place is safe, but what if we get found out someplace else, some other time?"

Tai expelled a long, low whistle, like he was thinking. Then he looked Nate in the eye. "Well, it might not be so bad, really. It forces you to face who you are."

"But in our business, we're never who we are. We're actors, Tai. The public, remember? From what I've seen, there are a lot of haters out there."

"Look, Nate—not gonna lie to you. Actors do keep *it* a secret to the public. I've heard stories of Hollywood parties where gay actors meet to just have fun together—and sometimes have sex. But most of 'em manage to play straight their whole lives. There were old movie stars, some dead now, who could have been found out, but the studios covered it all up. Or at least that's what I've heard. The studios don't like their product to be messed with. And that's what we are—product. They sell us, so they protect us."

Nate thought of Kerry and all the times he'd said nasty things about gay people. *I wonder if he would protect Tai and me?*

"Sooner or later, we're gonna be accepted. As Candy would put it, I just know it."

That little shared joke put Nate at ease.

Bart approached and plopped two enormous malts on the table. "Drink up, guys."

Tai squealed and pushed Nate's malt closer to him. "These things are far out, dude."

Bart laughed and said, "Burgers coming up soon." Then he turned to go back to the kitchen.

"Take a big slurp, babe."

Nate smiled. He could get used to Tai calling him that. He leaned over, put his lips around the straw, and sucked. *What a trip! I could get stoned on this, and there's not even any drugs in it.*

"Are you in heaven? Huh? Are you?"

"As close as I've ever been, Tai, as close as I've ever been," Nate garbled, not moving his mouth from his straw.

They drank about half their malts. Then Nate cut into the ecstatic silence.

"Okay, Tai," Nate said, pushing aside the malt for a moment, "what about today's stars? I've not heard of Troy Donahue, Sal Mineo, Tab Hunter, Paul Newman, Elvis or the like proclaiming undying love for men, or even any rumors."

"No, you haven't. But I have. Rumor has it Mineo and Hunter are gay. Those others? I don't know about Donahue—but he's pretty, though, isn't he? Newman's pretty firmly married to Joanne Woodward, so I think we can rule him out, although marriage is not always an indicator someone isn't gay. Elvis? Somehow I think there isn't a chance in hell, but if we could turn someone gay, I'd gladly give it a try with El." Tai flashed Nate a lecherous look.

"I haven't seen the Beatles, Jan and Dean, Donovan, or any other music star spouting they only date guys splashed across the pages of *Tiger Beat*. You remember, the mag that you and I make the cover of almost every month?"

"Okay, okay," Tai said. "You're right. And you're not gonna see us there either—not with anybody saying we like other guys. Trust me."

"I want to, Tai. But what happens to us if *Tiger Beat* or any other rag told the world about us? Girls, Tai, young, young girls *worship* us. Do you think they would still do that if they found out we're gay? And do you think their parents would let them?"

"It's okay, Nate." Tai took Nate's hand and held it to his cheek. "You're safe, babe."

"It scares me, Tai. I don't go home to a loving family every night. *Kerry!* is my family. It's the only thing I have. I can't lose that, Tai."

"Trust me, you're not gonna lose anything." Tai kissed Nate's fingertips.

The sincerity in Tai's voice, the look in his eyes, the warmth of his lips comforted Nate. *How can I not trust that?*

Bart brought their food. The burgers were huge. "Think you can swallow it all?" Bart asked, setting down his tray.

"Oh, I think we can handle it, big guy," Tai quipped.

They gobbled their food and slurped the malts. They were every bit as good as Tai had promised.

Wiping his mouth after the last bite, Tai asked, "Game for more unbridled merriment?"

"Sure, Tai," Nate said, ready to trust his friend forever.

"Good, 'cause Joe should be pulling up right about now."

Dissolve to: Exterior—the sidewalk

THEY PASSED onto the sidewalk. As they came through the door, Tai was startled.

"Tai! Hey, babe! What you doing here?"

Nate looked toward the sound. *Who is this? And why is he calling Tai what Tai calls me?*

Tai walked toward the guy, Nate trailing.

"Hey, Kyle," Tai said. "What brings you here?" Nate heard a strange mix of nonchalance, anger, and uneasiness in Tai's voice.

"Best burgers in LA, right?" Kyle said. His voice was breezy, but there was something false in him. Nate heard it. "Had a powerful hunger, man, and only one of Bart's burgers would satisfy it. How's Bart doing, babe? He won't know how to make just me a burger. He's used to doing two bacon cheeseburgers. Right, babe?"

Nate could see Tai starting to bristle. *And what's up with the babe? I'm Tai's babe now. They're no longer a couple.*

"Bart's fine, Kyle," Tai said. Nate saw and heard Tai gritting his teeth, his mouth set tightly. "I'm sure he won't have any trouble with your order. Bart would love to see you, I'm sure." Tai motioned toward the door.

"Great, babe, sure," Kyle said, starting to walk past them. Then he stopped. "But wait," he said, almost casually, although something in Kyle gave Nate the impression this was all planned, "who's your friend?"

Tai humphed. "Nate, Kyle…. Kyle, Nate." Tai spoke quickly, as if he was trying not to blow up and wanted to get this all over with.

"Nate? The heartthrob?" The tone in Kyle's voice made Nate cringe. "I've heard so much about you, Nate. And you are great on the show." He held out his hand for Nate to shake.

What an oily, smarmy, disgusting piece of shit this Kyle is.

Nate reluctantly took his hand, shook it once, and broke away. "Thanks, Kyle."

Let's please just get out of here. He pleaded with Tai with his eyes.

Tai grabbed Nate's arm and pulled him away from Kyle. "Joe's here, Kyle. Nate and I have to go. Enjoy your burger."

Kyle smiled a wicked smile—or at least Nate thought it looked wicked. *What's this all about? Is it really over between them? Or maybe Kyle is not accepting it's over?*

"Sure, babe. Enjoy the rest of your *date*."

The way he said the word stabbed Nate. Under his breath, Tai muttered, "Fuck." That one tiny word was full of fury. Tai pulled Nate toward the curb, leaving Kyle.

Nate started to question Tai about Kyle, but as they reached the curb, they saw Joe was talking to the driver of a long black stretch limousine. Through the restaurant window, they had seen the limo pull up earlier. No one had gotten out of it, which they'd remarked to each other as odd, but then they'd completely forgotten it.

"What's going on, Tai?" Nate was worried. Could Joe really be trusted?

"Don't know, but I'm sure it's nothing," Tai reassured him. And again, under his breath, Nate heard Tai mutter, "I'm just glad we're rid of Kyle."

Me too. And his babe. *The way Kyle said the word sounded clinging, almost dirty. Not like when Tai said it to me.*

The limo driver handed some bills to Joe, who then walked to Tai.

"Looks like you guys got some classier transport arranged for you, Tai. Enjoy."

Tai started to protest, but Joe got in his cab and sped away.

The limo driver walked up to them.

"Mr. Atua?" he said, holding out his hand. "I'm Eric. I've been instructed by Dana to be at your disposal."

Both boys were dumbfounded. They looked at each other and laughed, both from relief and at the diva, who had worked some of her magic once again.

Tai shook Eric's hand.

Opening the door of the car, Eric motioned for Nate to enter. Then Tai scooted in after him.

"Wow," Nate exclaimed. "Where'd the diva find a limousine, do ya think?"

"You kidding?" Tai countered. "Dear old daddy, don't ya think?"

"Right," Nate said, remembering Byron Stone.

Settling back into the plush leather, Tai said, "This is the life, babe, isn't it?"

"Yeah, groovy, man." Nate nodded. And when Tai's velvet *babe* came out, Nate knew the word was golden to him.

Tai laughed. "Listen to you. You're startin' t' get down with the lingo."

Enjoying their newfound luxury, the boys almost didn't see on a tray in front of them a small box, wooden with iron cladding, like a pirate's treasure chest.

"What's this?" Nate asked, pointing.

"Dunno," Tai said. Tai had mischief in his eyes. Then he rummaged into his pocket. "Got so caught up in Byron Stone's lux limo I forgot about this." He held up a key. "Eric slipped it to me. Guessin' this fits that padlock there." He indicated the lock on the chest.

Nate lifted the chest into his lap, then took the key from Tai. The lock clicked open with a turn. Nate lifted the box's lid.

Inside, on a velvet tray, there was an envelope. Across it, in an elaborate script, was "*Heartthrobs.*"

Nate took the envelope, ripped it open, and pulled out a handwritten card:

> *Heartthrobs... you have just opened the box of*
> *endless possibilities. Eric has been instructed to drive*
> *around aimlessly until you buzz him on the intercom*
> *(just pick up the receiver and push the button), at which*
> *time you can give him instructions as to where you want*
> *to go next. He is totally at your disposal.*
> *A luxurious limo, an obedient driver, two young*
> *lovers. What are the possibilities?*
> *Enjoy!.... The diva*
> *P.S. Nate... this is all my doing. Tai didn't know*
> *about my little surprise.*

For the first time that night, Tai seemed a bit flustered, not looking at Nate, just staring at the chest.

"Well…," Nate whispered tentatively, "it would be a shame to disappoint our hostess."

"I was hoping you'd say that," Tai said as he leaned over, placed the pirate's chest on the floor, and began unbuttoning Nate's shirt.

Scene 33

Fade in: Interior—the Berrigan apartment
Later that night

"So where've *you* been?" Paul Berrigan sprawled in the chair, drink in hand. Nate, on his way to his room, stopped and stared.

"I *ast* you a *q'estion*, kid," Paul slurred.

"What do you care?" Nate asked. Nate surprised himself. Talking back to Paul was low on his list. The dutiful son and all. The only time he'd even gotten close was the day he got back from the beach. *But with Tai on my side—and the diva—I guess I just feel like I have more courage.* "And why are you here? What happened to the divorce?"

"Don't *tal'* to me that way," Paul barked. "*I...* your father and *I...* your *man'ger. Tha's* two *goo'* reasons. An' for your *infuhma'ion* your *mothe'* and I *go'* back together."

"Well, goody for you. I hope you'll be very happy spending my money."

Paul gave Nate a *look,* and Nate decided he'd probably gone too far. Best to change the subject back to what Paul wanted to know in the first place.

"I got a burger with Tai, okay?"

"Tai?"

"Yeah, Tai."

"*Wha'*? You *coul'n't fin'* a date?"

"Tai's my friend. I like seeing him." *I want to tell him being with Tai is a helluva lot better than sitting in this hellhole. But best to leave that unsaid. And no way am I going to tell him how I really feel about Tai.* Nate smiled at that thought.

"Look, kid—*fin'* some girls—get out t' premieres. Party. Coul' use more *goo' press.*" Paul took a swig of whiskey.

"Yeah, well there aren't a lot of girls busting down my door for a date, *Daddy*."

"What about *'at* girl—*Cameron'sh* niece—*'at* you took to that opening *las'* month? A real looker, *sh'was*. You got some notice from that *li'l* outing. In fact, I even got a call with a movie offer after *'at*."

That info perked up Nate. He stepped farther into the living room, almost eager for this bit of news.

"A movie?"

"Yeah, some *B-movie* piece of crap. I *can'e'en 'member* the name. *Somethin'* with *purple* in it."

Suddenly, it dawned on Nate what Paul was talking about.

"You mean *Purple Twilight*? I got that?" Nate had read about the casting in *Daily Variety* and had set up the audition himself. It had gone well, but they told him they were seeing a few other guys for the role as well. *Wow! I can't believe I'm going to be in* Purple Twilight.

"Yeah. *Purple Twilight*. I turned *'em* down."

"You what?" Nate exploded. "I went after that all by myself. You didn't have the right to turn them down. Shit!"

"Hey. *Wash* your language. *Y'have* an image to keep up." Another gulp of whiskey. "In fact, *tha's* the *reason* I turned *'em* down."

Nate couldn't believe what he was hearing. *I manage to get something important, and Paul screws it up. I should have known. Why didn't I tell them I don't have a manager? Because they wouldn't have bought it. Paul is well-known around this town, for all the wrong reasons.*

"Was a goddamn B-movie. Nobody would have gone to *shee* it anyway. And *there'sh* no way Kerry woulda approved it. The director wanted *y'* to play a fag." He paused, then added, "*There'sh* no way my son… gonna be a fag. Unh-unh… not a chance in hell."

Dissolve to: Interior—the limo

THAT WAS hard. First I had to pretend that I'm much more experienced than I am—just to put Nate at ease over all this—and then Kyle shows up! I hope Nate got the message when I got rid of Kyle as quickly as I did. I wanted to explain, but then the limo thing and the diva's surprise and all that. It all just got away from me.

Tai sighed.

The phone in the limo rang. Tai picked it up, but before he could say hello he heard: "So—tell me all about it."

"Diva." Tai laughed. "We just dropped Nate off at his building. How'd ya know? You spyin' on us or something?"

"Eric and I are tight. I told him to call me on the car phone the minute you were alone."

"So the driver is your own personal CIA agent, huh?"

"All men are under my spell, Heartthrob. It's a given," she joked.

"And you weave quite a spell, Witchwoman."

"Cut the crap and fill me in. The date?"

"Oh, wow! Incredible. Fabulous, enchanting, captivating, heart-tugging, and pulse-pounding."

Dana giggled. "Been reading *Variety*, have we?"

Tai continued: "A five-star success! Socko! Boffo!"

Tai smiled, thinking of the evening. *I hope Nate's as happy right now as I am.*

"Okay, okay. Enough with the movie review metaphors." Dana giggled. "So, I done good, huh?"

"You bet." Tai whistled. "Outdid yourself. We wuz ridin' in style." *There's no way I'm going to ruin this by giving her a blow by blow. Tonight was ours, just Nate's and mine.*

"Don't care about the *ride*, Heartthrob. Wanna know if you two did the nasty."

"Unh-uh, Diva," Tai said, coyly. "Old Samoan custom… no kiss and tell."

"Come on," Dana pleaded. "You'd better tell, or my friend Eric the driver will leave your butt on the curb."

"Then so be it. I got m' Keds on. I could walk for miles." Tai switched to a German accent. "*You vill get nothing from me, Commandant.*"

She tossed his joke back to him. "*I vant answers, Mein Herr!*"

"Well, my lips are sealed. Sorry, Diva." He paused, then giggled. "Let's just leave it with a good time was had by all." Then he sighed. *So this is what love feels like? Real love? Not like that crap with Kyle?*

"Whoo-ee," Dana whooped. "Now you're talkin'."

Tai laughed at her enthusiasm.

"Tai—" Dana's voice turned serious. "I'm really happy for you both. You deserve it, my little Heartthrobs." Then she added, "And don't worry—your secret's safe with me."

Dissolve to: Interior—Nate's bedroom
Later

WHY'D YOU have to ruin it, Paul? If you'd just kept your mouth shut— or better yet—not even been here when I got back, I'd be happier than I've ever been. I'm in love, and nothing's going to rip that away from me, but I did want that role. And Paul, you are a shit. You had no right to take that away from me. I did learn one thing from this, though. There isn't a chance in hell you'll find out how I feel about Tai. You will not take him away from me.

Nate lay in bed. His mind would not let him sleep. He wanted to nod off thinking of Tai. Dreaming about Tai.

But Paul had ruined it. Purple Twilight *could have been my big break in features. Why, oh why, am I saddled with a shitty father and a hopped-up mother? If only. If only.*

Caught up in the depression that was his life, Nate drifted off. He slept a deep sleep, a sleep that cut him off from the world. At one point, he thought he heard the phone ring, but he was too drowsy to answer it. This sleep was like death. And it felt good because he wanted to shut out the world. The prison that this apartment was for him. Sleeping was release.

He was startled awake by loud knocking, knocking that could have waked the dead. "Wha'?" he shouted, still trying to keep his cocoon of sleep intact.

"Open this door!" It was Monica, sounding sober for a change.

"Go away," Nate shouted at the closed door. "I'm sleeping."

"Don't you have to be at the studio?"

"Not on Sunday," Nate yelled. She knew that. He never worked on Sunday.

"Think again, baby, it's not Sunday. It's Monday morning, and you've got to get up or you'll be very late indeed." Nate heard both concern and desperation in her voice. *She doesn't want me to get fired.*

Who'd pay for her pills? Still, if I've slept since Saturday night, maybe it's concern I do hear. She is my mother, after all.

Nate jumped out of bed. He was still in the clothes he'd worn on his date. He looked at his watch. He had only forty-five minutes to make it to the studio. As it was, he'd already missed morning class. Or what passed for morning class. Mostly, he, Tai, and Dana just checked in with the tutor when they got to the studio. The tutor would not be happy about his blowing her off this morning.

He ran to the door, opened it, and told his mother, "I overslept and woke up totally crazy. I'm gettin' in the shower now." He slammed the door, leaving his mother standing in the hallway.

As he let the cold water wake him up, he lathered his body. *How could I have been asleep for almost thirty hours?* Then it all came back to him. Purple Twilight. *I was so upset about losing that job, I got all worked up. Or worked down, I guess, because I fell asleep unhappier than I've ever been. Maybe I needed to sleep that hurt, that loss, off.* Then he thought of the role again that Paul had given away. He felt a dark cloud forming over him. *No, I can't do this. I have to get to work. Tai will be there. He'll cheer me up. And the diva. She always makes me laugh.*

Transition interlude: Interior—Stan Waldman's office
That morning

WALDMAN SAT at his desk, looking over the previous week's ratings. *Kerry!* was still in the number one slot. It was times like this, knowing the show was a big, big hit that would run for years, that made Stan Waldman a happy man.

Then Kerry Flanagan burst into the room. Kerry Flanagan—Stan Waldman's cross to bear.

He pasted a smile on his face and a fake lilt in his voice. "Hey, Kerry," Stan said. "What can I do you for?"

"Stan, what's this crapola you sent me?"

"I haven't sent you anything, much less crap, since Friday afternoon. But if you're talking about that, then I suppose the cover page will clue you in that it is next week's script." *Come on, Stan. Tread lightly. You don't want to unleash the beast that is Kerry Flanagan.*

"Don't get smart with me, Waldman. I know it's the script, and I know it's shit."

"Okay, Kerry," Stan placated. "What's wrong this week?"

"The whole idea—the bit about my reviewing that queer cook and his show."

"He's not homosexual, Ker. The censors would never allow that... he's just a little *sensitive*. It'll bring in the laughs."

"Sensitive, my ass. He's a prancing fairy, and you know it. And there will be no flamers on my show. You hear me? No fags. I expect this show rewritten. Get those no-talent so-called writers to work for the dough I pay 'em. And they better be quick because the table read is not going to wait."

Waldman sighed.

"And another thing. There are too many kids on this show. They pull focus away from me. I want at least one of 'em gone, you hear me? Fire the Berrigan kid. I've never liked him anyway."

Waldman smiled. Finally, something to report that would make his star happy. "I was on the phone earlier this morning about a deal that was struck. You'll be losing one of those kids you hate. So go have some coffee and relax."

Scene 34

Split screen: Interior—Tai, on the phone with Kyle
Early Monday morning

KYLE: D<small>ID</small> you fuck him?

    Tai: Did you not get it when I told you we were through?

    Kyle: Answer my question.

    Tai: I told you it was over between you and me. I thought we agreed on that point.

    Kyle: Bullshit, Tai, we didn't agree on anything… that *crap* was your idea.

    Tai: So….

    Kyle: Answer me—did you fuck him?

    Tai: Fuck *who*?

    Kyle: You know who. Your *friend*—your costar—the *Tiger Beat Heartthrob of the Year.*

    Tai: Surely you don't mean Nate.

    Kyle: Don't play dumb with me, Tai. You two. At *our* place. Looking all chummy. I saw you two.

    Tai: Were you spying on us? Is that why you showed up at Big Dick's?

    Kyle: Oh, yeah. I was staring into that window for a long, long time.

    Tai: We were just having burgers, dude. That's all.

    Kyle: And you needed a fancy limo to *just get burgers*? I'm not buying it, Samoan Surfer Boy.

    Tai: I don't give a shit if you're *buying* it or not. You and I are through—or rather, we never *were*. I can hang out with anyone I want. And speaking of hanging, I'm hanging up now.

    Kyle: Don't hang up on me, Tai!

    Tai: Yeah? What are you going to do about it?

    Kyle: Just don't hang up, or you'll… be… sorry.

Scene 35

Fade in: Interior—the studio
Monday table read

NATE RUSHED in and looked around, wondering what was happening. No one was there. Then he looked at his watch. All that sleep had made him crazy as hell. He wasn't late. He was early, early, early. Might as well make the best of it, he thought, as he surveyed the little world surrounding him. No one. He could make a little mischief. He grabbed his script, switched it for Candy's, and then put hers in his usual place. He gulped a breath, glad he hadn't gotten caught. Today would be fun. He'd be sitting next to Tai. Dana would be across from him, and together they could be totally professional while all three reliving Saturday night. *I wonder what Tai told Dana about it. I know Tai. He would have given just enough to satisfy her.* And that, since he knew Dana, was eating her up. He sat at his place, glanced again at his watch, and realized he had time to spare. He opened the script.

Within seconds, although Nate had burrowed into the script, he felt warm breath on his neck. Tai showed up almost immediately and sat next to him.

"Freeman won't like your switching seats, dude. You know how directors are." Tai sat, took Nate's hand, and squeezed it. "But I'm glad you did."

Nate looked into Tai's eyes and smiled. "I'm glad you're glad."

Candy clip-clopped in, wearing her clunky loud shoes she always wore to rehearsal, pulled off her rhinestone-studded sunglasses, and stuffed them in her purse. "Hm-hm-hmmm," she huffed. "Now, why would Marv want us in different places? I am so used to sitting in *between* my little loves." She put her hands on the two boys' shoulders and squeezed them together, offering her cheek to each. "Good morning."

Two simple words that said she knew exactly what was going on. As she sat, she chuckled.

She thumbed through her script, occasionally glancing at Nate and Tai, her face glowing.

"You don't fool me, my little darlings." She focused on Nate. "*You* switched the scripts, didn't you, my love?"

Nate blushed.

"You *did*, and I know why—you're in love, aren't you, my pet? With my little Tai. I just know it." Both boys looked away from her gaze. "Don't worry, dearies, I can keep a secret." In classic manner, she made the *zipping of her lips* gesture.

As she turned back to study her script, she murmured, "My babies are growing up. And it's about time."

"*What* is going on here?" Dana hovered over the table.

"Tai's cologne was making me sneeze, dear," Candy said, with a wink at the two boys. "I asked Nate to switch with me."

"She knows, Diva," Tai said.

"Thank God," Dana swore. "This secret-keeping is eating a hole in my gut."

"So you know, too, dear?" Candy quizzed Dana, then cast a faux hurt look at the boys. "So I'm not your only confidant?"

Tai reached across a severely blushing Nate to touch Candy's arm. "It's a new thing. Don't feel like we've been keeping anything from you. We still love you."

"Yeah, Can, you're our *granny*." From across the table, Dana held out her arms like she was hugging Candy, and then she blew her a kiss.

"How about *auntie*, dear?" Candy brushed her hair back with her hand. "Granny sounds so *old*."

"You'll never be old, Can. You're young as spring," Dana said, plopping down in her chair. The boys joined her with "We just know it."

They all laughed.

"Enough revelry," Dana said. "I have news that you all three must hear before it gets out to the general public. They will be clamoring for info, you know."

"Spit it out, Diva," Nate said.

"This is my last episode of *Kerry!*"

All talking at once, the three—Tai, Nate, and Candy—clamored for info, as Dana had predicted.

"No, my dear friends," Dana said coyly, "I have not been fired. I've fired them."

There was a long pause as that sunk in. Then Tai demanded, "Okay—now spill the beans, Diva."

"Well, as you all three, my closest comrades, know, my great love is *musical* theat*uh*. I took this part just to get something on my résumé." Dana, in true Dana-ness, grew more elaborate in her description. She was definitely an actress, playing her story for all it was worth. "They promised the *world* when I auditioned. I was promised a song every now and then, and my character was to progress to becoming a singing actress, in a school play, community theater, anything the writers could come up with." She paused for effect. She faux-frowned. "But then they hired the Heartthrob back." She let that sink in, like it was a lead weight she'd dropped. Then she went on with an air of fake graciousness. "Oh, don't get me wrong—I'm glad they did." She dropped the pretension and became the Dana they all three loved. "Because I love you dearly, my sweet." She batted her eyelashes at Nate. "But with Nate back, my role has diminished. A wisecrack here, a reaction there. No songs. No progression on the avowed storyline that would put me on my pathway to stardom. So my dear, dear daddy gleaned that I was a bit unhappy with my career." She looked at each of them, one at a time, letting that sink in.

"Cut the crap, Diva. Get on with it," said Tai.

She smiled triumphantly. "Daddy knows Sammy Davis, Jr. Big buddies with Sam. So Daddy talked to Sammy, and Sammy agreed to see me—he, his director, his producer, his choreographer—practically everyone who is involved with Sammy's musical *Golden Boy*. You probably know this already, but it's a big, big hit in NYC. Daddy flew me up there a few weeks ago so I could audition. They liked me. No, they adored me. After all, what's not to love?"

Nate saw Tai and Candy rolling their eyes. He joined them. Then Candy spoke up. "Go on, dear."

Dana took a breath and then spat out her news, finally. "I'm going to be in the chorus, but I also get to understudy the role Lola Falana plays, and with any luck, Lola will have to miss a few performances and my amazing talents will be revealed to the world. So, as much as I absolutely adore you, you magical, marvelous creatures, I must depart for my destiny, the bright lights of Broadway." She was gasping for air as she ended her barrage of words.

"I'm so happy for you, dear. You're going to be a big, big star, I just know it," Candy gushed.

"So how did you get out of your contract here?" Tai asked. "That had to have involved a lot of negotiating, a lot of lawyers, a lot of promises."

Dana smiled wickedly. "Byron Stone. Money *can* buy happiness."

Nate sat stone silent. He was losing her. He'd lost *Purple Twilight*, and now he was losing the diva. *What next? Will Candy drop from a heart attack? Will Tai suddenly disappear?*

Before he could respond to Dana's news, their director breezed in, and as predicted, he was not happy. "What happened here? You know I don't like change," he barked.

Candy sneezed, "A-a-a-a-choo!" She grabbed a tissue from the box on the table. "Trade with me, Dana dear. I'm afraid I'm not far enough away from that killer cologne Tai has on today."

Dissolve to: Interior—Nate's dressing room
A little while later

AFTER LOCKING the dressing room door, Tai planted a long, wet kiss on Nate's lips. Nate wanted to feel happy, but he was still lost in Dana's news.

"What's up? I thought you'd like that." Tai voiced his disappointment.

"It was nice, Tai, but—"

"But nothing." Tai grabbed Nate's cheeks and kissed him again, this time longer, more passionately. Resting his cheek on Nate's, Tai murmured, "You are sweet, sweet honey to me. I could do this all afternoon."

A banging at the door interrupted them.

"Hey, you clowns, I know what illicit acts are being performed in there. Let me in before I alert the authorities. My godfather's a cop, you know." Dana's insistent voice penetrated the door.

"Okay, okay," Tai said, unlocking the door. "Can't a couple of guys have a little privacy?"

The door swung open, and Dana rushed in, slamming the door behind her. "So, did you like the limo?"

"It was nice," Nate answered, with no enthusiasm.

"I really must have interrupted something big. You're not yourself, Heartthrob. What gives?"

"You."

"Me?"

"You're leaving us. It makes me sad."

"*Oh, you*," she said, pointing at him. "Quit your acting. I know you're happy for me. You're not gonna rain on my parade with your little fake pity party."

"No, really. I am happy for you, but here's the thing. I have two friends in this entire world—three if you count Candy, but she's not our age—and I don't like the idea that one of them is going thousands of miles away."

"It'll be okay, Heartthrob." She grabbed him into a hug. "Daddy's got a private jet, you know? I'll fly back when I can, and you and Tai can fly to see me." She broke away and stared him in the eyes. "And there's always the telephone."

"But it won't be the same," Nate said, dropping onto the sofa. *Is my heart breaking here? I never thought I'd get so wrapped up in the diva. But she grows on you.*

"Look, buddy boy." She sat next to him. "I'm not going anywhere—well, except to New York City—but I'll always be in your life, working my magic, meddling like a yenta, because you two are my boys." She pulled Tai onto her lap and cradled them both with her arms. "And when Dana Warrenton has friends, they stay friends, thick and thin, good times and bad times, LA or NYC. So just put a smile on that face. Erase your doubts. And tell me what happened in that limo Saturday night. Now. I have to, have to know."

For that fleeting moment, Nate was happy again. He wanted to believe her. He scooted over, making room for Tai to sit next to him, between him and the diva.

As Tai settled in, he said, "I told you it's private."

"Private, huh?" Dana smirked.

Nate blushed.

"Don't worry, Heartthrob." She grinned at Nate. "I don't know what went on in Daddy's car, but I *can* imagine. And that's probably hotter than anything you two little *boys* could ever do."

"Don't listen to her, Nate. She's just jealous." Tai kissed Nate on the nose.

"So—" Tai hesitantly drew his words out. "—are, uh, Eric, and, uh, the love mobile, available again, say, uh, this Friday night after the taping?"

"Sorry, Heartthrob," Dana blurted, "you two are on your own. Dad's going to be in town, and he has this thing about having his car available for his own use."

"Damn," Tai spat.

"Look," Dana said. "I have an idea—a little parting gift. Redeemable only if you both spend Friday night with me to give me a loving send-off. I'm flying to Teterboro on Saturday to begin my new, fabulous life. But if you'll party with me on Friday night, I can arrange another kind of party for you two for Saturday night."

"We're intrigued," Tai said.

"So, Dad's got a special arrangement at the Riviera in Palm Springs. You know, where Sinatra and Dino and the Rat Pack play and stay." Nate looked at her blankly. She shook her head. "What is it you don't understand? Rat Pack? Riviera?" She waved her hand. "No matter. The point is the folks at the Riviera make a suite available for Daddy dear whenever he gives them a nod. And Daddy will do anything his little daughter asks. You guys can manage a little getaway on Saturday, can't you? A little overnight for some kissing and some hugging and some loving. And golf. There is golf available. It is Palm Springs, after all." She laughed. "And all at Byron Stone's expense. Is your Mustang gassed up, Nate?"

"It can be," Tai whooped. "Wow, Diva, you're a total gas. Palm Springs, here we come."

Palm Springs? Nate tried to wrap his head around all these developments. *Why aren't I happy? Party with Dana on Friday night after the taping; Saturday with Tai, away from all this madness, away from the pills, away from the booze. I should be over the moon.*

But Dana is leaving. Going a zillion miles away. And no matter what she says, life is going to be different. And I don't like that kind of different.

Scene 36

Fade in: Interior—Nate's bedroom
Shortly after

MONICA WAS sprawled on the couch, Pall Mall in one hand, a drink in the other. Paul was in his usual position, drunkenly lounging on the easy chair, he, too, clutching a Scotch. *Nothing changes around here.* Nate swept right past them, heading for his room, when he came back from rehearsal.

He heard Paul slur, "Need to talk to ya, kid."

Nate ignored him. He went through the door of his room, slammed it, and threw himself on the bed.

How can Dana just up and leave? I know I should be happy for her because she's chasing her dream, but I don't want to lose her. She'll go to New York, become a big star, and she won't have time for me, no matter what she says now.

A loud, insistent pounding on his door shook Nate from his misery. But only for a second.

"Go away. I'm tired," he shouted, lacking energy, though. *Why can't he leave me alone?* It had to be Paul because Monica was so strung out by this time of the day, she couldn't manage to knock that loud.

"Open up." Nate ignored the order, knowing Paul was too drunk to do anything about his insubordination. Then Paul began his tirade again. "You nee' to get ya butt in gear, kid," he heard Paul say through the door. "The tutor called. Ya think you'd get away with skippin' classes? Not doin' homework? You wanna get in hot water with the state? You know they keep a close eye on you kid actors. Open this door, I say."

"And I say go away," Nate called from his bed. This time, Nate couldn't muster enough enthusiasm to fight with Paul. He could only hope his words would appease his drunken father. "I'll do the homework later. Tai told me what it is," he lied. "Now, I just need to rest. It's been a rough day." Then, despite his vow not to rile Paul up, he added, "Not that you'd care."

"Well, I'm tellin' ya now, ya better not screw this up," Paul, still outside the door, said. *The door's not locked. He could come in instead of just yelling at the top of his lungs. But that's not Paul's style. He'd rather act like a dictating goon than come in and hold a conversation.* "I gotta go for some 'pointments. Be late gettin' back. But I wanna see that homework in the mornin', ya hear?"

"Yeah, I hear," Nate said.

"Whadya say?"

"I hear you," Nate shouted. "Loud and clear, General." *He'll be so hung over he either won't be able to focus on anything I show him or he—and this is more likely—won't even remember to ask.*

"Get on it, I'm tellin' ya." *Paul always has to have the last word.* "I'm not gonna have you pulled off the show because you can't take care a' things."

And then there was blissful silence. Paul must have left the house.

I'm so sick of it all. I want a life like Tai's. His mother worships him, and his dad is cool. They care. And they don't get strung out on pills and booze. Even Dana's life would be better than this. Her mother seems to care about her. And her dad may be always out of town or busy, but he at least takes care of her in his own way. My shit-dad gets me fired from a movie I really wanted to do; Dana's dad gets her a spot in a Broadway show.

And with that thought, the thought of the diva's leaving came crashing back. He would do anything to get her to stay. Or better yet, he'd do anything to get her to let him go with her. To hell with *Kerry!* He wanted to run—run away from Monica and Paul, run away from Kerry Flanagan, run away from this life that wasn't a life. The only thing good right now he had going for him was Tai.

The phone jangled. Nate was so lost in his own misery, he at first didn't even recognize the ringing. After all, his phone rang so seldom. More now that he was with Tai, but still it didn't ring off the wall, like most teenagers' phones.

He almost didn't answer. He didn't want to deal with anything else, and it seemed shit was piling up on him daily—actually, minute by minute. But it was likely Tai on the other end of the line, and he needed some cheering up. He answered.

"Hey, dude." It *was* Tai. Nate brightened a bit.

"Tai, I needed to hear from you," Nate said. He hoped his voice had the smile in it that was on his face. The first time he'd smiled since Dana's news.

"Needed? Why's that?"

Nate wasn't about to unload on Tai. He wouldn't scare him away. He needed to hear his golden voice. "Nothing really, now that I'm talking to you. You make me happy." He never, in a million years, thought he'd be saying that to anyone, much less a guy. But it didn't matter; Tai did make him happy.

Tai chuckled on the other end. "I'm glad, dude. But you may not be so happy when I tell you what I have to tell you."

Nate's heart sank. *Why did I let myself get happy? I knew it wouldn't last. I don't deserve to be happy.* "What is it, Tai?" he asked, not really wanting to know the answer. What he wanted was to hear Tai tell him everything would be fine. He wanted to hear Tai tell him he loved him.

"About Palm Springs." Tai paused. Nate's spirit plunged. "I can't go. At least I think I can't."

"What's that supposed to mean? You think you can't?" *Why, oh why, is this happening? Looking forward to the weekend is the only thing holding me together.* Panic flooded Nate's body.

"My parents have plans that include me. I tried to talk them out of it, but they're pretty set on me being with them. My cousin's first communion is Sunday. There is a huge family to-do, and believe me, in my family, when two gather for anything, twenty-two follow. My mom and dad say I have to be there."

"Tai, I was counting on this weekend. I don't know if can hold up. Losin' the movie, Paul bitchin' me out because the tutor called, Dana's leaving, and now, no Palm Springs. It's gettin' to me, Tai." He felt tears welling up from deep, deep down in his gut.

"Wait. Back up. Losing the movie? What movie?"

"You know I auditioned for *Purple Twilight*?"

"Yeah. And you're saying you didn't get it? We both know that's the way of the business. Don't beat yourself up over that, Nate."

"I can't believe I didn't tell you this earlier. I did get it. But they called Paul, since he's my manager—at least that's what he calls himself. Anyway, he turned it down. So a role I won, a character I really wanted to play, someone I could sink my teeth into, is going to someone else. Not because I didn't get it, but because the man who's supposed to be looking out for my best interests is too stupid to know how important this movie is to me, to my career."

"Oh, Nate, babe, I'm so, so sorry. I know how much you wanted that. I would be so pissed if my manager did that to me. Luckily, Mama hired the best for me. But enough about this. Look, I'm gonna keep tryin' to sway my parents. I can whine with the best of 'em. Maybe if I whine long enough and loud enough, they'll let me miss this big event. Believe me, with a huge family of Catholics, there'll be other confirmations— plenty of 'em. Hang in there, babe. I'll get back to ya. It'll be good news. I may not break through the Catholic mafia attitude tonight or even tomorrow, but I'll get it done. Keep your fingers and toes crossed. I'll get this done. For you, babe. For you." A pause. "Now, I got homework of my own to do. See ya tomorrow. Slather those lips with Chapstick tonight because I plan to rough 'em up with some hot kisses tomorrow. Bye, now."

"Wait, Tai—" Nate called. "Explain the assignment to me. I gotta do it, if only to appease Paul."

Tai spent the next few minutes going over the tutor's instructions. Just that mundane explanation soothed Nate. When Tai finished, they exchanged goodnights.

Nate hung up the phone. The idea of Tai's kisses washed over him, washed away all the grief. But as he thought back over the conversation, he fixated on Tai's "Mama hired the best for me" comment. That just pushed Nate back over the cliff. *Tai has a manager who cares about him, not the money he can bring in. Tai's manager got him that Samoa gig. Maybe that movie wasn't the best offer he could have gotten for Tai, but it gave Tai a chance to see relatives and visit his home country and enjoy himself. Paul got me nothing for the summer break. And when I finally got an offer I maneuvered myself into, Paul killed that.*

I'm saddled with loser parents. Losers who will never be more than that. And I won't even have Dana to tell my troubles to. And Tai? The one thing I'm looking forward to, the Palm Springs thing, is going to be cancelled. All I want to do is leave it all. Just drift away from my life.

Nate looked at his alarm clock. It was only 5:00 p.m., far from bedtime. But all he wanted was sleep. Blessed sleep. To forget this horrible, horrible day. He decided a short nap would be okay. Maybe it would put his mind at rest. He could sleep twenty minutes, get up, get a bite to eat—even though he was not one bit hungry—do his homework, study his script, and then go to bed for the night.

He lay on his side and closed his eyes. When he opened them again, he was staring at the clock. It said seven o'clock. Two-hour nap. He hadn't intended for that to happen, but he could still manage to get everything done. Then he looked at the window. The sun shone brightly. It was far too bright for seven o'clock at night. He switched on the TV. The *Today* show was on. He had slept the last fourteen hours. So much for a short nap.

Then it all crashed back. The movie. Paul the manager. Monica the pill freak. Dana's leaving. Tai's family.

All he wanted to do was go back to sleep.

Scene 37

Fade in: Exterior—the highway
The following weekend

LONG WEEK. Nate felt he'd been the loser in a prizefight. The only thing that kept him going was Tai's *cheer up* mantra. Tai spent the week chanting that and then expounding on how much fun the weekend was going to be, a chance to kick back, let their minds go blank, and just enjoy. As good as that sounded, Nate wasn't convinced. *Cheer me up? That sounds like what bubble gum does. What's happening to me needs more than cheering up. I need a major overhaul of my life.*

But they were finally on the road to Palm Springs. Nate tossed Tai the keys to the 'Stang when he picked him up. He was afraid he would not be able to concentrate on the road, and the last thing he needed was a headline that read "Sitcom Star Kills Costar in a Fiery Crash." Now he was just trying to absorb Tai's constant chatter and hope it got him out of his funk. But all he could think about was the previous night.

Taping of the show went well, despite the fact that Nate didn't feel like he had a grip on anything. He'd spent the week virtually sleeping every minute he could find. He begged out of lunches at the commissary, telling Tai and Dana and even Candy that he had too much homework to catch up on, too much script studying to do. He was not certain they bought his ruse, but they at least backed off. Tai was the hardest to convince. But Tai loved him, and Nate figured that's what kept him from pressing too hard. So even Tai gave him his space. And he used that space not to do that homework or to study his script. All he did was sleep. Blissful slumber that pushed away his troubles for the brief minutes he had to himself.

But then the taping was finished, and it was time for the dreaded farewell party for the diva. It would be just the three of them, Dana, Tai, and him. Nate had mixed feelings about that. It wouldn't require him acting like he was glad for Dana in front of the other cast members, but it also meant he was going to have to play like Dana's leaving was one of the best things that could happen to her. *I may have won a Maggie, but I'm not that good an actor* was the thought that raced through his mind all week.

But when push came to shove, he played his part well. He was reasonably sure the diva didn't have a clue he was doing the best acting job of his life. He joked, he laughed, he told her he would miss her, and yes, by the end of the evening, he shed tears. But just enough tears to say "I'll miss you" and not enough to show how much his heart was tearing apart.

Given his history of the past week and hoping this Palm Springs trip would cure this depression plaguing him, he set three alarm clocks when he got home. He didn't want to sleep through till Sunday, which he was likely to do if he let himself do what he wanted to do, deep down. No, he was determined to pick Tai up on time, and together they would have a weekend to remember.

And now they were speeding toward State Highway 111. The scenery, Tai had told him, was supposedly breathtaking. But so far no beauty outside the car registered with Nate.

"Dude, we are lucky as hell. The gods are with us, I tell ya. You won't believe the promises I had to make to get Mama and Dad to agree to me missin' my cousin's thing on Sunday. As it is, we're gonna have ta rush back for the family dinner Sunday night. Tell me you don't mind. We got a whole night alone together, at least. And if I know Byron Stone, this place'll be lush."

It registered with Nate that Tai was talking, but he wasn't really listening. He was too lost in his own misery. Paul gave him the endless third degree about this weekend trip he was going on, and Monica? To listen to her, her *little baby* was going off to war. He talked 'em both down, mostly because he knew that Monica'd be sleeping it off when he left the apartment on Saturday morning, and Paul would already be ensconced in his Vegas suite with some redhead—or blonde or brunette— or whatever the color of the day was. But knowing they didn't really care, he wondered why they put him through torture when all he wanted to do was sleep.

"Copilot, this is Air Traffic Control. Are you with us? Do you copy?"

After Nate didn't respond, Tai reached over and punched him on the shoulder. "Nate, whazzup?"

Nate shook his head, trying to banish the negative thoughts. He looked at Tai. "Huh?"

"Lighten up, dude. We're on our way to luxury. Alone. Think of it. Just us two. Nobody hovering, spyin' on our every move. Granted, there'll be a passel of geezer golfers swarming around, but they won't bother us. Get happy, dude. You might even see your friend."

That statement startled Nate. He didn't have any friends— at least not in Palm Springs. He had Tai, he had Dana, and he had Candy. No secret friends lurking in the Springs. "What you talkin' 'bout? Friend?"

"I did some readin' up on this place, this Riviera. It seems Elvis the Pelvis has been known to stay there."

Nate cut his eyes sideways toward Tai. "So? He's not my friend. You know that."

"What I know is that, according to you, El came right up to you and talked to you at that movie premiere. Am I right?"

Nate smiled, thinking of that. "Yeah, he did. Wasn't much, but he's a really nice guy. Like I told you, he just wanted to tell me he liked me on the show. Blew me away that a big star like him would not only watch *Kerry!* but recognize me and take the time to come over. But that doesn't make us friends. Just makes him a great guy."

"Nate, Nate, Nate. Big stars don't just talk to everybody. Believe me, if Elvis Presley took the time at his own movie premiere to talk to you, that's a big, big thing. And I'm just sayin' we might run into him up here. But you're mine, all mine. Don't get any ideas." Tai laughed.

"Sure, Tai. The most famous and sexiest man on earth—a man who dates the likes of Ann-Margret, the sexiest woman on earth—is gay and wants me. I think you're safe, Tai." Nate reached over and caressed Tai's cheeks.

"Stranger things have happened," Tai said with a wicked smile and fake leer.

Tai's demeanor, his smile, the fakely sinister lilt in his voice all combined to lift Nate. *What the hell. I'm gonna enjoy this. Forget Paul, forget Monica, and forget Dana. This is me and Tai together, alone, and I'm ready for this.*

"You're right, Tai. Let's get this party started." Nate fiddled with the radio until he found Shirley Ellis blaring out "The Name Game." The boys sang along at the top of their lungs, and when she finished and the DJ went to a commercial, Nate, wailing over the drone of the DJ, sang out "Tai, Tai…." until he finished the entire name game with Tai's name. Tai countered with "Nate, Nate, banana fanna…." until he joyously gamed Nate's name. They finished and life was good. *For the first time this week*, Nate noted, but he quickly banished that thought. Then Petula Clark sang of the fun going "Downtown" and the boys once again sang along.

When Petula finished, Tai blurted out, "When you're with Nate and life is ever so great, you will surely go—to Palm Springs." Tai parodied Petula's song.

Nate added, "Just listen to the sound of old men hitting their golf balls and then, laughing at the fun you have—you know you can't lose." The words didn't rhyme or even make a lot of sense or really even fit the melody, but making up their own song was the most fun Nate had had in a long, long time.

"In just a couple of hours, dude, we're gonna be in the heart of gay heaven," Tai said.

"'Splain, yourself, Lucy." Nate was having so much fun already and totally enjoying the lifting of the black cloud over him that he couldn't resist his best Ricky Ricardo imitation.

"So rumor has it, m' friend, that old Hollywood used to—well, still do—go to Palm Springs in droves because it was far enough away from LA they could get away from it all and enjoy all sorts of *dee-licious dee-lights*. Lotta closet cases have homes here, tucked away in palm tree grottos, outta sight from the world. Lots and lots of orgies. Hotbeds of steaming sex. Real men doing real things to other real men."

"Sure, Tai." Nate laughed. "You're making this up, right?"

"Nah, dude. Bart told me. You remember Bart? At Big Dick's? He knows all about it. He's even been to a coupla those parties. You know Rock Hudson? He's *gay*, dude. He has pool parties at his mansion in Hollywood that are nothing but good-lookin' young hunks. In Palm Springs, there's a place called the Racquet Club, owned by a couple of old Hollywood actors. Bart says Rock Hudson and Tab Hunter and a buncha other actors—guys we always thought were straight and narrow. A lot of girls would be heartbroken if they knew they weren't—would party in their birthday suits at the pool there. You know Cary Grant, who was in that movie called *Charade* with Audrey Hepburn?"

"Yeah. That was a fun movie."

"Well, he owns a house in the Springs that has a wall around it so high that nobody, but nobody, can see what goes on inside it. Rumor has it that lots and lots a gay stuff is what's going on, dude."

"Tai, you kill me. I don't know if I should believe you or not. Rock Hudson? Cary Grant? Come on."

"It's true. Swear ta God." Tai held up his fingers in a Boy Scout salute.

"If you say so," Nate said. *I have so much to learn.*

"I *am* saying so. And if you see any gorgeous, tanned man-flesh at the pool that appeals to you, just remember this: you're mine, babe, mine, mine, mine." As he repeated the word over and over, Tai tickled Nate, one hand on the wheel, one in Nate's ribs.

This. This is right. No other word for it. I'm glad we're here at this very moment, pulling me away from everything that brings me down.

Nate's happiness was short-lived. His mind wandered and he found himself opening his mouth before thinking of the potential consequences.

"Why *me*? Tai, you're experienced. You've had other boyfriends." *Damn! I had to let myself go to the dark side.* But it was a question that had been eating at him.

Tai took his eyes off the road long enough to say, "Boy*friend*. Just one." Then he focused again on the road ahead.

"And that meant nothing, Nate. Kyle and me? Well, we were just experimenting. He had more experience than I did. Hell, I had none. So, in a way, he took advantage of me. But I let him." He paused a moment. Then he continued. "And I'm not sorry about it. I learned who I am, and eventually, I came to terms with it. It's not sex. That's just what happens. It's a way of loving, and love is never wrong. Yeah, the law may say it's wrong, but that's gonna be taken care of by the Civil Rights Act, ya hear? Everybody equal, that's what it says. And I believe it."

There it is again. Tai and his civil rights law. I hope he's right about how magical that thing is going to be. But change doesn't come overnight, and Tai doesn't seem to realize that. Nate shook his head, a tiny side-to-side tremor. Tai didn't see it; his eyes were on the road ahead. Nate's shake was not only an affirmation that he was probably right about that "taking a long time" thing, but it was also a motion to banish the thought from his head. Nothing was going to spoil this weekend. They were here, and Nate was planning to relish every moment, enough to last him a lifetime.

"Ya know what?" Tai asked. "From the first moment I saw you, I said to myself, 'There's someone I could love for the rest of my life.' And then I hoped and prayed that I'd get that chance."

This time, Tai paused long enough that the silence was deafening, Nate thought. *Should I say something? Should I ask another question? Is he doubting what he just said? Am I supposed to make my own declaration?*

Tai finally broke his silence with a honk on the horn. A honk on this deserted highway that only the desert lizards and buzzards were audience to.

"You make me happy, Nate." Tai reached over, took Nate's hand, and brought it up to his lips. He held it there, just pressing it to his soft lips.

Nate's heart filled. He could be happy if this moment lasted forever, for it warded off the evil his thoughts were often filled with. But he had to respond.

"And you make me happy too." Nate knew this was a binding moment, a time they would look back at, that place in their lives when they first married their feelings for eternity. And that thought gave him courage. "Believe me, there's not much room for happiness with Monica and Paul."

"They give you any grief over this trip?"

"They grilled me like Nazi inquisitors, but I pretty much told them nothing. By the time this morning came, Monica was too passed out to care, and Paul was long gone. I'd bet they're glad to get rid of me. And I'm happy as hell to be away from the pills and booze."

"Well, no hopped-up Mama, no soused-up Papa this weekend." He paused. "And no Samoan Mama, either."

"No way, Tai. You're not saying that. Mama Ruthie's the best mom in the world."

"Yeah, she is. But sometimes, you know, you just want a little freedom from the *mothering*."

"You'll never make me believe that. She cares about you, she accepts you for who you are… what more could you want?"

"You're right," Tai admitted. "I do have it good. I guess I'm just thinkin' 'bout all the beggin' and pleadin' I had to do to come on this trip. Nah, you're right… my parents are *the* best. And they *do* accept me. They don't know I'm gay, but when the time comes and I'm ready to open that closet door, I'm sure they'll be okay with it. At least I hope so. They're very strict Catholics, but they also totally buy into the 'Jesus is love' thing."

"Ya know what? I'd rather come out to Mama Ruthie than to Monica or Paul. Mama Ruthie might take a little time to absorb it all, but in the long run, she'll accept it because she loves you, Tai. Monica and Paul? Monica would act all wounded like she failed as a mother, and Paul would cuss a blue streak about how I'm throwing away my career. It wouldn't be pretty."

"Well, neither one of us is throwing away his career. We can keep this to ourselves, and the truth will never come out. As Candy would say, I just know it."

They both laughed at that, and the temporary cloud was lifted.

Tai slapped him on the back, then said, "Enough. This is our weekend… just you, me, and Byron Stone's luxury retreat at the Riviera. And Elvis. Don't forget Elvis." And Tai cackled another wicked laugh.

"Why does Stone keep this arrangement at this place?"

"The Riviera's the hippest, the most luxurious place in the desert. And it's close to the best golf courses in the world."

"And, according to the diva, her daddy does love his golf." Nate put his hand on Tai's leg.

"You tryin' to turn me on, dude?" Tai joked.

But the words were no joke to Nate. They immediately brought a rise out of him. He shifted in the Mustang's bucket seat, trying to accommodate this new development.

Tai leered at Nate. "Want me to take care of that for you? I only need one hand to steer."

"Oh, great. That's all we need. I can see the headlines in the Enquirer now: 'Teen TV Stars Perish Having Sex on the 111.' No, Tai, I can wait. We have all weekend."

Montage: Interior—Byron Stone's suite, the Riviera dining room

"CAN YOU believe this place?"

"It rivals the Malibu Beach Shack, that's for sure." Nate pointed out the wall of front windows. "The view's amazing." Nate stared out the window.

Tai raced up the stairs and started shrieking. "Check this out, dude."

Nate followed Tai's voice and found his lover—for that's what he was—sprawled across an enormous bed piled with pillows straight out of an Arabian night.

Tai reached up and pulled Nate next to him.

"Feel this," he cooed as he rubbed the silky, satiny comforter on Nate's cheek. He whispered in Nate's ear. "Turn you on?"

Nate laughed nervously. "Later, Samoan—I'm hungry." Nate jumped up. "Let's see the rest of the place and then head off for lunch."

"I'm hungry, but not for food." Tai leered at Nate.

"Save it for later, beach boy." Nate pecked Tai on the lips, and in doing so, he placed himself within Tai's clutches. Tai wrestled him to the bed, pinning him underneath him. Nate continued to protest, but he knew he didn't mean it.

Button by button, Tai slowly undressed Nate. He kept his eyes on Nate's. They seemed to burn holes in Nate's brain, telling him to surrender. And Nate fell for Tai's seduction. He relaxed and let Tai do what Tai had to do. And what Nate wanted him to do.

Tai covered Nate's abs with kisses, moving like he was striking keys on a typewriter, only instead of fingers pushing keys, Tai's lips were planting kisses. And when Tai finished on one side, he went back to the other, like he was moving down a page, typing his love for Nate over and over.

When Tai got to Nate's jeans, he fixed his teeth around Nate's zipper and pulled it down. Tai pulled Nate's fly apart, reached in, and pulled Nate's now full member from his pants. He took it in his mouth, encircling his lips around it, and plunged it deep into his mouth. Up and down and around and up and down and around, Tai worked his magic until Nate exploded. Nate shuddered, but it was a good shudder. He'd never felt that great before.

Releasing Nate from his mouth, Tai laughed. "And there will be more. Much, much more." He moved his face up to Nate's and kissed him gently. "Now, how about that food? I'm starving, and you're keeping me from eating. Well, eating food, that is." Tai's sly remark made Nate laugh.

"I don't think I was the one that started this, Samoan. But I'm glad you finished it."

The boys scurried downstairs. Off the dining area was a patio, surrounded by a multitude of lush plants.

"Hey, Tai, you see what I see? Look at that pool over there," Nate squealed. He pointed past the patio plants.

"Wow, man. Can you say skinny-dipping in the moonlight?"

"Only if you can also say, 'Please, Officer, don't arrest us' as he carts us off to jail for indecent exposure."

Tai pulled Nate's head to him and kissed his forehead. "But ah, babe, it would be worth it."

"Tell that to Kerry Flanagan."

"Shh. Don't mention Satan. This is *our* weekend." Tai motioned to the patio. "See the inviting loungers? If we push them together, we have a hot evening ahead of us, under the stars." He motioned to their surroundings. "Pretty secluded. No telling what two hot-blooded young boys can get into in the dead of night." He raised his eyebrows up and down lecherously.

Nate shook his head at Tai's joke. "That's it. I'm going to perish from lack of food while you stand around and make jokes. Let's head to the restaurant. You remember Diva called ahead and arranged everything for us. She says they have fantastic seafood."

"And it's all on Byron Stone's tab. Praise the Lord for divas with rich dads."

The resort restaurant was really nice. It was filled, however, with older men, dressed for their rounds of golf.

"This crab is fantastic," Tai exclaimed, cracking another crab leg.

Nate stuffed a shrimp in Tai's mouth. "Well, you gotta try one of these."

"Unbelievable," Tai cried, bits of chewed shrimp flying from his open mouth.

"What?" Nate laughed, wiping his face with his napkin. "Were you born in the rainforest? Didn't your mama teach you any manners, island boy?"

"Sorry, I get a little carried away sometimes when I eat. I just *love* food, dude."

"And I love you, *dude*." Nate stared into Tai's eyes. For a moment, they just sat, gazing and smiling.

Tai broke the silence. "Eat up. We got partyin' to do. When we get outta here, we'll do the tourist bit."

"Shouldn't we put on disguises or something? You know how those girls can be if they see us in public."

"Forget about the screaming girls. They aren't here, unless Grandpa coerced them into coming. And they're likely getting their tans on behind Grandpa's private wall around Grandpa's private pool. Look, guy, there are two kinds of people in the Springs. One group is average age seventy-five—they're not gonna care 'bout us. The other, well, just say they think like we do and we want them to care about us. There are beautiful bulging muscles out there, waiting for us to feast our eyes on. We might bump into Paul Peterson—you know the dude from *The Donna Reed Show*."

"Is he gay?"

"Not that I've heard, but we can always hope." Tai leered at Nate.

"Maybe I could turn him." He smirked, teasing Tai.

"Dudn't work that way, dude. Besides, you're all mine."

Nate's stomach jumped, thinking of later. Then he quickly added, "Well then—let's see what this town is all about."

Dissolve to: Interior—the suite

BACK AT the suite, Nate opened one of the take-out cartons they had picked up for dinner and inhaled. "There's nothing better than sweet-and-sour pork. I'm starving."

Tai nuzzled Nate's neck. "Yeah, you're always starvin'." Nate almost pulled away, but Tai turned Nate around and smothered him with kisses. Nate began to melt. Tai's hands explored Nate's neck, his back, his butt, and finally he planted one hand firmly between Nate's legs. "What's this, huh? Can I have my dessert before dinner?" Tai murmured.

Nate let his body answer for him.

Tai led him up the stairs and to the bed. Laying him gently down, Tai continued covering Nate with kisses as he tugged at Nate's buttons. Soon, Nate's clothes were undone.

"Lose these," Tai whispered, pulling at Nate's jeans.

As Nate peeled off his clothes, Tai shed his T-shirt and shorts.

The two stood and stared at each other. They drank in the sight of their lithe, supple, naked bodies.

Tai grabbed Nate and threw him down on the bed, then turned him over. He opened the drawer on the bedside table.

"Wow, man, the diva really thinks of everything. There's all we could ever need in here."

Tai opened a jar of Vaseline and took a glob out with two fingers. He smeared it on his hands and warmed it. Gently, he prepared Nate. Then they made love—unabandoned, hot. Love like Nate had never imagined. Love that joined them together not for the moment, but for all time. Love that made the world right.

And afterward they slept.

Waking up, Nate looked over at a window. It was dark. They must have slept a long time. He looked at the clock: 9:00 p.m.

Nate gazed at Tai. He looked so peaceful, so beautiful. A curl had fallen onto his forehead. Nate brushed it back. Tai slowly opened his eyes and grinned.

"Time flies when you're havin' fun, huh, babe?"

Nate chuckled. "Fun is too mild a word."

"Spill it... what ya thinkin' 'bout?"

"Well—" Nate wrapped his arms around Tai's neck. "—I was just thinking about you and the show, and how my life has changed. I met Candy. I met Dana. I met you. I can tell you now. Things really piled up on me last week. When the diva said she was leaving, it was the last straw. I'd lost *Purple Twilight*, and then Dana dropped her big bomb. I thought I wasn't going to make it through. I was looking forward to this weekend. It was the only thing keeping me sane, but then you called and said you couldn't go. There I was, no movie, no Diva, no you, and stuck with parents who truly don't give a shit about me except for the money I can make for them. For a brief moment, I thought of offing myself. Just gettin' it over with. Relief, you know?"

Nate's story was stopped dead by the look on Tai's face.

"Hey, I'm still here, aren't I?" Nate said. "I guess I do feel some sort of responsibility for the show—and Dana and Candy and… *you*—because I didn't think very long or very hard about that option. What I did was just sleep. You wanna know how many hours I've slept since Friday a week ago? A hundred or more. If I wasn't at the studio, I was in bed sleeping. And somehow it felt good. I was released from the suffering I was feeling. I was away from it all. But now. Now, Tai. I know I have you. And that will keep me going."

"I'm here, I'm yours." Tai gently kissed Nate. "And there's no reason to even think about such a terrible thing." He planted another sweet kiss on Nate's cheek. "Remember that."

Nate smiled.

"Now, how 'bout we take advantage of that patio? The moonlight. The stars. A little huggin'. A little kissin'. A little somethin' after that? But would you rather have our take-out before we commence with Act Three of *Love in Palm Springs*?"

"Well, I *am* hungry. You know me."

They eagerly ate their food, devouring it like it was a feast for kings, not even caring that it was stone-cold by then. When the last bite was finished and fortune cookies were read—Tai's said, "You will be happy tonight," and Nate's read, "A beautiful night is in your future"—the boys headed to the deck chairs. After pushing them together as planned, Nate cuddled against Tai.

They gazed up at the stars.

Tai pointed to the night sky. "See that bright one?"

"I see it, Tai."

"That's Taema, Samoan goddess of love. She watches over those in love to ensure nothing bad comes to them."

"Really?" Nate asked.

"Would I lie to you, dude?"

"Probably," Nate said, kissing Tai's nose.

Tai chuckled. "Well, Taema is a Samoan goddess. At least I got that right. I don't rightly know what she stands for, but I like my explanation, don't you?"

Before Nate could protest, Tai was smothering him with kisses again.

Could life be any better right now? Forget everything that came before this. This—me and Tai—will see me through. For now. For always.

Dissolve to: Exterior—outside the suite

ON A balcony above them, one condo over, behind a pot filled with tall bamboo reeds, a lanky, sandy-haired boy peered through the viewfinder of a Pentax Spotmatic. Nate and Tai were so lost in their lovemaking, they didn't even notice the flash of the camera.

Scene 38

Fade in: Exterior—the studio
The Tuesday after Palm Springs

NATE FELT a breeze through his hair as he steered the 'Stang to the NBC studios gate. He was still riding on the high that was their Palm Springs weekend. Not even getting home to an apartment in Monica/Paul chaos brought him down. Monica passed out; Paul nowhere to be seen.

Monday's table read had gone as well as could be expected. Nate missed the diva, but he had Candy sitting next to him, he had Tai at his other side, the script, what was left after all Jackass's cuts, was filled with laughs for him, and all was right with his world.

Neither Paul nor Monica gave him any hassles when he got home, and he went to sleep that Monday night, dreaming of Tai. Tuesday came, and like usual, Nate got ready and arrived at the studio early.

The guard rushed up to greet him.

"Hey, Jimmy." Nate waved, expecting the gate to open automatically as usual.

"Sorry, Mr. Berrigan," the guard said. "Mr. Waldman says you're not allowed on the lot. Word is, you've been terminated."

"What?" *Did I hear him right?* "What do you mean? I have the last show of the season to do. And I have an option for next season."

"That's just what I heard—nothin' official. You'll have to talk to Mr. Waldman. But I can't let you come in. Orders, sir. Sorry."

Dissolve to: Interior—the Berrigan apartment

NATE DROPPED Tai off at his house Sunday about midday. He hated to let him go. The weekend, too, too short, had been magical, a healing, soothing balm for Nate. They slept in that morning, went to the club for breakfast, came back to the condo for a little post-breakfast dessert—Nate was still in a bit of disbelief that he was so much in love with Tai and that what they were doing could feel so good and so right—and then they'd gotten on the road. The two-hour trip back to LA flew by with Nate driving this time while Tai chose the songs on the radio. Mostly, it was just a little bit of heaven on the highway for Nate.

He'd gotten home to his apartment soon after leaving Tai. Paul wasn't there. That was a good thing because he couldn't take any of Paul's questioning. Monica was dead to the world. It would have been nice for Paul to have been there making sure she wasn't actually dead. But Nate had been through this so many times, he just shook his head and walked past her to his room. He did all the homework he should have done the week before. He was on a high, and nothing was going to bring him down. He was still hurting about Dana's departure, but this weekend with Tai had made that pain a lot more bearable. He was energized and ready to take on anything Kerry Flanagan could throw at him because he was in love and he was happy and he was doing a job he loved—and doing it with the man he loved. Nothing was going to screw that up. Certainly not homework. So he dutifully did his due diligence.

After that, he saw Monica had put this week's script on his desk. It was usually just on the table when they arrived for the Monday table read, but they must have thought, since this was the season finale, the cast would want it early. Whatever. He opened it and read it through. He liked what he read. His role was center-stage this week. Or as center-stage as Jackass Flanagan would allow. He was eager to get to the studio Monday morning.

The day had gone well. Everybody seemed rested and excited to be wrapping the season. Before the formal opening of the read—the arrival of King Kerry—everyone chatted about summer plans. Nate was not happy he had no plans to report, but he knew he couldn't reveal he planned to spend every waking minute with Tai, hopefully most of it in bed.

Jackass arrived, and they began. Kerry, as Nate had thought he would, objected to almost every good line Nate had. He stopped Nate in the middle of each line and barked his orders to the writers, who sat sheepishly, nodding. Nate could see them shrinking with each cut.

Flanagan ordered rewrites, ordered a second table read at 1:00 p.m. sharp, and they were released for their all-too-quick lunch.

Tai and Nate agreed on the commissary and asked Candy to join them. She, however, was skipping lunch because she needed to phone her agent in New York. Despite her rule that summer breaks were for relaxing her old bones, she repeatedly opined, she was in negotiation to do a limited run on Broadway.

So Nate and Tai lunched alone, with Nate wishing they had some secret place they could go for dessert. They both knew their dressing rooms just weren't private enough for what they desired. And besides, there wasn't enough time before the second table read. Nate wanted to linger, languish, and love, love, love.

The rewrites were at the table when they all gathered again. And, as Nate had figured, many of his lines were gone, but some of the best remained. Kerry must have hovered over the writers, because he not only seemed pleased with the new script, but he didn't seem surprised at any of it. And Nate was happy Brian still got a few good zingers in directed at his dad. Anytime he got to one-up Kerry Flanagan with his character, he was happy.

The read finished, and everyone was released for the day. Nate got a brief time in his dressing room, saying goodbye to Tai for the day. Before things got too hot and heavy, they broke, Tai to a screen test for his summer project, Nate to home, since Paul had killed his summer project.

Tai refused to let that bother him. He was too happy with Tai. He eagerly looked forward to getting back to work on Tuesday.

But then this crap at the gate. *What is going on? Did Paul fuck me over again?*

He backed his car from the gate and sped away. *Paul is going to pay for this. There has to be an explanation, and he'd better be home when I get there to explain. His ass is grass. If he caused this, he will not only pay, but he will get his butt to the studio and make it right again.*

By the time Nate got home, his anger at Paul was defused, replaced by a feeling of unrest. *Paul is still in Vegas. He hasn't come home from the weekend. He wasn't there when I left for the studio, so how could he have done anything to get me fired? There has to be another explanation.*

Confused and dejected, Nate parked the car back in his slot at his building. Feeling like his feet were weighted down by twenty-pound concrete shoes, he got in the elevator. In a daze, he stood there. He was not aware the car hadn't moved or that the doors had opened again. It barely registered that another resident had stepped into the elevator.

"Going up, I assume?"

Nate heard the words but hadn't a clue what the person had said. "Huh?"

"Up? What floor?"

Nate murmured, "Five."

"Five it is."

A short ride and the doors opened. Nate just stood there.

"This is your floor, guy," the other rider said as he pointed.

Silently, Nate plodded into the hallway.

He heard, "Hey, you all right?" as the elevator doors closed once again.

No, I'm not all right. Life keeps piling shit on me. I've lost one of my best friends. It appears I've lost my job. And I have to go confront the two shittiest parents in the entire universe. That's if Paul has even bothered to come home. And what a shitstorm my news will stir up. I should just turn around and vanish. Take myself off the face of the earth.

He crept to his apartment. He slid his key into the door. His body was in slow-mo. His mind kept racing, though, faster than a NASCAR driver going around the track. *Why was I fired? What have I done? Why was I fired? What have I done? Why was I fired? What have I done? Why was I fired? What have I done? Why was I fired? What have I done?*

Like a robot, he slowly shook his head over and over. He pushed opened the door, slipped through it, and pulled it shut. In a daze, trying not to think, but his brain saying those words inside it, like a record with its needle stuck, he crept toward his room.

"*This* one's all *your* fault, you know, you little shit. What in *hell* were you thinking?" Paul's voice stopped him. Not angry. Quiet. Eerie. Menacing.

Nate followed the voice into the living room. He didn't know why. Paul was the last person on earth he wanted to see right then. But his legs didn't know that, he guessed. He almost laughed at that thought.

Paul sat, bottle of Scotch in hand. Monica lay draped across the sofa, a wet rag covering her forehead.

"What's my fault?" Barely audible. But he knew the answer.

"*You* got yourself fired *this* time, kid. Waldman called right after you left. Your mother was frantic when I got back. You see what it's done to her?" Paul gestured toward Monica. "You just had to do it, didn't you, you little fag? You and your *boyfriend* have been written out of the season finale, and your option for season four has not been picked up. Thanks to your sordid Palm Springs escapade, you two have been canned." Paul swigged Scotch straight from the bottle. "And you can't blame *me* this time!"

Nate expected that last statement to be shouted, bellowed, screamed. Paul delivered it quietly, and it was so, so much more effective. With his life ending, Nate inexplicably thought, *I should remember that line delivery for when I need it sometime. How can I be so detached?*

With my world blowing up.

Paul tossed a copy of the *Enquirer* to Nate. Nate scrambled to catch it. He was living on instinct. Someone throws something at you, you catch it. Doesn't matter if your life is over.

"I picked up this chronicle of your weekend caper after Stan called. Flanagan got a call before the story went to print. They wanted a comment. Stan did everything he could to quash this shit, but there was nothing he could do. This ain't old Hollywood, where the studios could pay off reporters, buy up photos," Paul said.

Nate stared at the paper. Splashed across the front page was *Gay Teen Heartthrobs.... Exclusive Photos Inside.*"

Shock. Total disbelief. Nate didn't want to look inside. What he and Tai did should not be splashed across some tabloid. What they did wasn't dirty. Wasn't wrong.

He almost opened the paper but was stopped by Monica finally speaking, a wail that pierced the quiet.

"Baby," Monica wailed. "What were you thinking? I know that article can't be true. It just can't be. Not my Natie."

Nate opened his mouth to speak, but Paul said, "Oh, it's true all right. The kid's a pervert—an out-of-work pervert, I might add."

Monica sat up.

"Paul, don't talk about Natie that way. He's our son. That article is obviously a fabrication. You know you can't believe a word you read in those rags," she said.

"Well, Mon, pictures don't lie. The kid is buck naked, for Christ's sake! They had to use all those heavy black boxes just to make the pictures decent enough to publish."

Monica emitted another sob; then she turned to Nate.

"What were you thinking, baby?"

Until that moment, Nate had just stood there, absorbed in disbelief and misery. Looking down, he saw but didn't see. *When did I open this thing? When did I find these pictures? Who would do this? What we did was private, for us only.* His eyes stared holes into these pictures of the most perfect and wonderful moments of his life. *And now here we are for all the world to see. For Paul to curse at. For Monica to use to fuel her drug addiction. Paul will get more and more soused as the day goes on; Monica will get more and more strung out. That's what they do. They don't need these pics to give them permission to do their drugs, drink their drink. But this—this—will make it so much worse. Because their meal ticket has just cancelled their dinner reservations. They don't care about me. It's all about the money. Whatever happened to the parents I was given? Why aren't they here to comfort me? To tell me they can fix this? To hold me? To tell me things are going to be all right? But no, those people checked out a long time ago. In their place are the clones who I know only as Paul and Monica.*

"Thinking?" Nate felt his eyes flooding with tears. "I'll tell you what I was thinking. I was thinking about my own happiness for a change."

Paul expelled a loud "Bullshit!" Finally, his rage came out. Nate knew it would. And he no longer cared how Paul felt.

"Paul!" Monica cried. *Yeah, Mommy. You tell him. Like you really care about me. What a joke.*

"That's okay. I wouldn't expect *him* to understand. Or care. Not about me. Not about his son." Nate wiped tears from his chin. "I wasn't thinking of Nate, the TV star who rakes in enough dough to keep his lush of a daddy drowning in Scotch. No, for once I was thinking about someone who deserves to be loved." He was getting angrier and angrier, raving, matching the rage Paul had just shown him. "Uh-huh, loved. Ever heard that word, Paul? No, of course, *you* don't know what that means.

Let me explain it to you. It's a simple word… *l-o-v-e.* Tai loves me, and I know I love him. *That's* what this weekend was all about. Love. Love I've never gotten from either of you vultures," he exploded. *That didn't solve anything. Didn't even make me feel better. But at least I did it.*

"Oh, baby!" Monica screamed. "You don't know what you're saying. That kind of love is wrong. And you're wrong about your father and me. I love you… I really do. And your dad does too. Tell him, Paul."

"Me? According to your faggot son, I'm not capable of love." Paul was quiet again. And that enraged Nate even more. Paul took another swig of Scotch. "How could I love a son who's a card-carrying cocksucker?"

"Paul," Monica pleaded. "Apologize to your son."

Paul's voice was calm, even, a touch of a smile on his face. "No. I will not. He's no son of mine." And he calmly took another drink, straight from the bottle.

"Then leave," Monica spat at him. "Get out of here."

Nate stared at his mother. *Why is she defending me? She can barely keep her head up, but for whatever reason, she is defending me against her drunken husband.*

"Paul, I'm going to say this one more time. Apologize to Nate. We need a united front here if we are going to get his job back."

Ah, so that's it. The trail always leads back to the money.

"Nate's confused," she continued. "He doesn't know what he wants. But we can convince him to give up this nonsense. Stay, Paul, and fight for our boy's job. Or leave. And you'll never see another penny of Nate's money. I'll see to that."

Wow. I didn't think she had that many lucid thoughts in her head. I guess when the topic's money, she can break through the drug-induced haze. Dollars, cash, gelt, dinero, francs, pounds, solid-gold bullion. Money, money, money. Obvious. All that concerns her. Not me. Not her little Natie. *Not whether her son is happy or not. It's all about the mighty paycheck.*

Nate looked at Monica; then he looked at Paul. How would this play out? Paul would likely stay. His love for the money would override his disgust at having a queer son. No doubt about that.

"Fine… I'll leave, but don't expect me back," Paul said. "And thanks to your pervert son, you two will be tossed out of here soon as his paychecks stop coming. You forget, Monica, I control the accounts. You tossed the divorce out of the courts, now didn't you? Your high-powered lawyer and his settlement never got off the ground, thanks to you. And I've been socking away the kid's money. I knew one day this roller coaster would stop. And I wudn't gonna be left with nothing. Have fun with your *feygele* son, Mon." Paul stood, turned, and walked straight for the apartment door. "Don't come crying back to me. I can't fix this one, and I wouldn't if I could. I'm not having any son of mine fucking another man," he said as he slammed the door behind him.

Monica collapsed, sobbing. *That was dramatic, now wasn't it? A grand exit, leaving me to cope with the leading lady, chewing the scenery to the hilt.*

"Get me my pills, baby."

Of course. First line of defense. Take another pill. Don't comfort your son. Don't tell him you love him and will always be here for him. Don't even tell him not to worry—even though there is a lot to worry about. Don't be a real mother. Just do what Daddy has just done. Walk out. Paul walked out of the house and my life. You stayed, Mommy, but you might as well walk out. Because your life and your pills are just one big step away from me and what I need.

With years of practice, Nate automatically picked up the pill bottle on the coffee table. He shook out a pill into the palm of his hand, looked at it, then pocketed the bottle. From the bar, he poured a glass of water, then took the pill and water to Monica.

"Here." His voice was cold as ice. He simply didn't care anymore.

Putting the pill on her tongue, then tossing back the water, she said, "Thank you, baby." She handed him back the glass. She lay back on the sofa and placed the wet cloth over her eyes.

Nate took the glass from her; then he picked up the bottle of Macallen Paul had left on the coffee table. He slowly carried them to the bar. He set the glass down, then looked at the Scotch bottle. Paul must have just opened it, because it was almost full.

"Not your son, huh?" He took a swig. It burned going down. Nate liked the feeling. Penance. The price he needed to pay for all that had happened. He knew. Oh, he knew from a long, long time ago. If he ever tried to be happy, it would all turn to shit. That's the price he had to pay for these two that called themselves his parents.

Scotch bottle in hand, he turned and slowly trudged to his room, one leaden foot in front of the other.

I should call Tai.

His first thoughts as he pushed the door closed.

Why? There's nothing he can do. I've lost his job for him. But he has a mother, a father who will help him through this. He doesn't need me.

Scene 39

Fade in: Interior—the Berrigan apartment
The evening after Nate's firing

"Nate, open up!"

A frantic Tai pounded on the apartment door.

"It's me." He shouted. "You have to talk to me. Why haven't you been answerin' your phone?" He pounded louder. "Open this damn door, Nate."

Despite his fear, his worry, Tai said the last almost quietly as he continued pounding. It was a plea, not a demand. From someone who knew the guy he loved and feared the worst.

Tai beat on the door, so hard that the door shook and he could see dents in it from his fist. He raised his foot to kick it in, when his leg stopped in midair. A voice from inside was calling faintly, like someone struggling to be heard, but not able to muster up any energy to shout out.

"I'm coming, I'm coming." The door flew open. Cigarette in hand, Monica, eyes red, skin blotchy and eyelids drooping, was standing in front of Tai. "*Wha's* this all *abou'*?"

"Where's Nate?" Tai demanded, pushing his way past her.

"How'd you get in *th' buil'ing*?" Monica pulled Tai's sleeve as he almost knocked her down, frantically looking for where Nate might be. "*How'd you get pas' doorman?*"

Tai stared at her with total contempt and jerked away from her. He strode toward the living room, looking into it, calling, "Nate, Nate! Where are you?"

Seeing that Monica had followed him, Tai stepped right in front of her. He leaned in, menace in his eyes. "I asked you where Nate is. Tell me."

"I'm... calling... th' police," Monica stammered. She stumbled to the telephone.

Tai jerked around and noticed the hallway. He raced down it, opening doors. A bathroom. No Nate. A bedroom with no Nate. The door at the end of the hallway was locked. Ready to break the door down if he had to, he heard Nate's pathetic imitation of a mother from the living room.

"If... you don' leave righ' now, I'm calling... the author 'ties."

Tai ignored her threats. Nate was the only thing on his mind. She could call out the National Guard for all he cared.

Standing in front of the locked door, Tai pounded, shouting, "Nate, open the door."

No answer. Tai resisted destroying the door, no matter how much he wanted to. He called again. "Nate, if you're in there, open up. I need to see you, babe!"

"Lea'm'son, alone," Monica said, now once again standing behind Tai. She'd apparently abandoned the idea of calling the cops in favor of stopping Tai.

"Nate? What's goin' on? You have to let me in, babe. Come on." Tai put his ear to the door and listened, tears streaming down his face. "I have to know you're all right." He wiped his cheek, but the tears continued. "Come on, babe. Answer me. You gotta believe me. I didn't mean for any of this to happen. I never thought Kyle would follow us. He's responsible for all of this. That shit took those pictures, sold them to the *Enquirer*." Tai's voice was breaking with each sob. He had to get through to him. "You've gotta believe me." He leaned against the door, his cheek wet. He felt helpless. Nate had to believe him. But Nate refused. One last try: "Open up, please... please!" Still no response. Then Tai stood upright and wiped his cheeks. "I won't let you shut me out, Nate. Open the door now or I'll break it down."

Complete silence engulfed Tai and Monica. But the quiet didn't last long. Tai was determined to make Nate listen to him and take him back.

The doorjamb gave a loud crack as Tai kicked it in.

"Y' can't do this, young man," Monica protested. But her protest was weak. She was totally useless, wasted.

The door flung open.

Tai saw him. A lifeless heap. His head facedown on the desk, a puddle of vomit.

Tai ran to him, jerked him up. Cradled him. Then barked to Monica, "Call an ambulance!"

"*I tol'you, lea'my son alone!*" Monica muttered; then she staggered to the bed and sat. "*You ha'no righ'to come barg'n'into my apartment.*" She took a drag off her cigarette, now just a stub. She was so out of it, she didn't even notice it was burning her fingers.

Shaking his head in disgust at Monica, Tai felt Nate's carotid artery.

"I don't know if I feel anything or not." He spoke aloud, but most certainly wasn't speaking to Monica. She was useless. Maybe he was thinking out loud just to stay sane and take care of what he knew he had to do.

He caressed Nate's nearly lifeless body—nearly lifeless because Tai had found a faint pulse. "Hang on, babe. I'm gonna get you help." Tai kissed Nate's cheek tenderly, sitting him back in the desk chair.

Wildly, he jerked his head around, searching for Nate's phone. It was on the bed stand to the right of the bed. Tai almost tripped over Monica's feet, prostrate as she was on the bed, as he ran to the phone. He grabbed the receiver. It was dead. He dialed *0*. Nothing. He tried again. And again, nothing. He pulled on the phone. It came loose from the wall. Nate had pulled the wire.

Oh, babe, he thought, *why didn't you call me? I could have stopped you. You didn't have to do this.*

He threw the phone against the wall. He ran from Nate's room. If his mother wasn't passed out, she would be saving her son right now. If his father wasn't, no doubt, in some Vegas stripper's bed, he could be getting an ambulance. But Tai was the only one—the only one who cared about Nate. And it was up to him to save him. He rushed into the living room, knowing the phone there was a separate line from Nate's.

The receiver was on the floor. Monica must have dropped it when she took her drugged self to yell at Tai. He reached for it. It was droning, "If you'd like to make a call, hang up and dial again," over and over. Tai leaned over to the telephone dial. He pushed the disconnect button. Then he dialed *0*. The time it took to make the entire rotation of the phone dial seemed like an eternity.

"Operator. How may I help you?" For a tiny moment, Tai felt pissed she was so calm when he wasn't.

Taking a deep breath, he said, as quickly as he could muster, "I need an ambulance. My friend's OD'd. I can't tell if he's breathing or not. Please, please get someone here fast."

"What's the address?" Again, she was so calm and collected. It really pissed Tai off. Didn't she hear how urgent this was?

Tai was so crazy over the thought Nate might be dead, he fought his brain to remember Nate's address. It came to him and he spat it out, thinking if his brain had worked quicker, they might have gotten here to save Nate quicker.

"I'll get someone on the line." The telephone went silent for endless moments. *What is she doing? This is taking forever. And my Nate doesn't have forever.* Finally, she came back on the line. "Someone will be there in just a few minutes. They're on their way. Stay on the...."

She was still talking when Tai dropped the receiver. As he ran back to Nate, he murmured, "Thank you, thank you, thank you, thank you."

He pulled Nate from the chair, and with him in his arms, Tai fell to the floor, holding on to his love for dear life. *He'll get through this. Nate's strong. They'll get here and bring him back to life. Nate can't die. I won't let him.* He rocked Nate back and forth. "Please don't be dead. Please don't be dead. Please don't be dead," he said, a mantra, a prayer to every god who'd ever answered a prayer.

Through eyes blurred from tears, Tai saw the empty pill and Scotch bottles, both having fallen from the desk.

"Come on, Nate. You've got to help me here," he cooed into Nate's ear. "You can't be dead. You can't leave me. I love you!"

"What're you doin'?" Monica had awakened from her stupor and was trying to pull Tai away from Nate. But nothing was separating them now. He used his shoulder and pushed her, as hard as he could, back onto the bed.

Once again prone from her drug-addled state, she mumbled a muddled, "Wha's wrong wi' my baby?"

After an eternity of promises to God, the Holy Mother Mary, St. Jude, Tagaloa, Vishnu, Zeus, Yahweh, Buddha, the Great Spirit, Gaia, and every god figure he'd ever heard about, Tai heard the door buzzer. He gently laid Nate on the carpet. Kissed his cheek. Whispered, "I'll be right back, babe."

Then his frenzy returned. He ran to the door and jerked it open.

"Thank God you're here!" he screamed. "He's in there!" He pointed toward the hall and let the paramedics follow with their gurney. When he came to the open door, he stepped aside, not wanting to be away from Nate any longer than he had to be.

One of the guys knelt to the floor and hovered over Nate, putting his ear to Nate's chest and feeling for a pulse. The other guy set his case on the bed. Tai saw him glance at the passed-out Monica and shake his head. He opened the case and was pulling out instruments while asking Tai, "What'd he take?"

By this time, the guy on the floor was checking Nate's vital signs with what his partner had passed to him.

Tai grabbed the pill bottle and thrust it to his inquisitor. "These, I think. And I also think he washed them down with Scotch. The bottle's empty." Tai grabbed the bottle and held it up. Tai began to sob again. "Help him, please. He can't be dead."

The tech looked at the pill bottle, then told his partner, "Valium."

While his partner worked over Nate, the tech shook Monica. She roused. "Is this your son, ma'am?"

With a bewildered look, Monica muttered, *"Officer, I want press charges…."*

The guy turned to his partner. "She's hopeless," he said.

"Let's get him up on the gurney," the other barked. He turned to Tai. "We'll get him to the ER."

The two men hefted Nate to the gurney, then strapped him in.

"Okay, let's roll," one said to the other. To Tai, he said, "You go with *us*. The woman's not in any state to do it. Maybe not even in this country."

Tai grabbed Nate's hand, running alongside as the guys wheeled him out.

"You're gonna be okay, babe. I just know it."

1998

"MY LITTLE darling," Candy gushed as she hugged Tai. "Come in, come in." She motioned Tai through the door of her suite at the Beverly Hills Hotel.

"Wow, Candy, these are some lush digs you finagled yourself into."

She pointed to a chair opposite a sofa. As Tai took the seat, she said, "I'm no fool. They wanted me here for this extravaganza, and I had my demands." She balanced on a cane as she sat on the sofa. Candy was getting on in years, but that cane, Tai suspected, was more a prop than a medical device.

She waved her arms around, like a queen granting an audience. "I've never made enough to stay here, but Kerry Flanagan is much richer than me. So when his people called—I want to say 'called my people,' but your Candy has no people anymore, never had many to begin with—I laid out my demands. This tribute to America's Favorite Comic is all orchestrated by Flanagan and his minions. If they wanted *me* as their main attraction, then this is what it took to get me out of retirement, out of my little pied-à-terre atop a hill in San Francisco and on a flight. I don't get out much anymore. I do have to admit I owe a tiny bit of my success to Kerry Flanagan. Those two Emmys I won doing his show make very nice bookends indeed. But there is no love lost between me and Kerry Flanagan. No, this is just another acting job. Perhaps the hardest of my career, for I will make the final speech at the gala tomorrow, praising our nemesis to the highest heavens, smiling all the way. After what he did to my little love, that will be the hardest role I've ever played. But his foolhardy firing of you two lovelies didn't seem to affect his popularity or the show one bit. Oh, how I wanted to just walk in and quit on the spot that morning, especially after what happened, but I couldn't afford the lawsuit. But we've talked about all this before. It's all water under the bridge now, isn't it? Life goes on. I could easily have declined Kerry's entreaty, but he's paying me a lot, and I get to see you lovelies again. And after all these years, you're happy, I just know it. I see it every time I'm with you. Far too few times, I might add."

"Candy, it took a long time to deal with everything, but yes, happiness is the order of the day."

"Tell me about your job, love. It's such important work."

"Well, we've only been operating for a few months, but I think we're making a huge difference. So many teens are in crisis, especially gay teens. If we can save just one, we've made a difference. People have taken notice. Donations are coming in. I think momentum will build, and we'll be around for a long, long time. I'm just thankful I'm in a position to do this."

"Ah, my sweet, what you're doing is God's work, I just know it. I was happy for you when you got out of the business. Even if it was forced on you, you took the blow well. Your college degree in counseling, your private practice, the success of your book—you are a marvel, my sweet. You've made my life richer just being in it. Many's the time I've lulled myself to sleep at night, thinking of your success. And now this. My darling Tai. Saving lives."

Tai thought of Nate. All this was for him.

"Enough about me, Candy. When does she arrive?"

Candy laughed. Her eyes twinkled. "You mean the queen of Broadway?"

"Who else?"

"I believe her father's plane touched down an hour ago. Byron may be eighty-some years old, but he's still a mover and a shaker in the business world, now isn't he? So his plane is always available. Too bad she's so busy, she can't avail herself of it very often. But she should be here shortly. In fact, she's probably signing autographs in the lobby as we speak. They frown on that here at the Beverly Hills, but sometimes die-hard fans manage to slip in."

And almost before Candy could finish her sentence, there was a pounding on the door.

"Well, well, well, speak of the devil," Tai said. He jumped up. "Do you mind?" he asked Candy, thumbing over his shoulder toward the door.

She thrust her cane at him, a queen waving her scepter. "Not at all, Sweetness."

Tai went to the door, looked through the peephole, and there she stood in the hallway in all her glory. He flung the door open.

"Diva!" he screamed, grabbing her in a bone-crunching bear hug.

"Watch it, now. I'm a Broadway star. You can't just molest me like I'm some call girl you ordered off the back page of some sleazy rag."

Tai and Dana broke apart. He still held her hands and looked into her eyes. "You never stop, do you?"

She flashed her snarky smile and rushed past him. "Where is she? Where's my Candy?"

She reached Candy as the older lady was maneuvering herself off the couch. They touched cheeks. "I missed you, darling, darling woman."

"I know you did, dear one." The twinkle in Candy's eye flashed again.

Dana took a spot next to where Candy had sat, pulling her down with her. "You've got to fill me in, Candy. What in the hell got you out of retirement for this… this… this three ring circus? This charade? This abomination? This assault to every value I hold dear?"

"Money, dear. Pure and simple. Kerry Flanagan is paying me bags of it. No one in the business wanted to do it. All his former costars turned him down flat. Doris, dear, dear Doris, after doing that mega-flop and enduring his shenanigans—I can't believe a star as big as Doris Day didn't do her research before accepting that role—won't touch this *tribute* with a ten-foot pole. I hear she vowed she'd never be in the same room with him again. Even our beautiful Pika turned him down flat. I was the only one left. So I made him pay dearly for my services. He can afford it, though, I just know it."

"You're still a hoot, Candy," Dana said, leaning over to kiss Candy's cheek.

"And don't forget the real reason you're here, Candy," Tai said. "You just told me you only came to see us." Then he looked at Dana. "Good thing your show just closed. Twelve-hundred performances and your understudy never got a chance at her big break? What's up with that?"

Dana gave him a dismissive wave. "I'm a very healthy gal, Samoan. Enough about my favorite subject—me—what you been up to? Still saving lives, one gay boy at a time?"

"Tryin' to," Tai said. He loved Dana so much. She had never lost her unique way of putting things. Well, only for a short time. After what happened with Nate. She was a wreck, he remembered.

"Well, you keep it up. The world needs more like you," Dana said. "Now, does this hovel have any champagne? I know I called from the plane and ordered a bottle to be sent up. Where, where, where?" She looked around.

"Oh dear, you needn't have. Kerry Flanagan is providing the very best. I didn't ask for it, but it was waiting in my suite when I arrived."

"No way am I drinking any swill that schmuck paid for. I feel a little dirty just sitting here in this room that's on his tab. No offense, Candy darling."

The diva has always told it like is. In her mind, anyway.

"None taken, dear," Candy said. "I know just how you feel. Hell, I feel just like you feel."

Tai and Dana both laughed. It was not often they caught their very proper Candy spouting a very unladylike word. Unladylike for her, anyway. Candy just stared at them and continued.

"Believe me, I'm having a ball knowing Kerry Flanagan is at my mercy. He's stewing over all this, I just know it." Candy smiled a knowing smile, wicked smile. "And yes, dear, your bottle arrived about an hour ago. It should be nice and cold by now."

"Then let's crack that puppy open," Dana exclaimed.

"Just wait up, Diva." Tai had been staring at the screen of his flip phone. "I've got a text coming in."

"You men and your toys," Dana said. "You always have to have the latest thing. I've never gotten a text on my phone, but as they say, it's old technology—from six months ago!"

"Well, you two are going to be glad I have this newfangled contraption because right about now—"

Tai was interrupted by a rapping on the door.

"Now who could that be?" Candy said.

Tai went to the door and swung it wide.

"My little love!" Candy pushed herself up and hurried to the door, followed by Dana's running shout of "Heartthrob!"

Tai stood patiently as the two women hugged Nate in tandem. "I told you they'd like your surprise. My *business trip* ruse worked, huh?

They bought it hook, line, and sinker. Scouting locations in Thailand. What a crock. We fooled 'em," Tai laughed.

Breaking away from his two favorite women in all the world, Nate said, "Oh, ladies, I *do* need to scout locations in Thailand—a film director's work is endless—but surely you didn't think I'd miss this little reunion?"

Nate kissed Candy on the cheek, Dana on the tip of her nose. Then he grabbed Tai into a hug.

Finally he spoke again. A sly smile crossed his face.

"I only have three friends in the entire world, you know!"

SUICIDE IS the second leading cause of death among teenagers.

LGBTQ youth are three times more likely to commit suicide than their heterosexual peers.

Ninety percent of teens who make plans for suicide give some kind of warning.

If you are contemplating suicide or know someone who might be, call

The Trevor Helpline

866 488 7386

For more information, go to

www.thetrevorproject.org

RUSSELL J. SANDERS is a man on a quest. In his travels all over the world, he searches out Mexican restaurants. A born and reared Texan, raised on Tex-Mex, he wants to try the enchiladas and other delicacies that pass for Mexican food in the far reaches of the world. He has been pleasantly surprised in Tokyo and Indonesia and left wondering in Rome and a few other places. Sometimes what the menu says and what you are served is not what is expected. But the joy is in the quest.

Russell's also on a quest to spread a very important message: love is found in many forms in this world, and being gay or lesbian or bisexual or any other variation is normal, healthy, and wonderful. He wants his novels to bolster the confidence of LGBTQ teens and change the minds or further educate all the others who may stumble upon his prose.

Russell's writing joins his long career of acting, singing, and teaching, adding to his passions for cooking and reading. He has won awards for his acting and directing and has taught theater to hundreds of teens. He has also taught additional thousands of teenagers the art of writing and the love for literature. He is always in the middle of a good story, whether reading it or writing it. And he can whip up a delicious meal in minutes. He does all this with the support of his husband, a man he has loved for over twenty years and married a few years ago. They are now transplanted in Las Vegas, Nevada. And to Russell's dismay, the Mexican food in Nevada is not too much to his liking!

Website: russelljsanders.weebly.com
Facebook: https://www.facebook.com/russelljsandersauthor

RUSSELL J. SANDERS

YOU CAN'T TELL BY LOOKING

When Gabe Dillon starts the year at a new school, one young man captures and holds all his attention. Kerem Uzun is the senior class president. He's friendly, popular, the son of doctors, of Turkish descent, and Muslim.

Soon Gabe's curiosity about Kerem extends to Kerem's religious practices. He's fascinated by the culture, philosophy, and rituals of Islam, but one thing worries him: many practitioners of the religion are outraged by proud gay men like Gabe. Kerem's cousin, Timur, an orphan who was raised alongside Kerem as a brother, is one of them. And he isn't the only one standing in the way of their budding relationship.

Gabe knows he can't choose who he falls in love with, and he's in love with Kerem. But is Kerem even attracted to men? Will he go against his fundamentalist cousin for a chance to be with Gabe? With so many forces trying hard to tear it down, building a romance will mean a struggle.

www.dreamspinnerpress.com

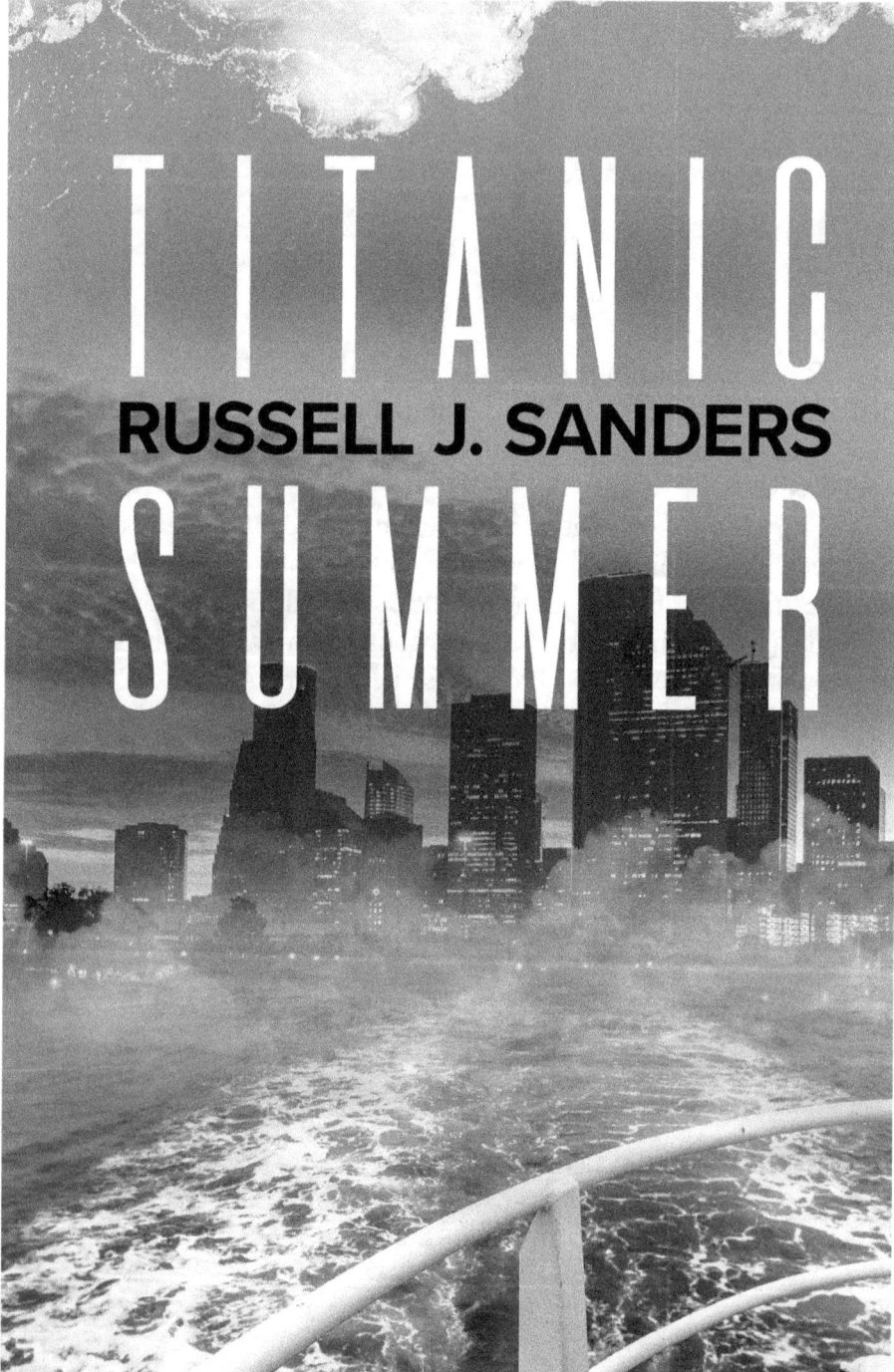

TITANIC
RUSSELL J. SANDERS
SUMMER

It's a summer of revelations for Houston high schooler Jake Hardy. Along with his estranged father, Jake embarks on a trip to Nova Scotia to visit the Titanic museum and the cemetery where the victims are interred. There, Jake's father's biggest secrets are revealed. Hurt and confused, Jake flees—not only from his father's confession, but from his own feelings.

Jake is gay.

Back home, the proposed Equal Rights Ordinance is polarizing people. As Jake faces a difficult choice about where he stands—and how far he's willing to go for his beliefs—he soon discovers that he's not the only one in hiding. When confronted with how his actions have hurt those he cares about, purposefully or not, Jake must learn to accept his friends, his father… and himself.

www.dreamspinnerpress.com

RUSSELL J. SANDERS

ALL YOU
NEED IS
LOVE

It is 1969 when Dewey Snodgress, high school theater star, meets irrepressible hippie Jeep Brickthorn, who quickly inserts himself into Dewey's life and eventually into his heart. Meanwhile, Dewey prepares to appear in a production across town, a play about protestors of the Vietnam War, where he befriends the wild and wonderful Lucretia "LuLu" Belton, who is also determined to follow her dreams and become an actress—whether her parents approve or not.

The show has a profound effect, especially on Dewey's father, who reconsiders his approval of the war after his son's performance. But Dewey knows his dad won't be so accepting if he reveals the love he's developing for Jeep, so he fights to push his feelings away and keep the peace in his family.

Still, Dewey can't ignore the ripples moving through society—from the impending Woodstock Festival to the Stonewall Riots—and he begins to see that the road to happiness and acceptance for him and Jeep might lead them away from conservative Fort Worth, Texas—and Dewey's dad.

www.dreamspinnerpress.com

RUSSELL J. SANDERS

COLORS

With a beautiful girlfriend, a scholarship to a prestigious musical theater school, and talent to spare, life is good for high school senior Neil Darrien. He's on his way to stardom, but then newcomer Zane Jeffrey secures a place in the school show choir, rousing Neil's envy. Neil soon sees there's more to Zane than a talented performer, though—he's funny and charming, and the two boys become friends. Neil's girlfriend Melissa doesn't like Neil spending so much time with Zane, and she draws Neil into her church. There, Neil is faced with a choice between righting a wrong and risking revealing a secret that could cost him everything he's worked so hard to achieve. As Neil's relationship with Melissa deteriorates, Neil starts to see Zane in a different light—one that has him thinking of Zane as more than just a friend.

www.dreamspinnerpress.com

The
BOOK
of
ETHAN

RUSSELL J.
SANDERS

Ethan Harker is the son of The Prophet, the stern, demanding leader of a small Southwestern polygamous community. Ethan has been groomed to one day take his place as the leader of this isolated cult.

But things happen that compel Ethan to flee his stifling community and find his way in the world beyond it. Totally out of his depth, he is sheltered by a remarkable group of people from a loving and accepting church. From them, he learns what family truly means and begins to construct a life free from the restrictions he's grown up with. Little by little he dismisses the assumptions he was taught about the "evil" people in the outside world.

Amid all this, Ethan realizes something about himself when he meets rapper Kyan, a boy his age. Although he's been brought up to fear and hate members of Kyan's race, he can't help falling in love with Kyan. Fueled by a new understanding and new friends, Ethan gains the strength and courage to conquer the confusing world he has been thrust into.

www.dreamspinnerpress.com

www.ingramcontent.com/pod-product-compliance
Lightning Source LLC
Chambersburg PA
CBHW051526260626
47170CB00003B/806

* 9 7 8 1 6 4 4 0 5 9 1 8 0 *